FORCE OF NATURE

S.L. SCOTT

Dedicated to My Amazing Team and Friends. You were there for me, cheering me on when I needed you most, before, during, and after the release of this book. It was noticed, appreciated, and you are incredible humans. I am so grateful to have you in my life.

Dear Kandace, I am so fortunate to call you friend. Although you are no longer on this earth, know that you still shine your beautiful light on so many lives and touch many hearts, including mine.
I love you, sweet friend. Rest in Peace #Shura

FORCE OF NATURE

Dear Rosa,
Take the Risk!

♡,

S. V. Scott
x

PROLOGUE

STRIKE

Our lips part the moment the shot rings out. A silent scream replaces the stars in her eyes, and she looks at me as if I'm the last person she'll ever see.

FALL

The snap of another bullet punctures the air, and my body curls around, shielding her as we hit the ground. Debris cuts into my hands as I cradle her head to break the fall.

PROTECT

A car door swings open, and a familiar voice commands us to get in. With no time to think, I act. Hopefully . . . outwitting death.

DEFEND

Our eyes stay focused on each other while we speed away
even as a gunshot ricochets off the bulletproof vehicle.
Hovering over her, I stay steady. Her body trembles under
my hands. "Breathe, Winter."
Her sweet scent covers me in a succession of quick exhales
and then slows when the words tumble off her tongue. "Are
we safe?"
"Yes."

For now.

1

Bennett Everest

Paris is gray. Everywhere I look—gray skies, gray sidewalks, gray buildings. I don't know what I expected before I arrived, but it wasn't gray.

When I volunteered for the job, I didn't realize I would be in the right city in the wrong season. I hear it's nice in springtime. Maybe I'll come back in six months and get something other than gray with the bonus from the deal I'm about seal.

To block the cool wind from hitting my neck, I pop up the lapels of my suit jacket and round the corner of the avenue. My feet stop when I see her.

Bourbon-colored hair that shines even under the light of the red bistro sign at dusk, a swan-like slope where her neck meets the top of her shoulders, a bright pink sweater clinging to her slender frame. Winter Nobleman is a burst of color on a cloudy day.

I pull the photo from my pocket and compare it to the woman sitting at the small table drinking coffee. It's her, and although she's attractive in the picture, it doesn't do her beauty justice.

Her father worries about her safety but seeing her sitting contentedly at a sidewalk café makes me wonder why. I look around as if to find something other than peaceful in this scene. I've yet to detect any threat of danger.

There's more to this story than I've been told. *Typical.* This seems too easy, which means it's more complicated than I was told.

This deal won't close unless I can get her home. How will I do that if she's staying away on purpose? I'm a good-looking guy and the right one for the job, or so her father said. So why does this suddenly feel like a fool's mission?

Get in.

Get the girl.

Get out.

Easy.

So what is keeping this gorgeous brunette here? Maybe she's purposely avoiding her family. But is that my concern? *Not really.*

Why she's here isn't my business, but closing the deal is. I'm confident enough to deliver this deal sealed with a kiss. So I'll just be honest with her. My job here is done if I can give Mr. Nobleman the assurance that his daughter is fine (*and damn is she fine . . .*), so he can continue with business and sign this deal. Then if she wants to fly back to Paris the next day, she can. An eight-million-dollar contract is worth a quick trip to Paris, but now it's time to close it.

I start walking, my pace slowing as I approach. The early evening still allows the last of the daylight to sneak in before night covers us in darkness. I watch her with rapt attention. Her lips understated and nude, long lashes painted black, drawing my eyes to hers and wondering if they're violet or blue. It was hard to decipher from the photos, and even though the file says blue, I can't help but want to see for myself.

What the—?

My feet stop, and I turn to face a bakery, pretending to window shop. Whoa! What is the obsession with macarons? It's a cookie, for fuck's sake. Out of the corners of my eyes, I watch as a man with a half-eaten baguette in one hand and bottle of wine in the other makes himself at home across from Winter. Although the cadence of his French is not harsh, her tone is.

Since I took Spanish in high school, my basic foreign language skills are useless. So I spy on them instead, keeping a sharp eye on his body language. The waiter returns and attempts to shoo him away, but when he wobbles on his feet to get up, his body lags back into the seat.

I don't have to speak the language to know the drunk is hitting on her. *Fucker.* The waiter returns, shouting a barrage of what sounds like threats, causing the asshole to stand. He leans over the table, making his motives more obvious despite her clear and definitive, "*Non!*"

When he doesn't get the hint, she leans back, appearing uneasy. *Fuck this guy.* I start walking, pounding the pavement with purpose. Weaving through the tables, I'm focused on them. She looks up when I arrive, her eyes going wide and lips parting just enough for me to see the tip of her tongue dip out and I catch a little pleasure in our shared second before it disappears.

Edging past, and with an elbow to the asshole's arm, I give her my best grin. "I'm sorry to keep you waiting, *mon chéri.*" I have no idea where that came from. Is *mon chéri* a candy or a real French phrase? I'm hoping for the latter, or now I'm going to look like the asshole.

As her sweet features are colored surprised, she replies,

"It's okay. You're here now, *mon chéri*. Remember how I taught you that you call me *ma chérie* because I'm a female."

I lean down, kiss her cheek, and whisper in her ear, "It's lovely to meet you, *ma chérie*."

The Frenchman tugs me back. Reeking of red wine, he slurs, "Who are you, *Américain*?"

"I'm her boyfriend, that's the fuck who." I square my shoulders and crack my neck, glancing down at his hand that he has the nerve to continue touching me with, and add, "I suggest you back up and keep walking. The lady's not interested, and I'm not a patient man."

I don't know why a little John Wayne slips into my tone, but it seems to do the trick. His hands go up in surrender still holding his prized bread and wine as he backs up. Too bad his mouth is still flapping. Dumb bastard. On the positive, I have no idea what he's going on about. I remain standing until he's down the street and still mumbling out loud.

"You didn't have to do that, you know?" There's a kick to her voice, a gentle tone with an edge to it.

I turn around to find Winter looking up at me. "Gray," I say.

"Gray?"

"Your eyes."

Looking everywhere but at me, she replies casually, "Overcast."

"Your eyes?"

"No, the day. My eyes are blue in the sunlight."

"I look forward to seeing for myself." I'm just about to get down to the reason I'm there when she laughs.

The tone is lighter than the church bells ringing in the distance, and she asks, "Do those quippy flirtations work for you?"

"Often. May I join you?"

She raises an eyebrow. "You got rid of one guy trying to talk to me so you could replace him?"

"He wasn't interested in talking to you."

"Oh, yeah?" Amused, she props her chin on her palm and watches me with a small smile. "Then what was he interested in?"

"Fucking you." Taking a seat at the table next to hers, I hold my hand up to get the waiter's attention.

That innocent pink sweater never fooled me. She remains indifferent, but she does ask, "Then what are you interested in?"

"Baseball that starts in the spring, camping in the fall, snowboarding in the winter, and boating in the summer." She rolls her eyes and sits back. I ask, "Why the eye roll?"

"Sports for every season. Typical male. When is the last time you spent time in a museum? Or maybe you never have? When's the last time you drank a cup of coffee out of a cup and saucer and enjoyed the scenery instead of getting everything to go?"

The waiter finally comes over, and I point at her drink. "I'll have what she's having. Coffee."

She says to him, "*Café, s'il vous plâit.*"

"*Oui*, mademoiselle. Monsieur," he replies.

When we're alone again, I say, "I like hiking and cold beers on a hot day."

"You like physical ways to occupy your time."

I take that as an invitation to readjust and sit a little closer. The way these tables are packed in here, it doesn't take much maneuvering. "I like being physical and hands on."

"Look, *Mister* . . .?"

"Everest." I hold out my hand.

"For real?"

"Very much for real."

With my hand wrapped around hers, she says, "I'm not available if that's the bush you're beating around."

"Available is a fascinating word to use."

She shrugs. "What can I say? I'm a fascinating woman."

"You sure are. You're clearly an American as well, so why are you in Paris?"

"People come to France to lose themselves in the culture, the slower pace, the joie de vivre of the city. Not that it's any of your business, but that's why I'm here."

"To escape real life."

"That's quite the assumption coming from practically a stranger."

"You know my name, so I think we're past stranger and 'practically' gets us one degree closer to friends." I wink, and she rolls her eyes again. The waiter sets my coffee down, and I add, "See how cultured I can be? Believe it or not, I'm even housebroken. So maybe I'm not the pig you make me out to be."

"You know what they say about first impressions?"

"What do they say?"

"Never trust them."

"And here I would have thought the opposite."

"Guess it's all in the way you look at things."

She triggers my sarcasm. "Glass half full or, in your case, half empty."

Pulling a few coins and bills from her purse, she sets them down on the table, and says, "It wasn't the coffee that told me who you were by first impression. It was your mouth." After snapping her purse shut, she says, "Bonsoir, Monsieur Everest."

2

Bennett

Winter doesn't make it twenty steps past the bistro before I toss money on the table and dash after her. She seemed serene in pink, but the woman has some bite to her bark. I like it.

It's easy to be distracted by her, but I'm here for a reason.

One reason only—to get her home so her dad will sign the media contract—but watching her walk down the avenue like she has no intention of leaving Paris anytime soon really makes me wonder again why he's alarmed.

Dressed in fitted black pants, she whips around on pink flats and plants her hand on her hip. "Are you following me?"

I stop with a good ten feet between us. Looking around, I reply, "I assume I'm free to walk wherever I want in France like I am in the States?"

"You are."

"Awesome." I close the gap and stand next to her.

"But you can't follow me."

"All right."

"Good," she says with a curt nod of her head. When she starts walking, I do too. Then she stops and glares at me. "I said you can't follow me."

"I'm not."

"Then what are you doing, Mr. Everest?"

"Walking *with* you."

"I don't want you walking *with* me."

"Fine."

"Good. Fine." She starts walking, and I keep pace next to her. Her arms fly out, and she yells, "What are you doing?"

"Walking *beside* you."

Her hands ball at her sides and she starts what sounds like swearing up a storm in French. *Feisty.* "Can you walk . . . not beside me?"

"If that's what you'd like."

"That's what I'd like."

"Okay, but only if you tell me what the title of your favorite song is."

"You don't even know my name, and you want to know my favorite song?"

"Yes, I do." I push my hands into the pockets of my pants.

"Why?"

"I think knowing a person's favorite song, or movie, or even dessert tells more about them than their name. It's more intimate."

"So Everest doesn't represent the man? It represents your ego instead?"

Her quick wit has me grinning. "My ego aside, my surname represents me in many ways, but it doesn't make up the whole of me."

She begins a slow stroll, and this time, she doesn't seem bothered by my presence. "Winter." Turning to glance back at me, she slows as if she wants me to catch up, so I do. Then we continue walking side by side.

"Winter," I repeat for no other reason than I want to hear how it sounds in the evening air.

"That's my name."

My attention darts her way, her words a reminder that she doesn't know who I am. I'm not sure what to say. I hate lying and, more so, starting in a place that could only lead to regret. I stop walking, pulling my hands from my pockets. "Winter?"

She turns back, her expression softening with a smile. "Yes, Mr. Everest?"

I should tell her.

I need to tell her.

I can't lie to her.

I shouldn't.

There's such an innocence about this moment we're sharing that I don't want to ruin it. Her smile grows as her blue eyes narrow in question. "Are you coming?" she asks.

"I thought you didn't want me to follow you?"

"I don't, but I haven't minded your silent company next to me."

Something is so captivating about this woman that I'm willing to play the role of her quiet companion to steal more time alone with her. I have a feeling the mention of her father's wish for her return won't go over as well as when I told him I would help make it happen.

Tucking my hands back in my pockets, I start walking again. The pinch between her questioning eyes releases, and a satisfied grin appears as we stroll together. "Winter is unique."

"I always thought it was my parents' easy way out. Do we name her December or Winter?" She does this funny mock voice and then laughs at herself.

"You were born in December?"

"Guess we're getting personal, after all."

The gray clouds part enough to see the sunset sneak through just before it drops below the horizon of the buildings. We reach an intersection, and when I look right, the Eiffel Tower reaches to the sky nearby. "Look."

When she looks, her expression lights up. "I don't think I'll ever get tired of that sight." With an eyebrow raised, she gets a devious glint in her eyes. "Have you seen it at night?"

"No. It's my first time in Paris."

"Wait until you see how magical it is at night. You'll always remember it."

"I have no doubt I'll ever forget . . ." My gaze goes from her and extends over her shoulder to the monument. We start walking again. "Winter is a beautiful name."

A small smile that hasn't left while she talks grows, a blush spreading like wildfire across her cheeks. She clears her throat, and then asks, "Since you know mine, what is your first name?"

"Bennett."

"Bennett," she repeats softly, then glances at me. "That's a very nice name, Mr. Everest."

"Thank you. I'll pass the compliment along to my mother."

An unexpected giggle escapes before a more longing version of my name rolls from her pink lips. "Bennett Everest." When her eyes trail over to me again, she lingers on my face, seeming to take me in as much as she can before the remaining light descends into darkness. "Sounds like a politician's name."

The thought makes me laugh. "Not with my past."

"We've all done something we're not proud of. Would it keep you from taking the oath of office?"

"Politics is not a path I'd choose."

She spins, her arms flying like a bird gliding through the air. "It's also a movie star's name. I just figured it would go to your head if I led with that one."

"It's like you know me already."

I like her laughter. It comes naturally as if I caught her off guard. "You look like one too," she says, keeping her voice quieter but focusing her eyes on me. "Tall. Dark hair. A face that's easy to appreciate and a voice that could hold the audience's attention for a few hours in a theater . . ." Winter doesn't stop, but she seems to divert to another thought she keeps to herself.

Trying to bring her back to me, I tease, "Only a few hours?"

"Maybe longer." She winks and puts her focus on the avenue ahead until we reach the next block. Turning toward me, she clasps her hands in front of her. Suddenly it's like we're on a first date and neither of us knows what to do—say goodbye or kiss instead? "This is me."

"You live here?" I ask, referencing at the classically French building across the street.

"No, but this is where we should part ways."

"For safety, I can walk you home if you like." Though the offer is absolutely true and well intentioned, I can't deny that I'd like to spend more time with her.

Glancing over her shoulder and then back at me, she sighs. "This has been quite an interesting . . . walk, but I should go. Enjoy Paris, Mr. Everest, and make sure to see Le Tour Eiffel at night. It's a sight—"

"I'll never forget. Like . . . this walk."

That brings her sweet smile back, erasing the worry. "Yes, like tonight."

When she takes a step away, I say, "Maybe we can see it together?"

"What is that?"

"The Eiffel Tower." It's hidden behind buildings, and I have no idea the distance, but I still point as if it's right there. She steals a glimpse in the same direction.

A debate whips through her eyes like the leaves that wave in the breeze. "I'm sorry. I've given you the wrong impression. I said I wasn't available. I shouldn't have even walked the three blocks with you that I did."

"Why did you?"

"If I recall correctly, *you* followed me."

"I recall it differently. Somewhere along the street, we started walking together, talking and getting to know each other. That's the version I'd like to remember."

"It's a good version, much more interesting than mine. Either way, I say adieu." This time, she hurries to cross the cobblestone street just as the lights on either side brighten for the night, her magic extending around her. Cupping her hand to the side of her mouth, she says, "'Dream a Little Dream of Me.'"

"What?" I ask. She wants me to dream about her?

"My favorite song. It's 'Dream a Little Dream of Me' by Ella Fitzgerald and Louis Armstrong."

I don't know the song, but satisfaction washes through me because she's shared one of her secrets. A Mini Cooper and a scooter drive by. When the street between us clears again, she asks, "What's your favorite song, movie star?"

"'Just Breathe' off Pearl Jam's *Backspacer* album."

"A classic in a different way. Bonsoir, Bennett Everest."

"Bonsoir, Winter," I say, pausing before I tack on her last name. I don't want to ruin the night by speaking a name I shouldn't know. I lean against the lamppost to watch her continue one of the longest goodbyes I've had the pleasure of being a part of.

A lip bite and eyes that share her inner delight can't hide how happy she is. I want to ask her where she's heading instead of going my own way. I want to ask her if it's normal for her to have such instant rapport with a stranger because I've never experienced anything like the past thirty minutes in my life. It was . . . easy. Her quick wit and the effortless sparring.

I give her a wave when she starts moving backward. She returns it and then walks away. When she peeks back, I nod once before she turns and disappears down the little avenue. It's not until she's out of sight that I realize I didn't accomplish my mission.

Pulling my phone from the inside pocket of my coat, I text my oldest brother: *This isn't going to be as easy I predicted.*

Hutton: *It never is. Where do things stand?*

To answer him bluntly, I'm a little disappointed she had to leave, encouraged that I might get to see her again, but standing alone on a street corner as of right now.

Me: *I'll fill you in tomorrow. I'm exhausted. Heading to the hotel to crash.*

Hutton: *Call tomorrow.*

Me: *Will do.*

I pull my earbuds from my pocket and insert them before I scroll through my music app. When I find the song, I buy it and listen while walking back toward the bistro where I can catch a taxi back to the hotel.

Lying on my bed an hour later, jet lag has set in, and I close my eyes as "Dream a Little Dream of Me" plays on repeat. It's an old song, one that I've never heard before, but as I listen, I catch the lyrics and see why the romance of it draws a woman who holds so much inside.

I can still see her so clearly when freedom caught up with her and she twirled right there on the sidewalk, blissfully unaware of the audience she had on the other side of the street. She didn't see the smiles on that elderly couple's faces or how I watched breathless while taking her in.

The more I think about tonight and how I didn't tell her who I was or that her father wanted to hear from her, I know what I did was wrong. But how do I take a rose and tell her not to bloom, to wait another day to breathe in the sunlight? To not breathe the freedom as she knows it?

My muscles relax and my body sinks into the mattress with images of pink—lips, sweater, shoes—tangled with blue eyes and hair spun of the finest silky strands. Maybe it's Paris, but damn, I've become a romantic. I'll blame the city and not the girl for the change in me.

Anyway, it will all change tomorrow when I expose the truth I kept from her tonight in the light of the day.

3

Bennett

Waiting for the sun to start setting, I occupy most of my day on the phone and handling emails. It's not the best way to spend a day in Paris, especially since it's my first visit, but with several large accounts recently signed, I refuse to drop the ball. Staying on top of my accounts is the secret to my success. It also keeps my brothers off my back.

I've earned trust from them and my clients. Word about Everest Media has gotten out. I used to handle all the accounts, but now I only have time for five million dollars or more, but when the Nobleman deal closes, that will go up to ten million. Being busy means business is booming and I love being a part of that boom.

A low ring trills from my phone. I tap the button to dismiss the alarm. When I stand, I stretch. Not getting a run in this morning because of the jet lag makes my muscles feel tight after a day of working.

I pull on a navy blue jacket that matches my pants. The stark contrast between the midnight blue of the suit and the pressed white dress shirt looks sharp. I opt to not wear a tie, but I still want to look good for Winter . . . *What the hell?* Did I just admit I want to look good for a woman I just met, a woman I have no business thinking about in any way other than a client's daughter?

Despite questioning my sanity, Winter is all class, so she should appreciate the effort. Fuck, she's messing with me, causing me to throw my common sense out the window.

Grabbing my wallet and room key, I tuck them in my pocket, keeping my phone in hand. I text my oldest brother while in the taxi. I didn't call Hutton like I was supposed to. *What would I say?* We walked three blocks and then said good night. I don't want to be peppered with questions I can't answer. The truth is, I don't know why I didn't tell Winter who I really am and why I'm here.

It didn't feel like the right time . . .

I'm attracted to her, which is understandable. She's a beautiful woman. But that's as far as it goes. I reach up to loosen the tie around my neck, but I'm not wearing one. *Is it hot in here?* I crack the window and take a deep breath of fumes.

Rolling the window back up, I hack up the exhaust fumes I inhaled from an old Peugeot that's rattling while trying to keep up with us. My driver seems hell-bent on winning this race when I just hope to survive the ride.

The taxi takes a sharp right, cutting the corner and causing me to tilt with it. "Fuck. We're not in that big of a hurry." Well, kind of . . . at least not for professional reasons. *Stay focused on this deal, Everest.*

When I see her, I'll tell her.

What if she's not there? What if I don't see her? Not tonight? Or ever again?

The driver eyes me in the rearview mirror but says noth-ing. One tight corner later and the car comes to an abrupt halt. *Thank fuck.* I pay the fare and hop out, trying to steady myself. I'm not sure if it's the car ride or the attraction I have for a woman with a million secrets that are stirring up my insides.

I bet it's the food. It's rich here. Buttered bread, cheese, and sauces seem to be on everything. I move to the corner but stop before I round it. What is my problem? She's a woman. *A normal woman.* Nothing more. A means to a signature on a contract I want to end my banner sales year on.

Fuck this.

I start walking.

And then I'm smiling.

Like a fucking fool.

The day had more clouds that seem to clear when I set my sights on her. Winter's hair is in a high ponytail with the ends swept to one side tonight.

Mindlessly dragging a pendant along a chain that dips to her chest, she has her head tilted down, her attention on the cream-colored pages of a paperback as she reads. A black sweater is wrapped around her this evening, and I start to wonder if the colors she chooses reflect her mood.

I hope not.

"Bonjour, ma chérie."

She looks up, a delicate smile already on her lips. "Bonjour, Monsieur Everest." Closing the book, she angles toward the entrance and waves for the waiter. "Please join me . . . if you can stay."

If I can stay? The invite surprises me, but I have no intention of walking away. Hope makes the blue of her eyes brighten in the last rays of the sunlight that streak down this street. It looks stunning on her—the sun and the hope. "I can stay."

"*Très bon.*"

It's kind of cute how she flips between French and English. Probably not so much when I do it, though I try when the waiter arrives tableside. "*Café, s'il vous plâit.*"

"*Très bien.*"

Winter holds her hand up. "Non," and continues speaking too fast for me to catch the rest. As soon as he leaves us again, she leans forward and whispers, "Do you drink wine?"

Typically, I don't. "Of course I drink wine. You know, it relates back to that whole being housebroken part."

She rolls her eyes, but the slightest shake of her head and squeezed lids reveals mortification. "I should apologize for my assumptions about you last night. I heard sports, and I unfairly lumped you in with a macho asshole I once dated. It's sort of a defense mechanism when I hear guys talk about sports."

I shouldn't like that she's been thinking about me as much as she has, but here I am enjoying every second of it. "I can admit that guys are generally assholes when it comes to sports, but I try not to be. I enjoy art, but that won't change the fact that I get into a good game and appreciate a beautiful woman. I drink wine when the occasion calls for it, playing sports, and working out." Her eyes dip from my face to my chest and lower. She's coy, a blush coloring her cheeks to match the sunset streaking the sky. "I also like when the same beautiful woman appreciates that I work out."

She drops her head into her hands. "Oh my God. I'm so embarrassed." Peeking over her fingers, she says, "I just got busted, didn't I?" Slinking down in the chair, she shakes her hands. "Please don't answer that."

The waiter sets two glasses of wine down on the table, and she proclaims "*Perfecto!*"

"Okay, now that's a word I do know. I took Spanish in high school."

The confession makes her laugh. Picking up her glass, she holds it between us. "To high school Spanish, men who like sports, and exercising so women can appreciate all that hard work."

My glass is tapped, and then we drink, our gazes locked together. "Oh! I almost forgot to ask. Did you love the Eiffel Tower last night?"

I'm not sure what to make of Winter tonight. She's completely different. Any reservations or hesitations she had last night are gone as if she's drunk, but she's not. From her eyes and her body, she appears sober. As for her thought process, I think I'm getting a peek into something unique. She's entertaining, to say the least.

I reply, "Unfortunately, jet lag won."

She gasps. "Oh, no. That's a shame. Well, hopefully, you're rested, and you'll see it tonight."

"Hopefully." I take another sip, my insides knotting in my chest. I'm not sure why—is it the truth burning me inside or that I'm starting to enjoy this lie of a life a little too much? "Are you hungry?"

"They have a wonderful pâté and tapenade plate."

"I'm thinking french fries."

I don't know why that amuses her so much, but it seems to. "They have great fries, too. Maybe I'll join you."

The order is placed, the wine refilled, and the sun goes down. "So tell me, do you come here every night?"

"No, but it is one of my favorite bistros in this part of the city."

I can't help wanting to know everything about her. She's a breath of fresh air and makes my heart beat faster. Although I think it's wiser if I pretend it was the taxi ride. "You must know the city quite well."

"I'm learning."

Any tidbit she's willing to give, I'll eat it up like it's the last morsel I'll ever swallow. I ask like I don't already know. "Is your family here?"

A long pause fills the space and then her right eyebrow lifts just enough to guess I'm probably pushing my luck. "My family is in the States."

"Do you always travel alone?" I really don't have anything to lose since our time is running out anyway.

"Who said I'm traveling alone?"

And then I remember. "Ah. That's right. You're unavailable."

That doesn't seem to warrant a response. I'd love to know more about that unavailability since she seems to not only take me flirting with her in stride but she also flirts right back. Her head tilts to the side, and she looks into my eyes as if she's reading me like a book. "What brought you back to the bistro, Mr. Everest?"

"You." This time I'm not lying, but I'm worried that telling the truth will make her leave.

"Are you always this forward?" By her inquisitive eyes and body language—leaning in, enough to show interest—she doesn't seem offended.

"Often."

"You gave that answer last night."

"I don't remember."

"I do. Flirtation, forwardness. Same thing. Same answer. Tell me, Mr. Everest, do women ever turn you down?"

"With these movie star good looks?"

"Funny."

"Quippy. I believe that's the word you used."

"So you *do* remember. What else do you remember about our short time together?"

The space is small for my large frame, so I shift a chair to my right and move in closer so the table is the only thing keeping us apart, and whisper, "I remember that asshole hitting on you—"

I'm not sure if it's relief or disappointment that washes through her, but she laughs. "He *was* an asshole, but I didn't expect you to say that."

"Oh, yeah?" I glance up as the fries are set down. When we're alone again, I move in. "I remember how the skies opened up for us long enough to watch the night set in. I remember the way your gaze lingered, and a sadness came over you when you stared at the Eiffel Tower, despite how much you seem to love the sight of it." Her lips part, and I lick my lower one in response before adding, "I remember watching you walk away until I could no longer see you and being worried that I should have insisted on walking you home."

"I was fine," she replied, her voice lower, her tone solemn. "Not much scares me these days."

"I see."

We keep looking at each other, but this time in silence. My heart starts beating in an unfamiliar staccato, and although cars are driving by and other patrons are around us, I wonder if she can hear it.

Taking a fry, she says, "You should eat them while they're hot. They're best that way." After biting it, she sets the rest down and picks up her book and purse. She seems to wrestle with something on her mind. "I should go."

"What? Why? We're sharing here. You can't leave in the middle of a plate of fries."

Her shoulders sag as a debate wars in her eyes. "I shouldn't have come tonight."

"Why did you?"

"You."

I got the answer I was hoping for, but I don't feel the

satisfaction I thought I would, not when she looks sad. "What's wrong, Winter?"

Watching her run the pendant along the chain again, I think it's a sign of anxiety. She says, "I don't know what I was thinking or what I'm doing. I didn't mean to give you the wrong impression."

"You didn't. You've done nothing wrong. Nothing to lead me on if that's what worries you."

"Being here is leading you on. Sitting here for two hours reading a book in hopes you might come . . . Everything I've done is wrong." She sighs. "I need to go . . . I *should* go."

"I'll walk with you, not follow, but *with* you. Give me to the corner to be a quiet companion again."

"I don't want you quiet. I quite like our conversations and the meaning under the pretense of nonsense. That's why I should leave."

"Someone once told me that every day is a new opportunity to take a chance."

"A chance at what?"

"Me." I was burying myself in this lie to spend more time with her, but the truth kept sneaking out as if she'd see it if I didn't say it.

"So if I stay, what happens then?"

"We talk about the weather, Paris, the book you're reading. Anything you want to talk about."

Leaning back, she seems to carry the world on her shoulders and uses the chair for support. "I don't even remember how to make conversation anymore."

"Why is that?"

"Look around. It's a beautiful city, but it's the loneliest place on earth."

"Why do you stay?"

"Because you asked me to."

I shake my head. "No, I mean in Paris."

"Ah. That. Well," she says, watching a couple passing by. "That will take more time than we have."

"I have all the time in the world tonight."

Her smile returns. "You're very charming."

"See? Now there's a reason to stay."

"No. That's definitely a reason to leave," she says, standing up.

I stand in response, tempted to touch her, to keep her here eating fries and drinking wine as if hours of daylight remain. I reach for my wallet and put money on the table.

When she glances down, she smiles and picks up a few bills. Handing them back to me, she says, "Do you always overpay?"

"I have no idea how much these French bills are worth."

"You're a lost cause, movie star."

"I am. Maybe you can help me."

In a standoff, we stay where we are. Pausing through several heartbeats, she then rolls her eyes. "Fine. Come on. I'll let you walk with me."

Chuckling, I follow her from where we were tucked away at a table. "Thanks for the favor."

On the sidewalk, she waits for me. "Ready?"

"Yes." *So ready.*

4

Bennett

It's not like I don't date beautiful women. I have a phone full of numbers I can call at any hour—day or night. Yet I can't remember the last time I actually called one of those numbers.

Not that this is a date.

It's not.

Nope.

It's a stroll. She's rubbing off on me. Not only do I roll my eyes that I used her word "stroll," but I rolled my eyes. I glance over at her. A little smile plays on her lips, whisking a shyness that seems to come and go across her delicate features. Even if she was snarky the first time we met, she's not this evening. As a matter of fact, she's like a whole other person not only from last night but also from what I expected.

The beauty has an indescribable appeal. There's the obvious—her attractive face, great body, and underlying confidence that sparks in a good debate. Magic encircles her, an aura that demands attention. I'm inexplicably drawn to her and it seems she might be feeling the same since she was waiting for me this evening. *What the hell has gotten into me?*

She stops a few feet ahead and looks back with concern knitting her brows. "What's wrong?"

"Paris."

A smile returns, and she comes back. "It has a way of doing that. One minute, you're strolling along the Seine. The next minute, you're in love—with the city, the music, the culture . . ." She turns her gaze to follow a car when it passes, and I hear her whisper, "Practically a stranger." Turning to me, she smiles. "I listened to your song."

I don't want to keep walking. Being with her feels so good despite the ending up ahead. "What'd you think?"

"I think you're a romantic at heart, Bennett Everest."

I shrug. "Maybe. I haven't thought about it before."

"I'm not normally like this."

"What are you normally like?"

She shifts, and then says, "Unhappy," before turning away.

Unhappy? Why is she unhappy? It doesn't take but two steps for me to fill that companion role again. What do I say to her? How do I delve into her life like I have a right to be a part of it? "I don't want you unhappy. I enjoy your smile."

She smiles for me. "I enjoy yours, too."

"Winter?" I realize not knowing the reason she's here and the reason she hasn't returned to New York might be more complicated than some superficial, easy out answer.

"Bennett?" she teases, mimicking me by bumping into my arm.

"You're visiting Paris?"

"No, I'm breaking in Paris."

"What does that mean?"

Waving it off like I'll let that lie, she says, "You really

should see the Eiffel Tower at night. How long will you be here?"

"Only a few days." *Please don't ask me why I'm here. I don't want to lie to you. Omissions are lies. I'm in deep already.*

Stopping in the middle of the sidewalk, she turns, pressing her hands on my chest. "You have to see it. You can't travel all the way from America and not see it at night."

She starts to turn away, but I hold her hands to me, wanting her right there. "Show me, Winter. Tonight."

Her hands relax in mine, and her bottom lip gets tugged under her teeth. Looking toward the other side of the street like she might find the answer there, she shakes her head. "I can't." Striking blues look up at me. "I wish I could. If we had met under different circumstances—"

"Like at the Louvre or maybe eating croissants along the riverbank? Those types of circumstances? Because I don't understand how it would be different from meeting each other at a bistro."

"No." Her hands disappear from under mine. "I don't know what spell we're under, but it's a bubble that's bound to burst. Why do I feel like we've known each other longer than we have?" *Why do I feel that she keeps reading my mind? This instant attraction . . . it's not me.*

"I feel the same if that makes a difference."

"It does make a difference, but have you ever heard of bad timing?"

"Is that what you think we have? That's a bit assumptive."

She shrugs with a giggle. "Well, you know me and my assumptions."

"So let me get this straight. Even though I'm not asking you out, you're ending us before I do?"

"Just saving you the trouble, in case you were thinking about it."

Scratching my head, I reply, "I don't think I've ever been shot down before I had time to take off."

Keeping her front toward me, she starts walking again. "There's something so magical about this city. Go see the Tower."

"And then what?"

"Think of me."

"Why don't you show me instead?"

When I start walking, she puts her hands up. "Because this is our goodbye."

"I don't want to say goodbye. Not yet." My brothers would tell me to let it lie, to let her go. To do my job and not get distracted. My sister-in-law Singer would tell me if it's meant to be . . . *Meant to be*? *Fuck.* Why am I acting like she's the last woman on earth?

"Then say au revoir." Her melodic voice is fitting for the idyllic scenery.

I should tell her who I am, but I hold back. I may not know what secrets this mysterious woman keeps, but I know enough to not tell her I'm here on her father's behalf. "Will I see you again?"

A soft smile graces her lips. "If wishes come true and fate has her way."

"Fate, huh? Hey, Winter?" Although she's walking away, her feet appear to move slower, fatigue or an equally heavy emotion coming over her. Stopping, she glances over her shoulder. "What book were you reading?"

Holding it up, she says, "*The Resistance.*"

"What's it about?"

She laughs, and it's quite a sight to see her expression so light, and the heaviness gone from her face. "A rock star who meets his match in a clever, and I might add badass, heroine."

"Sounds like some other people I know."

Catching my eyes, she laughs. "I don't need to save a rock star."

I can't stop myself. I roll my thumb over my bottom lip, and then ask, "What about a movie star?"

"Do you need saving, Mr. Everest?"

"I might if you're the one doing it. And I'm always happy to return the favor."

Her expression wavers between two emotions—intrigued and shy. Both look damn good on her. "I might take you up on that offer." Just when I think I've convinced her to stay, she starts walking away again. "Good night."

"Hey, Winter?"

Jokingly, she throws her arms wide. "What is it, Bennett?"

"I'll see you tomorrow." The promise secures her smile as if it's permanently in place. "Au revoir."

Her hair swings side to side when she turns around, putting her back that is rocking with laughter to me.

I remain on that sidewalk long after she's gone. Not because I think she'll return, but because I can still feel her when I'm here. It's a good feeling.

I didn't realize how far I'd traveled to the bistro, but the long walk back to the hotel is good for me. My head is clearer in the cool night air. I stay under the Louvre archways until I'm walking on Rue de Rivoli.

Inside the swanky hotel, chandeliers hang high from the coffered ceilings. Large planters of flowers stand guard along the walls. Modern art is juxtaposed to the historical elements that remain from the past.

Needing a strong drink, I detour to the bar, finding a place in a cognac-colored leather chair in the corner to sit and stretch my long legs. It would be nice to have bigger furniture. What's up with the small tables in this city? I set my phone on the brass top table just as a waitress sets a cocktail napkin down next to it. She dips down, and says, "Bonsoir."

"Bonsoir."

"Américain?"

"Oui." I guess I don't fit in as well as I thought.

"Would you like something from the bar?"

"Bourbon. Neat."

"Oui."

The bar's not crowded, but the brown paneling, leather chairs, roaring fire in the corner, and an assortment of liquor bottles on display appear to cater to a traveling business crowd. I don't feel bad for making a call because the atmosphere seems to be okay with it. I check my watch to calculate the time between Paris and Manhattan just as the phone rings.

"Why are you still in France?"

No greeting. Ethan is all business. He just goes straight in, causing me to chuckle. He'll never change. The middle Everest brother commands attention; whether he's in a bar or the boardroom, he owns the space with not only his presence but also his intellect.

My older brother, Hutton, garners his own share of interest but in different ways. My siblings and I have hair darker than the average brown like our mother, but Hutton is the darkest haired of us all and stands the tallest at six foot four. At six three, I'm no slouch, but damn him for that extra inch that he often uses to his advantage in business and in life. In contrast to his build, he's actually rational and has patience in spades. *Unlike myself.*

Unlike Ethan as well.

Ethan is ambitious, focused, and good at every fucking

thing he does. It's frustrating, but when it comes to the Everest brothers, the best was saved for last.

At twenty-six, I've come to respect my brothers and have learned a lot not only from my father, who owns his own financial firm but my brothers. Ethan, who became one of the youngest billionaires in history, was smart enough to bring Hutton and me along with him, making us richer than any man has a right to be.

Finances aren't everything though. My brothers may have found their matches, but when I think back on the beautiful Winter, being single has its perks.

The drink is set in front of me. "*Merci*," I tell the waitress before returning my focus to the call. "Things are . . . complicated."

"I don't understand why you're there in the first place. How does bringing Nobleman's daughter back to New York get our contract signed?"

"It happened so fast, and suddenly, I was on a flight in the middle of the night. It's a long story."

"I have time."

"Is Hutton there?"

"No, he's been buried in numbers for two days straight preparing for the end of year financials."

Taking a sip of the smooth amber liquid, I relish in the way the liquor warms some of the chill from my body. "Ethan, we were so close. Nobleman had the pen in his hand, ready to sign."

I recall the memory with clarity . . .

The lines in Nobleman's face have deepened. Stress. It's a bitch. He looks at me from across the conference table with his hands clasped on top. "I like your concept and the energy you've put into this project, Mr. Everest—"

I shift in my chair, angling toward the client. "I sense a but."

He delivers. "But it's a stretch for Nobleman Inc."

"Stretch? Or out of your comfort zone? I'm guessing comfort zone, Mr. Nobleman. But that's why you called me. That's why I'm here. You don't want ordinary. You're tired of settling for the same companies monopolizing the market and giving you poor service in return."

When he sits backs with a relaxed posture, I know I have him where I want him—one step closer to closing this deal. "And Everest Enterprises is different?" he asks.

"I'm not selling you a marketing package. I'm not telling you how to run your business or stepping out as a PR rep for your firm. Those other conglomerates try to cover all the bases but fail at the basics. Communications."

He crosses his arms in thoughtful reproach. "Communications?"

"Good old-fashioned media coverage. We'll make sure the equipment is top of the line, monitored on-site, and in place for all your major events. Last year you held two events and lost a signal halfway through your presentation. Our consultants will work directly with your communications department to create a plan that covers every aspect and then follow through with it from beginning to end."

Sitting up, he taps the portfolio my team customized for his business and says, "You've told me why we should go with Everest, but how?"

"How?"

"How much will it cost me, and how will you guarantee that the transition runs smoothly without interrupting our daily business?"

"I'll personally work with your team to ensure there are no disruptions and that you're treated like the priority you are to Everest Media and the parent company of Everest Enterprises. Because when you're working with one, you're a priority to all." I reach across to the head of the table and flip the portfolio open.

"Just sign on the dotted line, and we'll be here tomorrow to start the process."

Resting his arms on the table, he laughs. "You expect me to sign over eight million dollars in a four-year contract without negotiation? You have balls, Bennett."

"Big fucking balls, but I can back 'em, so I'm not moving from the price because it's a solid and fair price. I didn't quote you a rate to negotiate. I quoted you the best price from the start."

He pushes up, his fingers whitening against the glass top conference table. "There's something about you, Everest." He grins, and I know this is it. Holding out his hand, he says, "Pen."

I whip my Mont Blanc from the inside pocket of my jacket, and just as he's about to sign, his phone rings, distracting him from the task at hand. After glancing at the screen, he says, "I need to take this."

. . . Ethan listens to my retelling of the story, and then asks, "Connect the dots for me, Bennett."

Holding the phone closer to my ear when some patrons at another table get loud inside the bar, I reply, "He was distraught when he hung up. I tried to excuse myself, but he told me about his daughter. I couldn't leave. She hasn't been in contact with him for nearly a month and he struggles to concentrate on business because he's worried about her. Apparently, he knows through a PI that she's all right, but he doesn't know why she won't come home."

"A PI?" He sighs loud and clear. He's not wrong for being concerned. I was too. I still am, and I know more than I'm telling him. "Look, Ben," he says, "I get that he's worried, but that's personal."

"He asked about our connections in Europe."

"I hope he didn't ask Hutton. No way will he use his wife's association if it even has a hint of danger attached."

Hutton's wife happens to be a princess from a European country, but no way would we entangle her in this mess. Ethan's and Hutton's wives have become the sisters I never had, and I wouldn't do anything to endanger either of them. "I volunteered."

"I heard, but why?"

"He set the file in front of me and told me we'd have a deal if I bring her back."

"Who adds a clause like that to a business deal?"

"That's how worried he was, and I believed him." I hate to fucking admit it, but I've been told I'm easy on the eyes. "Here's the truth. My ego thought I'd have the contract signed by sunset."

"How'd that work out for you?"

"It hasn't." I steal another sip while I wait for the lecture.

"Arrogance aside, you have a good heart, baby brother, but remember there are two sides to every story. It makes you wonder what her side of the story is. Why would she go to this extreme? What happened to make her pack her bags and leave? There are too many unanswered questions, Ben. I don't like you being in the middle of this mess." I can hear his desk phone buzzing in the background, but he doesn't take the call. "You're there, so how do things stand with her?"

"They're complicated."

"You said that. What's complicated?"

"She's evasive when our conversations get personal. I can't figure out why she's here." I begin to trace the scene painted in the mural across the room, letting my mind go back to a few key things Winter mentioned. "She said she's here on a break." *Breaking* . . . is that the same thing as taking a break? "She's at the bistro each night. Tonight, she was waiting for me."

"Tell me you haven't hooked up with her?"

The word *unavailable* lands like a rock in my gut. "I haven't."

"Don't. Nothing will fuck up this deal faster than you sleeping with a client's kid."

"She's twenty-five, not a kid. I can tell you that much. And that's the thing. Nobleman made it sound like she's nothing more than a wild child out rebelling, escaping responsibility, life, but she's not like that. She's a little reserved and put together—her clothes, her hair, her makeup. Nothing's over the top. It's like he doesn't know her at all."

"Maybe that's why he's worried."

"I'll tell you, Ethan, it's almost like she doesn't want to be seen, but it's so damn hard not to look at her. Her eyes are this—"

"Ben. Stop. You can't do this. You can't do *her*. I'm serious. You need to come back to New York. We should have never gotten involved in this mess. Clearly, she's old enough to make her own decisions. You are not contractually obligated to bring her back to the States. We run our business ethically and stand behind our work. If that's not good enough for Nobleman, we'll pass on the deal."

His voice of reason sinks in, and I say, "It's still been a record-breaking year."

"It has."

"It's just disappointing—"

"I get that, but something feels off, and the last time I had this feeling, my wife's life almost ended." He sucks in a harsh breath. We don't discuss what happened back then. For him and Singer, it's best to keep it in the past. Winter's words come back to haunt me. *We all have something we're not proud of.* Ethan lives with a lot of regrets. Regrets he's trying to move past daily.

"You're right." I might not ever get answers to the questions I have for her no matter how much I want to know her secrets. We may have said au revoir like it wasn't a goodbye, but it needs to be.

Ethan's right. Nobleman's signature isn't dependent on me bringing her back. She's old enough and of sound mind to know whether she wants to be in Paris, Spain, New York, or wherever. It's time I return home. "I'll see you when I land."

5

Winter Nobleman

When I was a child, I discovered that not all Nobleman are created equal.

I am my mother's daughter, a bothersome sister, and an annoyance to a father too focused on business deals and my brother, the Nobleman who will run the company one day, instead of his daughter. My gender alone excluded me from contention. An old-fashioned man and his outdated ideals would lead me to where I am now.

It didn't matter that I worked harder than my brother.

I worked smarter.

I was salutatorian of my graduating class at my business school, earned scholarships from prestigious Manhattan firms, and a coveted internship with the biggest global shipping commerce company in the world.

It still wasn't enough.

Thinking about how I got into this mess . . . I wanted to prove my worth to him. The strategy was simple. Get the job. Get the man. Get the secrets that could save my family's company. Then walk away the hero. But in grand Winter style, I failed bigger and better than ever.

My father only saw me as a child who used to wear pink bows in my hair and obeyed his rules to a T. Until I purposely went against his wishes in a bad attempt to get his attention. I became his enemy when I did what he told me not to—I fraternized with the wrong people, mingled with wolves in sheep's clothing.

Good intentions, we all know how those turn out. The road to hell is paved with them, and hell is where I now reside. It may have the pretty package of Paris wrappings, but I'm not disillusioned enough to think I'm free.

Standing in this apartment ten flights above the street, I still wonder how I ended up in Paris?

The rose I found on my bed last night is a stark reminder. *It wasn't a choice.*

I plucked the petals instead of sticking it in water. This isn't a gift. It's a threat wrapped in velvety blood-red petals.

My small collection of books was on the floor when I returned. He's hell-bent on destroying any joy I might find to ease my mind. I picked them up and placed them back on the shelf after making sure the covers weren't too messed up.

I never predicted this outcome. I wasn't the hero. I was the pawn who unintentionally walked into a bigger plan, a plan I never knew was in place until it was too late.

Now I'm stuck in a game my enemy wants to win at the expense of my family. He may want their company, but when the mission is accomplished, it's my soul he plans to keep. His filthy lies fill my memories, his scotch breath burns my nose. "*You will never be free of me.*" His words haunt me.

My will is the least of his concerns, and now I'm trapped, but for how long? Regret nips at the back of my mind in the waking hours, and I find no solace in sleep. Weeks into this nightmare, I've learned where my family ties lie. Not with me. *With him.* Cowards.

They sold my freedom for a debt reduction. What will they sell next to wipe the slate clean?

I worry the answer might be the rest of me.

My anger has subsided into acceptance of my situation, resignation set in.

With every step I take, I'm watched. The photos left in my studio apartment last week, showing my shopping trip to Shakespeare and Co to buy books. The bra I liked but didn't buy in an expensive shop in the 9th arrondissement two weeks prior found wrapped in a pink box on the bed by the time I got back.

Groveling is not my strong suit. So it took everything I had to go to him on my family's behalf and dance with the devil once again. What I hadn't realized was that I was in over my head before I even walked into the restaurant. *I hadn't realized I was expendable. But twenty-six days in Paris has taught me that.*

What disappoints me the most is that I shouldn't have made this mistake. I shouldn't have trusted him. I should have never begged for mercy from a man without a soul. I'm smarter than that, yet here I am living with his limits and boundaries I can't escape.

I let the drapes fall, and the walls of my gilded cage close in. A new day is here. I either live it or die in it, but I'm not in control of it. So I try to look at the bright side and make the most of my time in Paris.

There's an ache in my heart, my constant companion, which nothing alleviates. *Perhaps today will be the day I die.* After all, I know the score. I'll live until he chooses I won't.

I walk back to the drapes and open them again, sweeping them behind the wall hooks. I can't let him win. Sunshine. *Light equals hope.* I need light in this dark time of my life.

Who knew I'd find it in an American in Paris? For the past two nights, I've felt—no, *I've tasted*—what freedom could look like. *Why'd I even bring up the Eiffel Tower at night?* Bennett has me acting foolish when I need to stay guarded.

Peeking outside once more, it's cloudy. *Again.* Very disappointing. I sit down and glance at my phone on the marble tabletop, the information I started reading earlier still there.

Bennett Everest.

Born in Houston, Texas.

Twenty-six years old.

Currently living in Manhattan.

Director of Media and Communications under the Everest Enterprises umbrella.

Why is he here?

Single . . . Ooh. Nice.

Net worth – five hundred million

Holy wow!

On paper, he's perfect. In real life, he's even better.

Taking the phone, I wonder why I'm making this call? *Yes, he's attractive, interesting, compelling . . . but he could be dangerous for me. If the devil finds out . . . would it be dangerous for Bennett?* Surely not. Surely that's just paranoia.

Exhaling a deep breath, I take a chance on . . . It's a risk. There are no two ways about it. "Everest Enterprises, how may I direct your call?"

I reply, "Mr. Everest's office, please."

"Which Mr. Everest, may I ask?"

I bonk my hand against my head. "I'm sorry. Bennett Everest."

"No worries. It happens all day, every day. Please hold and I'll transfer you."

A man answers this time, "Everest Media & Communications. How can we solve your communications needs?"

Funny. Punny even, considering my needs are the reason I'm calling. Loneliness has washed away my sensible side. "Hello, I'm supposed to meet Mr. Everest at his hotel here in Paris in less than an hour, but I've misplaced the name of his hotel. Will you be so kind as to help me out?"

"I'll be happy to contact Bennett and have him give you a call back."

"No. No. Um, I feel like such an idiot, and I can't blow this meeting. I thought it was on Rue deeee . . ." I drag it out hoping he'll fill in the missing information.

"Yes. Rivoli, I believe."

Let's see if it works twice. "I thought so. Laaaa . . ."

"Le Meurice."

"I should have remembered. It's one of the most beautiful hotels in the city. Merci." I hang up before he has time to ask my name. I finish the last of my tea and set the cup back on the saucer. The clatter lingers while I walk to the vanity and pull my necklace from where it hangs on the corner of the mirror. Clasping the locket in my hand, I can still hear her voice in my head when she used to say, "*Ring the bell and make a wish. You'll receive what you need.*"

I always thought it should rhyme, but my mother must have had her reason that it didn't. I shake the locket just enough to hear the familiar jingle inside, wishing I had the key. It was lost long before she handed it down to me. I bring it to my mouth and close my eyes to kiss it. "Wish me luck, Mom." It settles on my chest while I grab my jacket and purse. It's time to see a man about a tower.

Two blocks down from where I'm kept . . . *where I'm staying*, I correct as if I have a choice, I hop on the Métro. But the word *kept* makes my heart squeeze and my throat close as the night I woke up in the apartment flashes in my head.

My instructions were clear, the threat following

profoundly convincing. The sounds of brakes that need replacing pierce my ears as the train comes to a stop, saving me from another painful memory. Glancing to the platform, I see the station name in tiles and maneuver into the bustling lunchtime crowd to exit.

Parisians are known for their long lunches, but today, everyone seems to need to be somewhere and fast. Up ahead, I spot the green awnings and blue mansard roof of his hotel. It's one of the most prestigious in the city, and the central location can't be beat. Tourists may frequent this area, but I love the gardens across the street and being able to blend in with other people.

When I step through the first doors into the foyer, I look up and then move forward to take a quick spin through the revolving door. The chandelier sparkles above as I turn under it; the crystals shining like little beams of sunlight.

The bustle is kept at bay outside the fancy entrance. A couple stands at the check-in desk and two businessmen speaking German walk by me, so I move to the side, wondering what I should do next. Should I try to find out which room he's staying in or sit and wait?

I'm not even sure what I'm doing here or what I'll say when I see Bennett. He's a gorgeous man, but his genuine interest in getting to know me makes me feel human—not property or a pawn—drawing me to him once more.

Last night he told me that he'd see me tomorrow, but we said goodbye. *Did he stay another day?* I walk to the front desk. "Bonjour," I say.

The man in a suit so tight I wonder how he gets into it much less walks to greet me in return. "Bonjour, mademoiselle."

After trying my best ploys to get the information I want, he kindly and firmly shuts me down. So I sit on the sofa, dragging the locket along the chain, and people watch.

I'm too anxious to sit still for long, so I rely on the necklace in times like these. My mother's gift comes with memories from when she was alive, her locket a tie to a happier life.

Nora Nobleman needed the sun like I do, craved light even when she was stuck in a bed dying. On cold days, we'd draw the sun on paper and hang it on the windows like it was the middle of May instead of January and gray.

Holding the locket to my ear, I shake it lightly and listen to the little rattle inside and smile. It's not a real bell, but I like that we always pretended it was. To myself, I make another wish. "Please lead me to my destiny." I glance at the ceiling as if I'll see my guardian angel looking down on me. My bouncing knee stills and my cheek biting stops when momentary peace is found.

A painful hour later, I get up because I've lost my patience. Waiting for Bennett has been for naught. Maybe he left Paris. Maybe he'll be gone all day working. Maybe he's found someone else to show him the Eiffel Tower. Maybe he's upstairs now but waiting to leave until he meets me at the bistro later.

My mind is stuck in a Rolodex of bad thoughts and regrets. I have so many other things to stress about. A hot guy who looks great in a suit shouldn't be one of them. *Why am I here?* Just because he made me laugh once or twice doesn't mean I have a right to a third. This was another ill-conceived plan. This time I need to bail. Anyway, if it's meant to be, fate will bring us together again.

And hopefully, it'll be when I'm not in the middle of somebody else's plot. I take the time to push through the revolving door again just for the small thrill of it and glance up at the chandelier once more to catch the sparkle. But it comes to an abrupt halt when someone pushes in from a different chamber, causing me to look through the glass to the other side.

My grip tightens. Holy wow! A suit has nothing on Bennett Everest wearing running shorts and a fitted athletic shirt. I struggle to swallow normally, but this time, the sound echoes in the small, enclosed space.

In the opposite compartment from me, he laughs, but with his hands, he mimes push. "Oh," I reply, coming to my senses. "Yes." I push until I'm back in the lobby where he stands—wet hair stuck to his forehead, sweat pooled in the center of the shirt, a heart rate monitor bulging from under the fabric. A healthy glow skin deep in his olive complexion.

He wipes the top of his forearm across his forehead, making his hair stand up.

I've seen his eyes under clouds when evening meets night but seeing them in the daylight makes this trip worth the risk. Whiskey with golden sunset centers I could swim in for hours. He says, "Hi."

"Hi."

.

.

.

.

.

.

.

.

.

I should really say something else, but he's so much more handsome than I've given him credit for, and movie star doesn't seem to fit as much anymore.

Supermodel?

No.

Prince?

No.

Knight?

Cold.

A rock star?

Warm.

A fantasy?

Warmer.

A dream?

Warmest.

A book boyfriend?

Steamy.

Mr. Darcy!

Hot

Hot.

Hot.

Tilting his head, his smile grows as he looks down at me. "Winter?"

"Yes?"

"Do you?"

"Huh? Do I what?"

Chuckling, he says, "You didn't hear anything I said."

"Nope," I answer a little too proudly.

"All right, how about I start over. What are you doing here?"

"Looking for you." *Subtle, Winter. Really subtle.*

"You found me." His eyes are set on mine, a hint of cockiness slipping into the corners of his ridiculously adorable grin. "What are you going to do with me?"

"Ha! Cute." *So cute.* Too cute for his own good. I'm tempted to bite my fist. "I was thinking we could go to a museum and do other things before you leave." No threats prevent me from making new friends. No rules in place other than I'm bait. I don't even know what that means, so if I'm stuck in this city, I might as well make the most of it.

"I did a little sightseeing this morning and ran a few miles. I need to shower, so if you don't mind waiting—"

"I'll wait." I plop down on the sofa like it's the last round of musical chairs, and then inwardly roll my eyes at myself. *Cool it, eager beaver.* You're going to scare the man away with your desperation.

He taps his watch when an alarm rings. "You can wait here, or the bar is nice, but you're also welcome to wait in my room. I have a chair with a nice view, and we could order tea or coffee, anything you like, while you wait."

"That sounds nice." I hop up, and as we walk to the elevators, I ask, "So you're a runner, huh?"

That makes him laugh too hard. He shakes his head. "Seemed like a good way to burn through the day."

"Why did you want to burn the day away?"

"I have a date."

"Oh." I stop a few feet from the elevator. "I shouldn't keep you."

Turning back, he winks. "It's okay. You've saved me another crazy taxi ride by coming here instead. So about those few other things you want to do . . .?"

"Keep your thoughts where they ought to be. I was referring to seeing paintings and some sightseeing, movie star."

We step on the elevator, and he pushes the button for the fifth floor. "Are you sure you're okay with coming upstairs? I'm practically a stranger." I hear the teasing in his voice.

"Are you dangerous? I have enough psychopaths in my life." Truer words have never been spoken.

His laughter fills the elevator. "No, not dangerous, though I hear most women love a bad boy."

"I don't. What about murderer?"

"Nope."

I shrug. "Then I'll take my chances." I have nothing left to lose. There are worse ways to die than in the hotel room of a handsome millionaire who has a penchant for romantic grunge-era songs and french fries.

6
<hr>

Bennett

Winter Nobleman is striking at sunset, but when the clouds blew out and blue ran the expanse of the sky, she's stunning. Sitting in a purple chair near the window, she's trying really hard not to look my way. Talking with her eyes glued to the window, it's as if she's waiting to hear "Simon Says" so she can look at me.

It's quite adorable, actually. I haven't exactly been playing fair though. With my shirt in my hand, I say, "What would you like to drink? I'll order something."

She turns and her eyes go wide. "I, uh, er, um. Wine? I think I need wine."

I casually flex as I remove the heart rate monitor wrapped around me. It's just after two in the afternoon, but if the lady wants a drink, I'm not one to judge. "White or red?" I'm no wine connoisseur. I usually just drink whatever's offered.

Glancing at her watch, she replies, "White." Her gaze returns to me in a flash and stays put as I order the wine and a cheese plate. I catch her blues going lower, but they soon return unashamed back to my eyes. As soon as I hang the phone up, she cocks an eyebrow. "Are you going to stand around shirtless all day or take your shower?"

"Does me being shirtless bother you?"

"Not at all. Just curious." Her shoulders rise and fall quickly. Sitting back, she returns her attention out the window. "The view is nice, but I prefer the gardens."

Smirking, I stand in the doorway that leads to the bathroom, and say, "I don't usually pay much attention to views from hotel windows. I'd rather be outside than staring at it."

She angles in my direction. "Interesting."

"I won't be long. Make yourself at home."

"I will." This time, she smirks, and it's damn sexy on her.

I close the door and wonder what she'll do unattended while I'm in here. Not sure that room service will be quicker than I am, but I put it to the test and get in the shower. My muscles are tight from traveling, so I spend an extra few minutes letting the heated spray pound down on my shoulders before I get out.

After I brush my teeth, I consider shaving, but I don't want to keep Winter waiting any longer, so I skip it. It isn't until I finish in the bathroom that I realize my clothes are in the bedroom with her.

Shit.

Tightening the towel below my middle, I tuck the corners in the front and walk out. The chair is empty, but the bed is not. She doesn't even bother to lift on her elbows, much less look guilty for lying in the middle of it. The last thing I expected when I woke up this morning was to see Winter Nobleman lying on my bed. I might have dreamed about it, but the reality is even better.

"You said I could make myself at home, so I did. This bed is comfy." Her legs and arms move in the middle of the cream-colored blanket as though she's making a snow angel.

"That I did."

When there's a knock on the door, she points in that direction but makes no move to answer it. "Room service."

I hold my towel in place and open the door. The tray is set on the table and then the wine opened. After filling the glasses, the server disappears as if he was never here. And she still makes no move. Eyeing her, I raise my own eyebrow. "Are you waiting to be served?"

"Are you up for the task?"

"I can handle it."

She sits up, crossing her legs. So small in the middle of the large bed, I inadvertently smile from the sight. Maybe it's because it's my bed she's in as well . . . *maybe* . . .

With her eyes unabashedly roaming my body again, I give her a little show. The towel slips just enough to cause her mouth to open. But then I tighten the terrycloth around me and give her a little wink. "I bet you can handle me—I mean, the task at hand."

"What's the task at hand?" I ask.

"Bringing me wine."

"At your service." I take my sweet time crossing the room, giving her the full show without putting everything on display if you know what I mean. Her grabby hand takes the glass, making me laugh. "Hard day?"

"Every day is hard." The lightness of her voice and the fun that had been floating through the air dissipates.

"Always so cryptic." *Why is every day hard? Is she in some sort of danger?* Surely not. She's still as composed on my bed as she was at the bistro.

I expect her to finish her wine, but she doesn't even take a sip. She sets it on the nightstand and lies back. "I shouldn't be here—in Paris, in this room, here with you. I don't know you."

Her eyes follow me as I move to the open suitcase on the

floor at the foot of the bed. Squatting, I grab some casual clothes and look up. "Don't you?"

She sits up, fluffing the pillows behind her. After retrieving the glass, she sips from it and then returns it to the nightstand. "I looked you up online."

I stand and search her face for signs of what she's thinking and not saying. "That's disappointing."

"You could have lied. I would have never known the difference."

I have been. "I didn't want to lie about who I am to you."

"Why not?"

"I don't like to lie."

"Everyone lies, Bennett."

"That's a shame." It's a shame I've lied long enough to gain her trust so that she's sitting on my hotel bed like she's spending the day and maybe the night right there. It's a shame I can't bring myself to confess the truth to her even now when we're supposed to be honest, supposed to be proving that not everyone lies. But I'm still stuck on her words.

"I shouldn't be here—in Paris, in this room, here with you." Because even though she's walked away from me twice, and even though she shouldn't be here . . . *she is.* I don't know what to make of that. Do I push for answers or wait for her to expose what she's hiding?

She takes another drink, this time longer, closing her eyes as if she's trying to dull the pain rather than savor the notes. Tilting her head back, she opens her eyes. "It's probably best."

"Why are you in Paris?" I ask, hoping I'll get a better answer this time.

"I had dinner in New York and woke up in Paris. You never know where life will take you."

"Sounds adventurous." What I want to say is, *what the*

hell does that mean? But it's as though she's unsure what she can say, not being deliberately evasive. *I think.*

"Something like that." She takes a drink, not leaving enough to take another.

"Vague responses seem to be your specialty." I'm about to drop this towel but decide I should give her some warning. "Are you going to watch, or you want to give a guy a little privacy?"

"You have something to hide, movie star?"

Laughing feels good and lightens the mood. "Nope, nothing to hide, sweetheart." The towel falls, and she sits straight up. Her hair is a mess as her eyes go wide, absorbing the full picture.

For a woman who can have her choice of any man, she acts like this is the first time she's seen one naked. "Need some extra time to take in . . . well, *the extra*?"

Rolling her eyes, Winter falls back on the pillows. "And here I thought you were different."

I pull on my boxer briefs. "You can't expect me to pass up a perfect setup like that." Slipping on my jeans, I'm still chuckling. "I'm still not sure how we went from all the formality of the bistro to my hotel room and showing off our better parts."

"Two things," she says, watching me as I button my jeans and then pull on an undershirt.

"What's that?"

"First, a bistro is about as far from formal as you can get. Though I understand what you're saying. We weren't exactly at ease there."

"And secondly?" I pull on a sweater and then sit on the bench.

"I may be in your room, but I definitely haven't shown you my best parts."

When I look over my shoulder, she's lying on her side,

head resting on her elbow, and she winks. So fucking gorgeous. Such a contradiction. Sassy and confident. Dark and moody. I can't figure her out. What I need to do is stop thinking about her better parts or I won't be able to walk out of this room. "Ready to go, or do you want to stay in?" Plucking the front of my sweater, I add, "I can have this off faster than it went on."

Laughing, she sits up and swings her legs over the edge. "I just bet you can, but we have plans."

"Plans can change." After putting on socks, I lace up my Red Wing Chukkas.

"You're telling me." She pats my shoulder when she walks by and picks up her jacket from the chair. Cutting a piece of Brie, she eats it, and then says, "Come on. I want to show you my favorite statue." When she takes another bite, the lightest of moans escapes her lips.

I steal a few grapes from the plate but then squint at her. "Wait. You're forcing art on me?"

"Yes. Touristy stuff, too. It seems you haven't taken in any of the required sights in Paris since you've been here."

"You don't want to stay in, eat cheese, and drink wine?" I'm hungry, so I snatch a couple of bites of cheese and pop them into my mouth.

Grabbing me by the sleeve, she pulls me toward the door. "From the mess of papers on that desk, it seems you've been working when you weren't running. Let's go have some fun."

"Fine. Can't blame me for trying. You looked comfortable on that bed."

The door opens, but I stop to grab my wallet, check to verify the room key is inside, and then take my phone. Tucking them into my pockets, I step in and grab the rest of the grapes before the door shuts. Winter is already halfway to the elevator. "On a mission there, sweetheart?"

"Always."

Outside, we cross the street to the Tuileries Garden. I only know this because I have my own personal tour guide showing me all the statues she loves like *Standing Woman*. "Gaston Lachaise was an American." I'm elbowed. "Like you," she says with a smile.

"And you." I nudge right back.

She laughs. "Sometimes I forget. When you spend as much time as I do trying to blend in, you start to become a ghost of yourself." Touching the small waist of the statue, she adds, "Such a dramatic ratio to hips. Don't you think?"

Shrugging, I reply, "I guess."

"What do you see when you look at her, Bennett?"

Taking my time, my gaze swings between the statue and the woman beside it. "I see a woman who has desires and dreams but doesn't need someone else to fulfill them."

"I wish I could see her through your eyes."

"You can. Just close them." Her gaze hits me, and a scoff escapes. She's not very trusting, which is understandable since I'm still . . . well, I'm not sure what I am to her. "Just do it."

Huffing, she concedes. "Fine."

When she closes her eyes, I shift her gently in front of me and then pull her wrists slowly to her sides. She sucks in an audible breath, her back pressed to my front. She's soft in my rough hands and small against my large frame. I lean down to her ear, and whisper, "What do you see?"

"It's not what I see." There's an unfamiliar tremble to her tone. "It's what I feel."

"What do you feel, Winter?"

"Hope."

I inhale her perfumed neck, running the bridge of my nose along her silky skin. I'm tempted to kiss her, but instead, I ask, "Who stole your hope?"

She moves away, and the cold of the day invades. Her

fingers slide across her forehead as she paces. The severity of her distress hits me when she looks at me. "I . . . I tell you what I can, Bennett. The rest is just . . ." She crosses her arms over her chest, staring across the gardens. "Sometimes bad people have good intentions."

"Are you a bad person, Winter?"

"I'm trying to make things right."

"For who? Yourself? Someone else?"

"For everyone." She starts walking but turns back. "This way. I want to show you the Rodin."

And we're back to being practically strangers again. I follow her, keeping my pace a few safe steps behind her, giving her space, the distance I think will comfort her instead of me invading it. But she stops, silently waiting.

Her arm wraps around mine, and we walk the rest of the way entangled together like any other couple in the gardens today. I don't understand her. Complicated doesn't seem to fit how she twists my mind. I look into her sapphire eyes, knowing that's all I'll probably get. It's more than she wanted to give, so I consider that a win, a victory for today. With that small taste of who she really is, I'm already craving so much more.

I didn't catch a flight back to New York like I was supposed to. I stayed because this trip no longer feels like a contractual obligation but a personal mission. I've never been drawn to anyone like I am to her. Even now when we stand next to a work of art, I can't take my eyes off her.

I may not know much about art, but I know if it moves you, it's to be admired. *And damn, do I admire her.*

"*The Kiss,*" she says, her voice steady as if anchored in tranquil seas. "I dream of being kissed like this one day." She's too careful, struggling not to look for me as if I'm meant to be by her side.

I take the silent cue not only because *she* wants me to but also because *I* want to. Her shoulder presses against the front of mine. Her breathing steadies as if I'm the calm she needs. When she closes her eyes, I ask, "What do you feel, Winter?"

"Alive." I want to kiss her because I've never felt more alive than right here at this moment. I take things slow and kiss the spot just under her earlobe. Her hand holds me there before she angles into me, and says, "I can't."

7

Winter

I'm not in Paris to fall in love, like, or lust.

But that doesn't stop my heart from beating a little faster around Bennett Everest. I feel too much too soon for this man. I can search his name online as much as I want, but nothing prepared me for spending time with him firsthand.

Charming.

Funny.

Handsome. *Very.*

Great style.

Intelligent. Quick to pick up on wordplay.

Kind enough to let it go.

I'd forgotten the feel of caring hands, and what it's like to have someone listen rather than talk at me. Or shout.

I wonder if I've become complacent to the danger I'm in. I've become numb to taking precautions. I used to look over my shoulder every step I took. Now I brazenly step out with a man as if *he* won't notice. I hope *he* doesn't.

Just in case, I walk away, rounding the statue, and

pretend to admire the details of the sculpted bronze when all I want to do is sneak peeks at the man who seems to have come out of nowhere and made an unbearable situation more tolerable.

Bennett will leave any day, and I'll be left to endure this alone, watched like prey until the day comes when I have to play the part *he* commands of me.

Lure.

Deliver.

Walk away.

Job done. Then I'll be set free. *I hope.*

I wonder if Bennett will still be single. He's too good of a catch, but maybe I can look him up when I'm back in New York City. In the meantime, I'll enjoy him where I'm held captive. *It's sad how low my expectations in life have become. But it's better not to hope than to feel utter disappointment.* "What do you feel?" I ask.

Bennett changes as the hours tick by. As his comfort with me grows, his affection becomes more conspicuous. Leaning to the side, he sees me and smiles. What a deliciously devilish smile it is, too. "Lonely. Come keep me company."

I can't hide the smile he evokes as I come back and stand with him in front of the statue again. With my feet slipping between his, I start thinking about what it would be like to kiss those delectable lips. Would he embrace me like Paolo does Francesca in the statue—with passion, as if they might only ever have this one kiss? If it can't last a lifetime, can the memory carry the torch of their desire?

A high-pitched scream startles us, and we jump back from each other. A little girl with brown pigtails and an ice-cream cone turns red in the face and then screams again, this time followed by crocodile tears. Her mother rushes to her, griping about dropping the ice cream like she warned her not to do. Squatting down so she's eye-level, she wipes her tears and hugs her.

My heart shifts gears from racing to clenching, my mood souring just as quickly. "Could we go? Please?"

"Are you okay?"

I feel the prick of tears as the cold air hits me. "Fine. I'll be fine."

His hand is warm, so warm, defrosting my chilling heart and stopping me before I can get too far.

Compassionate.

"Winter, talk to me. What's wrong?"

"Talk to you," I repeat quietly to myself. I can still hear the little girl's sobs though they've lessened against her mom's shoulder. "That's not something ever asked of me since my mother died." The straighter corners of his shoulders round as they bear the weight of my confession. *Shit.* "I shouldn't have said anything."

"Why? Why is that something you should have to hold in?"

I like the concern that shines in his eyes. *He cares.* He doesn't even know me, yet he's showing more empathy than I've ever received. I could eat up the attention, losing my better judgment in the spoils of his kindness, and then leave him burning in the ashes of the betrayal. "You could become very addicting, Mr. Everest."

The right side of his mouth rises as the darkness of the pupils overtake the golden of his eyes, shamelessly drinking me in. Men can do that. They can wield their desires like a sword through innocent flesh and walk away unscathed from the battle. "And that's a bad thing?"

I've fought so hard to be seen as an equal to my brother and never was, but here stands this stranger serving it up on a silver platter and looking at me like I can be anything I want to be. He's willing to relent the difference in height to treat me as an equal. "It's too good."

"We're in Paris. If we can't indulge in the City of Love, where can we?"

Tapping him on the chest, I reply, "*Bonne remarque.*"

"And that means?"

"That means good point. We should get a coffee and éclairs before continuing our adventure. Oui?"

"Oui," he replies, "I'm starving."

"Come on. Let's feed you."

———

Sitting inside the cozy patisserie, we've finished our treats, and our cups are empty. Chatter doesn't fill every minute with him, but I like how easy it is to be with him. "You never told me how long you'll be in Paris."

He nods, looking down at his watch as if he's late and has to dash out the door. "I shouldn't be here now."

"What does that mean?"

"I was ordered back to the States yesterday."

"Ordered? Why?"

"Because my brother, the CEO, thinks I'm on a fool's mission."

"Are you?"

The intensity of his glare, the fixed gaze on me, stills me in my chair. "I hope not."

"What are you going to tell him?"

"That I needed to stay."

"Why did you stay, Mr. Everest?"

"I think you know." He moves his chair around to sit closer. "Is it bad that I want to kiss you right here in a dessert shop?"

"It's a bakery."

"Does it matter?"

"The kiss or the French word?"

He leans in, and I don't move a millimeter in my seat. I don't breathe. I just wait for his heat, his lips on me, his . . . My eyes fly open. "Did you just lick me?"

"I did. You had a little chocolate right there." His lips press to my cheek, and even though it's not where I want him to be, I'll take anything he'll give me because it feels so nice. And then I push him away playfully.

"You're silly."

"You need some silly in your life."

I think I might need more of *him* in my life. Reaching over, I take his elbow and pull him in again. With our faces just a few inches apart, I ask, "Did you stay for me?"

"I did," he whispers, "so let's make the most of it. I have two days."

"To live like you were never supposed to stay? I can work with that and make it so you never regret a single minute."

I'm tempted to kiss him, so tempted, but I don't. He's become the master of the tease, and I'm starting to enjoy the game. I lick my lips with his eyes glued to the small action and then stand abruptly. "Well, come on," I say, "we don't have time to lose."

"Yes, ma'am."

"Such a Southern gentleman."

"How'd you know I was from the South?" he asks as we walk toward the door. "Oh, right. You looked me up."

Oh, no. I've really screwed up. "Actually," I stumble over my words, trying to find something to land on. "You have an accent, Bennett. I'm from Manhattan. You may live in New York, but you're clearly not from there." I shoulder the door open and smile when I pass.

Happy.

Pure, unadulterated happiness. I can't recall the last time I felt like this.

The wind whips his musky oceanic scent around me, and I rush to find him. Standing under the burgundy awning with his hands in his pockets, he smiles just from watching me.

Carefree.

I see it in his eyes. Eyes can't lie.

I feel the same in my heart, letting it fill me and reach my eyes, too. Taking his hand in mine, I caress it, and with my smile too big to hide, I pull him with me as I walk backward. "The city is ours. What do you want to see?"

"I'm seeing all I ever need to of this city." He's quick, his arms going around me and pulling me against him. "What could we ever see that beats what's standing in front of me right now?"

With our bodies pressed together, I slide a hand under his sweater to feel his heart beating. "Yours matches mine."

He brings my other hand to his lips, kisses it, and says, "Maybe it's a sign."

"My mom believed in astrology, karma, and anything else involving a superstition. I gave up believing when she died. Though I still wish upon my necklace like she used to do."

Holding my hand as he lowers it, he gives it a light squeeze. "Would it be so bad to try to believe again?"

"You make me want to." A Vespa backfires down the street, bringing me from my daydream. I'm reminded of the little girl crying at the statue and now the scooter. Our bubble popped, an attraction building so fast that it probably would have burst on its own if given enough space and time to grow.

I sigh. *Who am I kidding?* I don't understand this attraction. And fear seeps back in. What if spending time with me puts Bennett in the crosshairs of *him*? He's almost too good to be true.

"You've gone quiet." *And very perceptive.*

"I . . . probably shouldn't make any commitments." Not wanting to seem too unstable, I add, "You know . . . being unavailable and all."

"You're a very quirky woman."

"I prefer unpredictable."

"That you are. But it's not bad to rely on something."

We start walking slowly at first as if the direction doesn't matter. *Does it?*

"My father once told me to be the hare. That, in real life, the tortoise would always lose."

"It sounds like you were caught in the middle."

"Caught between a dreamer and a realist. My dad was right." He keeps his gaze directed ahead, but he's not letting go of my hand, and I haven't pulled away. A squeeze became a safehold that he's apparently set on protecting.

Less than five hours together and I'm already beginning to feel something for this dark-haired man. How is that possible?

"Do you still talk to him?" The question gives me pause. For the first time since we met, something feels off. I drop my hand to my side and then tuck it into my coat pocket. It's noticed, and he's quick to add, "I've overstepped. I didn't mean to offend you."

"You didn't offend me, Bennett. It's just an odd question. Why wouldn't I be talking to my dad?" This is how I should reply even if it is a lie. "Wouldn't he worry about his daughter?" *Is my father capable of worrying about someone he can't even say I love you to?*

"I'm sure he does, but is there a reason he should?"

Yes.

He'd be furious at what I've done to protect him, but I

didn't do it to go against his wishes. I did it to save the Nobleman legacy. I pivot the conversation. "My brother, Braden, on the other hand . . . he hates me. Once my mother died, we ceased being civil to each other."

"I'm sorry."

"Don't be." I don't want to think of what's to come, or the price I'm paying for diving into the deep end, thinking I could swim with sharks. "Let's talk about other things. We only have two days, and my mom used to say that when you're with good company, it isn't about the destination."

The pressure releases from his expression, and he smiles. "Let's make it an incredible journey."

"There's so much to do. What do you want to start with?" He caresses my cheek, but before he speaks, I laugh. "I know where this is going, so let me rephrase that. What touristy thing would you like to see first?"

"I think I preferred the first offer."

"I just bet you do."

"How about you show me everything you love?"

"A man who lets a woman lead. You're a breath of fresh air, Monsieur Everest."

"As are you, ma chérie."

8

Winter

It feels like I've been here forever, stuck in a city I never asked to visit. The option to talk to my family was taken away with one threat; that which would end my father's life and ultimately mine for causing his death. It doesn't matter how much I try to hate him for his lack of love for me, he's still my father, the only parent I have left. I like to believe he would never intentionally hurt me, so it's easier to blame my gender for his disinterest in welfare.

A whisper tickles my ear, and Bennett asks, "How does it make you feel?"

I like that he cares enough to wonder about me. I felt uncomfortable when he asked me about my father, but then I somehow started talking about my mother and memories I haven't recalled in so long but seemed to come back as if they were yesterday. As if eighteen years haven't passed since she left me. I didn't know what to say because I can't tell him the truth.

We're in the early stages of what feels like something new —a new relationship, a new beginning, a new chance at love. A newness that blankets me like a cashmere sweater, feeling so good I don't want to take it off. "At peace," I reply.

I hate how much my answer exposes me, but that's what happens when someone tempts you to let your guard down while also providing a safety net as you're trying new things. And Bennett Everest is definitely something new I want to try. Leaning the side of my head against his, I whisper, "How does it make you feel?"

"Small."

"I get what you mean. I've seen the *Water Lilies* paintings online, on postcards, and on TV so often that I felt it might even be disappointing when I finally saw them in person the first time. But they're not."

"No, they're not. They're incredible like you."

"You're pulling out all the stops, Mr. Everest."

"When I go after something, *or someone*," he says, coming to stand at my side, "I always give one hundred and ten percent. Because if it's worth going after in the first place, it's worth giving it your all."

"You can be very charming when you want to be. Is that what you're doing? Charming me?" He doesn't realize I'm already under his spell.

"I'm spending the day with a woman who intrigues me as much as she attracts me. It's like a two-for-one."

"Two women for the price of one. Not so charming."

"No, that's not what I mean at all." We shift to our right to see more of the painting as a new crop of people walk into the oval room.

"Then what did you mean?"

"That I'm not attracted to one-dimensional women. They should have lives, goals, and dreams of their own instead of focusing on mine alone. Believe it or not," he says, "my ego is in check most of the time. I can handle a successful, confident woman who knows what she wants and likes. If I can satisfy her needs, there's no bigger boost."

"If. You said *if* when it comes to satisfying a woman? *If* isn't a part of the average guy's vocabulary. Doesn't matter how big or small, they all think they're God's gift. What makes you different?"

"There's nothing to prove when you can back up your words with skill."

The museum must have turned the heat on, so I slip my jacket down my arms. Fanning myself, I ask, "I didn't realize we were talking about sex."

"We're talking about life and fulfilling your partner's desires, but the same things apply to sex."

I like how he says sex more than I should—natural as if there's nothing to be ashamed of or nothing to hide in dark rooms, like *I'm not the slut I've been called.*

"You're not intimidated by a strong woman." I don't ask a question, and I don't expect an answer. He doesn't need to justify anything, so I say, "I guess I should have asked long before showing up at your hotel, but better late than never. Are you single, or have you been hiding a wedding ring somewhere in that wallet of yours?"

Pulling his wallet out, he holds it open. "Nope, no ring hidden in here." Waggling his left hand, he adds, "No tan line, no indentation, and no ring here either. I've been flying solo for quite some time now."

"Were you previously married?"

"No. I've had a few girlfriends, but no fiancées or wives in my past."

I don't have a right to feel this good about that, but I do. "Now that we got the first date questions out of the way, what do you think about the art?"

"So this is a date? Well, if that's the case . . ." He takes my hand and holds it like we do this every day as we walk into the next room together. Being goofy, he swings it between us, playing it up. I'm not sure if he's doing it for him, onlookers, or me, but I'm good with it.

My hand feels small in his and held with care just as he's treated me since we met. When we're standing alone, away from the crowd, he says, "I figured I'd make it official."

"Official, huh? And here I thought you were going to say a production since this seems to be for everyone else."

"Trust me, sweetheart. This is just for you and me."

I hate that I love when he calls me sweetheart. There's an edge to his normal tone that makes me think he takes no prisoners in bed.

"It's easier if we just call a duck a duck and a date a date," he says with a shrug.

"I want to trust you. Guessing games are never as entertaining as they sound."

"How about instead of guessing, we just ask what we want to know?"

"And answer anything?" I ask, starting to stress.

"Yes, just that easy. We can even take turns."

"What if we don't want to answer, or what if we can't?"

Facing me, he slips his hands around to the small of my back and pulls me close. If anyone saw us, we'd fool them into thinking we're a couple, just as I'm temporarily fooling myself. "Let's not overthink this. If you don't want to answer, then you don't have to. But know that I'm interested in you, Winter. And I want to know more."

My instinct tells me no, don't even try this. But when I look at him, I want to know more about him—everything the internet didn't tell me. I want to know the real *him*. And I want him to know the real me because when I finish paying my debt to the monster pulling the strings, there isn't any remaining doubt that Bennett is someone I would like to see again. "All right, I'll play along."

Rubbing his hands together, I see the devious glint in his eyes and start to get nervous. But what I've learned about Bennett so far is that the last thing he seems to want is to see me squirm. I wonder if that holds true in the bedroom. I hope not. "Bah!"

"Something funny you want to share?"

"No. Not at all. Sorry. If I let you inside my brain, you'll run out of here, and I'm enjoying your company too much to ruin the date this early on." I laugh to myself, and then he tickles my side. When I get louder and push off, he doesn't let me go and pulls me right back in as if I was made to fit against him.

I'm starting to think I might have been.

We're shushed by a lady with a name badge. Our laughter subsides, and I say, "You're going to get us kicked out if you keep that up."

"Let's live on the edge. It's not every day you can say you were kicked out of a museum."

Before he can tickle me again, I slip out of his reach. Stepping up to the painting, I let my gaze slip into the paint strokes. Keeping his words between us, he asks, "What do you do for a living?"

He comes out hitting hard, confirming my dread from earlier. *What am I supposed to say?* I've told him what I felt I could without giving the dirty details away. The more personal he gets, the more I'll have to pull away. Some secrets should stay buried. It will only get ugly from here, the details too bad to pretend I don't know better.

I like the way he sees me now. I like who I am when I'm with him, so I skirt around the issues. "I earned a business degree." It's one of the few things that never caused me shame, so I go with the truth. "I used to work with an acqui-sitions firm specializing in shipping, cargo holds, and docking rights."

"Really?"

Moving to his side, I watch as his eyes follow the lines of the large canvas hanging on the wall. But he turns, and by how his brows are cinching together in the middle, I can see more questions forming.

"I used to get that look a lot actually. I don't think most people associate a woman in that area of industry. I worked in an office most of the time. It's not like I was loading the ships at port, though I did once just for the experience. Prada are more flattering than work boots, especially since I'm on the shorter side."

"Everest Enterprises owns rights down in East Bay."

"Ah. That's where I know the name." Wiggling a foot in front of me, I'm quick to add, "My turn."

"I had no doubt that you're a badass who can do what-ever you set your mind to and do it in style." His smile, like the one he's wearing now, has become one of my favorite parts of the day. There's just something so genuine in the grins he shares with me.

"Stop being so good all the time. You're spoiling me."

"You should be spoiled sometimes. We all should."

"I bet women love to spoil you."

"I'm as rotten as they come."

"I suspected as much," I tease. But I know it's true. Bennett Everest doesn't lack for attention. Women notice him, eye him, smile and flirt with him everywhere we've been, including a woman who just purposely bumped into him.

The funny thing is, he apologized to her but didn't look twice. You know who he did see, though? *Me*. He makes me feel like I matter, as if I'm not invisible. *Not a toy for someone to manipulate.* He makes me believe in destiny as if I have a future ahead of me.

I don't know if I do or not, but Bennett sure makes me hope for more.

9

Winter

I can ask him anything, but whether he'll answer is a whole other story. Nevertheless, I'm greedy with this little taste of power, so I'm savoring every second.

Tapping my chin, I continue strolling down the length of the room until I reach the end. His eyes remain on me, studying me, trying to read my mind or body language. I notice. *I see him.*

So I drag this out in an attempt to unnerve him even though I should already know better. He's not a man easily intimidated. At least not so far. "Let me think." When I walk back and reach his side again, I ask, "Where did you grow up?"

He chuckles. Bennett sees right through me. I hate that I'm that obvious, but I gave him a softball question in hopes of getting one in return.

"I grew up in Houston, as you probably already know, but I'll do you one better. I went to the University of Texas in Austin—worked hard, played harder, and also earned a business degree. After a short stint in California, I returned to Houston to work for my dad. I built a small sales team. The job was easy to come by, but the boss was on my ass day in and day out." He laughs. "My dad was actually easy to work for, and the pay was decent for a recent graduate. My oldest brother was doing the accounting, so it was a family affair for the most part. My other brother, Ethan, was already in New York and brought me onboard."

His brother hired him because he was good at his job, but also because he was his brother. That's how families are supposed to work. Not like mine. I already have so many other questions I want to ask him, but since I'm willing to play by the unspoken rules. "You're up." Speaking of up, I crane my neck to catch his eyes. "How tall are you anyway? You're like a giant."

"Everything's bigger in Texas. I'll let you guess my height since it's my turn."

"You're a real comedian, Everest. So if it's not your charm, it's your humor. I swear I'm determined to find your Achilles' heel."

"Here's a secret," he whispers, the back of his hand straddling the side of his mouth. "I don't have one."

I believe him. But something has to make him putty in my hands. Food or drink? Fast cars or cigars? Kinky sex? What will make a man like Bennett Everest cave to a woman like me?

I stop and stare down at the white floor—my red shoes standing in stark contrast—as my throat tightens and my breath exhales with a sharp edge. "What am I doing?"

"Ummm . . . looking at art?"

Shaking my head, I close my eyes, squeezing them tight. "Not this museum. You?"

"Me? What about me?"

Spinning around to face him, I reply, "I'm trying to figure you out."

His hands move back and forth between us. "As I am you. That's why we're asking questions, exchanging answers, getting to know each other."

"No, it's not the same. I let my past in and started treating you like a game."

"I don't understand. Spell it out for me."

With a tight chest matching my throat, I do what I've never done before—lay my soul bare and expose what I hide from the world. "I started working an angle, but I caught myself. I stopped my thoughts from digging deeper because I do want to get to know you." I pause, unsure if I should say more, but I'm in too deep to stop. "I like you, Bennett."

"Good, because I like you, too." A smile starts to grow on his handsome face and holds steady before it spreads any farther. "But I'm still confused what this is between us. Pretending nothing is developing doesn't make it true. I don't date women who are in relationships."

"What happened to a duck is a duck and a date a date?"

"You're not seeing someone seriously. So when you say you're unavailable, you mean emotionally, correct?"

When all I want is to keep my secrets from him and enjoy the few days we have together, I sure know how to put myself right in the middle of the spotlight. My shoulders drop just like the pretenses I've been holding onto. "Save yourself the trouble and get out now."

He drags his teeth over his kissable bottom lip but then frees it. "You're just the kind of trouble worth getting into, Winter."

"I'm a mess. Can't you see?" *I hate being this raw. This open. This . . . timid.* I want Bennett to like me, to want me. Even though I know I can't have anything with him, he gives me hope.

"What I see is someone scared of the possibility of more—"

"I'm not scared of more, Bennett. I'm scared of . . ." I catch myself. "I'm telling you I'm screwed up."

"And I'm still here. And quite honestly, I have nothing to burn but daylight, so I might as well burn it with someone I find utterly fascinating."

"Fascinating?" I scoff. "I'm not that interesting. You just have vacation brain."

"And what's vacation brain?"

"With your day-to-day safely tucked in the States, you get to live another life while you're away."

"I don't take vacations. I like my job, going to work, and my life in general. So if I'm here, taking days off, it's because I want to be here." He pauses for a moment as if he's wrestling with something as well. How I wish we were simply strangers who met on a vacation, free to see where this leads. "Winter, what do you want me to do? Can I help you in some way? Fix something? Throw my hands up and be done with you?"

I lower my gaze to his chest, feeling ridiculous for starting this conversation in the first place. "No. You can't fix it or me, but I don't want you to leave."

Taking my hands, he holds them between us, gently rubbing his thumb over my knuckles. It's filled with the possibility that he's sticking around and we can get to know each other better. "Although I appreciate the heads-up, the warning doesn't scare me. Messed up, screwed up, emotional. These things come with life. We're all screwed up. Just some of us are better at hiding it. Life is full of surprises. Some good. Some bad. It's how we handle them that makes the difference."

He's so good. His heart is pure. He has an uncanny way of restoring hope where I thought there was none.

Wrapping an arm around my neck, he holds me to his side, and I've never felt safer in my life. I just want to burrow inside this comfort and not come out until all the bad is out of the way and I can move on with my life and possibly Bennett.

When I wrap my arm around his, he dips his head to the side on top of mine, and whispers, "You're a lovely package, but it's who you are on the inside that I like the most."

"Stop being all—"

"I know. I know. Charming." Hearing his carefree laughter puts my unsettled soul at ease. Our bodies break from each other, and he looks me in the eyes as if he'll make a stronger point that way. "You think I'm using lines or working you over, but I'm not. You just bring out the best in me." The added smirk at the end is a nice touch.

"Well, the best of you is downright romantic. That's all I'm saying."

Quirking his lips to the side, he narrows his eyes but then relaxes. "I don't know what to say to that, but as for the rest, I'm not going to read more into this conversation than it is. I like that you're being upfront." I notice his gaze darts to the far side of the room. I check over my shoulder, just in case. "I think the takeaway is that you like me. Guess what, ma chérie? I like you too, even more because you gave me something real."

From any other guy, I'd be on the fence about the pet name, but that a guy who loves sports and all those guy things says it wins me over every time.

We start walking toward the exit. "We've all made bad choices in our lives. All we can do is our best to fix them."

"There's a saying about bad choices make great stories. Let me tell you, I could write a series from all the bad I've done."

"Do you know how sexy it is that you know yourself well enough to acknowledge faults and want to do better?"

"Don't we all?"

"No," he replies, chuckling. "I've dated a lot of models and a few actresses—"

"Of course, you have." I sigh sarcastically.

"My point being that they rarely see their flaws because they're surrounded by yes people calling them perfect every day."

"I didn't have that luxury."

"Good. Neither did I, and I think we turned out pretty okay."

"Pretty okay?" I can't help but laugh now. "That's what we're striving for? Pretty okay?"

Taking my hand, he warms me from my fingertips to my toes. "Guess so." He stops, and says, "As much as I can appreciate the work that it took to create these masterpieces, I can only stare at them for so long. Are you ready to leave?"

I don't know why I find that funny, but I do, and I can appreciate his honesty like he respected mine.

In the middle of Paris, we start meandering as if we have no destination in mind. But I have plans for this man, things I want to show him that I've never done with anyone else. Maybe I was just waiting for the right person to experience them with.

I'm tempted to tell him everything—why I'm here, how I got here, the scheme I'm a part of, the devious debts that are due. Bennett Everest makes me want to confess my sins and then beg for forgiveness. Unfortunately, I think it's too late to cleanse my soul. Even by him.

The only thing that matters is what's happening right here, right now in the present. So before the goodness of the day disappears, I ask another question. "Have you ever eaten escargot?"

Not two hours later, the sun has set. As the lights dim, a familiar French tune wafts through the busy evening crowd. I've started to relax because the man I'm with has provided so much warmth and easy conversation, something I'd forgotten but had missed. He's a nice distraction to the mundane life I've been living, making me laugh before I forgot how.

"I'm starting to think that all people do in Paris is eat well and drink coffee all day and wine all night while watching the world go by," he says.

Having just taken a sip of my Pinot Noir, I choke. I cover my mouth with a napkin and try not to spit out the wine. That would not be pretty, and the last thing I want is to have red wine running down my chin. He tends to catch me off guard more than I'm used to. I think Paris has made me softer in more ways than my midsection. "Is there something wrong with that? Sounds like the good life to me."

"Nothing wrong with it, but when do they work?"

"They work around living instead of fitting living into their work schedule. It's a good lesson. One I never knew until I lived here."

"Speaking of you living here, when you said you're breaking, do you mean you're taking a break, a sabbatical?"

"I'm not sure how to answer that, Bennett." *He's too perceptive.*

"I've liked the honesty route."

I set the glass down and begin to spin the stem before glancing up at him sitting across from me. "I don't know if I can be that honest about everything."

That gives him pause. He looks away, but with a more determined tone, he asks, "Is the Winter with me now the same woman the rest of the world sees?"

"When I'm with you, I'm the person I want to be."

The waiter comes between us briefly and blocks me from reading his expressive eyes. My heart starts racing as I sit impatiently waiting, wondering what he'll say next, or ask, and if I can answer truthfully.

The waiter leaves after setting the dish of escargot between us. Peeking up, I wait for him to lead. Instead of peppering me with more questions, he picks up his fork, and says, "No time like the present." He pops a snail in his mouth and starts to chew, slowly at first, and then he swallows. "It's not *that* bad."

I can't let him show me up, so I take a deep breath and eat one. I don't love it, and I'm struggling to even like it. If I was alone, I'd spit it out, but he swallowed, so I will too. The right side of his mouth rises. "Not your cup of tea, huh?"

"Or coffee, wine, or ugh. No, I didn't like it. It's gross. Never make me eat another." He starts to laugh, and then I do.

Holding his glass up, he says, "Here's to no more snails."

"I will definitely toast to that."

With our eyes on each other, we both drink. He sets his glass down and leans in. "You know what I could really go for?"

"What's that?"

"A steak. A big, juicy steak."

God, he makes eating a steak sound like a sinful act. "That does sound good. I don't even remember the last time I had a steak."

"What do you like to eat?"

"I eat a lot of salads. Sad, sad salads," I say. The thought of a steak really does sound good, and my stomach growls. "God, I need a steak."

"I think it's time I buy you a proper dinner since this is a duck?"

I burst out laughing. "Yes, an official duck." And the best duck . . . *date*, I've ever had.

In awe, I stare at him. Nothing could have prepared me for where we ended up when we met a few days ago, but now that we're here, basking in each other's company, I don't want tonight to ever end. *How could I when I feel like I'm finally breathing again?*

10

Bennett

I've avoided six calls from my brothers today, but I should really take the seventh. Winter makes it so tempting to ignore it like the other times. I just know if I do, they'll send out a search and rescue team.

I hold the phone up. "I'm sorry, but I need to take this."

"It's fine," she says, waving me off like it's no big deal.

Excusing myself, I walk through the restaurant toward the door. Just outside, I stand among the smokers congregated out on the sidewalk. "Hey, what's up?"

"What do you mean, what's up? You were supposed to be in the office today," Ethan says. His voice is eerily calm . . . *Shit.*

"I sent an email that I'm taking vacation days." I release a heavy sigh. "I never take time off. I'm taking two fucking days. The company isn't going to fall apart in that time."

"That's right because it's my fucking company. What are you still doing there?" Ethan asks.

"I'm okay. Thanks for asking," I reply curtly. There's a

slight echo. I'm on a speaker. That means my other brother is there too.

"Glad to fucking hear it," Ethan remarks. "Wish you would have answered the first call, so I didn't have to spend my day worrying about you. Singer's called me three times worried sick."

Ah. That's when I realize this isn't about me taking a few days off. This is about their concern for my well-being. His wife is apparently not the only one worried. "I get it. You miss me, but I'll be back the day after tomorrow. In the meantime, I'm sightseeing."

"With Winter Nobleman?" Hutton's voice is distant. He's a pacer.

There are a lot worse ways he could have asked what I know he's thinking. "Look, sightseeing isn't fucking. I'm not having sex with her since I know that's what you guys think is going on here. But I do like her, and I also think there's more to this story than I was told by her father."

"So you're not sightseeing, you're investigating?" Hutton asks.

"No, I'm taking a few days off, and we're spending time together, getting to know each other. That's it." So far. No promises for later. "She's . . . fascinating."

"Oh wow, baby bro," Ethan starts, "sounds like you might be—Do I say it, Hutton, or let him off easy?"

Hutton replies, "Say it," then chuckles.

"Nooo." I'm already shaking my head. "No need to say it."

"In love."

"Asshole," I snap.

"So it's true?" he adds. "We've seen photos. She's—"

Standing under a streetlamp, I turn back, trying to see her through the window. "Beautiful."

"I'll tell ya. I fell for Singer the moment I saw her," Ethan says.

Hutton sounds closer to the phone when he says, "The moment I saw Ally, I knew we were meant to be more than a casual thing."

Winter spins a diamond in her ear, glancing around at everyone in the restaurant. The smile I left her with has vanished, and she appears unsettled. *From my absence?* "As much as I'd love to stroll down memory fucking lane with you two and relive your fairy-tale endings, I need to go"

"Yeah, yeah." Hutton laughs. "Don't forget about the deals we have signed since it looks like the Nobleman contract won't go through by the end of the year."

I'm quick to reply. "It's going through." The deal is a good one before he added that clause. I should be able to close it on merit alone.

"It's good to see you're still on track. Enjoy your time off, and we'll see you in a few days," Ethan says.

I tuck my phone away and head back in, keeping my eyes on Winter. As soon as she sees me, she exhales a breath, and the anxiety that I spied before disappears with it. A small smile reappears, but she seems to catch herself and takes a sip of wine as if everything's been fine all along.

I see through the act. I've noticed how she looks around as though she's expecting her world to fall apart, but she never looks disappointed to see me. I can say the same about seeing her. "Sorry. I needed to check in with my brothers."

"That's okay. I'm glad you're back."

"Me too. So where were we?"

"Drinking. Eating. Talking." Her tongue dips out and runs over the corner of her mouth.

This woman . . . she does things to me. Many things.

She takes the last bite of our shared crème brûlée and

then leans back. "I'm stuffed, and I've had a lot of wine. Basically, I'm in heaven."

The bill is set down without a word from the waiter. Our hands bump when we both reach for it. I'm quicker, though. "I'm not letting you buy me dinner. This meal is on me."

"Merci. The steak . . ." She moans while rubbing her stomach, and I swear the sound hits straight below my belt. "Just so good."

I set my card down, and it's swiped away before I have time to pull my hand back. Eager waiter. Back to the beauty at my side. "What do you have planned the rest of the night?"

"I'm hoping to spend it with you."

Glancing at the bottle, I find it's empty. Since I had a couple of glasses, she can't be that drunk. I think it's the full stomach. "I was hoping you'd say that."

While we wait, she asks, "Do you believe in love at first sight?"

"Have you been talking to my brothers?"

She shakes her head. "No, why would I have talked to your brothers?"

"It's nothing." I laugh under my breath. "Just a familiar topic."

Resting her chin on the palm of her hand, she has her elbow planted on the table between us, looking at me like I'm that dessert she just finished.

Lowering my voice, I ask, "Do you?"

"I didn't used to, but that's because I've learned the difference between love and lust."

"This is a lesson I'm not sure I've learned. Maybe that's why I get bored or burned. What's the difference?"

Her tone is friendly, but she holds me accountable. "You never answered my question, Mr. Everest."

"I was happily avoiding."

"Why is that?"

"Because I don't want to lie to you." Not any more than I have. I need to tell her the truth, and I need to do it tonight. Maybe confessions like that are best served after dessert.

Her breath catches, her lips still against the edge of her glass. She blinks and then takes a sip. When she returns the glass to the table, she says, "Lies are woven into the fabric of our lives. We were born of lies, and we'll die because of lies. Sometimes, I wonder if honesty exists."

She knows.

She knows I'm lying to her and sees right through me. The time has come. It's now or never if I want the slightest of chances to see her again, and I definitely do. I'm about to speak, but she says, "Just answer from your heart."

"From the heart . . ." She's right. Most women haven't always been interested in what I've thought or had to say, so this is different. Challenging. She's forcing me to dig deeper and find what is from the heart as opposed to the defensive answers flooding my mind, to ignore the script I was silently writing. "Okay. I—"

"Do you believe in love at first sight?"

"I'm beginning to."

I hadn't noticed that these little cat whiskers form when she smiles big enough for the joy to shine in her eyes. For a beautiful woman, she seems to have so many versions of gorgeous. Right now, as happiness overcomes her, she's breathtaking. *Speak from the heart.* "Yes."

Like the other two times, the moment passes, leading us to another more emotionally complicated transition. *Do we drop it?*

The waiter returns my card. She finishes her wine, and says, "It's time. We should go."

"Time for what?"

"Time to go to our next destination." When Winter reaches for my hand, I realize we have more time.

Time to get to know each other better.

Time together.

Time to kiss.

Time.

We have time.

"Ah. Right." When we get outside, I think about the times we've missed a kiss, a touch, or an opportunity, letting the heavier stuff slip under a full moon and stars that shine a little brighter here in Paris. Not in any rush as we begin to walk, I ask, "Where are you taking me?"

"Not far." There's that glint again. She's up to no good, and I like it. "A few blocks and then we'll be there."

"So you picked this restaurant for proximity."

"I picked this restaurant because I like it and thought you would, too."

"I do."

The streets are full of people meandering, tourists surrounding the area—other languages float through the air in the silence between us.

Listening to her is my favorite, so I ask, "Almost a month in Paris is a long time. Don't you miss home?" I don't even think she realizes how her hand tightens around mine, or that she's looking around like she's searching for someone specific. "What's wrong, Winter?"

I give her plenty of room and time to answer how she wants and when she's comfortable. I want to hear it from her, not learn about her from her father. I owe her that.

She points at the corner. "We'll take a left here, and then you'll see."

"I'll see that you're avoiding my question?"

"No." We round the corner and then stop. "You'll see that, which is way more interesting."

In the distance, down at the end of the long avenue, the Eiffel Tower sparkles as if it knew we were coming. "Now that is amazing."

"Right." She tugs me forward. "Want to get a closer look?"

How can I deny her this? Look at her smile—relaxed, at peace, and happy. It's like she was never anything but all of these wonderful things at once. I don't want to be the one to ruin it. "Definitely."

It's not a quick walk, but it's not too cold, and our hands are warm together. Any effect the wine was having at the restaurant is long gone and we're left with each other now, and that's enough.

Talk of the weather and stars, the Eiffel Tower, and the Empire State Building have all made it into the casual conversation. "I'm just saying, any woman would swoon if she were asked to meet atop the Empire State Building on Valentine's Day."

"But the foreshadowing ruins it."

"No," she says, shaking her head. "It's about the buildup. Even if you're sure the other will show up, there's always that one ounce of doubt that keeps you on edge until the last moment."

"So is it that edge, the adrenaline that sparks, or the romance that you want?"

She shrugs. "Maybe both."

"I can see that. We're drawn to danger."

"We sure are."

We reach the park, and as she admires the monument, I admire her. "I don't want tonight to end," she says, turning toward me.

"Me either."

Those missed opportunities replay in my mind—of how I wanted to kiss her at the statue, and when I almost kissed her instead of licking her at the bakery. "I don't want to miss another chance."

"Another chance to what?"

"Kiss you."

"You want to kiss me?" she asks as if it's not the only thing I've been dying to do since the first night we met.

"Of course, I want to kiss you."

She glances at the Eiffel Tower lit up against the dark sky, then back at me. "Okay."

Maneuvering around, I lean in, cupping her sweet face. "I'm not going for okay. I'm going for great." When her eyes dip closed, and I look at this woman in my hands—dark lashes against her creamy skin, pink lips not quite puckered but patient, and a splattering of the lightest trail of freckles across her cheeks, my heart starts beating against my chest.

Her eyes open, and when the clear blues capture my attention, she whispers, "Are you going to kiss me, movie star?"

"I am, but it's not every day you get to experience a first kiss. I don't want to rush it."

First touch.

The sweetest of smiles spreads across her pretty face. Just as she takes a breath, our lips press together.

First taste.

I sweep my hand around to her lower back and hold her, deepening the connection. Our lips part, and our tongues embrace.

First kiss.

Rich wine and the forbidden waiting to happen linger on her lips. I slide my hand up, weaving my fingers through her hair, slipping through the silky strands. When we part, our eyes slowly open. I don't move, not ready for it to be over.

The chill of the night invades our space, and our breath comes out like clouds. "How'd I do?"

When she smiles and reaches up to caress my face, she says, "Better than great."

In the shadow of the Eiffel Tower, I kissed her and suddenly knew I had to have more. "I don't want to be forward, and I'm trying my best to let what's happening between us happen naturally, but—"

"But we don't have all the time in the world. We only have another day." Her hands take one of mine between them, and she holds it.

"I want you to tell me what you want, Winter."

"I want you." The words come out quick, her heart speaking for her.

"I want you to stay with me tonight. Whatever happens tomorrow happens, but tonight, I want all of you."

Wrapping my arm around her shoulders, I lean down when she looks up and kiss her because I can and because when I do, she smiles afterward, making me want to give her a million more.

I still don't know if I believe in love at first sight, but I know this is the closest I've ever been. I also know that I want to give her a million more of anything her heart desires. And right now, I hope it's me.

11

Bennett

The taxi pulls to the curb, and the doorman opens the door. I step out and then offer a hand to Winter, not intending to let go until we're alone. Not for fear of losing her, but for pride in the fact that this beauty is choosing to spend her time with me. I want to make a show of it, but I don't. I try to play it cool.

Inside, we don't rush. We're not doing anything illicit. I push the button for the elevator and then nudge her lightly with my elbow. When she looks up, I ask, "Are you nervous?"

"Not at all. Should I be?"

"I am."

Rolling her eyes, she nudges me back. "No, you aren't."

I kiss her hand. "You just can't tell," I say, chuckling. "I'm good at hiding it."

"You're ridiculous is what you are." The door slides open, and when we step in, she quickly moves to the back corner. A tilt of her head. A wry smile. Her eyes only on me. I like everything about the sight before me. "What do you have to be nervous about?" she asks.

"I'm riding in an elevator with the most beautiful woman I've ever seen, who not only intrigues me but also challenges me."

"How's that?"

"I can't figure you out, Winter Nobleman."

She stiffens when the elevator door opens, so I check behind me. A couple waits for us to exit. Taking Winter's hand, I lead her out, giving them a friendly nod when we walk by.

She walks into my room first. The lights are on, dimmed, the food gone, but the wine is on ice with two clean glasses on a tray.

Slipping off her jacket, she sets it on a chair. The door closes automatically, and the hard lock makes her jump.

"You all right?" I set my wallet, key card, and phone down on the desk while watching her shut the drapes.

"Fine." She asks, "May I have a glass of wine?"

"Sure. I'll get it."

I pull the cork and pour the wine. "Do you mind if I use the powder room?"

"Make yourself at home."

With the wineglass in hand, she disappears, closing the door behind her. Something has changed. The particles in the air have rearranged, dissipating the lightness from before. Does she regret coming here, or am I reading the vibe wrong?

I pour another glass of wine for myself, though I'd really dig a beer instead. I consider calling room service, but if it's going to take a while, I don't want to interrupt our night.

The door opens, and she flicks the light off when she walks out. She's flipped her hair to the other side, and the wineglass is almost empty. It's only been a few minutes. Is she trying to psych herself up or get drunk? "Everything okay?" I ask.

"*Pretty* okay," she replies with what I think is a snort. Her hand covers her mouth as she cracks herself up.

My eyebrows shoot up. This is a turn I didn't expect. She comes to where I'm sitting in the chair and bumps my feet farther apart with the tip of her shoe. When I spread them, she sits on my lap, while setting the glass down and then wrapping her arm around my shoulders. "I've been thinking a lot about you."

Patting her hip, I ask, "Oh yeah?"

"The first time I saw you, I could have never imagined we'd end up here a few days later." She presses her palm to my cheek. "But that doesn't mean I didn't wish we could."

"You made a wish for me to bring you back to my room? And then what?"

Leaning down, she kisses me. With her forehead against mine, she sighs with her eyes closed, still holding my face to hers. "Do you mind if we just do this?"

I pull back. "*This*, as in sex? Like get it over and done with? Or just do *this* to distract you since something is clearly wrong?" I sigh and look down, my hands loosening from around her. "I'm sorry, Winter. I guess I misunderstood what was happening between us. If you're looking for something meaningless and void of emotions, you have the wrong guy."

"Do I?"

In the past, I might not have given every night I spent with a woman as much thought—both of us acting on instinct and need, but I thought tonight was different. Standing, I set her on her feet and move around to see her face. "I don't think you're naïve when it comes to me. I've been with women. I've had one-night stands. But that's not what I thought tonight was about. It may sound fucking ridiculous, but I guess I thought there was a shot we might see each other back in New York."

"New York? Bennett, I can't plan for tomorrow, much less New York."

I sit on the bench when she sits in the chair, curling her legs under her. "I want to spend more time with you whether we do anything tonight or not."

She rubs her forehead, seemingly in debate, but then she sets her feet down and comes to sit next to me. "I'm sorry, Bennett. You've been nothing but kind and respectful. I didn't give you the same courtesy. I do feel something. That's what scares me."

I reach over and take her hand. "Don't be scared. We don't have to do anything we don't want to. We can hang out and talk, or watch movies, French TV, or gorge on room service until we fall asleep. And if you want to leave at any time, I'll take a cab with you and see you home personally. Forget about tomorrow. I just want us to enjoy tonight. Stress free."

"I want that, too. How about we start with TV and room service?"

Reading her body language, I can tell she's genuine. Kicking off my shoes, I tug my sweater off over my head. "A woman after my own heart. Bed or bench?"

"Bed." She flips her shoes off, and asks, "Robe?"

"Closet." And just like that, we're back to easy. I know there's something beneath the surface that Winter isn't telling me, and that's fine. For now. But in moments like these, when she and I can so easily work a miscommunication out, I feel positive we can be more. She's strong and knows her mind but isn't manipulative in achieving what she wants. That's rare. *And welcome.*

She grabs the hotel robe from the closet and disappears into the bathroom again. I strip off my clothes, leaving on my boxer briefs. Dropping to the floor, I do ten quick pushups and a few sit-ups before popping to my feet and running my hand over my stomach. But I realize I can't stand here like an idiot no matter how sick my abs look.

I dive for the bed, and when the door opens, I'm kicked back under the covers with my hands behind my head. Basically killin' the stud pose. She tries to keep a straight face, but she can't. Her laughter fills the room as she tugs the belt on the robe tight around her waist. "Just hanging out there, huh, movie star?"

Just as she can't hide her smile, I can't hide mine. I flip the covers over as an invitation. "Climb on in." Reaching for the remote, I offer it to her.

"The water's fine."

I chuckle, looking her over. "It sure is."

Climbing onto the bed, she tucks her feet under and pulls up the covers. "Are you going to scoot over or hog the entire center of the bed?"

"I have to say, I'm quite comfortable right where I am."

She snuggles against me, one hand resting on my chest, the other under her. Clicking on the TV, she asks, "Do you always sleep in the middle?"

"I do."

"That's the sign of a man who sleeps alone."

"I'm not seeing the problem."

"Neither am I," she whispers with a gentle grin, and then places a kiss on my shoulder. The volume is turned up.

"I'm still full from dinner, but if you're hungry—"

"No. I'm not. I'm comfortable."

Wrapping my arm around her, I kiss the top of her head. "Me too."

"I'm missing my donkey shaved pencil. It has to be here somewhere."

"No. No, I got it. My ass is cold so give me a pen to fumigate the apartment." She bursts out laughing. We've been watching TV with the volume off for two hours and filling in with our own dialogue to soap style shows.

I don't think I've ever laughed so hard hanging out with a woman. She may have some high walls built to protect herself, but lying here, they've all but disappeared.

I thought her looking me up online would taint things, but it's not been like that at all. With her, I'm not a millionaire or the brother of a famous billionaire. I'm not the ladies' man or a high school football star. None of that seems to matter to Winter.

I have plenty of friends back home and in Manhattan, my brothers being two of my best, but Winter feels too good to be around not to consider pursuing a friendship. *Or more . . .*

The bottle of wine is empty, a pitcher of OJ half full, and a plate that has only cookie crumbs remain. With the robe hanging off one smooth shoulder, she points at the TV with a lollipop. "I think you won that round."

"You managed to use ass and apartment fumigation in yours without a thought. I'm saying you won."

"I'll take it," she says, and then pops the lollipop into her mouth. "Who knew a fancy hotel would deliver candy? I think I'm sugared up. Want to go for a run?"

"It's three in the morning. And you don't have running clothes or shoes. That's the candy talking."

Rolling her eyes, she falls back on the pillow. "Where'd your sense of adventure go, Monsieur Everest?"

"You're definitely drunk on sugar. I think you've had too much." I reach for the stick, but she smacks my hand and laughs.

"Maybe." Pulling the lollipop from her mouth, she points it at me. "You know what I think?"

Slipping lower on the bed, I angle her way. "What do you think?"

Her smiles fades, and her lips part as she takes a breath. "I think I'm ready for you to kiss me again."

"You know what I think?"

"What do you think?"

"I think I'd like that." I maneuver closer and lower my voice. "How do you want me to kiss you?"

She's very still like a statue. "I'm good like this." *Interesting.*

I try really fucking hard not to laugh. She's adorable. "Okay."

Her gaze darts to me. "I thought you were going for great?"

Taking her candy, I drop it in a glass of water, and smirk. "Always." I kiss her, not continuing a conversation I know neither of us intends to finish.

12

Bennett

Soft and welcoming. I love her mouth.

Her hands wrap around my bicep and then slide up over my neck. There's an insistence in the way she moves against me as if she can't get close enough. I give her what she wants and do what feels good, moving forward until her back is flat, and then separate her knees with mine.

As I press my body down, a little moan escapes her, making me harder than I was already. *Fuck.*

She holds me close as our tongues embrace, and our bodies begin a slow dance. One hand disappears from my ass that she was appreciating and tugs the robe open, revealing herself to me. Lowering to kiss her neck and then her shoulder, I whisper, "You're so fucking incredible, Winter." While she tries to slink out of the robe, her leg wraps over mine, holding me there. I finally sit up, so she can. "Let's take this off."

As soon as I give her space, she slips her arms from the robe and lays it on the bed under her. She lies back down before me in a light pink bra and matching thong. The pale color of the lace highlights a sheen as if the sun kissed her skin, and I can't stop myself. "Fuck, you're beautiful." The smile I receive in return is magnificent. Her surprise at my compliment shocks me, though.

A whispered, "You're so hot," leaves her lips. Her hands on my sides urge me back on top, so I move, kissing her again and appreciating the taste of her mouth, her skin, and the way she moves under me. Her body begs for more, and I start to memorize what makes her moan.

A kiss to the lips.

The spot behind her ear.

My hands on her waist.

Fingertips dipping under the lace and teasing.

Her breasts are firm and a good handful. I'd venture to guess a cup size, but it doesn't matter.

It.

Doesn't.

Matter.

The thought races through my veins, and I start to digest it. The size of a woman's tits has always been something I catalogued for entertainment, out of curiosity, and to engage my brain and not just my body. It's the same as every woman staring below the abs I work so hard to maintain to check out what the good Lord gave me.

But with Winter, it's different.

Like our time together, this just feels good. She feels good. With her, it's not a race to the finish. She's savoring my kisses to her neck and taking the time to kiss mine. She doesn't want a quick fuck before she ducks to catch a cab home. No, this is different.

New.

Better.

I don't want this feeling to end although I don't think I

can wait much longer before I explode. I ache to be inside her, so I whisper against the round of her breasts, "Do you want to—"

"Yes. God, yes. Please."

Lifting my head up to see her face, I smile. "I like you begging for me."

"I'd like you between my legs."

"I thought that's what we were talking about?"

"Your mouth first."

"First, huh?" She drives me fucking wild. As if I couldn't get harder, she opens that sexy mouth of hers and makes a request. Confidence is a turn-on. "I can arrange that." I slip under the covers and tug her legs until she's flat on her back.

Through laughter, she says, "You're so bad, Bennett."

"But I'll make you feel so good."

She takes a jagged breath when I pull her panties down. I admire the beauty before me. Soft and so wet already.

I spread her legs, and fingers weave into my hair, nails scraping lightly along my scalp. While I kiss the inside of her thigh, she gently nudges my head for more. I move to the apex of her legs and kiss her gently before I realize she's still, like a statue. *Again.* "Breathe, Winter."

Once I hear a loud exhale, I dip my tongue, tasting the forbidden—her salty-sweet essence. Her legs buck, and I hear a whimper. Checking on her, I look up, but she pushes my head right back down, causing me to chuckle against her softness.

Bold.

Confident.

Sexy as fuck.

Winter Nobleman has captivated me in every way— mentally, physically, emotionally. And when she moans again, I'm a goner.

I enjoy this late-night snack, leaving her breathless and

wet as she clamps her legs around me. Trusting me with her body and pleasure, I take it all from her as she trembles beneath me.

I did that. I'm the one who gave her every fucking thing she needed, and in return, she lies there, pulling me to her, kissing me, and through hitched breaths, she whispers in my ear, "That was the best orgasm I've ever had."

"More to come," I reply, "including me, ma chérie." I get out of bed, my briefs tenting. "Condom."

"I'm glad you came prepared," she says.

"I haven't come yet, but it won't take long with you looking that good." Grabbing a condom from my toiletry bag, I take my sweet time meandering back.

Winter's lying on the bed, arms wide, staring at the ceiling. "That felt so good."

Standing next to the bed, I ask, "Not great?"

"You and your 'great.' I already gave you the best orgasm award." Propping up on her elbow, she says, "If you must know, it felt amazing. You do not disappoint." Her gaze dips to my briefs. "Do not disappoint at all."

Now that I have her attention, I am not inclined to lose it. "I want you to undress me, Winter."

"With my eyes? I did that the first time I saw you."

I'd blame the wine, but her eyes are clear. "You're a bad girl."

"That's why I'm in Paris, but that's a story for another day."

"I like when you talk about other days we'll have together."

She sits up and runs her fingers under the top of the elastic waistband of my underwear. "It's tomorrow already."

"How about staying until daylight?"

A smile forms as she starts to take my briefs down. Peeking up at me, she says, "I'd like that."

"I like you," I reply, lifting her chin with my finger.

"Do you want me to . . .?" She leaves the question unfinished and looks down while running her hand along my erection instead.

"Only if you want to."

"I do." She slides my briefs down and licks her lips. Leaning forward, she touches the tip of her tongue to my hardness, making my stomach muscles clench in reaction. When she flattens her tongue and slides back up . . . *Fuck if that's not the sexiest thing I've ever seen.*

She takes me into her mouth, sliding down and back up several times, before I stop her. When her eyes connect with mine, I say, "I want to be inside you. I want to make love to you." I want to make this last all night yet race to the finish line. I take her bra straps and peel them over her shoulders. "I've tasted you. Now I want to see all of you."

Reaching behind her back, she unclasps her bra, and then slides the straps down her arms. She drops it on the floor, not embarrassed and not hiding herself from me, but shyness colors her face. Bending down, I kiss her, wanting to erase anything she feels that's less than spectacular.

She pulls me down onto the bed with her, and we move to the middle. Just as she's about to tuck under the covers, I lay my hand on her leg. "I want to see you the entire time."

Glancing at the nightstand, she asks, "Are we leaving the lights on, too?"

"Yes."

She sighs, not in disappointment but more adapting to the idea.

I start kissing her neck and moving to cover the spots that make her moan again. "Are you sure?"

"Yes."

Taking a second, I slip on the condom and then move

between her legs. Hovering above her, I realize I'm sort of nervous again. *What the fuck is wrong with me?*

Winter runs her hands up my chest and to the back of my neck. "Are you okay?"

I nod. I'm more than okay and that's what's wrong with me. I more than like her. Lowering down, I kiss her to settle my racing heart and find the peace I'm seeking. I move my hips forward, connecting us.

My breath escapes me as the heat of her body embraces mine. We move together, our eyes fixed on each other. The warmth of her sweet body feels so good that I start moving faster. I steal kisses but then rest my head down and let my body run off instinct.

She whispers in my ear, "So great, Bennett," making me smile. She's great for the heart.

I start kissing her again and then stop to push up enough to see her face. "You feel . . . so amazing."

Reaching up, she kisses me. The right side of her mouth slips up. "You feel incredible."

Her hips gyrate against mine, and we move, making love, and beginning to fuck because sex with her doesn't just feel good. Seeing her eyes bright with happiness, her body blushing across her chest, and sweat dusted across her skin. Steady becomes erratic, and we lose ourselves to the sounds of our bodies bonding.

Her voice builds with each yes she utters. When her head digs into the pillow, her back arches, and I help her chase the sensation. Winter's body tightens around mine, and her nails sink into my back as my name comes out on a moan.

The sight of her coming sends me over, sinking with her while murmuring her name, "Beautiful."

I don't lie there long before I roll to the side. She exhales loudly and even though her eyes are still closed, her hand finds mine between us, and our fingers entwine. I like watching her come back to the now. Her lids slowly lift, and she looks at me. Biting her lip, she rests her hand on her chest. "Hi."

"Hi." Slipping my arm under her, I hold her close and kiss her head. I tighten my arm around her, not ready to let her go, especially since she fits perfectly to me, all sticky sweet from the love we made.

Lifting up, she leans over and kisses me. "Of all the bistros, you walked into mine. It's not quite *Casablanca*, but Paris will do." I could stare at her all night, lying just like this next to her, and listen to her stories. "Did you ever see that movie?" she asks.

"No. We should see it sometime."

"Yeah, we should, but after some sleep and food."

"Deal."

"But first, do you mind if I clean up and take a shower?"

"Do you mind if I join you?"

She climbs out of bed, naked before me and not shy at all. "I was hoping you would."

We made another mess of ourselves in the shower. Fortunately, we soaped up afterward, which led to a whole other round of fun.

Exhausted and clean, we lie together in the dim light of the hotel room, our world contained for a few more hours. Winter's breathing deepened and steadied a while ago, but as I hold her, I don't want to fall asleep and miss this peace I've found.

We've slept together. I have to tell her the truth, but will she hate me when she finds out why I'm in Paris? I turn off the lamp and then work my way back into the center of the mattress again, enjoying the feel of her snuggling against my side.

In the dark, she asks, "Can I ask you something?"

Surprised she's awake, I rub her side, and say, "Anything."

A pause filters in, but then she adds, "Something's been bothering me, and instead of letting my mind spin, I thought I'd just ask."

All right. "Ask away."

"How did you know my last name is Nobleman?"

Fuck.

13

Bennett

Lying under the weight of her question, we're motionless, our breath the only sound in the room. I hate myself for doing it, but I do it anyway. "What are you talking about?"

"You said my name in the elevator earlier."

"Yeah . . ." *Please let it go. Please let it go.*

She sits up, but in the dark, I can only feel the motion. I can't see her silhouette until my eyes adjust. I miss the crinkles when she smiles. I prefer them instead of the glare I'm now getting, giving me the distinct impression that she is, in fact, not going to let this go. "I never told you my last name."

Grabbing an invisible shovel, I start digging myself into a deeper hole. "Sure you did. You must have."

"I didn't."

I sit up and rub her arm. *Please stay.* Whether she does or not, I owe her the truth. Just give me the chance to say it. "Winter—"

She moves out of reach when she climbs out of bed. "I think I should go."

"I think you should stay. We need to talk about this."

Although she showed no signs of shyness when we made love, she sure is now. Her pants are pulled on before I can get out of bed. "Winter, please."

Her hands go in the air, stopping me from taking another step closer. "No. I'm leaving, Bennett." She tugs her shirt over her head. "I don't know what's going on here, but I don't want to stay a second longer to listen to your lies."

"You stayed long enough for us to make love."

"Love?" She rolls her eyes. "I didn't trust my instincts when you said it. I questioned myself, that maybe I had slipped." Her gaze lands hard on me again. "I didn't."

"Let me explain." She's rushing, not running, so I seize the opportunity to reason with her. "It's going to take longer than thirty seconds. Can you please give me a few minutes?"

She grabs her jacket after slipping on her shoes and then glances to me. "No." Spying her bra on the bench, she snatches it and shoves it into her purse. "Everything about this situation is a warning for me to go."

"You're safe, Winter."

"I'm not safe if sirens are going off around us. Whatever you have to say must be pretty bad if you can't fit it into the time you've already been given." The silver chain of her necklace dangles from her pocket as she heads for the door. "Those lies must be eating you alive to suddenly have the need to confess your truth."

Trailing behind her, I ask, "Why'd you have sex with me if you questioned if I was lying?"

"I didn't know you were lying. You just confirmed it." After the rise and fall and a shaky breath, she doesn't look back, but says, "And sadly, because I'm lonely."

"Then stay and don't be. I like you, Winter. That's the truth. We can go back to New York together—"

"Oh, my God! That's it!" Spinning back, she points at

me, her eyes piercing mine. "Are you working for my father?" She closes her eyes, and says, "Did he hire you to sleep with me and torture me more than he already has?" *He's tortured her? What the fuck does that mean?*

"What you know about me is true. I work with my brothers. I'm from Texas—"

"I'm such a fool. You're probably some detective he's hired."

"I'm not," I reply, but she knows her father well since I know he did.

When I move toward her, she opens the door wide, and says, "Don't follow me. Please. Just leave me alone."

She starts down the hall, but I catch the door before it closes. "This is not what you think," I call after her.

"Tell my father . . ." She pauses and looks down at her feet. When she turns back, she adds, "You know what? Don't tell my father anything. I have nothing left to say to him." The elevator door opens, and I watch as she steps inside. Her eyes meet mine just before the door slides closed, leaving me standing naked for the whole floor to see. Fortunately, everyone's asleep at this hour.

The door closes behind me, and I stand there. What the fuck just happened? How could I let what was a tiny lie blow up to mass proportions? No one wins when lies are involved. I know this. I was taught better than I've been acting. Now I'm paying the fucking price for it. *Fuck.*

I have no idea where she's staying, but I sure as fuck don't want her leaving. I have to go after her. I pull my suitcase out from the bench and grab clothes to get dressed, pulling on underwear. Underneath a shirt, I find it—*the file!*

Shit. Should I really be using a file that an investigator provided, unbeknownst to her, to fix things?

Can I fix things with her?

Should I give her space and wait until morning?

I have no clue, but I do know this. If I push for too much, I may inadvertently push her away. Or has that ship already sailed? *Her fucking father. Why the fuck did I say her last name?*
Fuck.

I'm probably the last person she wants to see. She needs space. Women need room to let their anger breathe. I drop the clothes and grab my phone before falling back on the bed. I shouldn't need to call my brother with this, but even though I know he will give me a hard time, it's worth it if I can get an ounce of wisdom.

"Hello?"

I hold the phone out to make sure I called Ethan. The screen reads EE—Ethan Everest. Holding it to my ear, I reply, "Hello?"

"Bennett, it's Singer."

"Oh. Hey. I wasn't expecting you to answer."

"I know. Sorry. Ethan left his phone on the counter. I only answered because I saw your name pop up."

"No, it's fine. How are you?"

"I think I should be asking you that question."

Thinking about it, I try to reason through my stubborn emotions. Not good, quite honestly, but I won't worry her. "I'm fine. Is E around?"

"He'll be back in a bit. Do you want me to have him call you?"

She's the most kind-hearted person I know. I can ask my sister-in-law anything touchy-feely, and she'll never think less of me for it. "That'd be great, but hey, since I have you, do you mind if I ask for some advice?"

"Is this concerning a woman?" I hear the joy in her voice. I can imagine her smile. She lives for this stuff, and we've all come to appreciate her belief in happy endings.

"Yes," I admit. I'm a grown man who always has an

answer, but something about Winter has thrown me off my game.

"I'm all ears."

Pulling the covers over me, I say, "I lied to her, and she left."

"Why did you lie?" This is her MO. She listens open-mindedly before calling you out. And she will if she sees fit.

"Essentially? I knew she wouldn't talk to me if she knew the truth."

"*Oh*. That does complicate things." The phone goes quiet, and I give her a moment to think, hoping she might be able to help me find my way out of the mess I made. "So she knows you lied, but still doesn't know the truth?"

"Not fully."

"How much does she know?"

"That I know her last name even though she didn't tell me."

She hums as if she's pondering the situation. "But that's not the lie, is it?"

"No."

"I'm sorry, Ben. I don't know the full story, but it seems like nothing will be better until she does. Then you'll have a better idea if the relationship can survive."

"I know you're right. I just like her."

"I can tell. Hey, your brother's here."

"Thanks for talking with me, Singer."

"Anytime and good luck."

I'm going to need it.

The phone is handed over because Ethan asks, "What's going on, little brother?"

Thinking about what Singer just said, I start to wonder if I need more advice. She hit the nail on the head. There's no getting past this with Winter until she knows everything I've been hiding. "Not much. Just checking in. I'm going to fly back."

"Good to hear. Commercial or private?"

"I'd like the jet late afternoon, if possible."

"It's possible, but it's late here, and the office is closed. Text Zenny and let her know. She'll schedule it for you."

"I will, and then I'm gonna try to get some sleep."

"Everything okay?" He reads my tone too well.

"Fine." Suddenly, I don't want to get into it.

"Take care, Bennett."

"See you later."

We hang up, and I drop my phone on the bed beside me. My mind still loops through the things Winter said before leaving. She thinks I'm a detective tracking her on her father's dime. I wasn't tracking her down for him, but—fuck, is stalking her to get a contract signed any better?

Fuck no, it's not.

I hate that I broke her trust, the betrayal burning in her gut. I get up and find the file tucked in the suitcase, hidden from prying eyes. Flipping it open, I riffle through each piece of paper, looking for one thing—an address. I can go over there, try to talk to her, sit and wait until she's sick of me and allows me to share my piece.

Considering this PI knew where she hangs out at night, it's odd he never filled in the address to where she's staying. Weird. It's not like she seemed to be hiding where she was going each night. Why wouldn't he have it listed?

I have no way of contacting her—no phone number, no address, nothing but the places she frequents. Puzzling.

I'm pretty confident she won't return to the bistro, so that's out. Winter Nobleman could disappear into this populous capital city without another word or leave altogether, and I would never see her again.

Fuck. She already had trust issues because of her family,

and I just made it worse. I've screwed this up so badly I don't know if I can come back from it in her eyes.

The contract doesn't matter. I don't think it did from the moment I met her. Maybe that's a betrayal to her dad, but I'm okay with that. *Did he hire you to sleep with me, to torture me more than he already has?* Hearing her voice that . . . Does she actually believe that's what happened?

God. Is he capable of that? Of torturing her? I can't imagine it, but why would she lie? I have no problem betraying her dad? But betraying Winter? My chest is tight, and my stomach is tied in knots.

When she opened up about her feelings, she gave me her trust, and in one fell swoop, I lost it. I only have myself to blame.

I'll make this up to her, but first, I need to find her.

14

Winter

I hold everything I'm feeling in until I see the Eiffel Tower between two buildings. Anger. Hurt. Betrayal. Frustration.

Regret.

Regret.

Regret.

The dam bursts inside this taxi, and my emotions pour out, flooding my eyes and streaming down my face.

I should have known, so I only have myself to blame. I can't trust anyone. I knew this already. Least of all, my father. I wish I could believe he cared about me, but that's never been the case before. Why would he change now?

How did I not figure out Bennett's angle earlier? The hell I'm living in has blocked my better instincts. Who's good and who's bad eludes me. I can't believe I was so desperate for a friend, to be touched and treated like a human again that I let my guard down.

I'm so stupid.

The taxi stops, and I pay the fare before making my way

up to the small cell I lock myself inside each night. Who would have thought a luxury apartment building could feel like a prison. Am I imagining the danger I'm in? Maybe I'm not in any at all anymore. There's been no contact since the rose. Maybe these are just scare tactics.

Those tactics worked last time. I almost made it to the airport before the monsters who kidnapped me tracked me down. That threat and a gun had me returning to the toile wallpapered room.

Even so, I can't help but wonder how far I can get this time.

I unlock the door and let it close behind me with a loud click. I know this place by memory, so I move about in the dark—drop my purse on the table, toss my jacket on the chair. Toeing my shoes off, I'm about to take off my shirt, feeling dirty from being naked earlier, and shower, but the air shifts, and I sense him. His presence fills the room, causing my heart to thrum in my ears. A hand covers my mouth before I have time to scream.

Jutting my arm forward, I'm about to send my elbow into his ribs and then knock him to his knees, but his other hand clenches my throat, cutting off my air. Grappling at his hands, I'm hoping to remove one so I can breathe, but I'm lifted to my tiptoes instead.

As I struggle to breathe, I realize a cloud of his cologne typically warns me that he's here as soon as I enter the room. It didn't this time, as if he wanted to scare me more than an attack in the dark would.

His lips are at my ear, his breath hot against my skin. "I missed you, *ma princesse ténébreuse*."

I hate when he stakes claims, calling me his dark princess as some kind of play on my name. He never could stomach that I was a Nobleman, but he reveled in the dark of Winter. I was his dirty secret when he was my everything. He's a harsh reminder of the mistakes I've made. *I'll never trust my instincts again. How could I have been so naïve? Now twice.*

My body stops the fight, and my feet go flat to the floor. He releases my throat, and I drop to my knees, coughing so hard my throat burns.

A light switches on, and I turn back to find *him* sitting on the couch, arms stretched wide across the top and feet kicked up on the coffee table. His sandy blond hair is greasy, his grin matching it. He's a lowlife who likes to pretend he's someone. "You—" I start to cough again, unable to speak just yet.

A bottle of water lands on the floor next to me. He snaps his fingers and points to it. "Fetch."

"Fuck you." The words grind in my throat, the pain like fire shooting down my neck. I hate myself, but I need the water.

"Watch your language, Winter."

I drink despite the humiliation I feel for giving in. The water is cool, quenching my thirst and tamping out the flaming pain. I amble to my feet and sit on the edge of the bed. It no longer matters who we were before Paris, our roles have forever changed. Kurt McCoy is a different man, the one in control and I am his captive. He's so far gone from the man I thought I once loved.

I despise him. His arrogance. His cruelty. His determination to belittle me. He hasn't been missed, so why did he come tonight? "It's almost been a month."

"Three weeks," he replies indifferently.

"Three and a half. A month in two days. You brought me here and then left me. Why? And why are you here now?"

"Capri is lovely this time of year. The crowds haven't invaded like they do at the holidays. Anyway, I couldn't disappoint my friends by not making an appearance."

"You're an asshole." I hate how he never answers me. I

hate this night altogether. *Why now? When I'm already crippled by another man's deceit?*

"Surely, you know you've never been alone, Winter. I have too much invested in you to leave you to your own devices. A woman like you tends to find trouble around every corner."

"Corner office, you mean." I pretend to own an ounce of control, and snap back, "I found you right in your office. Easy as pie and played you like a pro."

Sitting forward, he rests his arms on his legs and studies me. Kurt never did know what to do with me. I used to amuse him, but like all cats, they get bored with their prey and eventually . . . I suck in a shaky breath, holding it until my throat releases. I hate the way the light hits his eyes as if he's savoring my slow death.

He stands and walks to the window. With his hands clasped behind his back, he says, "I was drawn to your spirited side. You came to me as a spy trying to steal information for your family. Stealing from me is unforgivable, a punishable crime, even if I did fall under your spell for a time."

Spell. The word makes me think of Bennett. I tense from the image of seeing him in my head—that smile, his engaging eyes. The way his touch makes me feel everything all at once.

"For a time?" I ask. Kurt has such a neat way of making years seem like two hours. That pretty much sums up what I should have realized long before I did. I was so desperate for validation that I turned to evil to earn a halo. *Hindsight and all that . . .*

Turning around, he sighs, his chest heavy under a blood red smoking jacket. "I played your games for too long—"

"Love was never a game to me. I just picked the wrong ally."

"Ally," he repeats, his bellowing laughter targeting my

heart right after. "Your angry rebellion to prove your father wrong was cute at first, amusing even, but never attractive. Did you really think I could love you? Your family doesn't love you, so why would I waste my time?"

Alone. Disparaged. Unappreciated.

"You wanted my name, Kurt. My connections. My inheritance—"

"I needed nothing from you. If I'd cared about any of that, I would have had you begging on your knees at the altar. Begging for *my* name." There's a growl to his tone, anger because I've hit a nerve.

"It doesn't matter how much money the McCoy family has, it won't change the trajectory of their legacy, or yours."

He charges me, my back and head slamming against the wall and rattling the crystal sconces. After forcing a final breath from me, he drops me, leaving me to slide to the floor. He can't kill me. Too many opportunities have passed him by. This isn't about death. This is about revenge. This is about setting the world on fire in hopes of finding a new beginning.

The McCoy name has been destroyed, and nothing he does can change that fact—not a deal, not blackmail, not a wife. Sadly, he still believes he can, and I'll pay the price, not with my life but with my family's if I don't handle him just the right way.

It churns my stomach, but I try my best to sound wistful while my back screams in pain. "You loved me. You did. It wasn't words to you. You felt them."

"And you were blind to the obvious."

I was. *He's right.* Under any other circumstances, I would have left the morning after we met and never looked back. It's fun to believe the lies we tell ourselves. Protection in the form of a coat made of words that provide the warmth we need when it's cold outside.

Using the wall as leverage, I hoist myself up, refusing to

show him how weak I really am. My body becomes a traitor as one single drop of blood falls from my nose to my chest. I don't realize it until his expression morphs, giving me a glimpse of the man who was easy to fall for when I was naïve.

"I hate when you hurt."

"Then don't hurt me."

My snarky comment doesn't faze him. He moves with less confidence and more humility when he approaches. Reaching his hand toward my face, he pauses, seeking permission. I'll never give him that luxury again. But I'm also not in a position to argue. *Stay strong. There's more at stake here.*

Holding me by the jaw, he scrapes the rough pad of his thumb across my face and under my nose. When he pulls back, blood covers it. With his eyes on mine, he licks it clean with two swipes of his tongue, a snake-like motion that warns of the evil inside.

And he's gone again, devoured by the monster he's become. How did I never see the sick side of this bastard before he turned on me? "You let another man touch you tonight," he says

My breathing stops hard in my chest. *Shit.* Now it's hard to breathe for another reason. I had become complacent, which must be the only reason Bennett got past my defenses. *Don't think about him. Show no weakness.* "Why would you care? I'm nothing to you. Just a pawn in a twisted game."

He angles back in fury, and I don't see his palm approaching until my head smacks the wall and my cheekbone burns with pain. "You. Are. My. Property. That's all you are."

I hold back the tears desperate to fall. *Show no weakness.* "You don't own me and you never will."

"I will until the tables are turned." And we're back to

business as if he didn't just inflict more damage. "You haven't asked why I'm here, Winter. How disappointing."

"I'm not dead, so I can assume that you came back to bat me around some more, toy with your plaything while inflicting deadly wounds in the form of words."

Sly gives him too much credit, though. Sinister. *Definitely.* "You shouldn't be afraid of my words."

He leaves the door open, so I peek inside his dark mind. "What should I be afraid of?"

"Me. Love extends beyond death."

"Love? You're not capable of the emotion."

"True," he says with a detached expression. *The man is despicable.* "But you believed I was at one point. So gullible, ma princesse ténébreuse."

I tuck my hands behind my back, trying to stop them from shaking. "Why are you here?"

"I thought you'd be happy to see me. Your mission is almost complete."

"What?" I give him too much power. He's dangling not only my future from his hands but my hopes along with it. I reach for the unattainable. "When?"

"Let's just be clear. This isn't over until I say it is." I stare at him as the freedom I crave remains firmly in his hands. His cold, angry eyes remain on me. "Winter, tell me you understand?"

"I understand," I reply, hope all but gone again.

"Good." He claps his hands together and then rubs them with the plan coming together for him. "You've done a fine job."

"I've done nothing."

His smile tilts toward genuine. "You've done more than you know. It's almost time for us—"

"Us?"

"The plan is in motion, thanks to you, but it's time to tie up loose ends."

"I don't know what you're talking about."

"And most of that is for the best. Trust me," he says, nodding like a pool shark about to take my money. "One last task and then you can return to your life again. You'll still owe me your life, but that's not a debt I'm collecting today."

"Then what are you collecting?"

"Everests."

15

Winter

As dirty as Kurt likes to play, he's struggling with the aftermath. The bruising. The bleeding. The pain he's inflicted on me.

With a stiff upper lip, though swollen, I remain awake despite his best efforts to knock me out. Hovering over me, he presses his erection against me. He gets off on power in the cruelest ways, and I was too blind to see until it was too late.

I never hated my father. I should have, but I didn't. That was a mistake. What I've endured for him is proof of that. Everything I've done is for his company, for him and my brother, to survive. That was the deal Kurt made with me, though being kidnapped and forced to agree put us on an uneven playing field.

A threat to my father's life was thrown in for good measure, and Kurt laughed that I could still shed tears for the man who basically abandoned me.

I'm strong. Stronger than Kurt ever thought I could be. I

die a little inside every day. One day, it won't be my body, but my soul that slips away, and until that day, I'll play by his rules and live this isolated life like he made me promise.

Bait. That's what he called me, but the term never made sense.

Until tonight.

Everests. He's after the Everest brothers, which means he's after Bennett.

I may not know what to think about Bennett's involvement with my father, but I still don't want him mixed up with Kurt.

So I'll take a hit and then another if it protects him. Bennett and I spent enough time together for me to see the real man. And with him, I was me again. I don't know why he lied, but I had no problem filling in the blanks before he could tell the truth. If I had only listened to my heart and his words, things would have turned out so differently.

I know deep down he's a good man. He's shown me how he cares—he listens, he asks questions, and he wants to make me feel not just good but great. Not giving him a chance to speak is another regret I'll add to my already long list.

If I had stayed, I'd be wrapped in his arms instead of bleeding on this bed in pain. I left because I felt betrayed, but the most unforgivable act of all is that I led Kurt right to him. I suck in a sob, knowing what this monster is capable of. Bennett's life is in danger because of me.

Kurt's hand touches my face, but I turn away, a sharp ache pulsing on my jaw. "Don't be mad, Winter."

Mad? I must have heard him wrong. "Should I be happy?" I still poke the bear. "Do you hit Chelsea?" I suspect he hasn't. Her milky skin would reveal the monster he really is sooner than the yellow undertones of mine.

He punches the mattress next to my head in frustration. "Why must you bring her into our time together?" he asks.

I thought he loved me until I found out there was another woman. I read about it in a gossip column. When she became his fiancée, I became his whore. Not by choice, but his drunken violence stopped and made me hate myself as much as he did that night.

Leaning down, he smells my hair, and groans. "You're my archangel, the one who will save me one day."

"What about your fiancée? I think she's more suited for the job."

"You're fire, and she's ice."

I'm dark. She's light.

I'm pretty. She's beautiful.

"She's the misses, and you made me the mistress."

"Don't be bitter, Winter. You get parts of me she'll never see."

Bitter, I mentally scoff. "The abusive ones." *The evil.*

Pushing off the bed, he tugs at his cuffs, but that won't remove the wrinkles in his soul. He pulls my phone from my purse, and demands, "Give me the code."

I struggle to sit up, the ribs on my right side hurting. Holding my hand over them to see if they're broken, I reserve a comeback. My resistance to Kurt bothers him more anyway. "Why?"

His tone turns harsh as annoyance sets in. "Give me the code."

"Why do you want to speak with him?"

The deadly stare of a shark has nothing on Kurt McCoy's glare. "Code."

My jaw aches, but I manage a solid, "Fuck you."

The case breaks under the pressure of his crushing hand. The screen will be next, but he stops, and his eyes dart to mine. "I'm tired of playing games with you." He stalks over with heavy footsteps that echo against the gilded walls of the room.

"I don't think so. I think that's why you started the game in the first place."

"Do I need to remind you that you came to me?"

"To talk, to work something out, not to be chloroformed, kidnapped, and blackmailed."

He shrugs dismissively and then holds the phone toward me. "It sounds so much worse when you put it like that. Now enter your code before I grow tired of you altogether."

Crossing my arms over my chest, I say, "He'll never meet with you."

"He doesn't have to."

"What do you mean? What are you going to do to him?"

"Why do you assume the worst of me?" *Really?* He doesn't understand why I would possibly think the worst of him? "As much fun as this has been, getting reacquainted, I must run. Maybe next time I can stay, and we can get reacquainted in a different way," he says.

"Never."

"I'm not asking, and I won't then either." He slips on his jacket and straightens his sleeves, making no efforts toward me. *Thank God.*

"What happens now?" I dare to ask.

"Your interactions and that pretty face are serving me well. Continue to do what you've been doing."

I lean against the pillows, tracking him as he moves around the room. "What am I doing?"

"Enjoying Paris."

"That's where you're wrong."

He reaches into his pocket and drops three photos on the end of the bed. "The photos say otherwise."

I peek to the foot of the bed, and my stomach drops to the floor. Bennett and me. "Why do you hurt me?"

"Because I like you, Winter, or I would have killed you already."

He stares at his reflection in the mirror. Sweeping his hair back, his eyes catch mine. "How long are you going to make me stay here?" I ask. "Why are we in Paris?"

"So many questions. It won't be much longer. And because Chel—look at me almost slipping. Let's just say, singling one out from the herd works better. And you've done well, ma princesse ténébreuse."

"What did I do?" He marches toward the door. "Tell me," I yell.

He takes a fast step forward but then stops and takes a deep breath. Straightening his jacket, he exhales, and then says, "Don't you ever raise your voice at me again. Do you understand?" I will not give him anything else of myself. "I'll take your silence as agreement." On a half-bow, he adds, "Bonsoir, Winter," and then leaves, slamming the door.

I bolt from the bed to lock the door behind him. I can't keep him out, but I won't leave the door to my life wide open. My lungs fill with clear air for the first time since I walked in. I can breathe again.

The ache returns and a pulse in my face causes me to rush to the bathroom. Standing in front of the large mirror, I see the damage he's done. It hurts worse than it looks, but maybe he meant it that way.

Blood is smeared from my nose to my ear, and the shape of his hand is still imprinted in the heat of my cheek. I pull my shirt off over my head and take inventory. The upper arm bruise will be easy to hide under my clothes, but my face is a whole other situation. My ribs. I press my hand over them gently. I'm hurt, but fortunately, I think it's only skin deep. My heart still pumps, and for that, I'm grateful to have another day.

I splash cool water on my face and dab a rag across it until I'm clean of blood and makeup. As I dry my skin, I think about Kurt's words—*singling one from the herd*. Does he mean Bennett?

Bennett. What was I thinking? I thought he was different.

As I continue to look at my face, I realize that I'm the one who put everything in motion. If I had been stronger a few years ago, I would have never walked into McCoy Properties. I would have never said yes to a date with a man I knew my father hated. I wouldn't be here now, trapped between my regrets and my will to live.

If I could go back in time, I wouldn't do this again. I would go back and change my fate altogether. With a second chance, I'd walk into Everest Enterprises instead.

I don't know why Kurt is *collecting* Everests—and I have no clue what that means—but I pray I diverted him. He's always been distracted by shiny objects. First me, and then Chelsea. I'm an old toy he still enjoys playing with since he apparently can't seem to leave me alone.

My palms go flat against the cool marble of the counter, and I lower my head, mentally and physically exhausted. I spy the time and sigh, finally finding the freedom to feel relieved. When I look into the mirror again, though, I know I need to put some ice on my cheek.

Kurt is always conscious about my eyes and not messing up my face. It's a face he likes too much to ruin, but I'm already ruined on the inside. Tonight he slipped with his hands like he did with his words. He made sure to humiliate me enough that I lost who I was when I was with him. Maybe I should be grateful for Chelsea. Without her coming into the picture, I'd still be under his thumb.

Pushing off the marble, I'm angry I could have such a thought, momentarily forgetting that I'm right back where I was, under his control. This time, I'm hidden in the shadows instead of the limelight of Manhattan's high society.

He destroyed my friendships. My girlfriends were too afraid to be around him and, in turn, me. I didn't believe them when they told me he threatened them, not even the day they walked away, leaving me in a hell I stupidly confused for heaven.

When I left him and his company, I began to rebuild my life, starting with a new job. The anonymous letter came not even a week after I started. HR cited concerns with my ties to Kurt. It didn't matter how I pleaded the truth; I was let go, believed to be a part of some espionage scheme.

Ironic, since that's why I applied for a job at his company.

Kurt McCoy was on a mission to rip me away from any life that didn't include him. Paris makes a lot more sense now. Since the minute I stepped into his office, he's been planning this all along.

Pulling a bottle of water from the small fridge, I hold it to my cheek. The icy cold is shocking, but I force myself to keep it there until my skin numbs.

I can't stop worrying about Bennett and what I've done. Even worse, what Kurt will do if he gets to him? I acted juvenile, letting my head spin instead of listening. I close my eyes and see Bennett so clearly in my head. That's the Bennett I know because he showed me who he really is. Gray days can't hold a candle to his sun. His six-foot-three frame has solid gold insides.

I wanted to know what redemption tasted like. He was my reward for being good all this time. And now, I've put him in danger like I did myself.

There's no debate about calling him. Kurt is probably tracking him down now, so I need to tell Bennett. I take the shortcut to try to fix things, to apologize, and then make sure he's on his way back to the States. The hotel operator answers, and I ask for Bennett's room. "Please take my call," I silently pray.

On the third ring, he answers, "Hello?"

"Bennett?"

"Winter?"

"Were you sleeping?"

"Are you all right?" he asks with the utmost care for me. "Where are you?"

"In my apartment. I need to talk to you." Will he think I'm crazy? I cringe at how insane I'll sound when I tell him the truth. Will he believe me? "This time, I promise I'll listen if you promise to hear me out."

Another pause and I start to think he's doing it on purpose to torture me. "When and where?"

"We can talk now."

"I leave later today, but I want to see you again."

God how I want that too, but is it safe? The three photos Kurt left behind lie scattered on the floor. The picture of us at the statue catches my eyes. A public place. That's probably best. "*The Kiss*." Checking the time again as if it's days later, I say, "Noon."

"I'll be there."

"Thank you. See you then." I hang up, not breathing easier but surviving, and that's key these days.

16

Bennett

Carbon.

A gray so dark that it borders on black. Dressy, but befitting the occasion. I only have this last chance to win her back.

Win?

Is that what I'm doing? *Is that what I want?*

Yep, it sure is.

I hate that Winter left hurt and angry. Betrayed. I've felt the same in varying degrees, but if only she had listened and given me time to explain. The words were right on the tip of my tongue until the blade of her assumptions hacked through them.

Yes, I think she'll like this suit best because I've seen the way she looks at me. Past the clothes she appreciates on my frame, she looks into my eyes with stars in hers. She's a romantic at heart from her favorite song to the book she was reading at the bistro. The door might have slammed behind her, but she's reopened it to hear me out.

I don't know what changed her heart and put this opportunity in my path, but I'm not going to blow it. I'm not only wearing my best suit but also my heart on my sleeve. I'll tell her the truth and hope she sees my earnestness through honesty. From there, I'll know where we stand, and if we'll get a second chance.

My suitcase is packed, and my computer stowed in the charging pocket. The high-tech traveler was worth the money I spent. It's weird to think about the money I've made and how I can buy anything I want. We didn't grow up poor, but we weren't spoiled either. I've spoiled myself a few times since —the apartment, the land next to my brother's down in Texas, that VIP backstage pass for my friends and me last year at an Austin music festival, and the suits.

But money can't buy everything. It can't buy things that matter like second chances. Second chances lie in the hands of the ones betrayed.

I knew what I was doing, or thought I did when I told her father I'd be the liaison to bridge the gap between them. Him telling me that I needed to do this for the deal didn't faze me. It sounded so easy that I didn't think about the emotions involved, selfishly, other than mine.

But the moment I saw her? Bright pink sweater. Long brown hair. A mouth that appears innocent in pink but depending on her mood can make you laugh or take a step back. She's cold water on a hot summer day. Refreshing and quenching with a sharp bite.

I slip my watch on and then call the front desk to have a car ready by the time I get downstairs. Looking around the room once more, I see the bed where we made love, her glass with remnants of lipstick still on the nightstand, and pink lace hanging from under the end of the comforter.

Grabbing it, I tuck her panties in my pocket and leave.

There's nothing here that needs me to stay. No, it's not the room or the city. It's the woman who I'm going to meet.

After I settle the bill, I walk out to the black sedan waiting at the curb. The driver loads the suitcase into the back while I slip into the car. The doorman instructs the driver to pull around the park, closer to the statue, and wait. I scroll through emails and reply to Zenny's. The plane will be arriving shortly fueled, restocked, and ready by one. Hours earlier than originally told. That doesn't leave much time with Winter, but I'll take what I can get.

Maybe she'll come with . . . I'll let her lead this conversation and see where we go from here if anywhere.

The car stops, and I get out, leaving my belongings. I don't see her as I walk the sidewalk to the statue. Looking left. Turning right. In the distance or waiting nearby, she's nowhere to be seen.

Will I be stood up?

Or did she set me up to make me pay for the betrayal?

I don't think she's vindictive like that, but who knows with a woman scorned . . . though scorned might be a bit much. She jumped to conclusions that I or the internet could easily deny. I thought she looked me up online. The last time I checked, it clearly stated I'm the Director of Media and Communications division of Everest Enterprises. I can't imagine it has changed.

Movement in the distance catches my eyes, which I then narrow to make out the figure. Surprised, I lift my sunglasses. Is that Winter? What is she doing?

Dropping my shades back down, I watch her running toward me yelling something, but she's too far for me to understand. People are parting on the path to let her by.

Arms waving.

Purse flapping around on her body.

Her sunglasses fall from her face, but she never breaks her stride to retrieve them.

Shit.

"What?" I call out, confused as to what's happening, and run toward her.

Thirty feet away, she screams, "Run! The other way!"

Twenty feet. "Run, Bennett!"

Ten feet. "They're going to hurt you." I catch her in my arms, spinning to keep her from falling. Her body is tense and she can barely breathe from exhaustion. A bruised lip. Fingermarks on her neck? *What the fuck?* Pushing me away, she says, "Go, Bennett. Save yourself. Go now!"

"Save me from who?" That's when I see them. Looking over her shoulder, my gaze lands on two men crossing the park faster than she did. "What the fuck?"

"Go, Bennett. Please."

Glancing once more from them to her, I say, "Not without you." I grab her hand, and we start to run to the car. The driver's eyes go wide when we approach, and he quickly opens the back door.

"Start the car," I yell several times. He shakes his head, not understanding what I'm saying. "French, Winter. Tell him in French."

"Umm . . . *Démarre la voiture!*" she shouts.

He nods and hurries back into the car. I slow and pull her forward. She ducks into the back seat, and I follow, shutting the door as the car peels away from the curb. Through the tinted glass, I stare at the men chasing us until they're out of sight.

Winter's holding her chest, her breathing erratic as she rests back on the leather with her eyes closed. My heart pounds from the adrenaline, and I catch the driver staring at us in the rearview mirror. I say, "*Aéroport. Tout de suite.*"

Elbowing me, she asks, "I thought you didn't know French?"

"I don't. I heard it in a movie once. I know *poquito*."

"That's Spanish."

"Oui." I wink.

She rolls her eyes, but a smile underscores it. Not enough to distract from her bruises, though. "What happened?" My gaze dips to her jaw area and then back to her pretty blue eyes.

A hand covers the bruise as if she'd forgotten about it, but then she pauses and takes a breath. "Hit a wall."

"With your face?"

Her eyes are bright, but the glare harsh. I still hold it because she's not intimidating me into moving on. "I'm sorry," she says, sitting up.

My heart had just started to regulate, but now it speeds up for another reason not related to running at all. "Why would you be sorry?"

"Because I dragged you into this," she says, signaling to the back window.

"Are those guys the wall you hit? Who are they?" She leans forward and looks out the window, then glances back, seeming to expect a car chase to ensue. I say, "This isn't the movies. This is real life. Ours, to be specific."

"Ours." She rolls the word around on her tongue, situating herself forward again.

I pull off my jacket because I'm sweating like a fucking pig. Thinking back to how I wore this to impress her, it seems frivolous compared to what just happened. "Do you have your passport on you?"

"Yes. Why?" Then it dawns on her, her eyes going wide. "Oh, no. I'm not leaving." She tells the driver to pull over. I tell him to drive, in English, but he gets it, and since I'm the client, he continues to drive. "I can't go with you, Bennett."

"Riddle me this, Nobleman." She shoots me another hard stare but doesn't say anything, so I continue, "You tell me to meet you and then tell me to run. For my life, I might add. Now I see someone has hurt you, but you're the one in control? No, it's not working like that anymore. Whatever game you're playing, you're losing. You're the queen of diversion, but now it's time to fess up because I'm not letting you off the hook anymore. Your life is in danger and now mine. So tell me, why are you in Paris, Winter?"

"Do you always shoot first and ask questions later?"

"And here I thought I was asking questions first. Is that topic too loaded? Let me try a softer approach, sweetheart. Who the fuck were those guys chasing you and apparently wanting to hurt me?"

By the way her mouth tenses tight like a little ball of yarn, she's offended. *That makes two of us.*

Waving me off, she says, "We don't have enough time to talk about it."

I text Zenny: *On my way to the plane. Have it ready to go. Add Winter Nobleman to the passenger list.* "We're about to have seven plus hours. Is that enough time?"

"I'm not going with you, Bennett. You can drag me along for the ride, but you're getting on the plane alone."

"I don't think so." I sit back and stare at her because I can be hardheaded too. I check out the angles of her face I missed the other times we've been together. She's stunning in any mood she decides to wear and owns it like she invented the emotion.

Her gaze lands solidly on my mouth and works its way up to my eyes. "You're not giving me a choice? It doesn't work like that."

"Tell me who those men were and why you're in Paris." We can play this game all the way back to New York.

"No."

"My life was on the line. Tell me why."

Her guard falls, and she looks away. "I'm sorry. I do owe you answers, but I can't give them in ten minutes."

"Give me something, like which wall do I have to hurt for banging you up?"

That earns me the slightest of grins, but I'll take what I can get right now. "They work for a man I used to work for."

"That changes things. Who did you used to work for?"

She looks back, regret taking over her expression. "Bennett." She looks down at her twisting fingers, then back up at me. "Listen, you get on that plane and go home as fast as you can. You'll be safer there."

"What about you?"

"I'll be fine. I always am."

"Not by the looks of it." I reach over, asking silent permission. She doesn't move away, and if I'm not mistaken, she even moves toward my hand. "Are you okay?"

With a gentle nod, her lids flutter closed. I move my finger along her jaw, and over the bruise so lightly I don't know if she can feel it, but I won't cause her any more pain. *Who the fuck hurt her? Why would they do that?*

It's not the time or place to do it, but I do anyway because the heightened emotions between last night have simmered to a low boil. I care about her, and this might be the only real chance I get to make amends.

I kiss her cheek and then again lower over the bruise on her jaw that looks like it's going to get worse before better . . . sort of like us.

"I'm going home, Winter, but I'm not leaving you behind." I sit back like this is settled, grumbling to get it off my chest. "You're so caught in your secrets that you don't even know what's best anymore."

"And you do? How?" Her hand flies to her chest. "How

could you possibly know what's best for me? You don't even know me."

Points have a purpose. She slams down the evidence substantiating the situation. She's not wrong. "How do I walk away? How do I leave you behind when two goons just chased you through a park in broad daylight? What would they have done if they caught you?"

"That's just it, Bennett. They weren't after me. They were after you."

17

Bennett

"Me?" I glance out the back window, feeling like we're being watched. "I've never seen those men before. Why would they be after me?"

"It's complicated."

"I can keep up."

She holds my gaze when it turns her way, but her expression falls, and she remains quiet.

Anger surges, and my hands clench into fists. "Why won't you tell me any-fucking-thing? What are you involved in that has you risking your life and mine?"

"Please don't make me say it."

"I won't, but you're getting on that plane."

Her mouth falls open. "You don't own me!"

I stare in disbelief. "Own you? Of course, I don't fucking own you. But you're not thinking clearly. You need to be safe, Winter, and you're clearly not safe in Paris."

"I'm not the one in trouble."

My eyes almost bulge out. "Really? Some fucker hit you,

and you think you're not in trouble?" I take a deep breath, struggling not to take the anger I hold toward whoever did this to her out on her. "Define trouble then? Do they need to rape or kill you in addition to beating you up?" *Really fucking struggle.* "I mean, what the fuck, Winter?"

The worst part is, she doesn't recoil. Someone's been abusing her long enough for her to take the hits blow by blow, and she keeps thickening her skin. I won't be the next one. "I'm sorry," I say.

When she looks at me, there's no hate. The glistening tears in her eyes reveal her fear, and she slides closer. "How do I tell you details when I know it will put you in jeopardy?"

"I can take care of myself. Let me help you." Taking her hand, I hold it. "Come with me. Get on the plane and fly home with me."

"I can't, Bennett."

"I'll protect you."

We approach the airfield. The driver shows his ID, and the gate opens. Winter sits forward. "You're flying private?"

"Yes. All we have to do is walk onto that plane and leave. Together. Whatever you're caught up in, I can help you get out. Look at me, Winter." Like broken ice adrift in the Bering Sea, her gaze doesn't rush over to me. I speak from the heart when I plead, "Come with me."

Her tears tip over the icy edge of her lids and fall to their demise, extending their reach in the threads of her red sweater. She wipes the next two away with the back of her fabric-covered wrists. "I want to, but I can't."

"Just tell me what's going on. Let me help you."

She sniffles and leans toward the window, looking up at the sky. "We had one perfect day." Turning back to me, she adds, "Have you ever thought that maybe that's all we were meant to be?"

"No," I reply, assuredly. I wasn't aiming for a smile, but given what we just went through, hers is welcome. "I'm drawn to you, Winter. I didn't tell you why I came to Paris with the intent to deceive you. And I'd never do anything to intentionally hurt you either."

"I know, Bennett. I know you'd never intentionally hurt me. I'm sorry I ran."

"I understand why you did, but please give me a chance to talk this out." I feel like I'm begging. Even though my day started with a taste of happiness because I believed I had time to mend fences, the chase certainly woke me up to the fact that there's so much more to this than meets the eye. How on earth could I have been the one who those goons were after? No one outside my family and hers knows I'm in Paris, much less would care for any particular reason.

"I want to talk to you, Bennett, please know that. I'm not in the position to, though, and I need you to trust me on that. Please." Something in her expression changes; a look in her eyes as she stares at the planes ahead of her.

"Those men have hurt you." I ask, "Why?"

"If I tell you, I'll be risking everything."

"Seems you already have."

My words are sharp, purposely directed to get a reaction, and I get one.

"I'm sorry, so sorry for getting you involved." Her top teeth gather in her bottom lip, and she worries it. "You can fly me to the moon, and he'd still find me."

"Then you'll come home with me. It's a fortress."

"Home," she whispers, though I don't think it was for my ears.

Bringing her hand to my lips, I kiss the top, and whisper, "I'll protect you."

Chasing the sunset, we've spent hours in peace high above the clouds. I relied on the steady whirr of the plane's engine and Winter's deep slumber to know everything was going to be okay.

Before she fell asleep, she wasn't talking to me, making me rethink the demands I made on her to leave. I'll weather the blowback. Her safety was and is more important than ruffling her feathers for a short time. There's no way I could leave her on that tarmac unprotected.

I'll let her rest for now because, apparently, she needs it by how hard she's sleeping. We have a lot to talk about when she wakes up. I just want to discuss it under the protection of Everest Security.

The flight attendant bends down. "May I get you anything, Mr. Everest?"

"A bottle of water, please." I'm about to plug in my earbuds, but then add, "And bourbon. Neat."

"Yes, sir."

I lean back to check on Winter across the aisle from me. She's stubborn.

Feisty.

Sweet.

Funny.

A little quirky.

A fighter. I just wish I knew what she was fighting. Or whom.

Smart. *So damn smart.* Making me wonder how she got tangled up in whatever is holding her hostage from her own life.

I've had my own stumbling blocks, but nothing to the point of leaving this world behind—friends, family, and the life I live. What is she hiding? Who is she protecting?

The attendant returns, setting my drinks down. "Here

you are, sir. Would you like a snack or for a meal to be served?"

"I'll wait for Ms. Nobleman to wake."

"As you wish."

"Thank you." I take a sip of the liquor, feeling the warm velvet rush through my veins. Watching her—lids closed, dark lashes curving up against the tops of her cheeks, wisps of hair hanging over her eyes—I find her stunning even in her sleep. Her mouth falls open, and a little rumble sneaks out.

Her snoring makes me chuckle. Good to know she has a flaw. Though it's so cute I'm not sure I can classify it that way.

Shifting, her hand falls in front of her, and I'm tempted to take it, to hold it, to comfort her as she struggles to hold on to those last few moments of peaceful sleep.

I don't. I take another sip instead and watch as her eyes open, slowly at first, with the sweetest of smiles following. "Hi," she says, her voice raspy and dry.

When her eyes find my water, she sits up, bringing the seat with her. "Do you mind if I steal your drink?"

"Not at all."

She gets up, tugging her sweater back in place, and sits next to me. Reaching for the glass in my hand instead of the water, she winks. I relent and watch as she takes a small sip and then a larger one. Resting her head back on the seat, she rolls her neck, facing me. "Did I snore?"

"No." It's an innocent little lie, the teeniest of fibs.

"Liar," she says, stretching over the large armrest to tap my leg.

I catch it before she has time to pull it away and hold her there. With our eyes focused on each other, she takes another sip.

"I have lied to you, but I'm not a detective."

"I know. I wasn't thinking clearly when I said that." She pulls her hand back and runs the tip of her finger around the edge of the glass several times before she looks back at me.

"I know your father because we were working on a communications deal." I can't read her expression because her eyes aren't on me. I hate it. "He's worried about you."

"He's not. You were just gullible enough to believe him. He doesn't matter to me right now." She finishes the drink and sets it between us, taking her hand from me and resting it in her lap. "You and your brothers are in danger. I knew who those men at the park were because they're the ones who kidnapped me."

I sit straight up in shock, the lap belt digging into my waist. "You were kidnapped?"

"That's the first time I've said it to someone who didn't do it."

Fuck the seat belt. I release it and stand, needing the space to pace. What is she involved in? "Winter, you need to tell me why and by who."

"I didn't know why until I met you." Her voice shakes just enough to hear the fear that's gripped her.

"Me? What do I have to do with it?"

"I was used to get to you. I didn't know, though. Please believe me. I would have never hurt you or put you in danger if I had."

"I don't understand. You didn't know me, and I didn't know you." My mind starts ticking through the conversations we've had and then back to what brought me to Paris in the first place. "Fuck me."

"What is it?"

"Your father. He's the key."

18

Winter

Bennett has been pacing the main cabin of the jet for the better part of an hour. Sometimes, he sits up front on the couch, speaking so quietly on the phone I can't hear him. The engine noise keeps his call private, but I know he's talking about what to do when we land and doesn't want to worry me.

I'm a wrench in his plans, an unexpected detour on his golden brick road. The man was born for success. Everything about him from his personality to his looks to his patience and humor draws you to him like a bee to honey. He's just as sweet. How, after finding out I had put him in danger, did he want to protect me? He should have left me in Paris.

I can't be his downfall.

I could never live with myself if he was hurt . . . *or worse*.

Will telling him the whole truth hurt or help the situation? I'm unsure.

But Kurt McCoy plays dirty, so I have to tell him every sordid detail.

Taking the seat next to me, he fastens his seat belt after stowing his phone in his pocket. "We're landing soon. Buckle up—"

"Buttercup," I finish. That earns me a smile. I soak it in, needing his light, his happy, and his charms back in my life.

"I have a million questions but need the security team to hear the answers. You're coming home with me."

"Come home with you and spill my lying guts, hoping the truth sounds more real than fiction? You should want me as far away from you as possible. Because of me, you were almost hurt today."

"I'm not afraid of getting hurt, Winter. Do you trust me?"

I settle into the soft seats and stare at my feet. "I don't even know what trust means anymore."

"It means that I tell you the truth, and you tell me the truth. I have your back, and you have mine." My throat thickens, my heart racing. "It means I give you my heart, and you give me yours."

"Is that what you want, Bennett?" I glance over. "You want to love me? I'm the most prickly pear out there."

"The prickliest pears taste the sweetest."

"Or die on the plant."

"No, they don't die. They bloom into the prettiest flowers."

"Stop being so damn charming. I almost got you killed, remember?"

"Nah, today isn't my day to die."

"Then what is it?"

Leaning forward, he kisses my bruised jaw, and then whispers, "Just the beginning."

We've landed, and a black SUV waits on the tarmac. A large man wearing all black stands at the base of the steps when we descend. Bennett greets him, "Lars."

The door opens, and I hurry to the back seat while they look around and then load in right after. Lars is up front, and Bennett slides in next to me. I stopped asking where I was going upon arrival. *I'm with Bennett* seems to be good enough for all of us.

I'm not sure where we're heading in our relationship, but I do feel a measure of comfort in his words. "*It means I give you my heart, and you give me yours.*" I've paid the price for trusting another man before, but I'm hoping my instinct is right to trust in Bennett. I already do, enough to consider giving him my heart.

I still worry about what he'll think when he knows the full story. I sank to new lows when playing by the rules didn't reward me. I can blame my father and brother all I want, but I'm the one who went to work for the enemy.

Nothing can justify my behavior, and it's time I face the consequences of my actions. A pretty face can't erase my dirty insides from the life Kurt made me lead under his lock and key.

I cover Bennett's hand, hoping it's possible to find our way out of this mess.

"A lot happened today," he says.

That's an understatement, but even his optimism rubs off on me. "And we survived."

"We did." An incorrigible grin arises. Bridging the gap, his hand lies seventy-five percent closer to me, palm up.

"You could have met halfway." Fifty percent would have been a good compromise.

"I don't mind going the distance for you, cactus flower."

And then I pool into a puddle of mushy feels on the floorboard of this SUV. Plucking my heart up, I wedge it back into place, and reply, "And here I thought you'd go for prickly pear, movie star."

"Nah. You're more than the armor that surrounds you."

Placing my hand in his, I study the size difference. His bear paw engulfs my panther paw, making me smile. He goes on to say, "You weren't born among the thorns, which makes me wonder why you grew them in the first place."

"My mother's death," I reply without thinking. I glance up to his whiskey eyes, holding my breath in shock of what I've admitted. I don't ever talk about that time, yet I have to him twice.

"That would do it." He slides all the way over until he bumps into me. Reaching around my head, he pushes the lock down, grumbling about it being up. When he rests back, our fingers fall into place, weaving together a bond built over days of getting to know each other. "I'm sorry about your mother, Winter."

"So am I, but there's nothing to be done now. There wasn't then either. Cancer fucking stole the rug out from under us. In her case, we didn't notice until we fell."

"Singer's mother fought breast cancer."

"How is she doing?" I ask, praying she's alive, and I didn't step in a landmine.

"She's doing well. The doctors are happy with her body's response to the treatment."

"That's good." I wish that was my case, but some of us aren't meant to have nice things. I look at the nails of my free hand remembering how my mom used to paint them dark blue like her eyes. She told me it was a warrior's color. Although I was only seven, she used to let me paint her nails while she would recite poetry from the heart. "*How do I love thee? Let me count the ways.*" I spilled the paint the day before she died. I say, "She died on a Tuesday. That was what she called Mommy-daughter day. Every week we spent that day together just the two of us. I found her passed away in her bed instead."

I hate how my voice trembles. Eighteen years is a long time to let something bother you. I'll need longer than this lifetime to get over her death. "She was buried the following Tuesday. I painted my nails black." I hold my hand up, the OPI Bubble Bath polish clean and neat, and the furthest from a warrior's color I can get.

Noticing the familiar skyline out the window, I ask, "Where are we going?"

"To my apartment."

"I don't have anything on me for a sleepover, not even a toothbrush."

"I have a spare."

"Clothes? I don't even have underwear. *God, how embarrassing.*"

A slow grin slides deliciously into place. Dipping into his pocket, I recognize the lace he pulls out. My mouth falls open and my eyes go wide. "I got that covered too," he replies.

"With my dirty panties?"

Shaking his head, he laughs. "We can wash your clothes for tomorrow."

"Well, what about tonight?"

"You can borrow mine."

"But you're a beast of a man. They'll swallow me whole."

His laughter deepens. "You know. I think you like how big I am." And then I get his signature wink.

I roll my eyes to play it off like he's just spoken pure insanity, but I do like it—the wink and his size. "Size doesn't matter. I'm not that shallow."

"Keep telling yourself that, sweetheart, and maybe one day you'll believe it."

"You know, sometimes I think you're the most charismatic man I've ever met. And then sometimes you open your mouth, and I just want to plug it."

"With what? Your tongue? I see how you look at me—"

"You mean the same way you look at me?"

"Maybe." He shrugs unapologetically. "Maybe not. I think we see things differently."

"Do we? How so?"

"I think you see men as prey—someone to con, someone to waste some time with, someone to fuck. See? You don't even balk at the suggestion. You'd be offended if I wasn't right."

"I can feign offense if you'd like." Covering my heart with my hand, I put my other to my forehead. "Oh, mercy me. Whatever would I be without a big, strong man telling me what to do?"

"You should have gone to drama school. You nailed it."

"I've had plenty of practice."

The see-saw of our emotions teeters the other way, and he says, "That's exactly what I mean. You don't have to practice with me. I'm not battling for control or one-upping you every chance I get. If this is who you are in Manhattan, I choose Paris."

Despite the fact he's still holding my balled panties in his hand, his words have such finality to them that I stare at him. "What do you want from me, Bennett?"

"I want you to end the battle before it begins. I understand you're outside your comfort zone, but I need you not to fight me every step of the way. We're on the same side. We're allies." His gaze lowers to my injured jaw. "No one is going to hurt you again, especially not me."

"Trust," I say, remembering how he said if he gives me his heart, I give him mine. He's been wearing his out in the open for all to see while I'm still trying to protect mine. "How do I learn to trust?"

"You just do it without any guarantees. Take the risk. Think how much better we can be as a team."

Squeezing his hand gently, and then with more assurance, I say, "Allies."

"You and me."

I wouldn't be alone.

I lean my head on his shoulder and he wraps his arm around me. Allies with Bennett is a good place to be. I don't need a man, or anyone, to feel complete. But for the first time in a very long time, I don't feel alone, and that's worth savoring. *That's worth fighting for.*

We spend some time in rush hour traffic before we finally pull into an underground garage. A gate comes down behind us with visible cameras throughout the garage. When we come to a stop in front of a gray steel door, it happens so fast that I'm not sure what to do other than sit tight.

The lock pops up, and my door opens abruptly. Lars says, "Right this way."

I glance back at Bennett, needing to know what to do. He nods. "It's okay."

Stepping out to Lars's right, I release his helping hand. He looks to his left and then escorts me to the open area by the door but tucks me behind the brick wall. I start to calm when Bennett joins me. "What's going on?" I ask, keeping my voice low.

"I said I'd protect you. Welcome to The Everest."

19

Winter

Not in front of the elevator.
  Just past the stairwell.
  Not near the door.
  Stay close enough to "save."

After Lars doled out the firm directives, I stay put right under Bennett's arm. Lars comes back down the hall to where he left us standing. "All clear."

"Thank you. I texted my brother, but can you update him on the clearance?" Bennett replies.

"Yes. I'm going up there now."

Lars continues to a door down the hall. Looking just beyond him, I see another door, and ask, "There's only one other apartment on the floor?"

"Yes, my oldest brother and the princess live there."

"Princess?"

"Of Brudenbourg," he says so nonchalantly that I still don't know if he's teasing.

"A *for real* princess?"

"Yes. A 'for real' princess." He throws in air quotes for fun as we walk into the apartment.

I stare at him. "I don't understand. You're not kidding?"

He chuckles. "No, why would I kid about her being a princess?"

"You call me sweetheart?" I don't even know what I'm asking, but I crave the answer like a kid craves candy.

Pulling me in, he kisses my head. "Because you are," he replies like the answer was always right there in front of me. "When you're not my prickly pear."

"I prefer cactus flower."

"Me too."

I force myself to look away from the gorgeous man next to me, my mouth falling open as soon as I enter the "apartment," which makes me want to use air quotes. I've never seen an apartment in Manhattan this big before. Rushing forward to the center of the living room, I stare out the large windows before me. "Good God, Bennett." It would be impossible to feel claustrophobic in such an airy, wide-open space. "It's like living in the clouds with no walls confining you." Finding him over my shoulder, I ask, "This is your place?"

"This is my place." The smugness isn't lost on me. But damn, he has every right to be cocky. My place is nice . . . at least I used to think so. But it's a ramshackle walk-up compared to this palace in the sky. From behind me, I hear him say, "I thought you did your research on me?"

I laugh. "I looked you up. I didn't research you."

"Ah, I didn't catch the difference earlier." When I look back, he's reaching into a cabinet. "Something to drink?"

"Whatever you're drinking."

The glass of the window is cold when I press my hands against it to see how far the view extends. Pretty damn far.

"What did Lars mean when he said he was going up now? Up where?"

"My brother Ethan lives in the penthouse. That's base."

"What's base?" I start to snoop around the place. "Nice view, by the way."

"Thanks." Setting a pitcher of water down on the island counter, he hands me a full glass. "Base is home base. Hutton's apartment down the hall is first base. Mine is second."

"But you're third born?"

"I know," he replies, shaking his head. "Missed opportunity if you ask me. They didn't." He chuckles. "Maybe it throws off the bad guys." He finishes his water in one long chug and begins to refill it.

"Bad guys?" I ask, my eyes going wide. Do they have more than the ones I've brought into their lives?

"Kidding. Kind of." And there's that wink again followed by a playful nudge as he walks by.

"I think it's too soon to joke about bad guys."

"You're probably right." Looking back at me, he signals toward the hall. "Come on. Let me give you a tour."

"Am I staying that long?"

"Is it bad if I want you to?"

Bumping against him, I say, "No. It's nice to hear." I walk ahead of him. "What's down here?"

"Probably a messy bedroom." I'm yards—yes yards, because this place is so damn big—ahead of him, making my way straight down the hall while peeking into each room I pass. Not his. Not his. Not his. "Palace," I mumble. *Goose*!

I walk into the cleanest bedroom I've ever seen. Not an item is out of place in the uncluttered space. The wood floors shine from a recent polish and not one wrinkle covers the duvet. Speaking of . . . "That's the biggest bed I've ever seen." I run and jump into the middle, ruffling up the blanket and sheets. Turning my face to the side, I say, "A giant sleeps here."

He chuckles from the doorway.

I roll over, propping myself up on my elbows. I glance at the clock on the nightstand and then back at him. "It's only five. I'm not going to make it to seven."

Coming to the end of the bed, he takes my ankles and pulls me toward the end until my butt is almost at the edge. Leaning over me, he rests his arms on either side of my head. "Do you think you'll be able to give an account of what's been happening to the security team tonight?"

"You need to work on your sweet talk."

"I'll take that as a pause for now on that topic." He laughs. "But how about kissing? Do I need to work on that?"

"It's been too long to judge. I need a reminder."

"Happy to oblige." He holds my gaze for a few anxious beats of my heart before he leans down and kisses me. My eyes fall closed, and my heartstrings reattach to his, and then it's over too soon. "How did I do?"

I wish we could kiss all day. He's just as amazing as he always is. "You're a talented man."

"I was inspired. I want to ask you something."

"Ask away."

He pushes my hair back from my face and strokes my cheek several times, his eyes fixed on my lips. "Are we together?"

When he trails his way to my eyes, I nod, ever so slightly and a lot squirmy. "Yes, I suppose we are."

"More than proximity?"

"More than proximity."

I'm rewarded with a slow, lingering lick across my bottom lip, a little tug, and then the sweetest pressure of his lips against mine asking for more. I wrap my arms around his neck and hold him right where he is. I'm sure it's the jet lag making me feel so much for this man. It must be the lack of sleep, delirium, the emotions ballooning inside. I hold my tongue before I say more than I should.

Permission granted.

Closing my eyes, I kiss him, my body relaxed but my hunger aroused. Pulling back suddenly, I ask, "Do you mind if I take a shower? I feel so dirty after flying."

A sigh escapes him, but he's kind enough not to let his disappointment show. "That way," he says, pushing up. "Towels are on the shelf along with anything else you need. I'll get you something clean to wear and leave it here on the bed."

I stare at him in disbelief. I hate the comparison, but I couldn't help the memory of when I dared to pull away from Kurt. It didn't end well for me. Yet here is this man, a little disappointed to pause things, but kindness and under-standing fill his eyes. I hug him tight around his neck. "Thank you."

"For what?"

"For being you. For being so wonderful to me."

"You deserve wonderful. You deserve more."

I kiss his cheek, and then ask, "What are you going to do?"

Rolling to the side onto his back, he throws one arm wide while the other slips under me. "Hang out waiting for you."

"As soon as I'm clean. I like that thing you do with your face and mouth. It's my favorite. But I'd feel better if I show-ered first."

He's chuckling. "One time and you already have favorites?"

I steal another quick kiss and climb off the bed. Kicking off my shoes, I send them flying in different directions. "Absolutely. Don't you?"

"I do."

"Are you going to tell me?"

"Yes." He eyes me as if he already sees me fitting snugly right into his life. "I'll let you know when the time is right." This gentle giant's gaze sweeps over me as he gets up. "Shout if you need me. I'm going to make a few calls."

"Okay." I bunch the bottom of my shirt in my hands, suddenly a little nervous. My chest feels tight when I realize how deeply I already care for him.

I'm unsure what to do with these feelings. I didn't expect him. I definitely didn't see a man that good finding me at my worst, and instead of turning a cold shoulder, he offered me his hand.

He leaves, and I'm left to my own devices, free to snoop as I please. "Shower, Winter." I take another quick look around the bedroom and smile. The furniture is a little different than I imagined for him. Back in Paris, I saw him surrounded by eighteenth-century French pieces curated to fit the opulence of the hotel.

Here, he's modern lines mixed with rich brown leather. Open, but warm. This room, and his entire apartment, is much more relaxed. Comfortable and not pretentious. If I ever had to describe Bennett, it might be the same.

The bathroom is big, just how I love it. The bathroom rivals the fanciest spas in Europe with white marble, wood shelves, and pale blue towels the size to fit a Viking. I smile, squeezing the plush cotton as I pass to turn on the water.

The water warms within seconds. Beats the pipes in my apartment, but that comes with living in a brownstone and trading modern conveniences for the character of our city's past.

I step under the spray, thinking I'm ready to trade my past for a new life. Closing my eyes, I let the water run over me, hair and all, washing away my makeup, the grime of the day, and hoping the threat I've been living under drains away.

Can Bennett really protect me? Can the Everest brothers take on McCoy if I give them the information I know? How will my family react to my return?

Bait.

I was nothing more than a worm on a hook for Kurt. I owe Bennett and his brothers so many apologies I don't know where to begin.

I did what I was told because I didn't know the master plan, but now I wonder what role my father has been playing. It seems too convenient that Bennett ended up in Paris from my father's request to check on me when Kurt is collecting them. Are they in this together? Bennett's right. My father is the key, but what game is he playing?

My father has shown me who he really is, but it's still hard for my heart to believe. Tears fall with the spray, rivulets stream down my body, the flat of my stomach, and tops of my thighs as they race to the drain.

Large arms wrap around me from behind. Kisses cover the exposed skin of my neck through wet hair. "Don't cry," he whispers against my shoulder before kissing it.

I curl into him, molding myself to his body wanting to sink into his arms, his heart, his life, his world. With my head still down, Bennett turns me around.

Standing in a soaking wet white shirt and dress pants, bare feet, and a silver watch that reflects the light from above, all I see is his heart worn proudly on his sleeve. I embrace him, my arms around his middle as tight as I can hold him.

The water rains down on our parade, and I'm so okay with that. I have him. I have him willing to weather the storm and a shower after a long day. He softens my sharp thorns and braves the planes of my prickly leaves. I'm the luckiest woman in the world. I say, "I don't deserve you."

"Sure, you do." An underlying smile elicits mine. He kisses my forehead. "I don't know what you've done that makes you so bad, but I feel you. I see you. The beating heart, the soft smiles, the stars in your eyes, and the love letters you write with your fingertips on my skin." He holds me tighter, sliding his big hands to cover my lower back. "And you know what?"

"What?"

"I feel the same, cactus flower." I'm kissed right where I need it most—on the lips. And I kiss him back, unbuttoning his shirt as he undoes his pants. When he's removed everything from his lower half, he bends toward me, raising his arms as I strip off the wet undershirt sticking to his skin, then he straightens up again.

The clothes are kicked to the corner and I'm pressed to the wall, my face cupped, his middle against me. As steam fills the shower stall, he turns his attention to my lower body and kneels before me. Lifting one leg over his shoulder, he then cups my breasts and squeezes while his mouth takes me between my legs. Then he looks up at me with what looks like reverence and says, "I don't deserve you."

And I melt.

Steam billows around me as I lean my head back, mouth wide open as I pant from the pleasure. I've never felt freer to react to a sexual act than the extent he allows me. Moans steadily escape me as his tongue dips inside.

I hold his head as my knees start to wobble, and my body begins to slide down the marble behind me.

His hands pin my hips in place, and he steals a peek up at me before diving deeper and teasing my pleasure right out of me. "Oh, God. That feels so good," I say, my voice feeble as I reach the edge of the orgasm.

"You deserve to feel so good, Winter. You deserve everything good." With one more lap against me, he has me sailing off the cliff to the heavenly skies into pure bliss.

Standing breathless before me, he holds my body as I get my bearings again. When I'm picked up, I wrap my arms and legs around him, our mouths making love as he carries me to the bed. The top of my head tips off the end of the mattress, and he kisses my body all over—chin, neck, collarbone, between my breasts, my ribs where he pauses. When I look up, I see a frown, and then anger crosses his face. He kisses me there again, this time tenderly before he continues leaving a kiss on each side of me before he goes lower to my belly. Spreading my legs, he kisses my inner thighs, and then I'm bare as he reaches into the drawer of his nightstand.

Returning before the cool air of the room sets in, he runs his hands up my legs and back down, lifting one up and kissing my ankles. I close my eyes, wanting his mouth selfishly savoring all of me again and relishing in the sensations. His body hovers above me, his erection pushing into the embrace of my body. Tilting my head back, I can feel his heated breath on my chest. And then I'm with him, moving against him and matching him breath for breath, thrust for thrust.

I scrape my nails over the back of his shoulders and greedily beg for more—faster, harder—*more.*

More.

More.

He focuses his strength on the goal, and like my head is on this mattress, I'm tipped over the edge the moment his fingers find my sensitivity, encircling my swell for him.

A groan follows as he finds what he's seeking deep inside me. I hold his head to me as my name flows like poetry from his lips across my chest. The kisses are less insistent, lingering longer, tasting the love we made until our lips meet again and our tongues slow dance.

"Dream a Little Dream of Me" plays in the back of my mind, and I kiss his temple before he has a chance to escape. I'm so close to saying those three words that I've never felt more than at this perfect moment. I love his weight balanced on me, and the connection we've made.

After another shower and getting ready for sleep, we slide under the covers again. The bed's so huge it doesn't even matter if he claims the center, but I still tease, "Bed hog," which makes him chuckle. He turns off the lights, and my eyes grow heavy, despite wanting to stay up and listen to him breathe and dream. Wrapped up in each other, I add, "We don't need this big bed when we're sleeping like this."

Spooning. It's been so long . . . *wait* . . . this might be a first for me. A satisfied smile splits my cheeks. Doesn't matter that he can't see, he can feel my body vibrating with happiness.

He kisses my shoulder. I let myself begin to slip into a contented sleep. Just before I'm lost to the dream world, he whispers, "This is my favorite."

20

Bennett

Ethan flips through the file in front of him, scanning the pages with the speed of a Jedi, possibly becoming one with the mind trick that tech billionaires develop after hitting it big. "This says she's been unemployed for a year."

"I don't know." I shrug. "We'll ask her when she gets up."

"How do you not know? You spent seven hours in the air and an entire night with her. How could you not have talked about the men who were after you?"

"Ethan?" Singer rests her hand on his arm, drawing his attention. When he looks at her, she adds, "Please be patient. You'll get your answers shortly. A lot happened yesterday, and they were tired." Standing, she moves behind him and rubs his shoulders. She looks at me, her smile full of empathy. "I don't want you fighting each other. This isn't business. This is personal. You must stick together."

"Where does that leave Winter?" I ask.

Ethan leans back, relaxing under the shoulder massage.

"If you trust her, so do we. As for how we proceed, we're relying on you to tell us what you want us to do. Aaron will join us when you're both ready to go over the details."

Aaron, Ethan's mercenary driver, has taken over security for the family in the last year. Making sure we're covered in some capacity is his top priority. Lars is the expert at securing locations since he was at one time a former Secret Service agent for a government figure. They make a hell of a team.

"In the meantime," Singer says, "we should go and let them start their day without an audience."

"You don't have to leave on my account." I turn to see Winter walking toward us tentatively. "I hope I'm not interrupting."

I stand quickly to greet her. Shielding her from the others, I adjust the baggy shirt back onto her shoulders as she tugs at the strings to the sweatpants, tightening until the fabric bunches at her waist. I lean down and caress her face. "Good morning, beautiful."

"Good morning," she replies, holding my wrists as I kiss her. When I begin to pull back, she holds me there. "I didn't know you had company."

"My brother and sister-in-law."

Running her hand down her hair, she lowers her voice. "But I look a mess."

"You look incredible. Anyway, they know about our circumstances when we left France. They're here to get security in place."

Her hand rests on her chest as she peeks around me. "All right."

I take her hand, hoping to calm the nerves making it shake. I'm ready to introduce her but stop. "We don't have to do this now."

"I'm fine. I really am."

I have to trust what she tells me. We also need answers,

and it seems we're only going to get them from her. "I'll be here for you every step of the way."

"Thank you."

Ethan and Singer are standing halfway between the table where we were sitting and the door. "Winter Nobleman—"

And then it happens too quickly for me to stop it . . . She curtsies and then takes Singer's hand, shaking it vigorously. "It is so amazing to meet royalty."

I cringe inside on her behalf but speak up. "This is my fault. Singer's not the princess."

Winter's head whips to face me. "What?" And then horror and embarrassment redden her cheeks and neck. To Singer, she says, "I'm so sorry. Bennett mentioned a princess lived down the hall."

Singer smiles and reaches for Winter's hands. "It's okay. I understand how this could happen." Tilting her head to the side, she adds, "Ally is the kindest person I know. And she has a good sense of humor. She'll enjoy this story, but she'll like meeting you more."

"Thank you." Laughing, Winter leans forward, holding her stomach, and then says, "I'm so sorry again."

"No worries. For real."

Hearing Singer say "For real" reminds me of Winter saying it last night. I think they're going to get along just fine.

"This is Ethan," I say.

"Wow, that's all I get. Thanks, man, for the stupendous introduction." He chuckles and holds out his hand. "Hi, I'm this guy's older brother and boss. It's very nice to meet you, Winter."

"Can you tell how much he loves being my boss?" I ask.

Winter nods. "Yes." Turning to me, she asks, "Any coffee?"

"Yes."

"We'll leave you two alone so you can wake up properly. Although I've always found it's easier to fly back and gain hours versus losing them, jet lag sucks," Singer says.

"Me too," Winter says as I walk them to the door. "Nice meeting you."

"You too." Right before the door closes, Singer adds, "Let me know if you need anything."

"We will. Thanks." I shut the door and then return to my girl. "How about a proper good morning?"

"I like proper, but you know what I like better? Improper. Right. After. Coffee."

I laugh, following her into the kitchen. "That's fair, but just know I'm going to hold you to that."

"I expect to be held in all kinds of positions."

Taking hold of her, I roam my hands over her back and lower until I reach the curve of her ass and squeeze. "Where have you been all my life?"

"Right here in this big city waiting for a giant to show up and rescue me."

"You didn't need a hero. You were doing fine on your own."

"That's because you don't know the full story."

"And that's something we're going over today. Let's get you coffee and get dressed. Can I make you breakfast?"

"Coffee's good."

"How about food? You need food, Winter."

"I'm not hungry."

"I'll toast bagels."

She shoots me a look that I think is meant to level me, but it makes me smile instead. "I don't eat bread or carbs in general."

"How do you not eat carbs? It's brain food."

Tapping her head, she says, "Yet I've managed to survive, cogs working at full speed."

"I watched you inhale cookies in my room and a fry."

"Those were one-offs. You make me crave things I shouldn't."

"I think your body wants carbs."

"My body wants you." She leans against the island, her body language challenging. She may only come up to my chest, but she's currently owning every inch of her height. Even adding a little with that raised chin of hers.

"And as much I like that, you can't survive off sex."

"We could try," she replies optimistically.

Wow, she's red hot this morning. "Did I leave you wanting last night? If I did, I'll make it up to you."

Wrapping her arms around me, she says, "No, but you can still make it up to me."

"Right after breakfast." I go to the fridge and open the door. Letting all the cold out despite my dad's voice running through my head about air conditioning the entire neighborhood when I was young, I search for something a no carb eating, feisty, sex-craving beauty might want. There's a limited selection since I've been gone, so I reach for the few things Singer brought for us and load them onto the island.

"Yogurt. Strawberries. Blueberries. Cheese. Pineapple cups. Eggs. Pick your poison."

Crossing her arms over her chest, she rests her hip against the marble counter. "Why are you so insistent I eat something when I'm not hungry?"

"Because I listened to your stomach growl all night. Because you haven't eaten in close to sixteen hours." Moving in, I pick her up by the hips and set her on the island before wedging between her legs and holding her by the ass. It has absolutely nothing to do with eating or feeding her, but just because I can, and I'm going to take full advantage of loving on this woman while I have the chance.

"Did you eat?"

"I ate a few hours ago."

Her eyebrows rise. "How long have you been up?"

"I don't know," I reply, checking my watch. "Four hours, I suppose. I ate and worked out with my brothers. Ate again then showered and got dressed before Ethan and Singer came over."

"You packed in a heck of a full day before ten. I must have slept hard. I didn't hear a thing."

"You got a good nap in on the plane too. Your body needs the rest."

She toils with the foil lid of the yogurt but doesn't open it. "If I eat this, can we go back to bed?"

"I have no problem with that compromise."

"Can I ask you something and will you be one hundred percent honest with me?"

I rub her back, and say, "Absolutely."

"How long can we be like this?"

"And by this, you mean what?"

"We're hiding in this high rise like Paris didn't happen."

"We're in my apartment because Paris did happen. We may need to perfect our ending, but we had a damn good start."

She kisses me and then rests her forehead on my shoulder. "We sure did. You'll stay with me when I talk to your security people?"

"I promised to protect you and to be there every step of the way, and I will."

Holding my face close, she says, "Anytime I'm in your way, just tell me. I don't want to be a burden, no matter how much I want to stay."

"You want to stay?" I can't hide the happiness that slips into my tone.

"If you want me to."

"I very much want." *You.*

"For a few days?"

I hate that she feels insecure. I need to do a better job of making her feel what I do. "Winter, I want you here so *we* can work through how we can protect you, and how we can make the threat against you go away. That's the first goal. But I also want you here for me. Call me selfish, but I don't want to contemplate the idea of you walking out that door and not being in my life. Just so you know, I want you here for more than a few days."

I expect a quip of some sort to come from her beautiful mouth, but she's strangely silent.

I'm not most men. I can handle her erupting moods and conflicting actions. I can handle the words she uses to stab others, wanting them to cut through the tension like a blade. I can handle anything she throws my way because underneath this defensive armor of hers, I still see the woman whose eyes light up from the sight of the Eiffel Tower sparkling at night. A woman who clasps her hands over her heart while admiring a statue of two kissing lovers. I see the woman who shared her darkest secret, the one that buries her under the memories and fell in love because she confided that secret to me.

She's the most beautiful woman I've ever seen when she drops her weapons and trusts me. I see when her expression morphs. The cynical look in her eyes lightens in the blue centers, the pinch of her lips releases, and her chin lowers. The tension in her shoulders softens, and her stance isn't so staunch.

I touch her cheek, and she lets me. "Will you trust me, Winter?"

Her eyes dip closed, and she licks her lips. When she looks up at me again, a swell of moisture fills the corners. "I do trust you. *Already.* That's what scares me."

"Don't be scared. We're in this together."

"And then what?" she asks skeptically.

"And then we finally get to live and be whoever we want to be."

"We, huh?"

I rub the side of her neck and then lower my hands to her hips, giving them a little wiggle and getting a giggle in return. "Did I overstep?"

"No. I like the sound of we."

"Good." I kiss her head, and then say, "I like the sound of you being here, especially that little snore you do."

Feigned offense jolts her head back. "I do not snore."

She pulls away, but I catch her wrist and bring her back in, this time dipping her. "Doesn't matter. I like it. You know why?"

She can't hide her smile, though I see her struggling to. "Why?"

"Because you have a great body."

I'm punched in the chest. "I meant why do you like that I snore, you big goof?"

"*Ohhhh.*" I knew what she meant, but it's great to hear her laughter. "Because it means you feel safe to sleep that deep."

"It's the bed."

"Okay." I kiss her. "It's the bed and not me. Gotcha," I tease with a wink.

As soon as I set her on her feet again, she's off down the hall. "I'm getting dressed."

"Your clothes were cleaned. They're in the bathroom." As much as I hate her walking away, she does a damn fine job of it.

But before she disappears completely, she turns back and sees me still standing there like a buffoon. She must feel sorry for me because she comes running into my arms, legs linked around me, and kisses me hard. When we stop to catch our breath, she says, "It's not the bed. It's you. Don't ever think otherwise."

Like a flower, she's slowly opening for me petal by petal, and it's a damn gorgeous sight to see.

21

Winter

My clothes are folded neatly in a pile on the counter. So neat that I wonder who washed and folded them. Does the giant have fairies and gnomes working for him? I wouldn't be surprised.

This apartment.

His success.

Him.

It's all a bit more overwhelming than I thought it would be when I was thinking about what I was doing on the plane. I'm still not sure if I made the right decision, though Bennett feels really right to me. But did I put us both in jeopardy by leaving Paris?

I don't know what Kurt wants with Bennett or his brothers. Did my father, or I put him on Kurt's radar? I'll never forgive myself if I'm to blame. Hopefully, we can get the answers before anything else happens because I'm not sure how long Kurt will leave me be, and I'm not naïve enough to think he'll just let the fact that I left go.

The cotton covering me comforts me. It's tempting to wear Bennett's clothes all day. There's the faintest scent of him on them from the drawers where they're kept. I hold the collar to my nose and take a deep inhale. My soul settles as he fills my lungs.

Reaching for the pink panties he was so kind to bring back from Paris, I roll my eyes and then look at myself in the mirror. My lip looks fine, which surprises me. The bruise along my jaw isn't huge, but it's changing to a new shade of anger—purple. A shudder runs the length of my spine, but I take a quick staggered breath to tamp it down, not wanting to think about that night.

Bennett makes me smile.

I have no makeup on and my hair isn't brushed, but the smile on my face . . . it's happiness unrestrained. That's what he's given me, which is more than I've had in the last eighteen years.

I leave the panties where they are and walk out of the bathroom. "Bennett?"

"Yeah?" he calls from a distance.

I meander down the long hall, peeking in each room to see if I might find him in one, but I don't. The handsome man is sitting at the table by the kitchen with a laptop in front of him working. He doesn't look up, engrossed in what he's reading. I pad across the floor until I'm across from him, breaking the concentration that carved lines in his forehead. "Hey, you didn't change clothes."

"No," I reply, coming around and sitting on his lap when he leans back. Tucked in his arms, I rest my head on his shoulder. "I decided to live in my boyfriend's clothes for my remaining days." I shrink my neck, realizing what I said a second too late. Closing my eyes, I stay quiet and so still, hoping he didn't hear me.

His mitt of a hand rubs my leg. I love watching him touch me like we've been together forever. "Boyfriend, huh?"

"I knew you couldn't resist." I get up but am pulled right back down.

"Like there was a doubt? I mean, just look at you."

I've been called pretty before by old boyfriends, over-heard my dad's friend at my sweet sixteen party talking about how much I'd grown up, and even from Bennett, but that he acts like he's the one who lucked out isn't a concept I'm familiar with. "What about me?"

"You're gorgeous, Winter. Everything about you is so beautiful. The way you laugh, your hair right now, and that mischievous grin you give when you have a good comeback. Your body is fucking amazing."

"No carbs."

"Yeah, so you say, but a little bread and a few happy pounds won't turn me away."

"Happy pounds? That's good stuff right there." The words and his hands on me. "Go on." I kiss his cheek as he runs his hand over my hip.

"Your eyes tell the story of your past pain, but your lips kiss me like there's no tomorrow."

My cheeks heat as I look down, but in Bennett style, he won't let me shy away even when it gets hot in the kitchen . . . or my face. Lifting my chin up, he pulls my gaze to his milk chocolate-y eyes. "I thought you were going to call me pretty, but you mentioned the other things you're attracted to."

"Those other things make up who you are. You are pretty —inside and out—but you're so much more. It's a disservice to the other senses if I only appreciate your beauty with my eyes."

Too obvious if I just flail right here on his lap and then melt away? I tighten my arms around him and kiss his neck. "Bennett?" I whisper. "You make me want to eat pasta again."

His laughter heals my soul in so many ways.

I lean back just enough to get the full view. It would be a shame if I didn't. He was made to be admired and in more ways than just physically, but when I see his smile, he just about does me in. *Again.*

"I've never been a good judge of character until I met you," I say.

He hums, pressing a kiss on me. His arms tighten around me, understanding I mean more than I'm saying, and then he looks into my eyes. "I won't abuse your trust." His deep and husky voice contradicts the sunny day shining through the windows but speaks to my core.

"I know we have a lot to talk about. It wasn't to put it off but to keep you safe. I don't know if I can, though." Shame washes through me. "I couldn't even keep myself safe."

"If your life and mine are in danger like they were back in Paris, we need to know the details."

"They aren't pretty." The irony of me using pretty again but not referring to beauty isn't lost on me.

He runs his finger along my bottom lip and then kisses it. "I can handle it."

"I'm afraid you won't look at me the way you are right now."

Lifting me up, he spreads his legs and brings me in. I'm not tremendously taller than him in this position, and he's still sitting down, but it's enough for his head to tilt back, giving me the advantage. "Look, Winter." He sighs and rubs his hand over his jaw. "If people are trying to kill you, or me because I'm with you, then we're in deep trouble. We all get involved in shit that wasn't meant for us at one time or another, so don't feel like you have to protect me from the truth. I can handle it, but more importantly, so can you." He stands up and kisses my cheek. "Honesty is the only way we're going to get through this."

This is how it should be. This is what a healthy relationship looks like.

Working his way around me, he heads into the kitchen. He adds, "I'm abiding by the same rules. I just hope you look at me the same as you are right now."

"In awe, but slightly cranky?"

"That's hunger. I'm making you food."

"And I'll eat said food on one condition."

With eggs on the counter, he grabs a bowl from a cabinet and then rests his palms next to them while eyeing me. "Lay it out for me, sweetheart."

"I'm taking you up on your earlier offer. If I eat breakfast, I get you right after."

"Scrambled or fried?"

"Over easy."

Pulling a spatula from the drawer, he cocks an eyebrow. "Are we talking about eggs or sex?"

"Maybe both, but let's start with the eggs."

He eagerly cracks an egg into the pan. "You got it."

I hop up on the counter and watch this man cook just for me, even seasoning the eggs in the pan. "No man has ever cooked for me before."

"What about boyfriends?"

"Definitely not. What about you?"

Sneaking a peek over his shoulder, he chuckles. "I've never dated a guy, so no."

This time, he has me laughing, and then he's focused on me. I push him playfully away and then pull him back by the front of his shirt and straight into a kiss. "Are you burning my breakfast?"

Spinning and scooping up the spatula, he says, "Nope." He gets a plate from the cabinet and serves it up. "Here you go." Retrieving a fork from the drawer under where I'm sitting, he presents it to me. "Ma chérie."

"Merci, monsieur." I take a bite, but stop, to ask, "What?"

"I just like watching you eat."

I inhale half and then say, "Little clouds of deliciousness. You're a good cook, Everest."

"I'm good at the basics."

"Trust me. You're better than good. You're great."

"You catch on quick. I find that so incredibly sexy. To keep my end of the bargain, I need to reply to a few emails while you eat. Set the dishes in the sink, and I'll tackle them later."

"When are we leaving for the inquisition?"

He sits down in front of his laptop again and laughs. "Funny."

"That's what you say now."

He types something but then stops and looks back at me again. "Nothing you say—"

"Will be held against me?"

"I was going to say, be used against you. I've had you as a girlfriend for, what, a few hours? I'm not looking to ruin it that fast."

Shaking a finger at him after setting the plate in the sink, I say, "That's good. Play the long game when it comes to the breakup. Gives my heart some time to recover."

"You're full of the funnies today, Ms. Nobleman." He tracks me while I walk along the wall of windows.

"I'm here to please."

"You can't say things like that when I have to work."

Giggling, I keep my eyes on this amazing view. "Well, don't work too hard. I have plans for you, including you being hard in all the right ways." Bennett needs to get some stuff done, so I go back into the bedroom and open the curtains before slipping off the baggy clothes and going back to bed. Jet lag is a thing, and naps are glorious, so any excuse will do.

I try for sleep, but when I close my eyes, I can only see Kurt's fist coming toward me. I hear the smack of his hand against my cheek and feel the pain erupt as if it just happened. I endure the punch to my ribs, the wicked snarl on his face, and struggle to breathe. *How did I once fall for this man?*

The bonus appearances of my father, often standing to the side doing nothing to stop the monster from hitting his daughter . . . A father is meant to be your hero, but mine would turn a blind eye or, worse, watch passively.

An expert could tell me what this nightmare means, but I already know.

My jaw starts to hurt, and I realize I'm clenching my teeth. Taking three deep breaths and slowly blowing out helps. I roll over, away from the window I thought would bring peace and pull the covers over my head.

———

As I float in that blissful state between sleep and wake, warmth cradles me in his arms and joy fills my soul. My back heats from the body holding me.

Safe.

Comfort.

Home.

My hair falls like a wave over my shoulder, tickling my back, as I'm roused by kisses in the crook of my neck. "Mmmmm." I roll over, and my lips are kissed before my eyes open.

Gentle hands find my breasts and hardness against my hip. Kisses cover my chest, and a hungry pulse beats through my veins. When I finally open my eyes, what I see is better than any dream.

I run my hand through Bennett's dark hair and let him ravage me. God, he feels amazing, too much at times, that I can't hold still. *Like now.* I arch up, and when his eyes find mine, he smiles. "Don't mind me," he says, "I'm just earning my keep."

Even freshly awoken, I can't resist him—heart and humor —and laugh softly. "I will never mind you earning your keep, but I think it's my turn to return the favor."

His hand flattens against my belly, keeping me down. "Nope. We're not doing that. We're not keeping tallies or tit for tats, though you have great tits. We're just doing what feels good and what feels right."

"You feel right."

"Get ready then because I'm about to make you feel so right that it might be wrong."

"Never."

I hadn't noticed the packet next to me until he swipes it and lies back, ripping the foil. Not two deep breaths pass before he's settling between my legs, making himself at home while over me. Reaching up, I hold his face and then lift to kiss him.

He comes down with weight while pushing in slowly. I suck in a breath and dip my head back as I lower my hands to his shoulders and hold on to him. I want all of him all at once. The stretch, the burn, the sweat, and the fall after.

His lips are at my ear, kissing behind it, tugging my lobe between his teeth. His breath sends delectable shivers through me as he pushes all the way in.

My mouth cracks open, and he kisses under my chin. The sound of the sensations we're creating is getting to him. His heavy breath takes over, and he's thrusting, moving and pumping, until I say, "I want to see you."

Opening his eyes, Bennett takes me in with wide pupils and a determined vein in his forehead.

We stare into each other's eyes as our bodies push and pull, tug and take. Speed is not the goal as we get off-kilter. The rush goes to my head as I struggle to keep my eyes open. Without my permission, my body constricts, and I'm falling headfirst into the beautiful abyss. Bennett dives in behind me, and when our lips meet again, it's with a promise of a kiss.

Bennett makes love a possibility again. He's affirming, which is refreshing, even though he claims he's selfish, but from sightseeing to sex, he puts me first every time. In the face of danger, he didn't push me away to keep himself safe. He brought me into the family fold to protect me at the expense of his own safety.

It doesn't matter what I throw at him; he's strong and undaunted, and patient like no other man in my life has ever been. But the way he trusts me makes my heart flutter and my mind feel at ease. *Something I never thought I'd experience.*

As we lie here, words aren't needed as an unspoken contract seals us together. In the golden light of the afternoon sunshine, I start to fall. Slowly at first, and then as if I've cannonballed into the bliss, I feel light and free to swim in this love because his heart is mine, and mine is his.

22

Winter

The hot seat is warmer than I thought. I tug at my collar and use my shirt to fan myself.

Bennett closes his laptop across the table from me, and says, "Don't be nervous. We're all on the same team."

"You don't know what I've done."

"Did you hire those guys to kill me?" His whole demeanor is casual as he stares at me.

"No!" My voice pitches anyway. "I would never do that."

"Exactly." Sitting back, he adds, "That's why you don't have to worry. I know you have your reasons. We're just going to ensure that everyone is safe moving forward and that the ones responsible pay for what they've done."

"That might be me." My stomach clenches as I speak the words I've been afraid to say in fear of losing him.

"What are you talking about?" More interest lies in his eyes, the lighter side of caramel turning to brown sugar.

The sound of the front door opening invades the apartment, and I startle when I hear, "About time you got your ass back into town."

Bennett stands. Tapping the table, he says, "It's going to be okay," then walks around to greet his brother.

He thinks this will be easy, that I'm clear of responsibility, but I've just confirmed one thing—he wagered before he knew the bet, and now he's the one I'll hurt next.

I stand and when I see another giant fe-fi-fo-fumming into the space. I'm starting to see why they need such large apartments. While Ethan has lighter hair than Bennett, his oldest brother is a shade darker—hair, skin, eyes—and handsome like both of them. The Everest genes don't mess around when it comes to good looks.

The woman with him is as beautiful as I would have suspected for not only a princess but someone married into this family. I whisper, "Do I curtsy?"

Bennett grins and then shrugs. "If you want, but you don't have to."

"Please don't," Ally says with a kindhearted smile, reflecting what Singer said about her. With something black in her hands, she comes to me and shakes my hand. "I've heard so much about you. I'm Ally. It's nice to meet you."

"You too. Bennett was telling me you're a princess."

"I am. I can't take any credit since all I did was be born to earn the title."

Bennett's brother leans forward to shake my hand. "Wait until you hear about the foundation she set up. She's incredible. I'm Hutton. It's nice to meet you, Winter."

"You too."

I take it no one lounges around these parts, and there's definitely no resting on your laurels in this family. The other thing very clear is how much the Everest men love and adore their wives. I've never witnessed such adoration. *How they must thrive on such devotion.*

"Now that everyone has met, how about we sit in the living room?" Bennett suggests.

The men move to the living room section of the open space while Ally holds her hands out. "I brought you a change of clothes. I've put in an order for a few more things that should arrive by early afternoon, but I thought a pair of yoga pants and a T-shirt could help you get by until the other items arrive."

Taking the stack of soft black cotton from her, I'm left speechless. As I stare at the clothes, I feel temperamental tears forming, so I wipe at my eyes, embarrassed. "Sorry. I've been an emotional mess lately for some reason," I say, trying to justify my overwrought emotions.

"No need to apologize. You've been through a lot. I can only imagine how you're handling it." She touches my upper arms and brings me in for a hug. Even though I just met her, the embrace is heartfelt, and for some dumb reason, my tears multiply. "You're a strong woman. This will pass, and you'll be free from these worries." Something in the soft lilt of her accent is so incredibly soothing. *How long has it been since I've felt such warmth and comfort in the arms of a friend?*

She leans back, her hands warm and comforting on my shoulders. "We're all here for you, Winter. Just let us know how we can help, and we will."

"I don't understand. How can everyone be so nice? You don't even know me."

"But Bennett does," she replies. "That makes you family." I notice how her eyes dip from mine. "He should have an ice pack in his freezer. You're not swollen, but it might help lessen the bruising. Come on, we'll look together."

Ethan and Bennett's voices are low, their dulcet tones heard, but their words indiscernible. I watch their body language from the kitchen. I've brought stress and danger to his doorstep, to all of their lives.

"Surprisingly, he doesn't have one. I can bring one down later, but for now, this bag of peas will have to do." She opens a drawer and pulls out a tea towel. There's such a comfort in the way she moves around like she's here all the time and then wraps the peas inside. "Ten minutes on. No guarantees it will help since it's already formed, but it's worth a try."

I hold the cold pack to my jaw. "Thank you. Everybody is so close . . ."

"We all hang out. Bennett's single." She catches herself, and says, "Well, was? I'm not sure what to say. I'm sorry. I don't want to intrude. I know how delicate these things are."

"It's okay." Knowing what I'm about to confess, I leave it ambiguous. "We're figuring things out."

Grabbing two bottles of water from the fridge, she hands me one. She's sharp and reads right through me. "I set up his kitchen the same as mine." With a laugh, she adds, "Before I started the foundation, I had a little free time on my hands, and you know a bachelor isn't going to get this stuff done."

"The foundation sounds like a lot of work. Do you do it all?"

"It's a lot of good work, good for the soul work. And no, I couldn't possibly do it all. I have a dedicated team of five along with volunteers. Singer volunteers part time. She works in publishing the rest of the time. She loves to read."

"I love to read too." I think about my books in the Paris apartment and how much those little novels brought me joy. Buying them felt more rebellious than any designer dress I bought on Kurt's dime and meant the world to me. "My mother really loved to read, and she passed her passion down to me. I started a collection in Paris."

Mentioning my mom causes me to reach for my neck, sick to my stomach that I left before getting the necklace. She must sense my sadness. "I'm sorry you had to leave your books behind."

"They aren't valuable, but they were a nice place to escape."

Rubbing my arm, she says, "I'm so glad you have that connection to your mother. That's a treasure you can carry in your heart."

"Are you close to your mother?"

"My mother was queen, so we didn't get to do a lot together when I was growing up."

She speaks of being royal as if she grew up in the suburbs and everyone relates. I love that she's unpretentious.

"Let me ask you something. My clothes were washed and folded magically. Would you know anything about that?"

"Not magic. Great amenities. There's a dry cleaner on the street level who did us a favor. There's also a spa on the fifth floor. Singer and I are headed down later for facials. Would you like to join us?"

I glance at Bennett, unsure what to say. "He says it's not safe for me to leave."

"In the building should be fine. You'll never be more secure than you are here. Even the windows are bulletproof."

"What does that mean exactly?"

Bennett replies, "It means it will take more than a few rounds to break the glass."

"So bulletproof really means it's bullet resistant?"

"Basically, it will give you enough time to get out."

Singer walks around the island toward the men. "Is it safe for Winter to go to the spa today?"

I don't know why Bennett gets this look in his eyes like sugar just invaded his veins, but it's adorably annoying. All three of them look back at me, then Hutton says, "That shouldn't be an issue." He glances at me. "Are you comfortable talking to us, or is there something we can do for you?"

They're so careful, treating me with kid gloves.

I hate it.

It makes me feel weak.

I love it.

It makes me feel like they care.

Sitting in a chair, I sit straight and hold the arms. A smile forms on Bennett's face, and he says, "I know you feel like this is an interrogation, but it's really not."

Hutton rests his forearms on his knees and clasps his hands together. "But we do need substantial detail to put security in place as well for us to decide what move to make."

Ally comes to the far end of the couch from them and sits near me. Patting my arm, she says, "It will be okay. I promise."

A knock on the door pulls their attention away, and I breathe again. Bennett goes to answer it. Singer comes around followed by the men we rode from the airport with yesterday. With a bag in her hand, Singer says, "The stuff we ordered—clothes, flip-flops, sneakers, some makeup, and toiletries—arrived."

Ally stands and peeks inside. "Great." Then she sits back down. "We can get you anything else you need."

"Thank you. I hate burdening you."

"No burden at all," Singer replies.

Lars and Aaron are reintroduced, the lead security team members. Aaron says, "I'll be taking notes for Mr. Everest and for our team, Ms. Nobleman."

He's not asking, but I say, "Fine," anyway.

Bennett's brother says, "Are we ready to get started?"

"I'm ready. Might as well get it over with." I'm not ready at all, but here we go.

Singer goes into the kitchen. I hear the faucet and then see her lean against the island, sipping water.

"Who were those guys in Paris working for?" Hutton asks.

My eyes leave the safety of Singer's and come back to the

group in front of me, and then I pick at the cuticle of my ring finger. Once I say it out loud, there's no taking it back. It will be out there . . . my life more at risk than it ever was before. But if it will keep them safe, I'm willing to make the sacrifice.

I suck in a hard breath and slowly exhale his name with it. "They worked for Kurt." I don't have to see them to feel the weight of their intense stares. "Kurt McCoy."

Silence carries through the air, and I look up, their gazes distancing as they process the name I've injected into their universe. They turn to each other, leaving me out of the private conversation held by their eyes.

A glass shatters, startling me. Looking toward the kitchen, Singer stands, her mouth open, a million emotions flickering through her eyes and contorting her face into horror.

Seeming to catch herself, she bends down. "I'm sorry, Bennett." She grabs at the broken glass and then jerks back, losing her balance. Everyone jumps to their feet and rushes to her. Blood drips down the side of her hand. "Damn it."

Ally and Bennett are helping her to her feet while I stand off to the side. They help her to the sink where she places her hand under running water. While I stand there, not wanting to intrude, Singer asks Bennett, "Do you have a bandage I can use until I get a better look at it?"

Bennett rushes past me and then returns with a first-aid kit that he spreads open on the counter. While he tends to her, she steals a look at me, a tear weaving down her cheek and dropping to her chest.

I move in slowly. "Are you okay?"

She shakes her head and then looks at Aaron. "I need Ethan." From her reaction, something tells me this is about more than a cut on her hand.

He replies, "I texted him."

"Thank you." Her voice is frail, unlike the vibrant woman I met earlier. "I'll meet him upstairs." She looks at Bennett when he stands back to his full height after bandaging her. "I'm sorry about the glass. I'll clean—"

"No," I say, moving in closer. "I'll clean it."

Hutton directs us away from the area while Ally walks by me, and says, "Don't worry. I'll clean it."

Singer says, "I'm sorry," again to Bennett as he walks with her toward the hall leading to the door.

His voice is low, his concern etched into his forehead. "It's okay."

"It's not," she whispers. "I need to see him first, and then I'll send him down."

"I understand. Aaron, go with her."

Ally stands near Hutton with a roll of paper towels. "I'll be up in a minute, Sing."

Clearly shaken, she nods her reply.

"I'm sorry," I blurt, hoping she feels better. I don't know why, but my gut tells me something is seriously wrong.

23

Winter

It's been an hour since Singer left, wounded by my admission. When Ethan showed up, I left the brothers by themselves. What did that interrogation last? One question. One confession. One minute before everything changed, shifting the warm welcome.

It's been quiet for a while. I'm not sure if contemplation is happening or everyone has left, but I stay in Bennett's room. I'm glad I kept on his clothes. There's more room to make mistakes and grow from them inside.

I push through the urge to run and avoid conflict or remain waiting in the master bedroom, especially since I'm not sure what I'm waiting for. I head toward the living room, not sure how many Everests I'll find.

Bennett stands from where he was sitting on the couch and drags his palms down the front of his jeans as his favorite song plays. "Hi," he says, his hand going up.

"Hi. How's Singer?"

"She'll be fine."

"I'm sorry."

"For what?" His eyes begin to narrow like he's struggling to read me. I relate.

"For causing her pain."

"You didn't, Winter."

I tap the tip of my shoe on the wood and clutch my hands in front of me. "I did." I look away. "I don't know how or why, but I've been feeling guilty this whole time, Bennett. This is her home. Would it be better for her, for all of you, if I leave?"

"No." His voice is quieter, not commanding the same attention as his frame. "Talk to me. Fill in the missing pieces. I sent them home so it could just be us. Us talking. You and me. Me and you. Please, Winter, explain how you're caught up in this mess that could cost me my life, my brothers' lives. Singer's and Ally's."

My chin can't hold its strength against this man. It hits my chest, and I whisper, "I'm sorry."

"I don't want your apology, damn it. I want answers."

Stubbornness braces my spine, and I look up at him, ready to tear into anyone who attempts to attack me. But I can't. Not him. "It's a domino effect, and I'm the one who knocked the first one down. If I had never gone to work for the McCoys, I would have never met Kurt. My role in this mess is the reason you were almost taken or killed."

"You saved me, Winter. What about that? You risked your life to help me. That doesn't matter to you?"

"It does because you matter to me." My lashes are wet from tears and I hate that I can't have this conversation without crying. Frustration, anger at myself, and the pain I've caused him and his family fill my lids until the tears topple over. I've carried this burden on my own for so long that to finally share it is so horribly painful. But the shame that comes with my admission is almost crippling.

"I may not have given the order, but I'm to blame, Bennett."

"Sit down." His tone is firm, leaving me no wiggle room.

I owe him answers. Now's the time, so I sit on the couch. "You can ask me anything. I won't lie to you."

He sits back down, a line digging deep between his brows. "See? Here I thought we were already past that."

"We are," I start, but stammer over a few breaths. "I just thought—"

"Allies. We said allies, Winter. Being on the same side, the same team, being allies means we stick together, and we don't lie to each other. I gave you time to yourself in the bedroom because I thought you needed it not because I thought we were over. Fuck, we've barely begun."

"I didn't doubt us. I doubted myself." Allies with him is so different than when Kurt demanded it of me.

"Because you doubted me and my reaction to something. You don't have to read into my expression. If you're unsure of something when it comes to us, or me, all you have to do is ask."

"Are you mad at me?"

"No. Why would I be?" he answers solemnly.

"The situation with Singer."

"You didn't cause that, and it's being handled. But I need to know your ties to Kurt McCoy."

"I worked for him."

It doesn't take but a split second for him to put the pieces together. "He's a competitor of Nobleman's." Scrubbing his hand over his face, he sighs. "Shit."

"Yeah. Pretty much."

He leans back. "This is what you hint at but don't say. You feel you betrayed your family by working for the competition?"

"I don't feel it. I know I did, and they know I did."

"Why did you go to work for the McCoys?"

"Because my father wouldn't hire me after I spent years in school preparing for the job."

Reaching over, he rests a hand on my leg. "They forced your hand. It's a specialized field. You didn't have much choice."

"I can tell myself that all day long, but it won't change my intentions."

"And what were those?"

"To get insider information from McCoy." I tap the toes of my shoes together. "Maybe in retribution as well."

"I understand the feeling of revenge. People have hurt my family . . ." He glances in the direction of the door like he expects someone to round the corner. When his eyes return to me, he says, "The McCoys have hurt my family and others close to us."

"I didn't know."

"We know you didn't. *I* know you didn't. But that he's involved with anyone around us is a threat to all of us. Did Kurt hit you?"

"Yes," I reply, wanting to bury my head into our happier times. As much as I hate confrontation and others being disappointed in me, it's time to face the truth and end this nightmare.

"You worked for him to get back at your family and to steal information. I get that, but I sense there's more to the story."

Honesty. No matter how much it embarrasses me. "We dated," I say, keeping my voice as low as possible.

He catches himself blankly staring at me, though I'm sure he has plenty of thoughts on the subject, and then stands. With his back to me and his arms crossed over his chest, he directs his attention out the window.

Rushing to fill the unbearable void between us, I add, "I thought he cared about me."

He whips around, his face showing his astonishment. "Kurt McCoy? You thought a McCoy would love you how you deserve?"

"You don't have to say it like that. I admit that I was naïve. I told you I'm a bad judge of character."

"Winter?"

"Yes?"

"I'm mad now." His voice is too calm to yell, his disposition not stiff or aggressive in stance.

"Are you holding it in?"

"Yes," the word comes out on a strangled breath.

"I'm so sorry I've brought this awful back into your life. I would never purposely hurt you."

Taking a deep breath and releasing a long exhale, he adds, "I'm not mad at you. What did you hope to gain when you went to work for him?"

"His operational plans," I say, the words spilling from my mouth. "I thought I could get them and give them to my father."

"What happened?"

"I'm betting you could answer that yourself."

Bennett is a thoughtful man. He takes calculated risks, and maybe spontaneous ones, but it seems when it comes to business, he's more on the analytical side. "He knew what you were doing, and you were the perfect prey." Sitting down again, he rests his arms on his legs. "Let me guess. He blackmailed your dad with the information he got from you? Thus dividing you and your father even further."

"And my brother. He despised me for the close relationship I had with my mother. He hates me even more now."

"I'm sorry it didn't work out the way you wanted. But

honestly, from what you've said, getting that information for your father wouldn't have changed things. As for the McCoys, they have no conscience or integrity." Bennett walks to the edge of the hallway. He's leaving? Just when I feel my heart start to shatter, he says, "The others need to know this information."

"What should I do?"

"I want you to tell us everything you know, and then when it's all said and done, we're coming back here, and I'm going to make love to you." His tilted smirk gives me comfort. "And if you're a good girl, I'll start face first."

He comes to me, lifts my chin until my mouth closes, and then with a finger remaining on my skin, he kisses me. Our lips are still pressed together when he asks, "How does that sound?"

"A deal I can't say no to." After he steals my breath away with another sweet kiss, I sink into the place where I'm most happy—his world and him. *Bennett. Bennett. Bennett.* This time when our lips part, he walks back, holding his hand out and waiting for me to join him. "Come with me, Winter."

All I have to do is take it.

The risk.

The opportunity.

The hand of the man who's more than I deserve.

When I reach out, he takes it and kisses it. "I'll protect you."

"Promise?"

"I promise."

24

Winter

In the hall linking the two apartments, Bennett places his hand on a black pad, and the wall shifts in and then slides to the side. Panic rises inside, and I ask, "Where are you taking me?"

"To the penthouse." He's not nervous at all, but his hand tightens around mine to put me at ease. "There's a lot of security in the building. Step back." The wall slides closed, and he punches in a code that opens the door to the elevator.

When we step inside, I ask, "Could someone hurt you and still get in?"

"There are precautions in place. When my hand is on the pad, it checks the points of fingerprints, handprint, pulse, and hormones. Through temperature, it can decipher between panic, threats, and regular sweat."

"How?"

"I'm not a science guy, but what I got out of the training is that we produce distinct levels of hormones in each situation." That he answers my flurry of questions shows the trust he's given me. I want to make him feel the same.

The door closes, and after he enters another code, I ask, "Did we only go up one floor?"

"Yes. We renovated last year and moved to the apartments under his."

The door slides open, and we enter. "Oh, wow!" I'm not sure what else to say as we walk down a gallery covered in framed black and white photos. The walls are black but lead to a bright space surrounded by floor-to-ceiling windows. So much of it is similar to Bennett's, but this place takes up the entire floor. "That is the most incredible view I've ever seen."

Singer comes down another corridor and smiles at me. It's not as happy as when we first met, but I'll take it. Taking my hands in hers, she says, "I didn't mean to react like I did. I'm so sorry for worrying you."

"Worrying me? No, please. I'm sorry. I didn't—"

"I know you didn't. There's a lot to tell, but it's not the time. That's history I can't change." She turns to their seating area—two large, deep blue couches face each other with light brown leather designer chairs anchoring them at either end. A wood table with uneven edges and prominent grain centers everything on top of an area rug. It's such a nice balance between masculine and feminine, formal to comfort. "Please, sit. Can I get you anything to drink?"

"Wine?" I don't even know what time it is, but it feels like a glass of white wine would treat me well about now.

"Sauvignon blanc?"

I appreciate the lack of judgment. "Perfect."

"Bennett?"

"I'm good," he replies.

Hutton and Ethan come in from the same hall where Singer had appeared. They stop talking when they move to sit. The brothers may tease Ethan about being the brains, but he does not lack in attractiveness. He and Singer make a stunning couple. As do Ally and Hutton.

I glance at Bennett, starting to feel a part of this family as well, wanting to be a part of them. Before I get too lost in that thought, Ethan says, "I think it's obvious that there's history when it comes to the McCoys and Everests." I nod as if he asked me a direct question. He didn't, but his green eyes focus on me. "The men chasing Bennett and you work for Kurt McCoy. Is that right?"

"Yes."

"You currently don't work for him in any capacity, correct?" Hutton asks.

"The word work is subjective."

Ethan says, "Please explain."

Singer hands me a wineglass and sits on the sofa next to her husband with a glass of sparkling water in hand. When his hand covers her thigh, the motion is one made of love and reacting to her without thought—on instinct. I've always found the small gestures of love more convincing than the grander acts. Those feel like they're made for everyone else.

I take a quick sip, and then say, "I used to work for McCoy Industries, a smaller division of McCoy Properties. A bad decision to spite my family in many ways and because of them in other ways." I continue to vomit my entire story, hoping to find relief afterward. "That bad decision was made worse by dating him. I know I shouldn't have, but I'll blame my age and how I thought I was smarter than my father at the time."

Hutton says, "We're all guilty of doing things we regret. What about after? You didn't cut ties?"

"In business, yes, but personally, he dragged me along for another six months."

Singer's voice is soft when she asks, "What do you mean he dragged you?"

The cut gets deeper and I can't stop the words from bleeding. "He had something on me—information about my father's company—and I thought that was what drove him. But then it was as if he lost sight of his initial goal."

"Which was?" Bennett asks.

"Me. He got engaged, but he became obsessed with me. He claimed to love her, but still pursued me. It was as if he wanted a fiancée but believed he had no reason to let go of me. I wanted nothing to do with him, and with every rejection, he came on stronger until he had what he needed to reel me back in." I take a gulp of my wine and then another, needing to numb some of these harsher truths. "I did everything to make my dad proud of me, to see me not as his daughter but as an equal to my brother. Kurt diminished all hope of that when he blackmailed me into being his whore." I finish my wine and cross my legs, defiant in their unreadable stares.

Bennett gets up and leans toward me. The sun rises and sets in his warm sunshine eyes. "Don't close down. You're not on the stand," he whispers.

I accept his words, though it's hard not to react the way I've trained myself to. He leans back but continues to rub my knee. "How long did that go on?"

"Six months. He lauded the information on my family's company over my head the entire time. He became physically abusive as if the emotional abuse wasn't damaging enough. When I stood up to him, I should have known he'd never let me walk away that easily." I'd been terrified, having no clue what he was capable of. Now it's too late.

"What happened?" Singer asks.

"He made his first move—a hostile takeover of my family's company. It was all my father had left. My brother invested his trust fund. Kurt was going to take it from them because of me. If I had never worked for him, Kurt wouldn't have the ammo. I basically handed him the keys to my family's legacy."

Bennett turns to his brothers, and says, "She worked in dock rights, shipping, and cargo holds," as if that says everything.

Ethan sighs heavily and rubs his temple. "I see. Same as Nobleman."

"What is it?" I ask, missing the connection.

Bennett replies for him. "Kurt McCoy's cousin tried to kill Singer and Ethan."

"What?"

"I don't want to talk about that," Singer snaps. No wonder she reacted the way she did at Bennett's. How can they even look at me? His cousin tried to murder them? *Oh God.*

Her husband wraps his arm around her. "We knew Kurt was running the company, but we didn't know the extent that he was following in his cousin's footsteps. We should have."

Hutton says, "I don't understand how you ended up working for him again. Do you mind explaining?"

"Kurt had been calling me for months. I finally took the call and begged him to show my family mercy. He told me to meet him for dinner. I saw it as an opportunity to plead in person." Worried to look Bennett in the eyes, I stare at the empty wineglass instead. "We had dinner and drinks, but by the time dessert was served, I wasn't feeling well."

Bennett stands, distressed—hands flexing, jaw clenching, and anxiety coursing through his muscles as he begins to pace, unable to stay still. "He drugged you."

I vaguely notice Hutton and Ethan, their reactions lost as I look at Bennett. He's so angry on my behalf, but I can't have him set out on a mission of revenge. "And then I woke up in Paris," I say, leaving out the in between.

"Drugged and kidnapped." His hands are fisted, his brown eyes burning, with anger. He mutters under his breath, "Motherfucker."

I stand and go to him. "I'm okay." I run the tips of my fingers down his arms until I meet his tight hands. I keep his eyes on me as I gently wedge my fingertips into his palms until he releases and weaves his fingers with mine. He looks away, redirecting his anger toward a painting on the wall. "Look at me," I say so softly, carefully. "Please, Bennett."

When he does, he says, "I want to kill him."

25

Winter

Fury fuels the fire in his eyes. "They're evil. The McCoys sold their souls to the devil a long time ago."

"There's more I need to tell you," I say, leaning my head against him.

Tilting back up, I rest my chin on his chest. "I don't want anything to happen to you."

"I'm fine. Nothing's going to happen." He takes a step back, calmer for the time being. When he sits, I do, too.

"Ben?" Hutton asks.

Turning toward his brother, he's annoyed. "I'm fine."

They hold each other's hard stare until Hutton seems appeased. "All right." Hutton redirects to me. "I'm not surprised that happened to you since we're dealing with a McCoy, but I'm sorry about it. Are you okay?"

I managed to bring these horrible people back into their lives, and they're checking on my well-being. Their kindness knows has no limits. "I'm, uh. I'm fine. Thank you."

"That's good," he replies. "Do you know why he kidnapped you?"

My hands start shaking from the memory, Kurt's bloodthirsty gaze coming back as if I can see him before me now. I sit on my hands, but my voice trembles still giving me away. "When I woke up in Paris, he told me he was collecting the debt I owed him."

"What's the debt?" Bennett asks.

"My life. He said he owned me, and I had to do what he told me to earn back my freedom. It wasn't threatening my life that scared me. Ultimately, I'm the one to blame for walking into his office in the first place, so my dirty deeds were always meant to catch up with me." My gaze pivots around the room at each of them as shame flourishes inside me. "I was used as bait."

Her voice wobbles on fear, but Singer still asks, "What were you supposed to catch?" She knows the answer, the tears welling in her eyes gives her away.

"I didn't know until it was too late. I swear I didn't." I shift uncomfortably in their spotlight. "I was told not to do anything out of the ordinary and live a regular life."

Ethan asks, "Why wouldn't he take your passport?"

"He took everything else of mine but gave me a copy. Until I tried to make a purchase and was denied for not having the original ID on me. Suddenly, my passport appeared on my vanity."

Singer says, "He trusted you?"

"I tried to escape once, but a threat and a gun was all it took to convince me otherwise. I was set up with an apartment, a phone, a credit card, anything I needed, except the freedom to leave Paris."

The first week is still stuck under my skin—*the quiet, the anger, the fear, the daily reminders of my incarceration*—like a virus I can't cure.

Singer looks at her husband. "How would that bait someone?"

Bennett sighs. "I fell right for it." I take a breath when the attention is off me. "Her father is the key," he repeats from before. "He's the one who got me to find her, claiming he was worried."

"He wasn't worried," I say. I can't seem to force myself to say the obvious.

Bennett does instead. "Your father is working for or with McCoy and set us up."

Although we were leading to this conclusion before, hearing it makes me feel sick again. As if I didn't hurt enough, my father and brother land another punch to my heart. Bennett kneels in front of me. With his hands on my knees, he whispers, "There are worse outcomes than finding someone you care about. It doesn't make things better, but we win, Winter, because we have each other."

My head falls to his shoulder as I embrace this man. He's right. "We win." This is true freedom. The murmuring around us comes to a stop when I lift my head. "I knew he was evil. I just didn't know how much. It's good to know where I stand."

Singer comes over and sits next to me, and Bennett takes the other side of me on the couch. She wraps her arm around my shoulders, and says, "Family is found in the ones who love you." I see her glance at Bennett and send the smallest of understanding smiles. "You are loved." She leaves it at that.

I cover her hand with mine. "Thank you." She stays while I wipe under my eyes. Catching Bennett's eyes, I say, "I never feared for my life, but I do fear for yours. The last time I saw Kurt was when I returned to my apartment after I left you. Kurt was waiting for me. He told me I had done a good job. I was confused since I hadn't actually done anything in Paris."

"You lured me right in," Bennett says.

"My father sent you."

"Same thing. They're working together and I fell for it."

"I still don't understand what he meant by collecting."

"What are you talking about? What was he collecting?" Bennett asks.

I bite my lip and then brace myself before saying, "Everests. He told me he was collecting Everests." I suck in a breath before I realize that they're all just staring at each other, speaking their own language through exchanged looks.

Singer breaks the silence, and asks, "But why?"

Ethan stands and walks to the window. With his hands in his pockets, his voice is scarily composed. "If I would have never started this damn company—"

Singer stands and goes to her husband. "You would have never met me." Wrapping her arms around his middle, she rests her cheek on his back.

Hutton adds, "And I would have never had a second chance with Ally."

When Ethan turns around, his arms wrap around Singer. "He's collecting us to avenge his cousin. How long ago did you work for McCoy Industries?"

"Two years ago."

"That doesn't add up," he replies. He begins to pace behind the sofa, running his hand over his chin, reminding me so much of Bennett.

Hutton retreats behind the other sofa, matching his brother's pace. "He had enough information to takeover Nobleman Inc. from what it sounds like. Winter was already gone from the company and they had been long broken up, so why would he get her involved?"

When Bennett stands, he says, "To get to me. I'm the easiest target."

I bolt up. "We had already met and had sex by the time

he first mentioned the Everest name though. *Ughhhh*," I groan, remembering my audience. I wave my hand in the air, hoping to erase the last part from their brains. I make the mistake of looking at Singer for support, but she just smiles. I roll my eyes, and say, "For Pete's sake. We slept together. Remember, I'm a whore, so this shouldn't come as a surprise."

No humor is found in the room, and Singer's smile is gone. Trying to hide how I really feel about myself in the shell of a joke is a defense mechanism. They're not fooled, especially not Bennett. Disappointment may be displayed on his face, but it's hurt I see in his eyes.

That's when I realize his brothers have stopped pacing. Bennett finally speaks, "Don't do that."

I turn to him with a lump in my throat, keeping me from speaking. My eyes must speak volumes because he replies, "You're not a whore because you slept with me, so don't belittle what we did. That whore business is caught up in your head. Assholes put that there. People who want to hurt you. I'm not one of them, so don't treat me like I am."

"I'm sorry."

"I'm going to take that apology, but from this moment on, cut that shit out."

"Okay." My answer is quick, maybe too quick, but when we speak from the heart, it's best.

Gently touching my chin, he angles my face to the side. "He hit you, potentially wants you dead, and he's collecting Everests for revenge." Bennett wraps his arm around my waist, and we face the others—together. Together. I don't think I've ever had someone so determined to not only stand by my side but also defend it. "All McCoys are dangerous, and if it comes down to us against them, we'll win."

I think back to the night I was determined to right a wrong. "I thought I'd be a hero. Instead, I was his pawn." As much as this hurts to remember, I have to continue for Bennett. I owe him, and all of them, the whole story. "My father told me he was given forty-eight hours to sell his company to the McCoys for bottom dollar, or they'd expose everything illegal Nobleman had done to stay afloat. Kurt and I had a toxic past, but he was determined to destroy my future, too. I still believed I would work at the company one day; that I would inherit it with my brother."

I meet Hutton's eyes. Again, there's no judgment on his face or any of theirs, but the tension is rising. I can feel it lashing at my insides. Bennett shakes his head. "It was a setup. Why would your father suddenly come to you to tell you this information, especially considering you weren't working there, and he knew of your past with McCoy. Your father and brother teamed up with Kurt, trading you for the company."

I don't feel sick anymore. I'm numb as the puzzle comes together. "Kurt had me meet him at one of my brother's favorite restaurants in Kip's Bay. Good food, but a dive. I should have made the connection."

"A place you go not to be seen," Ethan observes.

Nodding, I say, "I was dumb enough to believe it was because he didn't want his fiancée, Chelsea, to find out."

"Chelsea Neufield?" I didn't hear Ally walk in, but when she speaks, she comes around and stands behind Hutton, resting her hands on his shoulders. Taking her hand, he kisses it before turning back to me.

Little gestures.

My heart swells because Bennett showers me with those same types of little gestures that mean so much to me.

I ask, "How do you know her?"

Ally adds, "Not long ago. A month or less maybe. She came into the Everest Foundation office offering to be on our charity board."

"What happened?" I ask, my heart picking up speed, my gut twisting.

She looks around, seeming to pull the memory from thin air. Her eyes come back to me. "We don't have any board positions open, but when we do, we take them from our staff. Everyone at the foundation starts by working the phones. It's not glamorous, but answering our helpline is the most important job we have."

Bennett turns to me. "This is all a little too convenient, so let's map it out. Ethan and Singer have a past with Kurt's cousin. Kurt has a past with you, and his fiancée tried to make a connection with Ally, which is a direct line to Hutton." He takes a deep breath and exhales with a whistle. "I'm not a detective, though I've been accused of being one." He sends me a wink. "But McCoy has been attempting to close in for a while. When nothing worked, he lost his patience and went a different route."

Tapping my chest, I say the obvious, "Me." I move to the edge of the chair, gripping the arms. "May I get some water?"

Singer comes toward me and holds out a hand. "You don't have to ask." I take her hand as she leads me away from the group like a mama bear protecting her cub. That might be extreme, but I feel her warmth. We go to opposite sides of the island as she asks what I'd like. While she gets the sparkling water, I can hear the hushed tones and murmurs from the other side of the room.

Ally walks in, and asks, "How are you doing?"

"I don't know anymore."

"You're safe. They didn't get you guys in Paris, and they can't touch you here."

"How can you say that with such certainty?"

"Because this is our life. When you're with them, you'll never be safer. This building is a fortress."

"But out there isn't."

Singer puts the bowl of lemon wedges between us on the counter and rests her palms on the marble. "It wasn't easy for me to come to terms with this life and the changes required for me to fit into Ethan's life. He'd give it up if he could go back to the simplicity of life before he made his money, but there is no going back. So I had to move forward and accept that my life would never be the same either unless I gave him up. I can't deny my heart. He's worth the risks."

Ally squeezes a wedge into her water. With her eyes trained on the lemon, she says, "We always have protection. As for me, I'm used to it from growing up in a royal family, but you'll get used to it, too."

The assumption that Bennett and I will be together burns like a hot fire on a cold night in my belly. I want to feed the flame and keep it burning. Whispering, I ask, "How did you know you loved them?"

"Because I couldn't imagine living life without him," Ally replies. "My destiny was found in that man, and I've never been happier."

Singer says, "There is no life without him, not before we met, and not after we leave this earth. It's us. We were always meant to be, and he makes me laugh. Most of the world sees the demanding man behind the empire, but he's actually very charming."

"Bennett's charming." My cheeks heat, so I press my hands to them, trying to cool them down.

They both smile, and then Ally says, "He is. So are you. It's no wonder you were drawn to each other."

Singer comes around and covers my hand with hers. "You risked your life to save Bennett's, Winter."

"I didn't do enough sooner. The guilt eats at me."

"I know you don't see it that way, but every time I think about what could have happened if they had gotten him that day." Her hand leaves mine, and she holds it across her stomach. "I know I'll have nightmares about it."

"You saved him. Thank you," Ally says.

So many emotions have played through my heart today, but I'm blown away by how welcoming they are. It's been so long since I've had friends who are willing to fight for me. A lump forms in my throat, and both of them are quick to hug me. "It's okay," Singer says.

When we return to the living room, Lars and Aaron are there standing like guards in front of the window. They're very intimidating even when dressed casually. I'm tempted to salute them, but I resist.

I sit down and set the water on the table in front of me. "I wanted to say thank you to every one of you. You've seen my good intentions through my bad deeds and accepted me like I'm one of your own when I haven't earned that right."

"You don't have to earn it," Hutton says. "You're given respect until you lose it. Kurt McCoy doesn't live by the same rules. When you said you were a pawn, I'm afraid you were. But you saved Bennett at the risk of getting hurt, or worse, so now we need to make sure that you're safe as well."

"Thank you," I reply meekly. The care that fills the room is larger than this space can hold. They take me at face value, so I'll do anything I need to repay them.

The next question Bennett asks isn't one that's expected. "How did you know those men at the park were going to hurt me?"

Despite all that I've said already, this is the hardest for me to answer, and as I look up to say the words, I can't find my breath. All I can feel is darkness, menacing voices, rough hands manhandling me . . . the scent of humiliation. *Terror.*

26

Bennett

Cliffhangers are the worst, and when I swept her out of the room, I doomed the others to the edge. But what was I supposed to do? Leave her there to hyperventilate until she passed out?

Winter tugs at the sweatshirt she slipped into as soon as we returned. *My sweatshirt.* Barefoot, baggy clothes, clean face, and gorgeous. *My girl.* It's easy to pretend she lives here when she walks around like she does.

"Don't worry. They understand." This has become the longest day in history. "Everyone needed a break anyway."

"You didn't have to save me. I owe them the story."

"Tell me instead."

Her foot starts bouncing again, but on an exhale, she says, "They're the men who kidnapped me for Kurt. He doesn't usually do his own dirty work." She walks to the window, a great distraction that I seek for myself sometimes. "I heard the name Everest when I arrived at the park. It caught my ear. When I turned back to look, I knew who they were. Instantly. But they also knew who I was."

"That's why it was best for you to come with me. I know you didn't want to, but I don't regret insisting."

"Your insisting saved my life." Looking back over her shoulder, there's the smallest of smiles but no anger. "I don't think I've thanked you."

"Not in words, but I don't need them. You've shown me."

I come behind her and wrap her in my arms. When she leans back, I can feel her heart pounding in her chest. "I'm sorry I'm not who you thought I was when we met. I was . . . not myself. It took me a week after arriving in Paris to orientate myself and try to make sense of my situation—how I got there, how long I would be there. I took Paris as an opportunity to be someone else, to be someone who people on the street admired instead of how I felt inside. It probably makes me sound crazy, but the little excursions kept me sane. *Ish.*"

I turn her around and hold her face in my palms. "You're exactly who I want and need."

"That's what you are to me." She lifts up and kisses me.

Then I take over, kissing her because she needs to be kissed how she deserves, and because fuck, I need to have my mouth on hers, her lips parting, her tongue not sharp with words but soft with devotion.

As I run my hands up the back of her shirt. Her skin feels like cream and is scented with fields of strawberries I start to pull the shirt off, but she stops me, and her gaze moves behind her to the windows.

Protect her.

I promised I would, so taking her by the hand, we move to the bedroom. I take my time to lower the blinds and turn on a lamp, keeping it dim, and then find a condom. I don't want to ruin the mood by stopping later, but I don't want to rush through it either.

When I turn back, she's standing naked before me. The confidence she showed in Paris is on full display here. The only differences are the grayish spots that line one side of her ribs and her jaw. I'm going to repay that fucker twofold for touching her and then make sure that the company doesn't survive to the New Year.

It's not just the physical pain he's caused her that I worry about. She fights between the low self-esteem other men decided she needed and the cultivated strength of a lion I know she can be. Going to her, I take off my shirt and the rest of my clothes. Standing in front of her naked, to show her she has nothing to fear. We're equals. Equally vulnerable. I reach to caress her chin, and say, "I won't hurt you. Not ever."

Her gaze drops to the floor. "I don't remember what it feels like to live without pain. At least the bruises will go away."

"I can't erase the past. I can only promise you the future and *that* I'm waging my life on."

She holds me as tight as she can. "I don't want your life on the line. I don't want to lose you."

And that's when I realize that we may not have been together our whole lives, years, months, or even weeks, but my heart recognized hers the moment I laid eyes on her. Taking the days we've had and adding them to this feeling that we've known each other for a lifetime and cared about each other longer, it's easy for me to believe. "I'm not going anywhere except where you go, sweetheart."

Kissing her again, I pick her up and move to the bed to lay her down. She holds me to her, her arms locked around my neck. "You called me sweetheart, and there wasn't a hint of sarcasm." Sprawled on the bed like the lioness she is, she grins. "I think you like me. You might even more than like me."

"Busted. What gave me away?"

She glances down. I could be embarrassed that my dick is bumping against her leg, or by how hard she gets me, but there's no shame in it. She says, "You asked me my favorite song the night we met."

I climb on the bed and maneuver between her legs. Discovering the myriad of blues—cloudless springtime sky, deep ocean water, moonlight at midnight—buried in her eyes, I say, "I asked because I wanted to know."

"You asked because you *cared* to know. I don't know that I've had anyone ask me a question that tells you who I am so simply. I've gotten by with a pretty face and prettier lies."

She kisses my nose, then my lips, and adds, "I know that I was rebelling to get my father's attention. And I know why I dated the devil. So you and I may have met under terrible circumstances, but I don't regret a day we've spent together."

Kissing me lower, she rolls me onto my back, and wet lips trail down my chest. Her breath is hot against my skin when she stops above my abdomen to say, "One way or another, because of fate or destiny, we were meant to be together. If only for a week or for eternity. I don't know what's in store for us, but I regret not valuing myself enough to wait for you."

I move her hair, so I get the full view of her lovely face. "There's no point regretting what we can't change. I don't need to be your first, but I'm thinking last sounds pretty damn good."

"Charming." She smiles like she stole a kiss from her crush.

"Beautiful."

"Movie star."

"Cactus flower."

That makes us both laugh. But then her eyes dip closed as she slides between my spread legs. Peppering kisses around where I need her mouth, she teases, causing my eyes to fall closed. Keeping one hand in her hair, I sink into the mattress when she takes me into her mouth one torturous inch at a time. One of her hands covers the base while she uses her tongue and the lightest pressure of her teeth.

Fuck. No way will I last.

"Do you want me to come like this or be buried inside you?" I leave the question and then lie back, drifting back into the sensation. Her answer comes in the form of her mouth tightening around me. I place gentle pressure on the back of her head and let her devour me whole.

There's a freedom in falling, in letting yourself go as the heavier parts of life float in a different direction. It only lasts a few seconds, but there's magic in making you forget your problems for just a little while.

Winter looks up, a sexy grin in place. Her palms are on my abs, her fingertips tracing the ridges of my muscles. She lifts and slides up next to me, curling into my side. With my arm around her, my eyelids are heavy, the strain of the day beginning to get the better of me.

Her eyes are closed, but I kiss her head, rousing her once more. "I want to make love to you."

"Is it okay if we stay like this?"

"If we sleep, our night is fucked."

"Maybe we'll fuck all night instead of sleep."

"How is it possible that I met my match?"

That leaves her laughing. The sound is better than my favorite song. Rolling to the side, she rests her hands and chin on my chest. I open my eyes to find her sleepy blues looking at me. I want to devour her for the way she took me in her mouth, but for the first time in my life, lying next to a beautiful, naked woman isn't all about sex. This—cuddling, talking, trusting—is both soothing and an aphrodisiac.

Tracing my fingers down her spine and lower to her fine ass, I cup a cheek, and ask, "What?"

"I hate to bring the negative to bed with us, but I've been wondering if you contacted my father or if he contacted you?"

"Yeah, not exactly pillow talk." Shoving a hand behind my head, I lift enough to keep my eyes on her. I'm not going to deny her the conversation since it all has to come out eventually. "He contacted me."

"Because he set us up." The way she says that is so interesting. She's sees him for who he is.

"I stupidly believed he was worried."

"He plays a good game of poker." Rolling onto her back, she flops her arm across my middle while the other hand's off the bed. "How much was I worth?"

"The deal?" She nods. I feel like such an asshole, but I have to tell her. "Eight million."

"He wasn't going to sign the contract, Bennett." She drags her hand across my body and then rests it in her lap.

"I know that now."

"He doesn't have the money. The company is in dire straits." She sits up and straightens her legs on top of the covers. "I just remembered I told Singer I would go to the spa with them. I can cancel if you want me to."

I don't want to ruin her time with my sisters-in-law, knowing all of them could use the peace. "You should go."

"I'll just be gone for an hour or so."

"Take your time. Enjoy it. Do you mind if I tell the team what we've talked about?"

"Of course not." She leans over and kisses my head.

Just before she climbs out of bed, I catch her by the wrist. When she turns back, I sit up and give her a kiss. I can't believe those three little words are on the tip of my tongue. I scramble to replace them with four others. "You matter to me."

A sweet smile anchors her there, admiring me. She finally touches my cheek, running her thumb over my stubble, and says, "You matter to me." Stretching back, she kisses me before she leaves.

Smiling like a fool, I lie back with my hands behind my head. I think we kind of said it without saying it, but that will do for now.

27

Bennett

I pull the food from the bag and set the containers on the island. For a brief second, I wonder if she'll like what I ordered. Avoiding Italian, delis, burger joints, a repeat of steak from the other day, and knocking heavy carbs out of the menu made it tough to figure out what to serve for dinner.

Ten minutes later, the wine is on the table, the dishes, silverware, and glasses are set. Since I've lived in Manhattan, I've not had a woman to my apartment for dinner. I've always taken dates to restaurants. Before Winter, I never felt this need to impress someone, to bring them into my home, and to have them be a part of my life long term. I do with her.

Ally and Singer have stocked my place, so I light a few candles I discovered in the hall closet a few weeks ago and wait.

. . . And wait.

I should have ordered her a new phone today. Sucks not

having contact when I want it. Checking my watch, she's been gone an hour and a half. She must have gone for a longer treatment. Massages. Facials. These things take time.

When my watch ticks to forty-five after the hour, I take a sip of wine, and then I just finish it. That was a bad pour. This time, I refill it with more than four ounces. I go for six. Then drink some more until our glasses are even again.

Two hours . . .

I prod the chicken, and yup, it's cold. I get up and pace to the door and back a few times. "Fuck it." I call down to the spa.

"Good evening, Mr. Everest, this is Wendy. May I book a relaxation treatment for you?"

"No, Wendy. Thank you. I'm calling to touch base with Ms. Nobleman. Is she available?"

"No, sir, she left just about an hour ago."

"What do you mean?" I ask dumbly.

"Ms. Nobleman checked out and left with Mrs. Everest and Mrs. Everest."

"Thanks, Wendy." I hang up and call Singer. The words rush out as soon as she answers, "Is Winter there?"

"Oh hello, Bennett. Nice to talk to you, too."

"Hi, is she with you?"

"No—"

"Call Aaron. She's missing. I have to check the security video."

"Bennett—"

I hang up and turn to run for the front door but am halted when I see Winter standing in front of me. "Winter!" I grab her, pulling her to me.

Her arms come around my back and loop to my shoulders, her head tucked in my arms. "What's wrong, Bennett?"

"Thank God, you're okay. I thought something happened to you."

The door flies open, and Lars rushes in but stops abruptly when he sees us. "Is she all right?"

Pulling back, I look her over. "Are you all right?"

"I'm fine. What's going on?"

"You worried me. You said you'd only be an hour. It's been two, so I called the spa, and they said you left earlier. When I called Singer, she said you weren't there."

"Because I was on my way here. The door was unlocked, so I came in." Her eyes move past me, and she sees the table. "Is that for me?" she asks, smiling.

I take a breath and step away. Rubbing my temples, I try to figure out why I lost my shit. She was in the building. She was safe. Turning to Lars, I say, "My apologies. I overreacted. Everything's fine."

Walking to the door, he says, "You shouldn't leave your door unlocked, Bennett."

"I know. I left it open for her. Now that she's safe, I'll triple check the locks after you leave."

He chuckles. "And so another one falls."

"Another what?" We step into the hall.

"Brother." He shakes his head, still laughing. "Call me anytime. That's what I'm here for."

"Do you ever sleep?"

"No."

"You need a life, man. Watching over ours twenty-four seven can wear a man down."

"When all is calm on the Everest front, I'll take some time off. Until then, this is where I'll be."

"Thank you." We shake hands. "You're a good man, Lars."

I walk inside and see Winter standing near the windows. Looking out into the night, she has a wineglass in her hand, her sneakers still on, and a small purse strapped around her.

The sun set while she was gone, leaving my world darker

than how she left it. Lights are dotted across a sea of skyscrapers, but she stands as a testament to how bright my world can be with long silky strands that lead to the curve of her waist and toned legs under black leggings that dip out from a dark gray tee.

I could happily come home to this sight on a regular basis. Crossing the room, she looks back with blue eyes, black lashes, and happiness written across her face. "The spa had a version of warrior blue for my nails," she says, waggling her fingers. The color of her nails is just shy of midnight. I like how she admires them. Gives me more time to admire her.

"Warrior blue, huh? Very nice." When I wrap my arms around her middle, she leans forward, resting against me.

"I'm sorry I worried you. I thought being with the girls in the building . . . I don't know what I thought. I wasn't thinking. I'm sorry."

Out of the corner of my eyes, I catch sight of a flicker above her head, and when I look out the window, it's just in time to catch it again. I narrow my gaze to home in but there's no flash. "It's okay. I let my mind get away from me under the current conditions."

She raises her arms around my neck. With the glass in one hand, she curls the other around my nape, looking up at me. "How long do we get to pretend that we can stay here forever?"

"Another day?"

It's the slightest of nods, but I see enough. "Just a little more time. That's all I'm asking for."

Does she not see how much I like her being here, how I try for restraint when all I want to be is inside her, touching her, kissing her until her lips swell from pink to red? "I could keep you here forever if you want."

"What if you lose interest?"

"I know when I have something good."

"And you see me as good?"

Pushing my fingers through her hair, I caress the back of her head. "I see you as a part of—" The explosion is deafening, the window cracking against the pressure as I spin, shielding her behind me. "Run!"

"Where?"

Another flash in the distance and a shot is fired. I grab her arm and sprint for the exit. The glass splinters across the panel, and when I open the front door, it explodes behind us. "Run to Hutton's."

We run, and I land hard against their door. Typing in the code, the lock is released, and I burst inside. "Ally? Hutton?"

Panicked, Winter says, "I left her at Singer's."

"Hutton?" I shout once more, but there's no answer in return. "Elevator."

We run back to the hall and I flatten my palm, activating the black pad and an alarm. When the door slides open, I pull her in, and type the code to close it. "Get in."

Inside the elevator, she asks, "Is it safe?"

"The safest place we can be until we get downstairs." I grab my phone and type: *Code five. Penthouse.* "Was Ethan home?"

"No."

I press the button for the top floor and then text: *Abort. I'm going in.*

"What's going on?" She cries, huddling in the corner.

"When the door opens, do not leave the elevator. Stay to the side so no one can see you."

"Bennett?"

"Three. Two." The door slides open. "One." With my arm stretched out, protecting her, I lean back just in case there's gunfire or an attack. When we're greeted with silence, I run down the hall. "Singer?"

She comes running around the corner, and I catch her in my arms. "The alarm sounded."

"We have to get out of here." She grabs her purse from a table as she runs to the safety of the elevator. "Where's Ally?"

"She went home."

"Fuck! We just looked for her." I press the code, and the door shuts again.

Looking at me, she asks, "What's happening?"

She moves to the corner with Winter and wraps her arm around her just as Winter starts sliding to the floor terrified. "It'll be okay," Singer whispers to her.

The elevator stops back on my floor, and the door opens. "Ally!"

Ally gets in, soaking hair and in a short bathrobe. When I press for the door to close, she says, "I was taking a shower."

"You're in one piece?" I ask.

"I'm okay." She and Singer hug each other. "I'm glad Hutton's at work."

"I'm sure he's already left." I am never going to hear the end of this. My brothers will be fucking maniacs to deal with.

The speaker in the elevator beeps once, and Lars's voice comes through. "Is anyone injured?"

I look at them, doing a quick assessment. "No."

"The penthouse and your floor are on code five. The elevator will come straight to the second floor where I'll be waiting."

Singer's phone rings. Her voice is shaking when she answers, "Ethan?"

When tears start rolling down her cheeks, I take the phone from her. "She's fine. We're heading to the panic room."

"What's going on?" His breath is puffing. He must be running.

"You can't come here."

"Bullshit. If my wife's there, I'm there. Tell me what happened?"

"My apartment. Three rounds. The glass held long enough for us to get out."

"Fuck!" His shout echoes through my ear and probably half of Manhattan. I hold the phone away reflexively.

His anger is palpable but not stronger than mine. I catch Winter's eyes glued to mine and reach for her, but the elevator stops. "We're here." I disconnect and hand Singer the phone. Reaching down, I help Winter up, holding tight to her hand.

Lars is waiting with two men behind him. While he faces us, they're turned away, armed and on guard. "We're not detecting any activity from the outside or on the top floors. Go in," he commands. Singer, Ally, and Winter rush out of the elevator and into the panic room. I trail them into the state-of-the-art, full metal and concrete-built compound. As soon as Lars closes the vaulted door behind us, I see Winter stop.

Standing in the middle of the room, Winter looks around, and says, "Oh my God! No!"

28

Bennett

Singer and Ally have been here a time or two. An attack on the building hasn't happened but once before, but we've had several false alarms, so they're familiar with the shelter.

The way the panic room is set up, it can serve as an apartment for all of us for up to four months. After that, oxygen and food get rationed for one more month. If Manhattan is bombed, this shelter will survive.

As for Winter, who's trembling like a leaf, I go to her and bend down to look her in the eyes. "We're okay. You are all right. Try to take a deep breath." She hangs on every word, her grip on my arms tightens and her nails begin to dig in. "Breathe, ma chérie."

Her lashes are clinging together under the weight of her tears. "What is this place?" Taking another deep breath, she exhales slowly.

I can hear Ally talking to Hutton and Singer to Ethan, both of them taking to opposite sides of the large living space. Knowing they're safe, I turn my focus back to Winter. "It's a panic room. For safety."

"This isn't a room." Her nails loosen from my skin, and she begins a slow scan. "This is an underground prison."

"It's not a prison."

"We're locked in here, right?" She rushes toward the door and tugs on the handle.

"We are. For safety."

"You keep saying that. Stop saying for safety." Pulling as hard as she can, she raises her voice. "I want out. Get me out, Bennett."

"Not until we get the all clear." I go to her, but she slaps my hand away.

"Open the damn door!"

"Calm down." Her eyes are crazed, her pupils wide. "What's wrong, Winter?"

"I want out. Now!" She puts her feet on the door for leverage and pulls back the handle as hard as she can. Her feet drop, and she yanks again, her body shaking with desperation. "Let me out!"

Holy shit. "Are you claustrophobic?" *What do I do*? I run and grab her around the waist, her body flailing and hitting my arms as she screams at me to release her. When I do, she falls to the ground and curls over her body. Her head tucks down over her knees, and her body stills under the trembling.

When I touch her back, her arm flies out to push me away, so I leave her be, turning to look behind me. Singer puts her hands out for me to stay put. Ally comes with her. They don't look stressed or panicked like how I feel inside. Helpless to help Winter.

Slowly, they ball up on either side of her. They don't touch her or say anything. They just match their breathing to her lengthening breaths.

The sound is all we hear for a minute before Singer looks up and nods at me. I move in, not sure what to do and not wanting to upset Winter. Squatting in front of her, I wait until she looks up, her body following suit as she sits on her legs bent under her.

Winter may have tucked away in terror for only a minute, but it felt like an hour. I know McCoy's to blame. *Fuck. What did he do to her?*

When she looks at me, I see the horror of humiliation filling those beautiful baby blues. Caressing her chin, I run my thumb over her cheek, and say, "Don't cry."

She sits up, and I swoop in to catch her. Her arms come around my neck, and I lift her, kissing the side of her head as I carry her to a couch. With her head resting on my shoulder, I sit, cradling her to me.

Her eyes are closed, so she doesn't see Ally or Singer getting up and giving us privacy when they disappear into one of the bedrooms. Resting my hand on her neck, I try to check her pulse without her getting wind of the covert operation. It's calming, which is good, so I kiss her forehead.

She says, "I was packed in a crate."

My heart rate spikes from the confession, but I'm not sure where to go with this. As if it will make a difference, I whisper, "When?"

"The night I was taken to Paris."

"Kidnapped," I correct.

She lifts her head, but her arms don't loosen. "Kidnapped," she says so softly like the idea itself is unfathomable. "He drugged me and shoved me in a crate. A crate . . ."

"Fuck." *He's a dead man.*

"I woke up, Bennett. I woke up and realized I was in a box with very little air on a private plane, not nice like yours. It didn't haul people, and it smelled."

I hold her tighter, my apologies built in every touch. How could she survive that and come out the other side? She did. She is still doing it.

"I found light in the bottom corner and wedged myself, so my mouth was as close to that pinhole as possible, but it hurt too much to stay that way."

"Winter?" Her eyes look up, and I can finally see the peace she has with me returning. "How did you survive?"

"I begged for my life. The lock was removed, and I was taken to the bathroom to relieve myself as if I hadn't already. I had no choice. The fear was too great."

"Was that sick fucker there?"

"No. When I saw the interior of the plane—dirt, grime, other crates—and the men on it, I thought I was going to die." I wish I could erase that memory. *And then I want to kill the men who did this to her. Every last fucking one of them.* "They groped me. The harder I fought, the more it entertained them. I remember wondering if they would stop if I gave in, or would they take more. Would they take all of me?"

"What did you do?"

"I continued to fight. I'm too stubborn to give them the pleasure of my death." A small smirk shines, reaching her eyes. "Fuckers."

My girl is a beautiful badass. "You're incredible."

She sighs, the devious glint in her eyes now gone. "They grabbed me from behind, though, and covered my mouth. I was shoved back into the crate just as I passed out. Four against one. Not great odds."

"Did they . . .?"

"No. They knew better."

Stretching her neck to the side, the Winter I know emerges, and she eases off my lap, taking a deep breath. I stay seated, and ask, "What does that mean?"

"I was Kurt's property. I still might be. I don't know. What I do know is that nobody touches Kurt's belongings without paying the price." She starts looking around and spies the kitchen. "Water?"

"I'll get it." We walk into the small sectioned-off space together, and I pull a bottle from the fridge. I twist the cap and give her one while I take another. She's rattled, the after-effects of the attack upstairs and her panic attack here wearing off. I drink half my water when she drinks.

Leaning against the counter, she says, "Kurt knew we slept together."

"How?" I finish the water, trying but struggling to keep my anger controlled. Squeezing the bottle, I crush the plastic in my hand.

Winter pauses and then wraps her hands around mine that's still holding the bottle. She doesn't need more worries. I lower my shoulders and keep the fury hidden inside. Predicting it's safe to proceed, she says, "He followed us and he had photos."

Photos—*Shit.* "Of us?" *Am I the reason he beat her?*

"At the park, not from your room," she replies as if that's better. I haven't asked if he touched her, but I can't move on without knowing.

"He hit you . . . I'll never forgive myself for letting you leave that night."

"You couldn't have stopped me. Stubborn, remember?"

She's letting me off the hook, but imagining what she went through, picturing him touching her, hitting her . . . I raise my fist up to punch the wall, but she steps in front of me. "Bennett."

My fist shakes in the air, my anger needing a release. She reaches up, and as she did before, she embraces my hand and then lowers it. "It's a concrete wall. I don't want you to ever feel pain because of Kurt."

"Too late."

"No. It's not. Together, we can fight through this."

"Together." *Together.* I let it sink in. Hearing her say the word, hearing her talk about a future together starts to diminish my hate with her love. I hug her and kiss the top of her head. "Together."

"I've been thinking about that night."

"Yeah?"

"I'm glad you didn't chase after me. You were naked, after all. I would have worried about you freezing off your good parts."

"My good parts?" I laugh. My quirky, funny girl knows how to ease the tension in a room. "Now's not the time to argue that I have a sparkling personality and a smile that has made you weak in the knees."

"Very true. You have a talented tongue too."

"You must be speaking of my conversational skills," I tease.

"Not at all, though I can credit you there as well."

She takes my hand and twirls under it. When she stops, she's facing me again, so I lean down and kiss her neck. "You're no one's property. Not ever."

Her hands were roaming the front of my body, but stop on my shoulders and pull me close. "Not even yours?"

"Not even mine." Disappointment causes her shoulders to slump. I can't take seeing her sad. "Don't doubt how much I care about you. My heart is already yours, and I've called you mine, but you'll always be free."

"I don't want to be anymore."

"What does that mean?"

"I want to be yours, Bennett." There's a plea in her tone, a fear in her eyes.

"I'm not going anywhere, Winter, but—"

"But? Don't say but. It's been amazing this last week."

"A week. Yes," I reply, rubbing my hand over my jaw once. "I see you in my life, and I want you to be a part of it. But a lot is still unsettled, and we'll never be free to be together how we want until it is."

"Kurt?" *That fucker won't be a problem for much longer.*

Her father crosses my mind, the truth scraping across my tongue. "And your family."

She crosses the room and sits on the couch. "I don't ever want to see either of them again."

When I sit, I pull her legs across my lap. Rubbing her shins, I say, "I'll support whatever you decide."

"I've decided." She smiles. "I've never dated anyone like you. You truly support me."

"That's the difference between me and those assholes."

"You have more differences than that."

"Oh, yeah? Like what?"

Touching my cheek, she says, "This face can't be beat."

"Tell that to Joey Kendall in the fourth grade."

That makes her smile. "You, sir, are hands down the most handsome man I've ever seen. But it's not your face that has me falling. It's your heart. Let me ask you, Monsieur Everest. Is it made of gold or steel?"

"Depends on the day."

"Today?"

"Steel because I want to protect you like the walls around us."

"And tomorrow?"

I drag her onto my lap, making her laugh. Holding her waist, I shift her onto her back and lean over her. I kiss her delectable lips once, twice, and then reply, "Gold, because although I'll never own you, don't ever doubt that you're mine."

29

Winter

Bennett has become so ingrained into my life in such a short time that I think we missed a few steps along the way. Does it matter? Would this happening over months or years bring us closer than we are now? Or have these tragic events linked us inexplicably?

The cogs click as the bolt releases, and the vault door opens. Ethan rushes in with Hutton, their wives running into their arms. I lean my back against Bennett, out of the way.

His hand clasps around mine, and then he leads me to the door, but Hutton stops him. Although he's still hugging Ally, he holds a hand out. "Thank you."

"No need." Bennett glances at me and then shakes his brother's hand. "We clear?"

"No. We'll be driven to different locations tonight."

When Ally steps to the side, Hutton brings Bennett in and pats his back. "Seems you've pissed off the wrong people."

"Or the right ones." When they step apart, Bennett adds, "I have no doubt it's McCoy."

"Ethan has the team trying to locate him." An intensity has taken over his features—his eyes darken, his brows pull together, his hands fist. "We're about to be separated for the night. No calls. They might be traced. Don't go anywhere unless you're with Lars, and we'll meet at a secure site tomorrow."

We take the stairs down one level and enter the parking garage just as Singer slips into one SUV and Ally with security in tow gets into another. After escorting his wife, Ethan comes back, and asks, "Are you both okay?"

"I'm fine," Bennett replies.

I nod, my heart pulsing in my throat as the cool air swathes us.

"You saved her," Ethan says, "You did, little brother."

"I did what you would do."

Aaron and Lars appear calm, but they start to herd us toward the vehicles. Before we split up, Ethan adds, "Get to the safe location and I'll see you tomorrow," and then gives his brother a hug. "Thank you, Ben."

"Take care and see you tomorrow."

Lars moves me to the vehicle with light pressure on the back of my arm. I climb into the large SUV, and Bennett slides in next to me. The doors are shut and locked, and as soon as he climbs in the front passenger seat, we're off.

"Where are we going?" I ask, tugging at a straggling cuticle.

"I don't know."

"For how long?"

"I don't know, Winter. I've never been shot at before. I don't know how this works." The glass slides up between the front and middle row, giving us privacy.

There's a growing distance between us despite how close we're sitting. "I'm sorry."

The comment surprises him, and he looks at me quizzically. "I'm not mad at you."

"You have such an incredible family, and because of me, their lives are in danger."

"Because of you? No. This started before you, remember? Someone tried to kill us this time and stupid enough to attack one of the most secure buildings in Manhattan. Everybody who lives in that building was in danger. So I am mad but not at you."

"You should be. I'm mad at me."

"It won't solve anything, so I'd rather spend the energy fixing this mess than dwelling on it."

"Why are you always so reasonable? Get mad, Bennett. Get it out," I shout in the small space.

He takes a deep breath as he turns toward me. "You're picking a fight with the wrong guy."

"I'm not picking a fight. Your family could have died tonight, Bennett, and that would be on me."

"No. A sick fuck fired shots at my home because they're evil. And *that's not your fault.*"

"But your brothers . . . they must want me gone—"

"Why do you hate yourself so much?"

The question smacks me, stinging my heart and stopping my breath. "What are you talking about?"

"This mess was caused because you hate yourself enough to burn everyone who gets near you just to prove you're right."

"I don't do that." I cross my arms over my chest and look out the window. A memory of my mother comes back, one I haven't thought of in years.

I hate this bed, the one she's been left to die in, in the room on the other side of the house. Climbing up on the bed next to her, I look at my pretty mama. "Do I look like you?"

"Do you want to look like me?" she asks with the smile she always gives me. Love.

I nod eagerly. "Daddy says I do."

"He's right." She taps the button of my nose. "You're going to live a beautiful life, Winter. Promise me that more than anything else, you'll live and love and learn. Those are the things that make you a survivor. Those are the things that you need to hold on to when you have nothing else."

. . . The lights outside the vehicle race by as the memory fades into my reality. I lower my head, rub my eyes, and mumble, "How do I hold on to a life when everything else fails me?"

"With a helping hand. We all falter at one time or another." Bennett's rich and comforting voice warms me. "We fail. We make mistakes. We learn. We move on."

His words are so similar to my mom's. "We live. We love. We learn." Her words and his meld together. *She would have loved him.*

Bennett's phone rings. When he looks down, his head angles, and he turns the screen away from me.

Curious, I ask, "Who is it?"

"It's . . ." He pauses and lets it go to voicemail. When his eyes reach me, he says, "It was your father."

"What? Why would he be calling?"

"I don't know."

"He knows I'm back. I have no doubt he's working with Kurt." Crossing my arms over my chest, I add, "I wonder if he's in on the attack."

"Sadly, I think we both know the answer to that. Do you want me to listen to the message?"

"It's your phone."

He turns away, directing his gaze out the window, and

holds the phone to his ear. It's the longest thirty seconds of my life. Traffic in Midtown Manhattan during rush hour is faster. An indecipherable mumble follows when he pulls the phone from his ear.

"What did he say?"

"He knows you're back."

"No surprise there," I reply sarcastically and roll my eyes. "What else?"

"He said he's leaving a box of your mom's things with the doorman." Now I sit up, interested. Very interested. "If you don't pick it up tonight, he's throwing it in the trash tomorrow."

"What's in it?"

"He didn't say specifically. Just said it's your mother's stuff."

I grab his arm. "We have to get it."

"We're not getting it."

Releasing him, I say, "Bennett—"

"No."

"I can go if I want."

"Yes, you can, but I'm begging you not to, Winter."

"It's my mother's belongings."

"It could be a trap." Shrinking back to my side of the SUV, I stare at him in disbelief. He reaches over and touches my leg. "Don't go."

"But—"

"Please. Please, Winter." His eyes plead with mine as he leans forward with his head lowered. "I almost lost you today. I can't take this chance."

The pain in his voice makes me want to soothe his concern. That I'm causing that pain breaks my heart. "I'm sorry." I reach for my neck and rub. "I know I should let it go. It's just stuff. It was a dumb thought. I just . . . I don't have my mother's necklace anymore because I left it in

Paris. This box might be the only thing I ever have of hers again."

Covering my hand, he studies me. "If he left the box with the doorman, we won't see him."

"My father is a manipulative, egotistical asshole, but if it's a trap, he wouldn't leave it in the lobby."

"That's true, but I still don't think this is a good idea."

"He wouldn't risk anything in the building where he lives."

"I agree."

I watch the world pass by outside, trying to figure out what my father even has left of my mom's. He threw out so much after her death. *Why now? Today?* I hate asking this of Bennett, but I think it would eventually tear me apart to know things of Mom's were thrown away instead of me cherishing them forever. "I want it. Doesn't matter how small or big it is. If it was hers, I want it. I can stay in the car, and we can have the doorman bring the box to me. Please."

Bennett contemplates that idea for a moment and looks at me, really looks into my eyes. Then he shakes his head at the same time he rolls down the privacy glass. "Lars, we're making a stop."

30

Winter

Listening to his steady heartbeats soothes the anxiety trying to cripple my strength.

Live.

Love.

Learn.

Take strength from the man beside you.

I can do this.

Through the window, I recognize the neighborhood. I lift my head from Bennett's chest to prepare—mentally and physically—and use his love as armor around me.

Lars says, "I still don't think this is wise."

"I'll be quick, and then we can leave."

Bennett's hands go up. "Whoa. Hold on. What happened to the doorman coming to you?"

The vehicle pulls to the curb. Glancing at the building, nothing has changed. Twelve stories. Clear glass with arched windows. Red brick exterior with cream-colored trim. A familiar doorman dressed in teal, still here after all these years. Same as it ever was.

When Fred doesn't make a move, I pop the locks. "I'll be fast."

The privacy glass slowly rolls down. "You're not going anywhere. Lars can get the box."

"It's a box. Right there. I see it on the counter just inside the door."

He says, "Lars, will you get the—"

"No."

"This isn't a time to be stubborn, Winter."

"Stubborn would be getting it without a conversation." I can tell he's not going to be convinced. I look back at the box on the counter. There may only be twenty feet between the damn box and us, but Bennett's concerns are warranted after the past forty-eight hours. "Fine. Lars can get the box."

"Would it feel better if I say it? Like you're still winning?" I hear his amusement in his tone.

"Yes, actually." I fold my fingers together and straighten my shoulders.

He mumbles, "At least I know what I'm getting into," then adds, "Lars, will you get the box."

"Yes."

Leaning forward, I add, "Thank you, Lars."

"Stubborn," Bennett mutters from beside me. I'm okay with it.

We watch as Lars walks inside and talks to Fred. As soon as he puts his hands on it, Fred is quick and pulls the box back.

The elevator doors open, and my father and brother enter the lobby. I shrink, sliding down just a little on the leather seat despite the privacy glass. I'm tapped on the hip. When I turn to Bennett, he says, "They can't see you. You're safe inside here."

I don't know why I'm on edge. Is it seeing my family for the first time since my kidnapping, or is it that they helped organize it? I know. My heart just aches thinking about it.

My father is paler than I've ever seen him, feeble in ways that start to temper my anger. I'm not sure if it's age or his body rotting him from the inside out, but I turn to Bennett. "He doesn't look good."

Bennett doesn't say anything. I know he's struggling with his own anger toward that man, and I'm surprised he's been able to hold himself back. His knuckles are paying the price —whitened fists rest on his thighs.

When I turn back, my asshole of a brother takes the box from the counter and steps back. His mouth is running. By his expression, he's pissed. "He's not going to give the box to Lars," I say.

His hand finds mine, and he takes hold. "You're not getting out of this vehicle, Winter."

Turning back, I'm met with worry. I give his hand a squeeze. "I know."

Lars stands well above my father and brother, and by size alone, he's intimidating. To most. "Braden's a dickhead to fight this." As if my brother can hear me, I say, "Give him the fucking box."

"Are you willing to leave without it?"

"You know I'm not." I don't look behind me because I also know he's probably fuming over this situation.

Fred argues with Lars as well and comes around the desk, pointing toward the door. Lars relents and comes back to the vehicle. Coming to the other side of the SUV, Bennett partially rolls down his window. Lars says, "They're not giving it unless they can talk to her."

"I'm right here." Both of them turn to me. "I can talk to them. I have a few things I want to say as well."

Bennett's eyes narrow. "You're kidding me, right? They

had you kidnapped, not knowing if you were going to be raped or killed or both."

Lars says, "We can't stay here. The area has not been secured." He looks down the street and then the other way before returning to us. "We have to leave it."

"It's my mother's."

He replies, "I understand, but it's not safe for us to be here."

Bennett releases me and runs his hands through his hair, stressed. He knows how important this is to me, but says, "He's right. I'm sorry, Winter." When he turns back to Lars, he signals toward the front. "Get in."

"No." I shoulder the door open and dash from the vehicle as Bennett swipes to grab me. "Winter!"

Lars is hot on my heels by the time I reach the door, drawing everyone's attention from inside in the lobby. I swing it open, and Lars catches it. He doesn't say a word but follows close behind me as I enter.

Fred greets me with the same unfriendly tone he's had for years, "Ms. Nobleman." No eye contact, only acknowledging me out of obligation to his job.

I smile as polite as I can, trying to kill him with kindness. "Fred."

Braden stands before me like someone who's gotten away with murder. I survived. I'm sure to his disappointment. He says, "The queen herself decided to grace us with her presence."

"So glad to see you too, brother. Still living with your daddy?"

His laugh has lilted more toward a cackle as he holds the box hostage in his arms, taunting me. "While I've been saving the family farm, I hear you've been traipsing around Europe."

"You could have called," my father says.

"Why? You knew where I was." Held captive in Paris. Shot at in New York. I have a feeling he's known all along, just like Bennett's theory on him being the key.

"And how would I know that?" His eyes move above my head as a gentle caress curves around my shoulder. I look back. I didn't hear Bennett enter the lobby, but I'm glad he's here. With him on my side, maybe this won't be so bad. One can hope.

"Mr. Everest," my father says as if he's greeting a peer on the golf course. He reaches to shake his hand, but Bennett doesn't move. He doesn't even bother speaking to him.

A spark of recognition strikes Braden's eyes, and his expression morphs, suddenly very interested in us with dollar signs floating in his eyes. *Asshole.* The grin that splits his cheek is . . . wretched . . . not finding another word that fits better for that creepy expression owning his vapid features. "Good going, sis." Turning to Bennett, he adds, "She bagged an Everest. Guess getting Mom's looks paid off."

Bennett steps forward, but my hand whips out against his arm. "It's okay."

My brother doesn't know when to shut up, though. He adds, "You brought backup."

"I brought my friends. Do I need backup from my family?" I don't know how our mother could produce that beast, but then I remember that my father insisted he "be a man" and suck in his emotions. He sucked so hard he lost them altogether. "I'll take the box now, Braden."

My father stares at me like he's seen a ghost. "In this light, you look so much like her."

"Nora. You can say her name. She loved you even when she shouldn't have. You should give her the respect she deserves for trying to survive you."

Braden spits, "You're such a bitch."

When he bobs forward like a school kid threatening others on the playground, Bennett steps in, and says, "Keep your distance from your sister. Do you understand, Nobleman?"

"Is that a threat, Everest?" His slithering tongue lands hard on the *T*. My brother is the worst human ever.

They hold their own against each other, but I'm not worried about Bennett. He's clearly in the power position. His voice is smooth and deep, laden with menacing undertones. "That's definitely a fucking threat."

"That will be enough, Braden." My father's voice catches us off guard, and I see him still staring at me. I'm the ghost that's come back to haunt him. I'm the warrior my mother raised.

Despite how little I feel in his presence, I stand my ground, but a shaky breath exhaled reveals my fear. I've never lived up to anything this man has expected of me. I was set up for failure the day I was born. Seeing him now, after what I've survived, I wonder why I cared. So much life wasted trying to appease him. No more. "I want the box."

My father's arms open, and a smile that almost appears sincere slides into place. "Winter, I've been worried out of my mind." He comes to me . . . *He. Comes. To. Me.* Miracles never cease.

I stand there stunned, unable to will my arms around him. No tears come. Not even a loving embrace can erase what he's done to me.

He pulls back and taps his legs nervously. "I've been meaning to ask if you've received anything that might concern the company?" His nonchalance is anything but casual. Every word articulated has an underlying meaning.

"What do you mean?"

"If you received anything . . . there was unfinished business with your mother." He waves his hand as if he's shooing a fly away, then smiles. "Then I suddenly remembered maybe Winter can help since you were close to her."

"You were married to her." I see a flash of irritation before his fake grin returns. I say, "What unfinished business?"

Braden steps forward with the box again, taunting me behind my father's back. "This is just trash, but you can have it if you give us what we want."

"I don't know what you want other than me dead."

Neither of them even bothers to feign innocence. I shake my head. At least I know the truth.

My father says, "Have you received anything from your mother? If you did, you need to give it to me right now."

From my mother? "I only had my mother's locket, so I guess you're shit out of luck."

When I turn to leave, my father says, "The locket! That's it. You always did wear that piece of junk."

I take a breath, pausing before I turn back around. "I'm surprised you noticed. I thought I was invisible to you."

"Never invisible. Something your mother left me to deal with. Always right there." It's impressive how my father can say cruel things in such a sincere tone. "A thorn in my side."

The reference makes me recall Bennett's words—*You weren't born among the thorns, which makes me wonder why you grew them in the first place.* My father is the reason I grew them. Braden sharpened them.

Unlike them, Bennett cherishes me. He appreciates my prickly side as much as my soft petals.

My father steps closer. "Where is that necklace? We can trade. This box for the locket."

I cup my throat feeling the bare skin but am quickly

reminded he's one of the reasons I no longer have it. I would never give it to him. "Why do you want it?"

"I'm losing my patience. Where's the goddamn necklace, Winter!" His commanding tone echoes through the lobby.

Bennett steps around me, and stares down my father. "I'm losing patience as well. Give her the box."

"When she gives me the necklace."

I say, "I don't know where it is. I lost it."

"Lost it?" His expression tightens, pained even. "You stupid girl."

Bennett takes my hand. "It's time to go."

"Big man," Braden says sarcastically, "Are you going to save her, Everest?"

"I don't need to save her. She's doing fine on her own. I'm just here for moral support . . . Or to fuck someone up if they try to fuck with her."

I do a double take. It's not that I didn't know my giant could indeed fuck someone up, it's that he's so gentlemanly to me. He's also right. It's time to go by about eighteen years when it comes to my brother and father. I reach for the box once more, but Braden pulls back. "Necklace or nothing."

He's going to make me fight until the bitter end. Tears pierce my eyes because as much as I knew they didn't love me, it hurts when the truth finally sinks in. But I won't let these tears fall. Not over him. Raising my chin, I turn to my father, and say, "Everything I ever did was for you and to save a company you ran into the ground. I made a deal with the devil to get him off your back—"

"The fuck you did," Braden spits. "Before you claim to be Joan of Arc in this fucked-up mess, let me make it very clear, sister, that we saved our own necks. So you standing here is only a stroke of luck on your part, and well played on fucking the mark."

"Fucking the mark" makes no sense to me, but Lars and

Bennett are suddenly in action. Lars says, "Step back, Winter."

Bennett blocks me from my father and Braden, and then says, "Get in the car."

This time, I push my stubbornness aside and listen because something's wrong. I turn to leave, but Braden has to open his mouth one last time. "You think you're so important. You're not, Winter. You're nothing, just like that woman you idolize in your head."

I whip around, my anger getting the best of me. "Don't talk about her like that. She loved you."

"She's dead, and now that you managed to get the one thing that mattered to me taken away, you're dead to me, too."

I want to hit him. I hate him so much. "The company? Money. That's all that matters to you?" I've lived through years of this abuse, and I'm over it. "You can have all of it since your inheritance wasn't enough." Inheritance triggers a faint memory . . . my trust fund. I didn't get it on my twenty-fifth birthday. With Braden still staring at me, I add, "It's tainted, just like you."

"That's all you got?" he asks, egging me on for more.

"That's all." Before I leave, I take one more solid look at them. *Hard. Cold. Callous. Cruel.* That's all I see in them. There's no winning with them, only losing. "You're evil," I say, "inside and out, just like the McCoys."

The box is dropped, the sound of glass breaking shatters my heart. Braden's eyes are wild with rage. I've seen that look before. He's so much like Kurt that I don't know why I never saw it before. They're two of the most hideous humans, both consumed by greed and revenge. Braden says, "You said you'd sacrifice for us. Time for you to step up."

"What are you talking about?"

Bennett's hand tightens around my wrist. "Winter, go. Now," he grits between his teeth.

But that brother of mine . . . "Did you really think Kurt would let you get away with this? Like he'd be fine with you fucking his enemy?" He charges me but hits a wall named Bennett. Lars grabs him from behind and throws Braden down. As I rush for the door, I look back when my brother yells, "You've doomed us all to death, you whore."

A light flickers in his eyes, a dawning of a new idea. "Oh shit," he says, his head hitting the floor. "This is your plan. Fuck us over by fucking that guy for the big payday. *Fucking hell.* Why didn't I see this coming, you clever cunt?"

I stop in the doorway but don't turn back. "You're wrong." *I would never hurt Bennett.*

He chuckles maniacally. "He was hired to track you down. Should've figured you'd fall for him. Your heart is as weak as mother's." His words are cut off as I let the door close behind me.

The leather is cold, and even though the heat is on, I'm frozen to the bone as I slide across the back seat. Angling toward the building, I take one last look at my so-called family, welcoming the pain of the door behind me as it digs into my back. My brother's soul is lost. I just hope it's not too late for mine. I need someone who believes in me, someone who sees through my defenses and bad decisions.

I need Bennett. I'm safe in his love. *Treasured.*

I watch as Bennett picks the box off the floor and tries to leave, but my father blocks the door. What the hell? They start yelling . . .

But that's when I hear the click of the handle. I sit up to look behind me, but the door flies open, and I'm yanked into arms I don't recognize. A cloth covers my mouth too fast for me to scream and too drowsy to fight.

Life leaves my limbs, and my body becomes a rag doll as

I'm dragged into a waiting van. Bennett dives across the backseat of our SUV, but the door is closed, shutting him inside. The van door slides shut, blocking my view.

The sound of squealing tires against the cement and yelling are the last things I hear, the men who kept me in the crate the last I see before my world goes black.

31

Bennett

The sound of gunshots fills the cold air, the echo bouncing between the buildings. "Drive! Drive! Drive!"

Rubber skids against cement as the pedal is floored, putting the vehicle in pursuit. The passenger side door I flew through slams closed just as I tuck my legs inside the vehicle.

Sitting up, I see Lars running down the street in front of the SUV still shooting until we pull up next to him. He jumps in, and we're going again. "What the fuck?" he shouts. "Why was her fucking door unlocked?"

He presses his phone to his ear and starts calling out GPS coordinates. "Faster," he demands. I'm not sure if he's talking to the driver or the person on the other end of the line. When his head whips around, he tells me to buckle in.

I ignore him, needing to be able to jump out when we catch them. But the red lights on the van are heading out of range too fast to catch.

"Don't lose them," I say from the back as I drag my hand over the leather where she sat. Winter was here. Right here.

"Fuck. They came out of nowhere." I feel numb with her gone.

"We'll catch them," Lars says, turning back again.

"They chloroformed her, Lars." The words claw up my throat as I realize she's helpless. "She can't fight."

"She'll fight," he replies. I'm thrown against the door where she was taken from when we make a hard right. "Buckle in, Bennett." The car turns left down an alley.

We all realize it at the same time. "Don't stop," I say, not accepting this is over.

The driver glances at Lars as the SUV slows down. "We can't catch them. Their lead is too great, and the vehicle won't—"

"Don't you fucking give up. Don't give up," I shout. "She needs us."

He says, "The traffic's too heavy, Mr. Everest."

"Then I'll get out." I get up, but Lars shoots a command.

"Sit down. I can only keep track of one of you right now. It's either Winter or you. Choose."

"I choose Winter." I sit back with adrenaline still coursing through me. One more turn and their taillights are gone. Vanished into a sea of red lights and horns honking. "No! No. Find them."

"There's traffic ahead, but I don't see any vans, sir," the driver says.

"Find them!" The vehicle comes to a stop due to traffic, and I jump out, running as fast as I can. Lars calls my name, but I weave between cars and keep running until I hit the intersection. Standing in the middle, out of breath, I turn in circles, scanning every vehicle. I don't care that the traffic light is green or cars are driving around me.

I only care about Winter. "Fuck!"

Lars runs up next to me, huffing. "Sidewalk, Ben."

"She's gone. Into thin air. Gone."

He pushes me from behind. "Get out of the fucking street."

I step into a crowd of gawkers, some taking my picture, some filming the spectacle. Pushing through, I find space in front of a law office where I try to catch my breath. The muscles in my thighs start to give, and I squat down. "They took her from a car that was supposed to protect her."

Lars leans against the window, and his head drops down. "I fucked up."

"They'll kill her this time. They didn't last time, so she doesn't have a chance this time."

"She does," he says. "She'll fight."

"When she wakes up," I remind him.

He nods, but his eyes stay trained to the surroundings. "It's not safe out in the open. We need to get to the vehicle."

"It's not fucking safe in there either." I stand back up and start walking down the street. I don't even know where the SUV is, but I keep moving.

His phone buzzes every two seconds, alarms sounding. Lars finally answers, "I have him. Where are you?" There's a pause. "We'll meet you around the corner."

As soon as he hangs up, he's on another call, telling someone what happened. Tapping me on the shoulder, he signals to go left. The SUV speeds down the alley, coming to a stop in front of us. The locks are popped because apparently now they're fucking using them, and we get in.

The driver reverses as Lars relays what happened again. I hear him say Aaron's name. That means Ethan's gotten wind. My phone buzzes, and I huff before answering. "Thought we weren't supposed to call each other?"

"I'm on an untraceable phone." I expected a lecture, but that's not what I get. He says, "I don't know what to say, Bennett. We're gearing up."

"I promised I'd protect her. I promised her, E."

"I know. Aaron's tracked your vehicle and is tapping into cameras to find the van. We already have a photo of it. We'll find her."

When we drive away from the area, I collapse onto the seat, knowing there's no chance of finding her now. "What just happened? She was here, right where I am, and then she was gone."

I'm not asking him anything, but he says, "We'll find her. I promise."

"Before she's dead?"

"You can't think like that. I've been there, and it won't do you any good. I need you to focus. Are you with me, Bennett?"

"I'm with you. I'm here," I say, raking my fingers through my hair.

"I told Lars to take you—"

"I'm not going to the secret location. I can't sit and hide while she's . . . *Fuck*. I'm not resting until I have her back."

"I was going to say you're going to the operations center. You can sleep in the panic room while the glass is being replaced on the building."

"I just met her, but . . ." She more than matters to me. *I love her.*

"I know, Ben. She does too. I'll touch base soon."

"Okay." I hang up, and lying on my back, I stare out the far window as the tops of buildings flash by. "Where are you, Winter?" I whisper, closing my eyes as I try to summon the connection that was built out of the blue. My heart reached for hers, and hers danced with mine in the moonlight of a Parisian bistro. It was the perfect setup for romance; something she'd read in a book but instead shared with me. "Where are you, ma chérie? Stay strong and please believe that I'm coming for you." I send that into the universe, hoping it lands with her wherever she may be.

"ETA—two minutes. Don't waste time. Be ready to get out. I don't know if the building has been secured since we were going to do that after dropping you off at the secret location," Lars says.

I sit up, and my shoulders fold forward; her loss is a defeat weakening my muscles. The SUV comes to a stop in the garage, and I hop out at the same time as Lars. The operations door is open, and we step inside.

The metal door slams shut, and a bolt is turned, locking us in, and the world out. I step up behind a security guard I don't recognize. Lars has never been good with introductions, but if he's here, he's on the team.

The guy points at the lowest monitor on the wall. "We hacked into the city's camera system. You never saw the van come up beside you because it came from this T-street. From the lobby, our SUV blocked them entirely from view." He looks up at me. "But here's what puzzles me. There was no way for them to track you. This SUV is unmarked and recently went under complete inspection, bulletproofed, the whole nine yards."

I say, "It was her father or her brother."

I'm working this out in my head, but Lars says, "Depends on what they would gain from that. Is she worth more to them dead or alive?"

"After what we just witnessed, we know the answer." We bend to get a look at the video capturing the van at different points, but then it disappears. "How can it vanish even from the camera?"

The silence builds as he rewinds and then replays it. Lars says, "Again." Again. And again until Lars points at the screen. "Pause it right there."

"What is it?" I ask, leaning in closer.

"The van."

"Where? I don't see it."

"That's just it." His heavy sigh brings our attention to him. With his hands on his head, he walks to the other side of the room. "They were right fucking there. They turned their lights off, and we drove right by that alley."

"What?" My head whips back to the camera. "Play it again."

He rewinds the footage again and plays it in real time. The camera covers the alley from one end to the other. When it pivots back to the where the van was last seen, the lights are cut just as they turn. "Fucking, fuck, fuck, fuck!" I slam the bottom of my fists against the wall. There will never be a pain like the loss of Winter, so the blood caused by the jagged edges of the concrete means nothing to me. "I could feel her near." I scrub my hands over my face. "What have we done? If she dies . . ." I struggle to say the words, but the truth hurts, and I'll take every ounce of this guilt. "It's because of me."

After two hours of watching the same footage, we still have nothing to go on. The camera never caught the van leaving, but after sending a team to investigate the alley, we're still left empty-handed.

Ethan arrives just after midnight. He looks tired, but he's here. "Any leads?" he asks. The door closes behind him, and he walks straight to the monitors.

"None so far," I say.

Lars, looking worse for the wear, sits in a chair with a laptop. "We're coming up empty. We checked with the Noblemans but even threats didn't ruffle them. We did retrieve a text message between Braden and McCoy just after we arrived at the building, though. But we haven't broken the code."

"What does it say?" Ethan asks.

He changes screens. "Season's Greetings."

"I've read it a hundred times and nothing." Bolting out of the chair, I smack my head. "You say it, and I just solved it."

Ethan crosses his arms over his chest. "And?"

"Winter. The season. *She's* the season. Greetings means she's there. They're seeing her, greeting her downstairs. Her brother fucking tipped the kidnappers off. That's how the van was there so fast. They were already plotting it."

Beginning to pace, Ethan works through things. "They tried to shoot her or you, maybe both, through the window of your apartment. But you got out."

"He called my phone, but I didn't answer."

"He still couldn't track your phone."

"So he lured us in."

Ethan says, "They didn't get you in the apartment, so they were ready for you when you left."

"They knew her weakness, and they used it against her," I add.

Lars leans back. "Her mother."

Nodding, I sit down. "The box was a decoy . . . the bait like she was. She showed up, and her brother texted them."

"Boom." Ethan exhales, exhausted. "They were there and got her, but where will they take her?"

"Wherever McCoy is."

Lars asks, "We tracked him. He's still not stateside."

"Fuck."

Ethan stares at me. "Where is he?"

I say, "Paris."

32

Winter

My lungs constrict, and I rise, gasping for air, but am jerked down by restraints. Blackness fills my vision except for the dim light that filters the outline of the mask covering my eyes. I reach, but my arms ache in response, the restraints around my wrists confining them above my head.

Wild heartbeats thump against my chest as panic sets in. I'm tempted to cry out, to scream in hopes someone will hear me, but fear of who that might be is stronger. I pull my hands toward my body again, but I'm stuck. The low rattle of metal makes me think handcuffs, but the wide bands around my wrists make me realize it's the kind for sexual play.

Oh God.

I wiggle my legs, and they're free. When I spread them wide, I discover I'm on a large mattress covered in soft and silky sheets, the luxurious kind that covered my bed in Paris.

Closing my eyes, I try to focus on something happier— Bennett's handsome face and great laugh when I stole his fry

—and regulate my panting breaths to calm my heart before it explodes from my chest.

"You can relax," a female voice says with distance between us. "You'll be fine."

I'll be fine? Fear sprints through my veins. My mind ticks through what happened while I was out. Soft fabric stretches over my breasts, but bra straps don't cut into my skin. The sheet slips over my legs with ease, but I can feel a pair of underwear covering me. I try to remember what I was wearing when I was awake last.

New York.

Night.

Yoga pants. Sports bra. T-shirt.

Bennett's face before the door closed and I passed out.

Drugged . . . *Kurt.*

I'm careful with my words, not sure who or what I'm dealing with. "Where am I? Who are you? Why am I tied up?"

"I expected something more original. Those questions are boring."

"Not to me." I try to sit up again. When that's too hard to do, I rub the side of my head against the pillowcase to get the mask off to no avail. "Let me go. Please."

The mattress dips beside me, sending my pulse to skyrocket through the roof. A hand lifts my mask, but I don't find the relief I was expecting. Her smooth hair is shinier up close, her eyes greener, her skin tanner. "Chelsea?"

"We've not officially met."

I glance down at my chest, suddenly feeling more exposed than before. A vintage Blondie T-shirt I bought on the left bank is covering me. That's when I look past her and around. My apartment . . . *Paris.* Oh my God! My heart picks up the pace again. I never woke up on the plane this time. I don't know why that bothers me. I should be happy to be alive, even if only long enough to beg for more time.

My thoughts turn, and I focus on every part of my body, taking inventory of any unwanted sensation. I exhale, closing my eyes, thankful that I don't feel violated beyond my current situation.

"I dressed you," she says, "but you even make street clothes look good." I'm not sure how to respond, so I stare at her, waiting for the ambush. She removes the mask altogether and runs her fingers through my hair to the very tips letting it fall gracefully down around me. I can't read her eyes. The pupils are large, but they're void of emotion, maybe resigned. Drugged? She adds, "I've heard enough about it to want to feel it for myself."

Angling away from her, I say, "I don't understand."

"Neither do I." Sitting there, she appears to contemplate her next move. "I'm never enough for him." She walks across the small one-room apartment and looks at herself in the mirror. I recognize her dress as the Agostino I bought out of spite last month. It was five thousand dollars, and I didn't bother having it fitted. I never intended to wear it because it could walk the line between evening and wedding, and I never wanted to give Kurt the wrong idea. I just wanted to burn through his money. He never said a thing.

She says, "I can appreciate a beautiful woman." Turning back, she looks at me. "But how do I compete?"

The dress doesn't fit her properly, the small cap sleeves keep dropping. "What are you talking about? Why am I restrained?" I yank at the chains again, my wrists beginning to burn from the tight cuffs rubbing against them.

With my head lifted, I watch her open her clutch and pull out what appears to be a tube of Chanel lipstick. When she starts to apply it, slowly, so she doesn't color outside the lines, I realize it's the same color I wear. My gaze flicks to the vanity where I always kept everything organized and notice the empty space. Holy shit, she's a psycho. *Is she single white female-ing me?* "Please let me go, Chelsea."

"I didn't like this idea, but you know Kurt."

"What idea?"

Without missing a beat, she continues, "He's always such a drama king." She snaps the lid closed and drops it back in her purse. "I won't be the one who kills you, Winter."

My head bolts back up. "Kill me?"

"I may be second best, but I'm willing to stick this out until I'm first." Waggling her hand, she displays a huge diamond ring on her finger. The one that gutted me the first time I saw it on the society page. "I got the ring. Eventually, I'll own his heart." She stands and comes to the side of the bed to gaze down at me. "In the meantime, we have dinner plans."

"We do?"

Laughing, she pats my arm and then turns away. "No, silly."

While she's walking to the door, she looks back after snapping up her purse. "I see why he's fixated on you. Maybe we can spend some time together when I come back to study your personality."

"Study?" Is she . . . *trying to become me?* "Chelsea, don't leave. Let me go. Please don't leave. Who's going to kill me?"

The psycho stops and turns around. "That is for you and your god to decide, not me." She walks out of view, and I hear the door open. "Please," I shout, tears stinging my eyes. "Don't leave me. Don't leave me like this."

Then the door slams closed, and I drop my head, tears sliding over my temples into my hair. *Kill?* Someone is going to kill me?

I won't welcome it. I'll fight until my last breath is ripped from my chest because for the first time in my life, I have something to live for. *Someone to live for.* I squeeze my eyes closed and let thoughts of Bennett meander through my veins to settle my mind so I can think clearly.

Looking up at each wrist, I tug once more to see how hard it would be to break from the bed. The posts are at least five inches thick. My wrist will break before those will. I'm stretched too far to reach either cuff with my head or teeth.

"Fuck!" I shout frustrated, digging my head into the pillow and kicking the covers off.

That's it! "Help me! Help! Help! Help!" I shout at the top of my lungs. "Help—"

The door opens and my words and breath stall in my throat. Kurt comes around the corner like he lives here. "Winter, shhh. You're going to get us in trouble."

"That's the point."

He smiles, and it actually appears genuine. When he sits next to me, some kind of strange emotion invades his dark eyes. "Oh, God." *Happiness.* That can't be right. He's happy to see me? I remember that expression from when we first met. My body shrinks away as much I can when he reaches to touch my face. *What the fuck is happening?*

"Yes, I'll be your god, Winter. I'll be everything. For you." He looks down at my shirt disapprovingly. I find an ounce of pleasure in his displeasure.

"What are you doing with me?"

"Such a loaded question." Running the tip of his finger up the middle of my belly and dragging the shirt with it, he stops just before he exposes my breasts. His gaze flicks up to my eyes. "It was good having Chelsea by my side and you in my bed—"

"That was never my choice."

He laughs humorlessly. "We see things differently. I remember a woman with potential in her eyes asking for a job. Who gave you that job?" When he runs his hand under my shirt, my body recoils from his touch.

"Joyce in HR."

"I did!" he snaps, pressing on my bruised ribs. The rejection apparently stings, despite me thinking he couldn't feel anything but contempt. He stands to examine my face and then frowns. "The bruises are healing, but I didn't mean to hit you so hard." Grabbing my face, he squeezes enough to cause pain as his thumb digs into the bruise on my jaw. "You make me crazy, and I lose myself."

"There's no denying who you really are anymore." I try to turn away from him, but he holds me there. "Why am I here?"

"Because I miss you," he replies, leaving me exposed on the bed.

"You have Chelsea."

"I don't want Chelsea. She's predictable." Ironically, I got the exact opposite vibe from her.

I shoot daggers with my eyes. I hate everything about him, even the way he walks across the room like he's actually the god he believes himself to be. "What do you want?"

Unscrewing the top from a bottle of scotch that he always keeps stocked here, he glances at me over his shoulder. "You."

Everests and me. I don't dare utter their name, hoping he's been sidetracked enough to forget about them. I'll take the hit for all of them, and for Bennett, I would do anything. "You didn't want me. That's why you proposed to Chelsea."

He pours the liquid into a crystal glass and turns around again. With his eyes locked on my body, he swallows, drinking me in with the liquor. Running his thumb over his mouth, he catches the extra drop that escaped the glass and licks it.

Setting the glass down, he moves to the other side of the bed and lies next to me. Staring up at the fabric canopy, the back of his hand rests against my hip. I would move, but I have no doubt he'd find me again. "I made a mistake," he says, rolling to face me. "If I apologize, will you take me back?"

"What?" I spit that response before I have time to compose a less violent reaction. "This is coming out of the blue, Kurt." I've never seen this side of him. He's almost . . . human.

"I know. It disappointed me as well. I think I might have a heart, after all, and I'm willing to give it to you to care for. That's romantic. You like that, right?"

I'm stunned. I even raise an eyebrow in disbelief. Kurt McCoy is a narcissistic psychopath who's more deluded than his crazy fiancée. I need to outsmart him, which means staying calm and sounding strong . . . *Take control of this situation. This is life or death.* "What about Chelsea?" I ask, trying to sound unperturbed as if I'm glad he wants me and not her. *Play the game, Winter. Play the game. But don't acquiesce or he'll know.* "Chelsea loves you, Kurt."

"She has no spine. She doesn't have an original thought in that head of hers. Not like you. No, she doesn't have your spirit, the fight to survive, or a soul that's tainted like mine. I knew you were made to be mine when you took that first step into my office. Darkness attracts darkness, ma princesse ténébreuse."

I prefer Bennett's sweetheart to Kurt's princess, Bennett's light to Kurt's dark.

"You're confused," I say flatly. "You don't love me, and I don't love you. That's not what we ever were. I used you to get back at my father. I stole your insider secrets to win back his love."

"You think you used me, but I won. I outplayed a player.

I can respect that you tried, and it doesn't matter where you are in life, you'll always be mine."

"I'm not now, and I'll never be. I'm not yours. I'm not even my own. You threw me out as bait in the middle of Paris but never told me who to lure. No, you don't love me, Kurt, and I don't love you."

"I do, and you do. You always did."

"No, I just didn't know any better." *Now I do.* I don't know why I'm confessing this to him, but it seems like maybe he needs to hear it.

"You now love an Everest?"

Yes. Flutters fill my tummy, but I hold down any sign that will give away how much I love Bennett. I hope to see him again one day, so I must lie better than I ever have. "Love was never meant for me. I'm buried under too much darkness."

"I want to scrub you clean of your sins and his finger-prints from your skin. I will own you again, Winter." His hand clamps down on my throat, and he starts to squeeze, fear shooting through me as I yank at the chains.

My eyes begin tracing the pattern in the French fabric above to find a safer place in my mind, but he finally releases. "No one will ever own me again," I say, coughing.

"I can give you everything you ever dreamed of."

There's no malice in his expression when I glance his way. He seems to believe what he's saying. He's playing his best game yet—the human one—but I'm too wise to fall for it this time. "You can't give me a real family, and you will never love me like I deserve." I close my eyes and the words *you aren't Bennett* float through my head. "You tried to kill me. How is that love?"

"Your nine lives prove your pussy is mine. We're meant to be together. And I can give you your family back. I can make them love you. You will have me. You'll want for nothing."

When I see how hopeful he is, I know there's no real question being asked. Only a demand. Some things will never change. If I refuse him, he's never going to let me live. I'm never going to walk out of here. So I do have a choice, but both of them end in my death—body or soul.

It doesn't matter how he tries to pretend we're friends, lying on the bed next to me like I'm here by choice. I pull at the chains binding me to the bed, a reminder to him of what this really is.

He sits up, turning his back to me. He knows how I feel about a future with him. Once I left, I only looked back when I was forced to. He's incapable of accepting the truth. A heavy sigh falls across his shoulders, and he stands, straightening his shirt. "I must go, or I'll be late for dinner."

"With your fiancée."

"She might be my fiancée, but you could be my wife."

Lose-lose is what that is. There's no other way around it. He's never actually said the word love because he has never known it. I can play his game to live a little longer or die trying to get the answers I need. "Why did you kidnap me?"

Returning to where he left his drink, he lifts it to his mouth but pauses. "This is your last chance, Ms. Nobleman."

"Last chance?"

"To live." With his back to me, he finishes the liquor in one swift go and sets the glass down. He looks back at me, and says, "You have until I return. Then I want an answer." The room is left ripe with his anger in his absence.

And I'm left to decide if I want to live or die.

33

Winter

Curling onto my side, I try to go back to sleep, but when I realize I'm free, my lids fly open.

Chelsea sits in the chair with her legs tucked under her, the white evening gown flowing over the side and pooling on the floor next to her sparkling shoes.

A puff of smoke fills the air above her, causing me to look down at her hand. The cigarette needs to be tapped, but her eyes are on me with black streaks staining her cheeks. "Who's Bennett?"

I don't reply, but since I'm unchained, I get up cautiously. She doesn't seem to mind. She's a mess, and my gut tells me that's not good for me. An empty bottle of red wine sits on the table and what looks to be the last of it in a glass next to it.

She repeats her question and then takes another long drag of the cigarette, her eyes never blinking or leaving mine.

"A friend."

"A special friend if he's worth mentioning in your sleep,"

she adds, ash falling on the dress and burning the silk fabric. The black dots meld with the red wine she's already spilled. "Did you know that you can't buy happiness?"

She's a woman on the edge of a breakdown, so I proceed cautiously. "I learned the hard way."

"So did I." She smiles as if we're bonding. "I didn't know you were here until today. I didn't know . . ." The smile falls away and takes a sip of wine. "As soon as you arrived, he was on edge. Anxious to see you. When I confronted him, he slapped me."

Moving closer to the large wardrobe, I reach for a long yellow skirt on a hanger dangling from the corner, and then move slowly like we're friends spending time together. I'd prefer jeans or pants, but I'm not pushing my luck and stick to the closest option.

"That was before dinner," she says, leaning her head back on the golden velvet wingback. "Kurt ended us right before the third course was served because you agreed to be his again."

Oh, no. My stomach tightens while my breathing picks up. I keep my eyes on her while slipping on the skirt. "That's not true, Chelsea."

"What is the truth, Winter? Tell me how you got entangled with the man I'm supposed to marry."

"We were dating, and I fell for him." The words are sour on my tongue, but the truth isn't always tasteful. "I thought he loved me, but then he met you."

That brings a lazy smile to her lips, and her lids drag down and slowly back up. "I fell for him, too. I love him." She eyes me.

A row of flats are tucked under the wardrobe, the lavender suede pair that tie around my ankles are the closest. I won't have time to wrap them up if I can get to them.

"Your love is true. He should value that." I step closer and start to toe them out from under the dark space.

"He values a challenge. That's not me. You'd be surprised how many men are afraid to approach a beautiful woman. He walked up, and I begged him to take me with him." She scoffs and then takes another drag. "I'm pathetic."

One shoe is close enough to slip on. "You're not."

"That's *his* word for me." She picks up the glass and finishes most of the wine.

"You deserve better."

My actions catch her attention, and her eyes dip to the shoes. "Do I?"

"Yes. I was where you are now, but I got out. You can, too."

She swivels her legs down, and her feet touch the ground. "There's no getting out. Women like us are used and tossed away to age ungracefully while the men we love find a younger, prettier model for their arm."

"You will only get what you settle for, Chelsea. You can do so much better than Kurt."

She throws her glass and it shatters under the window. "Is that what you did, Winter? You turned him down because you didn't want to settle? You're a liar! Everyone knows it. You were begging him after he chose me."

"I wasn't."

Raising her voice, she says, "You did," pointing a finger at me. "He would tell me how you were so desperate that you would let him fuck you anywhere. You'd beg him."

I slip on the other shoe; the straps twisted uncomfortably under my feet. While trying to remain calm, I reply, "He forced me, Chelsea. That's not a lie. That's the truth I have to live with every day of my life."

"What are you saying?" She crosses her arms over her

chest, the sleeve slipping down on the right side. "Are you accusing him of raping you?"

Closing my eyes, I remember meeting him like it was yesterday. I was so bright-eyed and innocent to the real world. I was the perfect prey. "I was a girl with daddy issues who would accept any advances as a substitute."

When I see her lower her defenses of him, I add, "He didn't rape me." Our history races through my mind. "He blackmailed me instead, presenting my options like I had a choice when I knew I had none. So yes, Kurt fucked me how he pleased, even if he gave me the option of where. But I never begged."

"He blackmailed you how?"

My mother's locket catches my eyes, hanging from the mirror behind her. I want it. I look back at Chelsea, hoping she doesn't notice. I'm not sure where her heart lies right now —precariously balancing between a breakdown and her love for a man who doesn't love her.

I take small steps forward, determined to get the necklace around my neck before I leave this place for good. As careful with my words as my steps, I reply, "My family's company. He could have destroyed it, but he didn't."

"He didn't because he had you." She's connecting the dots.

And for the first time, I exhale all the guilt I've carried around for years. Rubbing my wrists, I also ask, "Did you release me?"

She's very approachable in her sorrow, looking for a friend in an enemy. Sadly, she's just another woman used by that disgusting man. "I did. He never hit me before tonight. For this, he'll kill me," she says, losing the energy to fight.

I understand the hopelessness. I've been living like that for years because of him, but I'm not willing to die with her. Expending the weight of what I took the blame for, I take the chain from the mirror and drop it over my head. It's a risky move but one worth taking, not only for me but also for my mother. She deserves to be remembered. I walk toward the door.

"You can't leave, Winter."

I turn back to see the broken woman before me. It's then that I realize she's right. I can't leave. Not yet. I've been in her shoes—alone, hurting, with nowhere to turn. I take a cleansing wipe from the vanity and go to her. "Let me help you." If anyone ever needed someone in her corner, it's Chelsea at this moment.

She tilts her head back, and I wipe gently across her cheeks, removing the mascara streaks from her face. She doesn't move, but her eyes stay on me the whole time. I whisper as if someone else will hear us. "I got out, and you can, too." Her heart is good. I just know it is, so I treat her with the kindness I wish I had been shown. Tossing the wipes on the table, I then hold out my hand. "I'll help you."

As if the prospect of leaving overwhelms her, she sits on the edge of the chair, pushing her hair behind her shoulders and adjusting her slipped sleeve back into position. "He's going to kill us."

"We have to fight." I'm so close to the door, and here I am, giving my freedom away by waiting. But this may be the only chance she's ever given, so I stay. "I'll help you."

"Promise?" She grabs her shoes and slips them on.

"I promise."

Taking her clutch in one hand, she holds my hand in the other. "I want to go home. I want to see my family. I don't want to live this life anymore."

"You will, but we need to go."

"He's been living next door to you the whole time."

I take a shuddering breath. So much makes more sense

now. I have no doubt my apartment had cameras to spy on me too, even if I never found them. "Is he there now?"

"Yes."

There is no escape. "He'll know we're leaving."

"No. He took a sleeping pill earlier after he made me pour him a drink. He needs both to sleep." The monster can't sleep with his dirty conscience.

"So we need to be quick and quiet." She nods as I open the door of the apartment and peek into the hallway. It's clear.

"I want to finish college. Kurt made me quit when we got engaged."

I hold my finger to my lips. I'm not sure where the monsters reside, but I don't want to wake the sleeping beasts. We tiptoe down the hall as quiet as mice.

But not quiet enough it seems . . . I hear the click of the knob before I hear him. "It's a little late to be going out, Chelsea. Come here." Kurt snaps his fingers, commanding her like she's his pet. "I see you made friends—"

"With your obsession." She holds my hand and looks back.

"Obsession." He rolls the word a few more times.

Squeezing my eyes tight, I gather strength from my mom and from the man who wanted nothing from me, but who I am. I look down at my hand wrapped around hers and see the deep blue painted on my nails. It's not a coincidence I chose this color for the first time since my mom's death. I know she's here with me, watching over me. Now I need to be the warrior she believed me to be.

With my other hand, I hold the locket and start walking again, taking Chelsea with me.

"Winter!" Kurt's voice slaps our backs. The cock of a gun follows. Chelsea stops and looks back again, causing me to stop. He asks, "How does that make you feel, Winter? To have a man willing to dispose of anyone in our way to have you?" I don't look back, not one millimeter. I won't give him the satisfaction of seeing my face. But I do tighten my hold on Chelsea, praying she sees him for who he really is and not the Prince Charming she wants him to be. Two more snaps and then another command, "Here! Now, Chelsea."

I look at her. "Don't go. Stay with me."

Sobs wreck her frail body. "I'm not strong like you."

"Don't go. Please," I beg, my hands starting to shake. Do I let her go? Do I save myself? Looking at her, I see so much of who I used to be—clinging to anyone who pretended to love me. I was wrong. I didn't need attention like that. I needed the patience to find the attention I deserved. I know how this ends for her. "He'll kill me, and then he'll kill you. Maybe not today, but he will be the end of you."

"Chelsea!" His voice booms, causing us to jump.

Then time slows, my breath heavy in my chest when the elevator dings. The hall goes quiet as the brass doors slide open ahead.

Thirty feet.

Two doors.

Three seconds.

Weapons drawn.

Lars's eyes land on me as he rushes from the elevator with a gun leading the way. I can't find comfort in the rescue because Bennett runs right after. Our eyes meet, and my free hand flies in front to stop him from coming closer when the fire of a bullet echoes from behind me. "Nooooo!"

34

Winter

Chelsea screams, and her body crumples next to me. Another shot is fired as I'm dragged to the floor with her. Our hands stay clasped as the brightness in her eyes fades, seeking that life she spoke about. "Chelsea?" I cry, trying to get to her.

Red blood spreads across the white dress like ants spilling out of an anthill. It all happens so fast and flows slowly through each thread covering her chest. A heavy form lands behind me and rolls me to the other side before I can take a breath.

The soulful eyes I could stare into forever look back at mine as gunfire fills the air. That incredible smile that had me hooked from the moment I saw him shines, but then disappears as he jolts, falling forward. His back arches in as he lands on top of me. "I love you," falls from Bennett's lips as his weight comes to rest.

"No—" I'm about to scream again, but Bennett's hand covers my mouth. He kisses under my ear, and whispers, "Be still. Play dead."

Oh, thank God. "I thought you were dead," I say in a quiet sob, but then do as he says and close my eyes. Chelsea's fingers still clasp mine. I can't see her, but I know she's hanging on.

Bennett's phone is on the floor and 112 on the screen. His body remains still as his finger presses send. I hear the emergency call answered just as a door slams down the hall.

Lars's deep voice penetrates my soundless tears when he yells, "Move."

In one giant jump, Bennett pulls me to my feet, and I'm ripped from Chelsea as we run toward the elevator. He lands with a thud against the wall, my body crashing into his before we change places. I say, "Get Chelsea."

"Lars has her." Tucked in a corner hidden from view of the door, Bennett's hands roam my body as he checks to make sure I'm in one piece. Wanting to protect me from the whole wide world, he uses his body to shield me. Cupping my face, he finally asks, "Are you okay?" I turn my gaze to the sky, seeing the sandstorms roll into his eyes and concern forcing a line between his brows. "Winter." He pauses, and I catch a glimpse of pain shade his expression.

Holding his wrists, I finally release my anguish. "We have to get her to a hospital."

"We will, but we have to get out of here first."

Lars runs into the elevator with Chelsea in his arms, Bennett punching the button as I maneuver around to see her. Moving her hair away from her face, I lift on my toes. "We're going to get you help." I take her hand and warm it between mine. "Okay?"

The elevator finally starts its descent, but through the quiet, I hear her hard swallow. Though her body is limp in Lars's arms, a small smile appears before she rests her eyes. I look at Lars, and he silently reassures me.

"I texted the police the address and to send an ambulance," Bennett says.

Reaching up, Chelsea rests her hand on my shoulder. "You should forgive yourself."

"I can't." I shake my head and then lower it in shame. "I caused this. I set everything in motion."

"With good intentions, Winter."

"The road to hell." I take a harsh breath, inwardly scolding myself. I never related to a cliché more than I do now. My legs feel weak, so I move to the side and grab onto the railing, holding myself up.

"When these doors open, Lars will go first, and we'll follow," Bennett says, "There will be a car—"

"No, they need it. They have to get to a hospital."

He glances at the numbers as they light up above Lars's head. "I need you safe." His phone vibrates, and he starts typing again.

The elevator stops, and the doors open on the second floor. Lars is a wall of a man with a woman in his arms staring down at an elderly couple. The man shrinks under the stare. The woman on his arm grabs the fur at her neck, and her mouth falls open. Lars's deep voice vibrates against the elevator. "We'll send it back up."

Bennett hits the button to close the doors, leaving the stunned couple behind. Then he continues like we never stopped at all. "You're going to walk out the front door like nothing is wrong. We can't put other lives at risk."

"Why didn't we take the stairs?"

"Because they did."

"They . . ."

"Kurt and his men," Lars says. "Showtime."

The doors slide open, and Bennett's hand covers my lower back. We start walking, pretending we weren't just in a gunfight or have a bleeding woman in desperate need of a doctor. "Black SUV at the curb," he says under his breath as we pass through the people in the lobby.

I look down at the cold, checkered marble floors when I see a couple's eyes go wide. "I lost my shoe, and there's blood all over my skirt."

"No one cares about us. Keep walking."

Lars and Chelsea are in front of us, but once we reach the doors, he stops to wait. He's still trying to cover us when he should only worry about Chelsea. "Take the car. Go," I say, pushing his back as we exit onto the sidewalk.

"Winter!" My name bleeds off the sharp-edged blade of Bennett's tongue.

"No. They need to go. We'll be fine."

Bennett eyes me and then glances to them. Seeming to go against his better judgment, he shakes his head. "Take it, Lars."

"Go inside until the next car arrives," Lars replies. He runs for the car and climbs in the back with Chelsea.

I catch her gaze one last time. She raises her hand up, so I raise mine. The door closes, and the car pulls away.

Paris is cold in November, reminding me of what I'm wearing, or the lack of. As the chill sets in, sirens sound around us, bouncing off the walls just as two policemen race toward the hotel. "Shit," Bennett says, and then grabs me and pulls me into a kiss.

Safe.

Deep.

Passionate.

Real. So raw, reflecting how I feel for him.

True and honest.

Full of promise and a future.

Our lips part the moment the shot rings out. My silent

scream swallowed by Bennett as I look at him, praying this isn't the last kiss I ever get from him.

The snap of another bullet punctures the air, and he curls his body around me, shielding me as we fall. Protecting my head from hitting the ground, his hands slip into my hair

The sound of tires ram the curb and the back door to an SUV swings open. A man jumps out of the front seat with a gun, covering us, and Ethan yells from the back, "Get in."

We're up on our feet in seconds, and I climb in with Bennett hot on my heels. The door closes, and the vehicle takes off to the sound of metal ricocheting off the SUV. Barricaded in Bennett's arms, I don't move, and I don't look away from the only person who makes this life worth fighting for.

"Breathe, Winter." Bennett's steady hand touches my trembling body, my shoulders quake to the fear inside.

What we just survived begins to sink in while the walls of the SUV start closing in. In a succession of quick exhales, I try to regulate my breathing to match his calming eyes. When my breathing stabilizes, the words come tumbling off my tongue. "Are we safe?"

"We're safe."

I finally breathe with ease, and then say what I wish I could have back there, "I love you, too."

He leans in and rests his forehead against mine. "You love me, sweetheart?"

"I do." I wrap my arms around him, wanting to breathe in his entire being so our souls will forever share the same universe. "I love you."

I wish things were different. I wish I had never dragged him into my mess to clean up. I wish so much that I'm not sure I'll survive this regret, or that we will. When this is all over, how will he look at me? Will he still care? I can ask a billion questions, but deep in my heart, I know the answers.

I see them written in his eyes. Yes. We will survive this together.

Kissing me quick, he says, "I love you, too."

"Hey, that's great and all," Ethan says, leaning forward and looking at us. "I'm all for love, but there's a psychopath loose in Paris who needs to be found—"

"We need to get Winter to the hospital," Bennett says.

"What?" I ask, confused. "Why?" And then I look down at my forearm.

Taking hold of my wrist with one hand and my elbow with the other, he examines it. "Fuck, Winter, are you okay?"

I was cold, but figured that was the adrenaline rush subsiding. It's not a long gash, but it might be deep. "Will I need stitches?" I ask, feeling a little woozy.

"Maybe," Ethan answers. "We need it checked, and then we're out of there. I've set up extra security."

"I promised to help Chelsea, Ethan, I need to be there."

He says, "It's dangerous, Winter. The longer we stay, the bigger the risk."

Bennett groans. "Why are you doing this?"

"Because she has no one else. I know you're worried, but Ethan said there would be security. I'll be fine," I say, touching Bennett's arm. "They'll check my wound and then we'll see to Chelsea, okay?"

"No. It's not okay. You were hurt. *Again*. I'm still trying to deal with that. I'm fucking furious that fucker took you. I can't lose you, Winter."

Cradling his face, that strong, scruff covered jaw, in my hands, I kiss him. "I'll listen this time. I promise."

His brother says, "Ben, we'll have eyes on her every minute."

"Yeah, I know. I know," Bennett moans. "Extra fucking security. Got it."

"Okay," Ethan says to me, "you need to do exactly what

we say. We don't know what we're walking into, but as I said before, we have bulked up security."

I sit back knowing I'm not telling the truth about being fine. My heart is still beating overtime as I think about what happened. My arm is throbbing, but I'm so thankful to be alive and in Bennett's arms once again.

35

Bennett

Eight hours at the hospital waiting for more information has worn us down. Hearing Chelsea was in recovery after surgery was good news, but the silence since has been deafening.

Winter paces the private lounge in a pair of slip-on shoes a nurse offered her. The cut on her arm wasn't very deep after all, so they've stitched and bandaged it and told her it should be fine, but there might be a scar. We've each napped at some point or another, but she's back on her feet, trying to run a path into the tiles.

Ethan's been speaking with the police just inside the door, and I'm stuck staring at the stained grout, hunched over in a chair next to Lars.

He laughs lightly to himself, making me look over. With nothing obvious entertaining him, I ask, "What?"

"She asked me how she looked in the car because if she was going to die, she wanted to look her best when she shows up at the pearly gates."

That makes me sit up. "Chelsea? What did you say?" I'm

not going to rush to judgment, but I think we need to take things slow. She was with Kurt, after all. But Lars must see the same thing that made Winter want to help her.

Lars is calm, wearing a slight smile that's rarely there. He looks over at me, and adds, "I told her she looked too good to die. When she asked what she had to live for, I said when we get back to Manhattan, I'm taking her out on a date."

Surprised, I reply, "Um. Wait a minute. Let's back up here. You asked a woman out although she might have died in your arms?"

"She wasn't going to die. I wasn't going to let her." He shrugs. "Anyway, she's pretty."

"I'm not sure what to say. You either have the worst intuition about women or the best game I've ever seen."

"Game," he says with a smug nod.

The door opens, and the doctor who performed the surgery enters the room. As if told to, we all stand at the same time. He looks around, not sure who to speak to, so I volunteer for the job. "How is she?"

His French accent is thick, but his English is great. "She did well. We've been monitoring her closely for the past few hours. She's stable, so we're moving her out of ICU to a room. Monsieur Everest requested a private room, and one has been secured."

"What about her injuries?" I ask.

Touching his chest close to his shoulder, he explains, "No major organs were afflicted. The bullet was lodged into the muscle, and she lost a lot of blood. She's very lucky. One inch lower would have done damage she might not have survived."

"When will she be moved?"

"She's already being moved."

Winter asks, "Can I see her?" She joins my side.

"It's fine for you to wait with her. We only ask that you let her rest," he says.

"I will. Merci," Winter replies and looks up at me, the first signs of joy returning.

I hold her to me and kiss her head. "She owes her life to you."

Looking back at Lars, she smiles. "She owes it to him. I owe mine to you." Her arms come around me, and I take the embrace, needing it more than I would have thought. "We've been through a lot for practically being strangers," I tease.

"Strangers," she repeats, laughing. But then she rests her chin on my chest, and her smile is prettier than any sunset I've ever seen on Lake Austin. And those are some damn gorgeous sunsets. "I love you."

"I love you so much."

Running my hands down her back, I take a second to look at her before she leaves. "Those words have never been easy for me to say, but this time, it's different. It's the first time I feel them, and I feel them fully for you. So they come easier. I joke about us being strangers because we haven't known each other long, but I feel closer to you than I've ever felt for anyone else before."

"I feel it too, Bennett. I feel full of happiness that made me feel guilty when we met. You know what? I don't feel guilty for loving you. And if we hadn't been set up, I truly believe we still would have found our way to each other."

"We were always meant to meet, baby."

"I like being your baby, your sweetheart, your ma chérie."

"I like being yours." I lose myself momentarily while kissing her. Then the lights come back, and the sound of others return to full volume. Our lips part, but our hearts stay entwined.

Lars places a hand on my shoulder. "They said Winter can wait in the room, but they only want one visitor at a time. If you don't mind staying a little longer, I'd like to see her right after."

"Of course." Winter releases me and pulls a long necklace out from the collar of her shirt and starts dragging it mindlessly along the chain. "You got your necklace back."

Holding it out to look at it, she says, "I made sure to grab it before we left the apartment." She opens the locket and stares at the tiny photos. "I don't know why my father wanted it. He never cared about these pictures before." I look down at the photos of her mother on one side and Winter as a baby on the other.

I take it in my hand to get a closer look. "Your mom was beautiful."

"In the lobby, my father stared at me like he was seeing her again," she says.

"You do look a lot like her."

"I'd seen him just four weeks prior. That's not enough time to pass as if you're seeing someone for the first time. It just makes me realize how he never saw me at all."

"I see you."

"Yes, you do." She smiles and leans against me, admiring the pictures. "Thank you."

"You're a smiley, happy baby."

"I was shaped like a potato."

"Happy. Healthy. Loved. Cute as a potato." I smirk. "That's how babies should be."

She takes her necklace off and rests her head on my arm. "Don't you think it was weird that he wanted it? That they wouldn't give up the box unless I gave it to them?"

"Yes. I don't know if they were wasting time until the van arrived to kidnap you or he actually wants this necklace."

She lifts it and looks at it in her hand, her thoughts lost on it as she stares.

The little tinkering sound it makes when she rattles it has me wondering. "Is it worth a lot?"

"I don't think so. She had it made, but it's just silver."

"Have you ever looked up the stamp on the back?" Peering down to get a closer look, I read, "Browning."

Leaning in, she gets a closer look. "Browning. I never noticed it before. I think I took so much for granted since I had it most of my life."

The longer she stares at it, the more tension that grows. I finally ask, "What are you thinking?"

"He was upset I'd lost it. The silver isn't worth enough to justify what they've done to me. That means—"

"It's not about the silver."

A heavy pause hangs between us. She glances at me and then opens the locket, popping open the tiny silver frame. The photo stays in place. As if she has to justify it, she says, "It's old."

"It's okay."

She nods and uses her nail to pry the little photo from sticking to the locket. I see her shoulders fall like mine do. "There's nothing there." Showing me the blank shining silver, she says, "Well, that's a letdown."

Watching her put the photo back in, I ask, "What's that thing you say when you shake it?"

"Ring the bell and make a wish. You'll receive what you need." I listen as she shakes it.

"What makes that sound?"

Shrugging, she replies, "I don't know. I never had the key."

"Do you think it's anything?"

"Braden used to tell me it was one of his baby teeth so I never wanted to open it."

She hands it to me. I turn it over in my hand, the chain

hanging over, and jangle it again. Fascinating. "What if it's not?"

"I guess we find a key to fit it when we get back to New York and find out." She turns to the door. "I want to be there when Chelsea wakes up."

I pull her back to me and kiss her on the head. She smiles and a faint blush crosses her cheeks when she looks back before we leave.

Lars opens the door, and we walk together past the security detail outside the door. A nurse leads us to Chelsea's room and gives Winter instructions before she steps inside and tends to her. Winter stays in the doorway and takes my hand. "You're staying at the hospital?"

"Yes," I say, looking around the room. The nurse excuses herself and marks on the chart when she exits. I add, "We'll be in the room down the hall. Victor will be stationed here. Let him know if you need anything, and he can contact us. All right?" I reach around her and pull us together. "I won't leave until you do."

"Thank you."

Then I kiss her head again, so fucking thankful she's okay. "I'll check in on you later."

"Okay," she whispers.

I'm about to go, but something in my gut tells me to stay. Leaning inside the room, I look through the open door. Chelsea has lost some color, but she looks peaceful while she sleeps. The machines have a soft whirr to them, and her heart is steadily beating. The rest of the room is standard for a hospital room. Nothing catches my eyes, but something feels off. I can't leave her here. "I'll stay."

Winter looks up at me when I take her from the room and tuck her behind me. She says, "You're tired. Get some rest."

"I shouldn't leave—"

"You should. Victor's right here. I'll be fine."

Ethan comes down the hall, and says, "How is she?"

"She's doing well. Asleep right now," Winter replies.

I step in but keep my voice down. "Have they found McCoy?"

Ethan says, "No. They've sent out the photo. We'll have more interviews tomorrow, but after that, we're getting on the plane and heading home." To Winter, he adds, "Chelsea's parents will be here by morning to stay with her until she can travel back. We'll also station a guard while she's here."

"What about after that?" Winter asks.

"Her parents have money, Winter," Ethan says. "They've turned down my offer to fly her home and said they'll handle it. As for security, they don't trust us, and it's understandable. They're confused about what happened. Kurt was engaged to their daughter. They have a lot coming at them and don't know who to believe." Checking his phone, he starts texting. When he's done, he's distressed. "If they want my help, they'll have it."

"Thank you," Winter replies.

His attention is elsewhere. He starts typing again and then walks away. "I need to make a call. Are you staying?"

Putting the necklace over her head, I set it so the design faces out. "We're staying."

He nods. "Walk with me, Bennett." While heading toward the exit, he says, "Look, I need to get back tomorrow. Singer's not feeling well. She's with Hutton and Ally. They'll help her until I get back, but I want to be there for her."

"You should go if she needs you."

"I'll talk to the detective once more before I leave. By the way, one of the renters had a camera in the hall. We've been cleared of any wrongdoing."

"I was worried we'd be stuck here for a month dealing with it."

"Nope. You're free to go since you already gave your statement." He pats my back. "You doing all right?"

"Hanging in there."

"Don't hesitate to call if you need anything tonight."

"I won't and thanks for being here." I give him a hug, though we pat it out before it gets mushy.

"She's a good woman. Her heart is in the right place," he says.

"She is, and it is."

"You're a good man, Ben."

"I am," I say, laughing.

He steps back with a guard behind him. "Take care, little brother."

"You too, big brother." I shove my hands in my pockets and return to Winter. "I think I should wait in the room with you."

"I don't want to scare her. She doesn't know you."

"Still so stubborn, but you're probably right this time, so I'm not going to fight you on this."

"Really?"

"Yup. I'm too tired. I'm going right down that hall and sleeping. If you need anything, you know where to find me." I kiss her cheek and start walking. "And Victor is staying outside the door. Yell if you need him."

When I turn around, she calls, "Hey, you!"

"Yeah?" I ask, looking back with a raised brow.

"I love you, movie star."

"Good thing I love you too, or this would be awkward." She rolls her eyes and laughs. "Bonsoir, ma chérie."

36

Winter

When Chelsea stirs, I sit up. Her eyes open, and I move to her side. "Hi," I whisper.

"Hello," she says and then clears her throat.

I reach for the pitcher of water and pour some into a cup with a straw. "Here."

She takes a sip but starts coughing, a little water dribbling. A nurse rushes in and fusses about, so I step back and give her the room to work. When we're alone again, I stand by the bed and hold the railing.

She watches me. A lot like I've been watching her.

"How are you feeling?"

She grimaces. "Like I've been shot. Will I be okay?"

"Yes. The nurse was just here. The doctor will be in soon."

"Did you get hurt?"

"I'm fine. Bennett and Lars, the man who carried you, arrived and . . . well, they saved us from what could have been much worse," I say shakily. I've thought of the scene over and over again during the past however many hours, and I'm still trembling.

"And Kurt?" By the way her voice quivers, I know she doesn't really want to know the answer, but I just don't have it in me to lie anymore.

"We don't know where he went. But the police and the Everest security team are looking for him. They'll find him, Chelsea. They will."

She looks away for a moment, and I see her suck back a sob. So, I add, "I don't know if you want this, but you have a friend, Chelsea." She doesn't say anything, so I keep rambling, "If you want. There's no pressure—"

"I'd like that."

"You would?"

"Yes. You saved my life, Winter. But I don't understand why."

I've thought a lot about this over the past few hours, and I don't have an answer other than saying, "It was the right thing to do."

Her body lies so still that if the monitor wasn't beeping along to the beat of her heart, I'd be worried. "After I saw what he did to you, I tried to talk him into letting you go."

Standing there, I'm not sure what to say. *Thank you*? I don't know. My gut twists over this one.

She adds, "I believed his lies that you were the one stalking him. I wanted to believe anything he said. He loved me supposedly, but after he broke up with me at dinner, I saw you differently. I saw some of you in me. Once in love with a man you thought cared about you, but then discarded for someone else. I had no idea he could be so cold. So vicious."

"Is that why you came with me? Because you thought I was pathetic, and you didn't want to turn out like me?"

"No, I saw how strong you were." She struggles to take a

deep breath, and I know I need to let her rest rather than discuss all this. I'm about to get up when she says, "You gave me hope that I could be more than I was. I see what he sees in you."

"Who?"

"Kurt." She coughs. "You're more than a pretty shell. Your heart shines." I grab tissues for her and reach for the call button, but she stops me, glancing at the monitor. "I'm fine."

My fingers tighten around the rail, and my eyes well with tears. I tilt my head back, not wanting them to fall like the fool I am, but when I look at her again, two tears fall like heavy raindrops from my chin. Her hand covers mine. It's cold, but the emotion that comes with it is warm. "Thank you," she says.

"How can you thank me when you were shot?"

"I lived because I was shot. I'd be dead if I lived another day of that life." I cover her hand, and she adds, "So yes, I owe you a thank you."

I bend down and gently embrace her. "You're going to get through this."

"I hope."

"Hope is worth hanging on to." Standing up, I give her a sympathetic smile. "You should rest. Get better, Chels, and when you're up for it, call me when you're back in the city."

"I will, and Winter . . . Thank you for staying with me. So I wasn't alone."

I'm not sure if she's referring to the apartment or the hospital, but either way, I still want to hug her. So I do. She has so much to get through. *To live for.*

Just before I leave, she says, "Do you think you could put in a good word for me with Ally Everest. Kurt was the one to encourage me to work there. I now know for his own access to the Everests, and I'm afraid, me being selfish, I snubbed my nose to actually working for charity." Tears fill her eyes.

"But I've come to realize that everyone needs a hand every now and then. You gave me a second chance. Maybe I can help others get their second chance, too."

"Answering the helpline?"

She nods.

"I'll talk to her, but let's get you better first."

"Thank you."

I quietly exit the room, and Victor stands from leaning against the wall. Pointing toward the other room, I say, "I'm going back to the other room."

He asks, "Should I come with you or stay?"

The room is within sight. "Stay here to make sure she's safe. I'll be fine. I'm just going right there."

"Oui."

I walk down the hall. Victor's eyes are still on me, but when I see the bathroom, I detour. "I'll be quick." Inside, I bend down to check for feet in both stalls. All clear. Then, I mentally scold myself for being paranoid.

I can't walk around in life fearful that Kurt will find me. I can't let him control my life like that any longer. Stopping in front of the mirror, I take in the shocking sight of myself. Earlier, I purposely avoided the mirror, but now I can't avoid it anymore. I wet a paper towel and dab under my eyes. My makeup has long worn off, but residue remains. At least the bruising is receding. It's still ugly, but it should be gone soon.

Tossing the towel in the trash, I finger comb through my hair and then fluff. There's nothing else I can do to save it. It's just funny that Bennett still looks at me like I'm beautiful when I'm in such disarray.

The handsome charmer.

The thought of him makes me smile, and I realize that's all I need—him and the happiness he brings me. Ready to get back to the slumbering giant, I choose the second stall.

As soon as I push the door open, a hand clamps down over my mouth as I come face-to-face with Kurt.

I scream as my eyes go wide. The sound muffled as Kurt grabs the back of my head with his other hand and forces me backward at an aggressive speed too fast for me to grab hold of anything.

There's nothing to help me, my arms flailing until I reach out to push him away by the face. My body slams into a full-length mirror, and he releases me, letting me fall like rain to the ground. I cry out in pain as shards dig into my hands and knees.

"You turned your back . . . me. Dismissed my feelings . . . weren't good enough for you . . . *I* wasn't good enough . . . the nerve to take what's mine and turn her against me. Did you think . . . get away with it? Did you not learn your lesson the . . . "

Kurt's words are mumbled, my hearing going in and out. My head pounds from the impact, and I stay hunched over. *My back . . .*

Lifting my hands, glass stabs into my palms and blood runs down my wrists. He might have finally broken me into pieces like the slivers of mirror surrounding me.

I hurt everywhere, but he hasn't broken my will to survive. I'll never give him the satisfaction. Kicking me to the side with his foot, he says, "Get up, Winter. Get up."

His voice becomes clearer, his hateful words taking me back to when I first arrived in Paris. He wanted vengeance. I thought it was against his enemies, but it wasn't. It was against me.

I'm the only woman who ever left him. Though he filled me with shame, I still walked away. I left because I knew my deeds were never dirtier than the emotions he felt for me. The devil craves fire, and I was his flame.

He could never predict that his inflicted pain would

make me stronger. I'm not a flicker that will burn out. I'm the ember that rises from the ashes.

He plays rough.

He plays to win.

He plays for entertainment.

I look up at him, the man who claimed at one time to love me. He never hurt me until I was gone, until I was no longer his. I've choked on Kurt's hate, and then I tasted Bennett's love. I'll fight for love. I'll fight to win. "You won't kill me." There are no doubts. None. Bennett loves me. I know that with all my heart, so I'll fight.

"Yeah? Who says?" Kurt squats down and pats my head. "Who says, little girl."

Fight.

"Me." Snatching a piece of broken glass, I swing, cutting him across the neck, and then kick him away from me. Using the sink, I pull myself up but slip on the glass. I land hard with the corner of the porcelain jabbing into my stomach but catch myself before I fall. He roars and reaches for me, taking hold of my ankle and tugging.

One swift kick to the face with my free foot sends him rolling back again. I push off and run for the door despite the glass biting into my skin.

Bennett's smile, laugh, love—I fight for me, for my happiness. I fight for him.

"Help!"

Yanked backward by my hair into Kurt's arms, his hand covers my mouth while he holds a gun to my head. "What did I tell you about my property? No one touches what's mine in life or death."

Victor stands, flicking his eyes nervously between Kurt and myself, his shaking hands aiming a gun at me. The door across the hall swings open, and Lars and Bennett rush to a halt. Tears swell in my eyes as I stare into Bennett's. I close them, hoping to always hold on to the warmth his bring, letting his love wash over me.

"I'll kill her." Kurt's voice tremors for the first time ever. There's no way out, and he intends to take me down with him. My mind races as he moves into the hall, forcing me with him. "Keep your hands visible and stay back. If I die, she dies."

Bennett raises his hands, but his eyes never leave mine. *I love you* spoken freely between us, the sweet words silently shared over and over.

My feet slip, and his grip tightens around me, leaving bloody footprints in our wake. He's losing a lot of blood. *Good.*

Oh, God! Is it mine?

And then things seem to go in slow motion.

I'm pulled back as the metal shakes against my temple.

Such a big man when he's in control and a coward when he's not.

Hospital security runs down the hall but stops behind Victor.

One uses his radio, but the feedback makes it indecipherable.

I hear Bennett's growl. "I'll make sure you die a gruesome fucking death, McCoy."

I love you, Bennett Everest.

"You have to catch me first." *Not brave words. Words of a fool.*

And then everything speeds up again. When they're out of sight, I'm swung around, and with the gun still pressed to my head, he says, "Run."

I have two choices: Run and be shot by this maniac or fight for my life.

Strike

With all my might, I'm swift with my arm, swinging it
forward and jabbing my elbow back.

Fall

Kurt stumbles. I turn around with the glass still piercing my
hands and shove him as hard as I can.

Protect

Shots fire, and I duck, pieces of the ceiling falling around me.
I shield my head and run for cover.

Defend

Kurt rushes me, slamming into the door before I can open it. "We'll die together."

Time slows as the gun rises, our eyes locked on an eternity I refuse to live with this man. I take my last shot at living this life. Leaning in, I kiss his cheek to surprise him and grab the gun. "Not today. Not ever!" I drop to my knees and lean back with the gun pointed at his face.

"Ma princesse ténébreuse."

"The tables have turned."

37

Winter

Kisses cover my palm, and I open my eyes with a smile on my face even before I see who it is. I don't need to see Bennett because I feel him—the kisses and his love all over me—with me while I slept. "Why are you so sweet to me?"

He stares at me with half a smile and then gets up from the side of the bed and hugs me. I wrap my arms around his head and hold him. The attack, the almost being killed part of our evening, and the stress he must have felt when I was taken in New York are all taking a toll on him. The weight of his pain comes to rest on me, and I welcome it wholeheartedly if I can make my giant happy again.

When he tries to speak, he's too choked up and tucks his head into the nook of my neck. "Hey, look at me." Making eye contact, I see the shine in his eyes, and ask, "Are you okay, babe?"

"*Are you* is the question I should be asking."

"I am now." I caress his face with my bandaged hands.

"Everything's going to be okay. Have you been here all night?"

"Where else would I be?" He leans his forehead against mine. "Don't scare me like that again, okay, Rambo?"

The concussion Kurt caused was diagnosed as mild. I'm fortunate I didn't have more damage. I survived. I'll also survive a few little cuts and a mild concussion. "Tell me about it." I giggle, but that hurts the ribs on my backside, so I stop. That concern lingers in his eyes, so I smirk, and try for a joke. "Don't worry. I'm *pretty* okay."

He takes a deep breath while taking me in, then a chuckle follows. "What am I going to do with you?"

"Give me another chance?"

"Another chance? You've had me since the moment we met. I'm not getting rid of you, and there's no way in hell you're getting rid of me."

I look down, pulling at a loose thread on the blanket's edge. I can't play coy around him though. He has me wrapped around that big pinkie of his. "I've made a lot of bad decisions in my life, but you're the best decision I've made yet."

"Who's the charmer, now?"

"You. Always you."

"Nah. I have plenty of flaws."

"Like what?" I ask.

He kisses my hand before his confession. "Sometimes I leave the toilet seat up, but sometimes I remember what my mama taught me and put it down."

"Ugh. That's all you got?" I roll my eyes and laugh. "Humor me. What else?"

"I don't always use a chip clip before shoving the bag back in the pantry. And my brothers used to steal my fries, so they're sacred to me now."

"Your brothers or the fries."

"Ha! The fries," he jokes.

"You were willing to share with me."

"I'll let you have anything you want, sweetheart."

My cheeks feel hot, so I push down the covers on one side of my body. No relief. It's official. It's him. I adore him.

"What about your flaws? Got any?" he asks.

"Plenty. I brush my teeth four to five times a day."

"Is that really a flaw? C'mon. Give me something good."

"Okaaaay." I tap my upper lip a couple of times. He's transfixed, a smile hanging around like a drunken moon in his eyes. I'm not the only one who's smitten. "I pick at my cuticles when I'm nervous. I kick my shoes off and leave them wherever they land until I need them again. I save the wire hangers from the dry cleaners because I hate to throw anything away, and sometimes . . ." I suck in as deep a breath as I can without it hurting. "I read the end of a book first."

"Nooooo," he says sarcastically. "You rebel. Why do you think you do that?"

"If something happens to me before I read the whole book, I know where the characters are left in life. Hopefully, in their happily ever after." Pushing past the embarrassment, I add, "I also only read stories with a happily ever after, so there is that."

"Why do you only read happy endings?"

I take his hand and hold it on my lap. "Seems like a good way to go."

"You're not going anywhere if I have a say."

"Have I told you how much I love you?"

"Say it again."

"I love you, movie star."

Leaning down, he kisses my head. "Now that's the best confession of all. I love you, ma chérie."

"Bennett?"

My breathing comes staggered, regulated by fear. My heart races, and I try to get my bearings. The curtains aren't heavy enough to keep out the daylight. It slips through the crack of the blinds.

Clean lines.

Warm browns.

Home.

My love runs into the room, concern written all over his face. "What's wrong?"

I'm not sure how to answer. I used to be a lot more stubborn, feisty even. I've learned that I don't have to have my guard up at all times. I'm safe to lower my walls and let in loved ones.

Loved ones.

Loved *one.*

Bennett.

He comes to the side of the bed while I try to catch my breath. Sitting down with a sigh, he rubs my shoulder and leans in to kiss it before asking, "Another nightmare?"

"Yes." *Another* nightmare. The last week has turned my life upside down, more than it was already. Although we're back in Manhattan, my days and nights have been filled with visions of what happened. I can still feel the cold gun pressed to my head. I can smell the Scotch on Kurt's breath. I can see the blood that once covered my body. I keep experiencing the sensation that I can't get away, that I'm slipping on glass and blood. I hate it. I hate *him.*

I have another appointment scheduled to talk to somebody, somebody who didn't live through it, somebody who can hear my story and hopefully help me move past it one day.

There's still unfinished business that lingers like a wet shroud, a trial, blackness trying to snuff out our light. I was once a dark princess. I blamed myself for everything that happened, for causing a chain of events I attribute to wanting my father's approval. Through the pain and suffering I caused others, that I've caused myself, I'm finally ready to take responsibility for my part but not for the aftermath.

I look up at the man, a bright knight in shining armor, a giant in size and heart, a movie star in my sky, and I can't help but want for this to be over for him, for me, and for us. So I sit up and crawl into his lap, wrapping my arms around his neck. I don't lean my head on his shoulder. Instead, I look him straight in the eyes. "You made me a steak salad."

"Huh?" His nose crinkles in confusion, but I much prefer the smile that accompanies it to the concern that was there.

"The night we were attacked at your apartment, and we had to leave. You made me a carb-free dinner."

He laughs. "You caught that?"

"I did. I'm sorry we didn't get to eat it. It looked really good."

"Stop apologizing. You didn't mess up our dinner plans. You just made them a little more exciting."

I kiss those delectable lips and then whisper against them, "You made an effort for me. I've never had anyone care that much before."

"You're making me feel guilty."

Surprised, I tilt my head. "Why do you feel guilty?"

"Because it wasn't entirely for you. The meal was, but dessert . . . I bought brownies, and they're full of carbs, in hopes that you'd let me eat them off you."

Giggling, I raise an eyebrow. "You want to eat brownies off me? Isn't that a bit crumbly?"

"Mixed with whipped cream and . . . *fuck*. I'm getting hard."

"Who knew brownies were the way to your—" I clear my throat, feeling him harden beneath me. "Heart."

Kissing me below my ear, he knows the way to my . . . heart, too. "It's not the brownies getting me hard, sweetheart." Running a finger along the top of my breasts, he elicits a moan from deep within, making me crave more.

"Can we just stay here all day and ignore the rest of the world?"

"I wish we could."

The troubles of the world sneak back in to burst our bubble, and I rest my head on his shoulder. "How long until we leave?"

"Just over an hour."

"I guess I should get ready," I say, though I don't move a muscle. I want to stay here all day. The building may be the most secure location on earth—even more so with Ethan's *upgrade*—but Bennett's my safe place.

Standing, he doesn't release me until my feet are firmly on the ground. That's something I find myself doing less of lately. Bennett Everest keeps me floating on cloud nine. At one time, I was willing to do anything to save my family's fortune, money I realize they lost a long time ago. Before Bennett, money didn't bring anything but pain. Knowing I have him means more than having a check I can't cash. He believes in me. He loves me—flaws and all.

Just as I'm about to slip into the bathroom, he catches my hand and twirls me back into his arms. "I'm working in the living room if you need anything." I hate how he worries.

My sweet boyfriend can't help it with that big heart he carries around. I kiss him, and he grabs my ass. I swat him away before we lose an hour in the shower getting dirty. "For practically being strangers, you sure are handsy."

"You love my hands on you."

"I do. And your face." I could really use all of him on me and in me right now. "Do we have to go?"

He chuckles. "Yes, but once we're home, you're mine. All mine for the rest of the night."

"I can't wait." Giggling, I start the shower and then undress, but stop and hit the button to turn the glass from clear to private. This place is decked to the nines. I love it here with him, not only because of the security but because of the family. Although I don't share their last name, I've become one of them. They've accepted me with open arms, and that says a lot about how much they care for Bennett and his happiness.

Forgetting my hair clip on the nightstand, I open the door to the bedroom. I stop when I find him sitting on the bed, his head down, and holding my e-reader. Returning to him, I stand between his legs and lift his chin up. "What are you thinking about?"

Holding up the e-reader, he says, "You had to leave the books you love in Paris. And you haven't been back to your apartment here. Sometimes I wonder if you're happy. If you're really okay. With me." He always checks on me. I don't think I could sneeze right now without him making sure I don't need a visit to urgent care. It's wholly unexpected and has stolen my heart in the best of ways.

This is love. This is what love is made of. Love is Bennett.

"My books weren't collectibles, but novels I loved. I can buy more. Don't worry about me. I'm happy. Everything in Paris was just stuff. I brought what matters most back to New York. *You*. You make me happy. You make me feel safe."

His arms come around me, and he pulls me in to kiss my belly. "We can thank my brother for the security."

"I meant my heart, my soul, my well-being is safe in your arms. I'm spoiled."

"And I plan to spoil you rotten."

"Like you." I laugh.

"Yes, just like me." He stands, kissing my head. "Go

shower. I have work to do and then I think we should pay your place a visit."

My whole body sighs under the weight of that thought. I've put it off, but he's right. "All right, but I don't want to stay long. I love it here and now that it's more secure than ever, thanks to Ethan, I want to come back and cuddle for a while."

"I'll make sure to tell him how much we appreciate it, but Ethan lives for the security stuff. So figuring out how to lock down the building was a challenge he got to geek out on and get done in record time. His brain works in crazy ways."

I linger in the doorway to the bathroom. "I can't say I'm not impressed. Not only are the windows coated in mesh made from some kind of extraterrestrial technology," I tease, "but the steel panels installed mean business. Yep, I must say you Everests are impressive."

"*We* Everests?" he challenges with a look that begs to play.

I don't want to be late, though, so I feed the ego. "You, babe. *You* are impressive."

"I thought that's what you meant." He chuckles as he leaves the room, but I hear him in the hall as he walks away. "Fifty-four minutes. Shake that sweet ass, sweetheart."

This apartment was the first finished and Bennett included me when we could move back in as if I'd always lived there. Ally and Hutton's place is supposed to be done today. It will take a couple of weeks to finish making the security adjustments to the penthouse. They're staying in safe locations until the apartments are cleared for them to move back in. Every pane of glass on the top two floors will have a steel panel that slides down when something gets within twenty feet of the building up here.

I pray it never comes to that, but I feel positive about healing the wounds that caused my claustrophobia. I just chalk it up to go along with all the other damage Kurt caused and make sure I'm not only honest with myself about where to place the blame but to talk truthfully with Bennett and my therapist when those fears arise.

The box from my father had photos from my childhood, my mom growing up, her wedding pictures, and Braden as a baby. Broken glass from a framed picture of my mom holding me as a baby is scattered at the bottom. I dusted it off and put it in an album.

I try not to let my heart ache, but I'm mourning all three of their deaths these days. It's easier to think of them gone forever than to think of them at all.

When McCoy Properties filed bankruptcy a few days ago, Ethan bid and won a portion of their Manhattan portfolio, including the building across the street from The Everest.

In a stroke of irony, the properties were sold the same day Kurt was denied bail for being a flight risk and locked in a French jail awaiting trial.

I'm not sure about the amenities or quality of life in a French prison, but I suspect it will be nicer than he deserves. I have never wished ill will on anyone before, but he and my brother are tied these days.

Journaling has helped to make sense of everything that's happened to me. Seeing it on paper gets it out of my head. Reading my story makes it clear how easily they manipulated me. I regret ever walking into the McCoy offices, but the shame rests squarely on my father's shoulders.

Kurt sang to the police the first night he was arrested in hopes of a reduced sentence. They hadn't offered a plea bargain, but he was still begging for his freedom as if he could persuade them. He's met his match.

I received a message the following afternoon from Lars. My father and Braden had been arrested that morning for kidnapping, conspiracy to commit a felony, and a list of other charges I lost track of. It didn't take long for Braden to make his one call. With the company funds cut off and his inheritance burned through, I sent the call to voicemail.

I never heard from my father.

The evidence the police have gathered so far will put them both away for a very long time. They just spent all the money they have on bail, so getting an experienced lawyer is out of reach.

It may have taken me years to realize, but now that I see I was never going to get the love I deserved from him or be treated as an equal to my brother, I knew what I had to do. I've realized that their love is conditional. Unlike the Everests' love—unconditional. So I have a process to follow.

Acknowledge the problem.

Address it.

Solve it.

Survive it.

I've done the first two. Now it's time for the last two.

Under the shower spray, I wash my body and exhale, reminding myself to breathe. Don't let the betrayal win. I'm healing through love, but I will not give another second of my time to their hate. They will never change, so I have to.

38

Winter

It's been almost two months since I've been here and now nothing about this apartment feels like me anymore. The deep yellow couch and rich violet velvet drapes, the brushed bronze lamp, and the turquoise accents are so pretty, each piece chosen to make a statement. I bought it all, paid for it with my hard work and long hours, but now it reminds me of the apartment in Paris.

Too busy.

Too cluttered.

Too much of everything.

A pretty bow on the shell of the life I was leading.

A facade.

I prefer clean lines and warm leather these days. Sunlight that brings out the gold in soulful eyes and arms that wrap their love around me.

I was always searching for something to make me feel whole, to make me feel loved, to make me feel anything but shame in what I'd done. I never found it in a man, especially not the ones who were supposed to protect me. I found who I was when I turned toward the sun, soaking in his rays.

Bennett Everest walked right up to that table and into my life. He didn't accept anything less than all of me and loved me more for it.

That's a real man.

So I'll spend my life giving thanks in the ways he deserves —kisses, support, laughter, and love. I turn to find him waiting by the door as if needing an invitation. He's invited into my life. Wherever I go, I want him with me.

I pause knowing someone else has been here. My belongings touched. This feeling in my gut twists, but I carry on. Get in. Get out. I empty the basket of mail I've collected while I was gone onto the coffee table. "This place feels like a betrayal to what we're building together."

"Our life," he says, not missing a beat. He walks around, looking at the décor and the few photos I have displayed on the coffee table. Picking up my favorite, he says, "I like this one of you and your mom. We should put it in our living room." Glancing up, he holds it out for me.

"Just like that, you want my stuff mixed with yours?"

A question was never asked or a conversation had about moving in with him. We just fell into a life together. It's a life I don't ever want to fall out of. It's a relationship I'm willing to work for when the honeymoon dating stage is over.

"Just like that."

I want to hug him, bury myself in his arms, and disappear for a little while. "I'd like that very much."

"You can bring anything you like. I want your input. I want your touch. I was even thinking we could put a few photos of us around the place." The simple offer awakens a swarm of butterflies in my stomach. After setting the frame down, he sits on the couch. "I want it to feel like your home as much as mine. I know you didn't choose it, but it's safe and—"

"I love it there. I do feel safe, and we have great neighbors." Moving around the sofa, I wrap my arms around his middle and look up at him.

"We do." His smile makes my heart happy. He also makes it incredibly hard to stay on task. "I'll look around for a few items I want to keep, but I've lived without most of it for so long, I think I'm ready to get rid of everything."

"What about the apartment itself?"

"Including that. It's time to close the door forever." I shuffle through the mail that arrived after I was kidnapped that night. Just acknowledging that I was taken is another step on the healing staircase. I had my rights taken away, my choice, my life. "It's time to part ways. So you're totally good with having a full-time roommate?"

He sits back patiently. "If it's you, I've been all in since the moment I saw you in that pink sweater at the bistro."

"I was wearing pink?" The sweetness causes me to stay because I don't want to miss a word of this.

"I remember thinking you were the only thing I saw under that overcast sky. A burst of color on a rainy day."

"You need to stop being so romantic, or we're going to be stuck here hours longer than planned."

Sitting forward, ready to leap at an invitation, he asks, "In bed?"

I burst out laughing as I continue to sort the mail. "Later. We have work to do."

"What's this?" I look over at the envelope in his hands. Three addresses, crowd the front, and two red undeliverable stamps.

"Huh." I take it from him and turn it over several times. The date is from December of last year. "I'm not sure, but someone has tried to get it to me for almost a year now." I rip it open while reading the different stamps and the addresses marked on it. "This was delivered to the house where we lived with my mom. Then it was sent to the apartment where my father raised us. I guess Fred turned it away."

"Interesting. It finally made it here."

"The return address is a lawyer's office." I pull out the paper inside and unfold it. The first thing that catches my eyes is a silver key. My mouth falls open because so much makes sense now. "This is what my father wanted from me."

"What is it?"

"The missing key to the locket." Tears flood my eyes when I see my mom's signature at the bottom of the letter written on a lawyer's letterhead. The law office sounds vaguely familiar, but I'm more interested in the letter itself to dwell on it. Covering my mouth, I silently read:

Dearest Winter,

Happy Birthday, my sweetest daughter. This letter is to find you on your 25th Birthday, so if you're reading it, that means it made it safely to you.

I want you to know that you will always be with me, and I will always be with you. Ring the bell and I'll be near.

Stay the warrior I know you were born to be, strong and brave like I raised you because sometimes life doesn't turn out the way we plan. If that happens, here's the key to set them straight again.

I love you,
    Mom

· · ·

Shifting the paper from my lap, a tear just misses it. "My mom was amazing."

"You got more than her looks."

I feel strong, stronger than I've felt in years because of this man sitting next to me and my mom always being in my heart. Despite the bad that's happened, I feel like the luckiest woman alive.

I pull the key off gently, not wanting the tape to rip the paper.

Bennett peeks at me. "You're not wearing the necklace."

"No, but I want to try the key as soon as we get home."

"We can go whenever you're ready."

I read the letter one more time before folding it and tucking it back into the envelope. "Be right back."

In my bedroom, bras, panties, and shoes are strewn across the bed. Makeup scattered on the vanity. Purses on the floor. I didn't leave it like this, so someone has rifled through my belongings. I can't see the fingerprints of the burglar, but I feel violated the same as if he touched me himself. The saddest part is I don't know who to blame—my father, Braden, or Kurt. How did I ever accrue so many enemies?

"None of this stuff matters," I remind myself. "It's just stuff."

"Find what you need?" I glance over my shoulder to find Bennett just inside the room and nod. He looks around, but his eyes are quick to return to me. "Let's not stay long." He's kind enough not to amp up my fears.

"Yes, I agree." When he returns to the living room, I move into the closet and bend down, shifting a box of socks out of the way. It's a good hiding spot, and I can tell before I find what I'm looking for that they never found it. I pull a dark wood box not bigger than a shoebox out and smile. My mother's jewelry box was given to me before she died. We used to pull every piece of jewelry out and wear it all at once.

Most of her jewelry was inherited, but my father did buy her a few pieces. I lift the lid and pull out the broach. He gave this to her on the day my brother was born. I always loved it. Diamonds and pearls. She never got a gift for my birth because of his disappointment but look who won in the end.

I return to the living room with the box in hand and sit down next to Bennett on the couch. I've come to recognize that look in his eyes, the one that worries about me, so I reassure him before he has a chance to ask. "I'm okay."

He nods, accepting that answer at face value. When I stand, he does as well, picking the picture frame up from the table again, and asks me, "Got everything you want?"

Taking his hand, I lead him to the door. "I have everything I need."

My hands are shaking, but not from fear.

"A key, huh?" Ally asks, resting her elbows on the kitchen island.

Bennett rubs my back but doesn't say anything. He understands the significance of what this means to me.

I ready myself and then insert the key into the bottom of the locket and turn gently. The lock releases silently, but I can feel it give and the back pops open just enough for me to wedge the sides apart. Inside is the tiniest capsule I've ever seen.

"It was there all along. That's what made it ring," Hutton says.

"Metal against metal," I say, touching it with the tip of my finger.

Ethan had an overseas call and excused himself, but

Bennett, Ally, Hutton, and I stand around the kitchen island, staring at the little treasure.

Bennett leans down to get a closer look. "So the key was never lost. Your mother just waited until the right time to give it to you."

"My twenty-fifth birthday," I say, holding the capsule in the palm of my hand.

Hutton leans in and says, "Whatever is in there must be important to wait this long."

Ally's arm comes around me. "This was meant for you, a gift from your mother."

Quietly to myself, I whisper the words of my mother, "Ring the bell and make a wish. You'll receive what you need. *Huh.* Not what I *want*, but what I *need*. What do I need?" I've never taken the words to heart. *Until now.*

His scruff is thicker today, and his eyes deep in thought as he rolls the locket around in his hand. "Browning. I was sure the jeweler's stamp on the back meant something."

Ally rests her hip against the stone top counter. "The answers you need might be in there, Winter." The attention turns to the princess who's become a cherished friend and already like a sister to me.

"Why am I scared?"

She says, "We're here for you, but I have to tell you that I'm dying to solve this mystery." She fists her hands into balls and shivers excitedly. "Come on. Open it."

I unscrew the little metal container and pull out a piece of paper. Flattening the rolled-up strip on the counter, we all lean in, and then I gasp. "Is that an address?"

"It is," Bennett says, grinning. "Come on. Let's go solve a mystery."

39

Winter

Excitement fills the air as the four of us head for the door. I pull the purse strap over my head and anchor it on my hip. "You guys are cracking me up."

Hot on my heels, Ally says, "This is fun. We're like the Scooby Gang, solving mysteries and fighting crime together."

Hutton looks at her quizzically. "You watched *Scooby Doo* growing up?"

"No. We didn't get it in my country." She shrugs. "But it comes on one of the cartoon channels here and I lost three hours to the gang the other day."

"Fighting crime, um, yeah, let's not encourage Winter." Bennett holds the door open with a grin. "I'm hanging up her superhero cape. I'm quite fond of her in one piece."

Elbowing him in the stomach playfully when Ally passes, she says, "So protective these days."

"I have a lot to protect." And there's that wink that makes me smile.

"Such a flirt," I add with a tug of his shirt.

While Hutton deals with the security to get us in the elevator, Bennett envelops me in his big arms. "Oui, oui, mademoiselle."

"I dressed up as a French maid for you one time, and it's forever going to haunt me."

"I was referencing our time in Paris, not the other night."

My cheeks flame and I giggle. "Ah. Most of Paris was good." Ally laughs, and as we descend to the garage, Hutton holds her and kisses her on the head. These Everests sure know how to charm a girl and win her heart. I add, "Oops. Pretend you never heard that."

"Too late," Hutton groans. "It's seared into my memory. Not what I want to know about my little brother."

"Not so little," Bennett banters.

"Let's not go there," he counters while we laugh.

We enter the garage to find the waiting SUV. With Kurt's and my family's situation not settled, we still take precautions. You know, like riding around in bulletproof vehicles. Normal stuff like that. I shake my head because nothing is normal about my life these days.

Hutton gets in first and then Ally. I wait until after her, the memories of being snatched through the door too vivid to wash away some days. Another issue I'm working through with my therapist. It's only been a couple of sessions, but she says I'm making progress, so I lay my faith in the process and Bennett to help get me through the tough times. It's incredible to have people I can rely on and confide in. I've not had that in a long time.

Driving through Manhattan, we already know where we're headed. Bennett places a call, settling my anxious heart. I feel at home with them and savor the sound of the banter and laughter that fills the car as it fills my soul right along with it. It's only been a short time, but these are more than friends. They're my family.

"Winter?"

"Yeah?" I turn to Bennett who's standing on the sidewalk with a hand out.

"We're here."

"Oh." I slide out. "I was lost in my thoughts." While the others get out of the SUV, I look up at the New York Public Library. "Will they let us in?"

"We're about to find out."

The four of us head inside and wind our way to The Berg Collection Reading Room. I stand admiring the room with Ally when she whispers, "Singer would love the smell."

"I do, too. Old books, paper, history. It's all here. I wish I could bottle it."

When Hutton and Bennett return, Hutton says, "They usually only allow access by appointment only."

"Oh, no. Will they not let us look?"

Bennett steps up as a woman waves us over. "I made a call on the way over. I also made a large donation in your mother's name."

"You did?" A sweet ache heats the middle of my chest, a lump forming in my throat. I lean against his chest, my head down. His generosity never ceases to amaze me. "Thank you."

Rubbing my back, he leans down. "It's for a good cause."

Two hours later, we're still stumped. The librarian has been happy to help, but we're out of ideas when she comes back to check on us. "We close in an hour. How are you doing?"

"Nothing makes sense," I say, rubbing my temples. "Why would my mom send me here?"

She leans in and looks at the locket on the table between us. "This is very pretty."

"Thank you." The key dangles from the chain, but I slide it to the side to turn the locket over and set it next to the capsule and piece of paper. "My locket had this address hidden inside. So we thought there would be a clue to help us, but we're still baffled"

"May I?" she asks, taking the locket in hand. "It's Victorian in design. So lovely." Turning it over, she reads the stamp, "Browning. Elizabeth Barrett Browning. She lived during the Victorian era." While she's talking, I shoot a glance to Bennett whose smug grin says it all. He did know. "We have some of her poems in our collection and have copies of her published books, though they don't have monetary value. We have them for reference purposes."

I stand, my fingers pressed against the solid wood of the table. "May I see them?" I grab the piece of paper with the address on it and follow her to her desk. While she types into her computer, I look at the scrap again. "She would have never ruined a book of value, a first edition. But she might if it's a newer copy." The librarian eyes me disapprovingly. "My mom loved to read."

That seems to satisfy her, and she stands. "I'll be right back with the books."

I return to the table and sit, my knee bouncing anxiously. "This is it. I know it."

Holding up her crossed fingers, Ally says, "I feel it, too."

The librarian sets a small stack on the table, then moves her eyes from the scrap to the books. "The paper looks similar to Browning's most popular book of poetry. This particular book is used for research if anyone needs it. I don't think I've ever had anyone ask for it, though since it's not a collector's edition."

"This would have been eighteen years ago or longer."

"Ah," she says, "I've been here twelve."

My heart starts racing as she fans the pages with her

thumb. "Here we are. 'Sonnets from The Portuguese XLIII.' A perfect match." She presses down on the page. "I'm not sure if I should be thrilled to solve the puzzle or charge you for the damage."

When she starts to laugh, the others do as well, but I'm too stunned to react. "A perfect match," I say, looking at the scrap and how it fits the page. Taking the book, I read the poem, though I know the words by heart, "How do I love thee? Let me count the ways. My mom used to recite this to me while we painted each other's nails." I didn't know I had any more tears left to cry, but happy tears bubble up from the memory.

Bennett moves his chair closer and wraps his arm around me. "I love you."

Too choked up to say anything, I stare at his hand covering mine and relish his love.

He leans forward, squinting his eyes. "What's that?" Pointing at the open page. I bend over the table to take a closer look. Written along the inside crease of the spine are tiny words in ink. "That's a bank!" Bennett says.

"A bank? What is that number after it?" I ask.

Ally says, "A box. A safe deposit box."

Bennett's chair tips back when he bolts upright. He's quick to pick it up and grab my hand. "We have to go."

The librarian startles but picks up the book and hands it to me. "Take it. We can replace it."

"Thank you. Thank you so much for helping us!"

Holding the book to my chest, we rush from the library to the SUV parked one block down. The bank is in the Financial District, and we're hitting rush hour traffic. Tucked inside the vehicle, I say, "Now I'm stressed."

"We'll make it," Bennett replies.

The fun we had on the way to the library has turned serious heading to the bank. It's not like we can't go tomorrow, but if we can make it today, we'll know our next move as opposed to running through imaginary scenarios all night if we don't.

As if my mom works her magic, the traffic clears in our lane, and we cruise through the green lights. At the curb, we file out, and I hurry inside with fifteen minutes to spare before closing. "Hi, where do I go for safe deposit boxes?"

The guard directs us to a desk, but when I look back, Bennett and the others have stayed behind. He says, "This is all you."

I want to shout my love for this man from the rooftops, but I don't have a moment to spare, so I'll show him later. As soon as a banker greets me, I say, "I have a bank deposit box."

She smiles. "I'll be happy to help you. What's the number and name?"

"1753." I go with my mom's name. "Nora Nobleman."

She types in the information and then peeks up at me. Types some more and then leans toward me from the other side of the desk. "Do you have a key and ID?" *Damn it.*

"I have my ID. Nora's my mother. She passed away."

"I'm sorry for your loss." I take it as a good sign that she's still waiting for my ID.

I dig it out of my purse and set it between us. She analyzes it while I add, "I don't have a key."

Pushing my ID back, she digs a key from the back of the drawer, and says, "It's password protected. Do you know what you need?"

"What I need?"

"That's the question I'm supposed to ask you, Ms. Nobleman," she replies with an endearing smile.

What I need . . . *like in the phrase.* I roll the question around in my head, trying to remember everything my mother ever said to me. "Love? Mother? Mom? Nora? Am I limited?"

"I'm not a computer," she says with a sympathetic laugh. "We're only limited by the bank closing. Unfortunately, we close in ten minutes."

I tap my nails nervously on the desk. "My name?"

"No, I'm sorry."

Help me, Mom. What do I need? She didn't know Bennett. I look back and see the others waiting patiently. I don't want to disappoint them. What can it be? The click of my nails draws my attention, and I see the polish I had painted again the other day, "Stay the warrior you were born to be. Warrior blue. I need to be strong. I need to be a warrior."

She pushes the key over to me and stands. "You'll have privacy in the room, but please note we close in a few minutes."

"Wait, what?" I pop up from the seat. "What did I say? Strong? Blue?" I gasp. "Warrior? Oh, my God!" Tilting my head back, I whisper, "Thank you, Mom."

"Yes, Ms. Nobleman. Right this way."

Looking back at Bennett, Ally, and Hutton, I jump and squeal, totally giddy. "Yes!"

I'm given a round of applause and take a bow. "I knew you could do it," Bennett says.

We did it, Mom, I praise, my heart full knowing she's been with me all along.

I'm quick to the room, knowing I only have two minutes. Locating the box, I stick the key in, my mind going wild with what could be inside. After I set the heavy metal box on the table, I lift the lid while holding my breath.

Then I release it, deflated when I find another envelope from the same law firm. "Okay, what is this?" Opening it, I pull out the folded letterhead and spread it flat on the table, reading it slowly.

And then again. Until the security guard knocks on the door. "Closing time."

I glance from him back to the paper, reading the title once more before I fold it and stuff it back into the envelope. I don't know what to think, and I'm too nervous to assume it's what I think it is.

When the glass door opens, I rush from the room and straight into Bennett's arms. "You will never believe it."

40

Bennett

Night surrounds the legal offices of Everest Enterprises, and I keep the blinds closed because I don't want anyone to see us in here. I also keep Winter away from the windows.

"I've put in a call to Mrs. Nobleman's lawyer," says Reegan, Everest Enterprises' lead legal eagle. "He drafted the document, not leaving any room for interpretation. It's straightforward. Based on the legal language, if Winter claims her rights under this document, she'll own Nobleman Inc."

This confirms what we suspected. Winter hasn't said much in the past ten minutes as shock fully sets in. Still staring at the paper, she finally exhales. "Um . . . huh."

Ally smiles and leans over. "Winter?"

"Yes?" She glances over at her.

"Do you have any questions?"

"I do." She looks at Reegan. "Do you mind repeating it for me?"

Laughing, he replies, "Not at all. So this paragraph says that Nora Nobleman grants her stake in the corporation to the sole designated receiving party. This is where your name, Winter Renee Nobleman, has been filled in. This document is signed by her, your father, her lawyer, and has been notarized. It's official and will hold up in court."

"And that means?"

"That means if you sign here, you accept the agreement and can enforce it." He glances at Winter, and then continues, "This paragraph notes that if you deem the company is not being held to previous standards of better business set forth in this paragraph—mishandling of funds, treatment of employees, poor decisions and bad deals, you can take back the rights from the current CEO and dismiss him without severance. How has the company been performing? Do you have data from the past five years?"

Winter grins. "I sure do."

Her stint as a corporate spy with insider information has finally paid off.

She rests her elbow on the desk and gives the document a closer look. The office is so quiet I can hear her whispering to herself as she rereads each line. Again. Finally, she angles toward me, and says, "We have some firing to do."

I chuckle. "We do indeed."

"I remember when I showed up the Monday after I graduated with my briefcase in hand, my résumé tucked inside, and a head full of optimism." She glances up at me. "I thought for sure I had done everything right. I thought my father would finally see me as an asset to the team."

I ask, "What happened?"

"I did everything the right way by setting up an appointment with HR and letting him know I was taking the opportunity seriously." She looks down at the file in her hand. "He wouldn't take the meeting, and he told human resources to cancel theirs after they kept me waiting for two hours. For two hours, I sat inside those doors, making the receptionist uncomfortable with my presence as the family battle played out before her."

"What an asshole."

We waited until morning to take this next step. It's a doozy for her. She drags the locket back and forth on the chain, and says, "You know what the worst part was? I actually believed him. He told me if I got the degree he wanted me to, the internships, and worked hard to pay my extra expenses, I would earn a place at the company. I did it all and still wasn't accepted like my brother was without doing half as well."

"You did it for you. Not him. You were proving you could. If he couldn't see the value in what you had to offer, it's his loss. But this will ultimately be his biggest loss of all. He's about to lose his company, but more importantly, he loses you."

"You're an incredible man. You've given me your support from the moment we met. With you, I feel like my old self, a better version, and that feels damn good. So thank you."

I gently massage her neck and then kiss her head. "I would have never let you slip into the competition's hands. Not in business or personally. One of the things that first struck me about you was your obvious intelligence. As I've gotten to know you, I'm in awe of your gutsy attitude, your passion, your need to fight for what's right. Your compassion for Chelsea is admirable. To help her wasn't a choice for you. It was simply what you did. You, Winter, are an asset in so many ways, one I always intend to cherish."

The elevator doors open, and Ethan arrives with Reegan, Aaron, and Lars.

Winter asks, "I've been thinking about last night. I stayed

up all night reading and rereading every line in this document. My father's signature means he acknowledged the agreement. Why would he do that?" I sigh, blowing out a bit of frustration. "I worry I might never know since my mother can't tell me, and there's no one else listed. Did you find out anything else?"

Ethan moves around to the front. "Once we knew where to look, we discovered more."

"Of course," I say, "skeletons aren't meant to stay buried when covered in lies."

Reegan hands Ethan an envelope. Ethan pulls the papers out and shows them to her. "Your mother and father started the company as partners and shared fifty-fifty. She worked there until she had children and then decided to stay home. Your father would run the day-to-day operations, but big decisions would be made jointly. The initial contract was amended when she took a step back to include that her approval was needed regarding decisions involving one million dollars or more."

She takes the papers from him and smiles, pointing at her mother's signature. "She had such pretty handwriting. It matched her heart." After a quick pause, she says, "I'm catching the drift. Basically, he made decisions without her approval, which puts him in violation of the amended contract, giving me the right, as her designated representative, and the power to end his reign."

"That's correct," Reegan says. "And since the profits have been squandered for personal gain, that's how we double down on the claim. This contract gives you full ownership, including the debt, unfortunately." He glances at Ethan and takes a step back. "And there's a lot of debt."

The silent exchange is not subtle, but then Ethan says, "Not more than the company is worth, though, so that's good."

I say, "They tried to have a sister and a daughter killed for whatever's left. Life never meant anything to them."

"*My* life never meant anything to them." She presses to the side of me, quietly studying the company name in silver lettering on the bleached wood doors.

I take her hand. "This isn't going to be easy, Winter, but you're not doing it alone."

Ethan steps toward the doors. "We should probably go in and take care of business while the element of surprise is on our side. Are you ready?"

"I don't think my mom's lawyer is coming, so I'm ready." She lifts up on her toes and kisses me. "You'll have my back?"

"Always."

Winter hands the paperwork back to Ethan while holding the copy of the contract she found in the safe deposit box. She opens the door. The receptionist looks up in surprise to see the crowd, her eyes darting among us. "May I help you?"

She doesn't even know who Winter is, for fuck's sake. I have to remind myself not to punch her father's and brother's fucking lights out when I see them. Winter says, "I'm here to see my father, Ross Nobleman."

"Oh. Um . . ."

"Winter Nobleman."

"Is he expecting you?"

"No. He never saw me coming."

She picks up the phone, but Winter is quick to cover her hand. With a smile, she says, "I want to surprise him."

"I don't think that's a good idea."

Winter heads for the glass double doors and pulls them open. "Don't worry. This won't take long."

Winter leads the way through the cubicles and past a row of offices with large windows. When I look back, Aaron is keeping the receptionist company. More importantly, he's keeping her from giving a warning.

Winter stops at the door and knocks once before walking in. "Hello."

Her father looks up and frowns. First, his gaze lands on the locket, then drifts from her to me, and to the others as we all file into his office. "Leave the door open," I say.

"What are you doing here?" he asks. Wow. He just does not give a fuck. Crazy. If she weren't so strong, I'd worry about her reaction, but my warrior is fierce. She's weathered worse than the contempt on his face.

She moves in even closer, standing on the other side of his desk. "You couldn't find what you were looking for. But guess what? I did. Right here in this memento. Mom has always been watching over me. Something you never did."

His feigned innocence doesn't bode well for him. "That necklace is a piece of junk."

"Junk that's worth a lot . . . worth everything really. To you and to me."

Trying to intimidate her, he stands, presses his hands to the desk, and raises his voice. "What are you getting at, Winter? Say it and get out."

She pops the paper open in front of her and holds it so he can see for himself. "The truth always comes out, and it has. You need to vacate the premises in five minutes or I'm calling the police."

Snatching it away, he reads. "What is this?"

"Your execution."

He balls up the paper and throws it at her face. *Fuck him.* I rush to knock him on his ass, but Lars and Ethan grab my arms, holding me back. "She can handle this," Ethan says.

Her father laughs. "Yes, keep your animal under control."

Winter hasn't moved. She never even flinched when the

paper hit her. What kind of life has she had that she doesn't even react to his hostile act? "Winter?"

She angles back. "It's okay. It's just taking him a minute to process that his life is over. I've had years to get used to his absence. I can spare him the time to realize what he's losing."

Nobleman laughs again, but it never reaches his eyes. He knows he's in trouble. He looks at me, and says, "You can have her, Everest. She's no good just like her mother." Directing his hate back to Winter, he adds, "I married her for money and got it all, every last cent her family left her." He grabs his jacket and slips it on. "You coming in and claiming the company means nothing. A contract I signed under coercion will never hold up in court."

"And how exactly were you coerced?"

He takes his phone from the top of the desk, and replies, "She caught me in bed with another woman, a younger more beautiful woman." Winter's indifferent expression slips, but he continues, "She was going to die anyway."

"Shut your mouth." Her voice is steady, but I see how her hands tremble. God, I want to help her, but she's a warrior, and this is her dragon to slay.

"What's the big deal? She wasn't meeting my needs. That's grounds for divorce. I saved her the embarrassment."

Winter rushes toward him, but I catch her before she makes it across the top of the desk. "It's okay, sweetheart. He's not worth our energy." Holding her around the waist, I can feel every heavy breath of hers. I hold my mouth to her ear, and whisper, "Tell him the good news."

A knock on the door draws our attention. Aaron appears with an older gentleman in a gray suit. The man says, "My apologies. Traffic is brutal today." He holds up a file. "I brought the contracts, and my signed affidavit confirming that both parties were in their right mind when they signed the agreement."

Her father looks as if he's seeing a ghost. Guess he is in a way. *His past.* It's come back to haunt him. This is how karma should work.

Calmer, Winter says, "My mother may have put up with your shit, but she ensured I wouldn't have to. As her designated representative, I have the right to take the company away from anyone mishandling it."

"You can't do that." He has the balls to cackle.

"I can. And I am. You may have seen me as a nuisance, but my mother raised a warrior. Your five minutes is up. Get out."

Their eyes stay locked for a time, but the chicken shit turns away first and starts rummaging through his desk.

Reegan clears his throat. "That's company property."

A vein bulges in her father's forehead as he glares at him. He finally walks to the door. "You'll be hearing from my lawyer."

"I look forward to it," Winter replies, following him out. "If you can afford one."

Braden comes running down the hall. "What the hell is going on?"

"You're fired," Winter says, and then snaps.

"You can't do that!"

Reegan holds up the balled-up paper. "She can as the rightful heir and owner," he says.

Her father grabs Braden by the arm, treating him like the toddler he is. "Come on. There's so much debt that no one is getting paid, much less her."

He catches up to his dad, a worried wobble to his tone. "I don't understand. Why does she get the company?"

"Shut up, Braden."

Her brother circles back and charges Winter. "Fuck that bitch!"

Just before he reaches her, I hold up my hand, letting his

throat meet my palm. I push back and then squeeze. "Assault is a violation of your bail."

Grabbing his arms and yanking them behind his back, Aaron subdues him and slams him down on the ground. "Oops. He fell." I suppress a laugh. With a knee to his back, Aaron says, "Call the police."

While Ethan makes the call, I walk over, putting the toe of my shoe right under Braden's nose. "Better get used to this position. Have fun in jail, fuck face."

Winter stands alongside me. Although we're all enjoying the power play, she squats down and tilts her head to the side to match his. "The worst part is I can't even shed a tear for you anymore."

"I don't need your fucking tears."

"How about my help?"

His expression morphs. *Pitiful.* He actually looks hopeful. "You'd do that?"

Winter stands back up. "No. You're an asshole."

Her father hightailed it before Braden hit the carpet. It's okay. Jail will sort him out as well.

She walks away and we follow, but Winter stops outside the door, looking around at the employees. "Are you all right?" I ask.

"He's such an asshole."

"He is." Braden Nobleman makes me thankful for my brothers. Sure, we give each other shit, but we always have each other's backs.

"You know," she adds, her nose scrunched. "I thought I'd feel more satisfied, but no matter how much I wish he cared, he just doesn't, and that's the harsh reality."

"Maybe the grand finale will give you peace of mind." I take her hand, and we start walking.

"What's that?"

We make it outside the building just in time to see them

being led away by the police. When her father sees her, he yells, "You slut! You're having me arrested?"

She shrugs. "Oops."

Curse words are slung her way as we walk down the sidewalk toward the car. "How did that feel?"

"Very satisfying." She smirks. "Even though it was her husband and son, I think my mom would be proud of me."

I kiss her hand. "She would be so proud of the woman you've become. And let's face it, I'm a catch, so she'd love me, too."

Giggling Winter is one of my favorite sides of her. "Okay, movie star. You win. You're quite the catch, and I fell for you the moment I saw you fake eyeing those macarons in the window."

"You caught that, huh?"

"I caught you, which is better than any cookie."

I chuckle. "Is this how life is always going to be with you?"

She winks. "Pretty much. Is that okay?"

"Pretty okay indeed for practically a stranger."

"I can live with pretty okay." I hold the door open for her as she climbs in, and asks, "What about awesome?"

"You're right." I pop an imaginary collar. "Awesome just feels better." I climb in, and Lars shuts the door behind us before loading in the front.

Rolling her eyes, she laughs. "You're nuts, you know."

"Nuts for you." I shake my head at myself. "That was so bad."

"It was, but you're still just as charming." She rubs my leg. "So what do we do now?"

"I have a few ideas."

41

Winter

I didn't expect to spend June in Paris, but here we are. Again, I can't say by choice. Kurt McCoy's trial has lasted for almost two weeks. While his lawyer dragged me and whatever reputation I had through the mud, I had to sit there and take it from him, like I always did.

This time though, I will win. Just like how I won Nobleman Inc. I was traded to clear my father's debts and to be used for Kurt's deranged pleasure. His deceit was spun wide enough to trap us all in the McCoy's web. All for money.

Sitting here as the officers lead Kurt away in handcuffs and chains, we've learned that what he had done to the Everest family and me was again only for shipping slips and cargo holds. He couldn't care less about avenging his cousin. Guess all the McCoys were raised under the same umbrella of hate.

Hearing the details stated so blatantly, so coldly, made

me nauseous. Singer stayed for a few days but flew home to spend time with her mother. Since she's pregnant, the trial was too upsetting for her and being in the vicinity of a McCoy made her ill as well. Ethan stayed to see the trial through.

Twenty-five years in prison for the attempted murder of Chelsea. Ten tacked on for torturing me last November. The US has filed to try him for a list of additional crimes. We'll see if they win the extradition.

My father's and brother's trials start next week. I'm not sure how I'll feel, but I'll be there in the front row to watch their demise. Yeah, I'm not above hoping for a little revenge myself. I'm still working on the anger issues I have when it comes to my ex-family.

I look at the hand that clings to me and give it a squeeze. Chelsea gives me a tight smile, but it's a victory that should make her smile. "Guilty," I repeat the verdict.

She's a changed woman these days. After she was cleared of conspiracy, she began taking a couple college courses and works part-time at the Everest Foundation answering calls. It's a job she takes seriously and has already helped other women get the help they need.

Lars, sitting on the other side of her, asks, "Are you ready to go?"

She nods. "So ready."

We give each other a hug, and she says, "I'll see you back in Manhattan. Lunch soon?"

"Yes, I'll see you then."

She's strong and never looks back at Kurt when she leaves. I don't think I'm weak. I'm just too in love to hide it from anyone, especially him. He stares at me as I give Bennett a kiss. But like any other time I kiss this man, nothing else in the world exists.

"Did you just kiss me to show me off to your ex-boyfriend?"

He's quick, another thing I love about him. "I did." We don't lie about anything anymore, not even who ate the last fry. I wholeheartedly admit I'm addicted to those delicious little carbs.

"I'm good with that. Let him live with that image of us for the next thirty-five years." Bennett takes my other hand and stands. "I still don't think it's long enough."

"If he's made to serve the full sentence, it will do." And it will, too. I don't want to wear this anger around my neck anymore. I need to trust the system, and, as Bennett says, karma to finish her job.

While we walk out of the courtroom, Ethan says, "I'm flying back tonight. Are you staying a few days or heading home?"

I look at Bennett, and ask, "What do you want to do?"

"I think we'll stay a few days."

Sitting on the rooftop of Le Meurice Hotel under the summer sky, I sit back and enjoy the show. The Eiffel Tower sparkles like the stars above, and the most handsome man I've ever seen with the kindest soul sits across from me.

The champagne glasses are empty, but Bennett doesn't refill them. Instead, he says, "I have a surprise for you."

As if right on cue, "Dream a Little Dream of Me" begins to play, filling the sultry air, and he takes my hands. Twirling me out and bringing me back in. He catches me, and we begin to sway to my favorite song. "You know how to romance a girl."

"You haven't seen anything yet."

"You always were a force of nature."

"And you were a force to be reckoned with."

"You reckoned all right, I reckon." I wink.

"Funny girl."

An arm tightens around my waist when he brings me even closer. I'm never more at ease than when I am with him. I even let him lead.

He spins me around until my feet come to an abrupt stop with my back to him. My breath catches, and my mouth falls open. "Bennett, what have you done?" Rushing forward, I stand in front of the small cart stacked with the books I collected when I was here in Paris, books that kept me company when I was so alone.

Picking up *The Resistance*, I hold it to my heart. Being able to escape to another world, to other characters' lives rather than my own, kept me alive in some ways. These gave me moments of joy in a very dark time.

I can't ever say this to Bennett because he might take this the wrong way, but I had a serious crush on Johnny Outlaw. Seriously hot book boyfriend material. And I remember thinking I had met my very own Jack Dalton as I walked back to the apartment the night I met Bennett. He may not be a rock star, but he'll always be a movie star to me. "This is the book I was reading when we—"

"Were on our second date."

"You remember."

"Every minute," he says.

My eyes fill with tears as happiness fills my heart. He wraps his arms around me, and I finally ask, "How did you get my books?"

"The trial is over, and they weren't held as evidence, so they let Lars in. Was there anything else you wanted from the apartment?"

"No, this is more than I thought I'd ever have."

"You're more than I thought I'd ever have, Winter."

When the next song begins to play, he kneels on one knee in front of me. I try to cover my mouth as it hangs open, but he takes my hand before I can. While "La Vie En Rose" drifts around us, he says, "We're not atop the Empire State Building and it's not Valentine's Day, but I wanted to tell you that I love . . . God how I love you so much."

"I love you, too."

"I was captivated by your beauty when I first laid eyes on you. Drawn to the free spirit who showed me her Paris, I fell in love the first time we kissed because I'd never tasted love before. And I knew then that your soft lips were the only lips I'd ever taste again. I found my home in you."

He kisses my hand and then brings out a ring box. "I once heard, from a very wise and beautiful woman, that if you make a wish, you'll receive what you need." He lifts the lid to the Tiffany blue box and then holds my hand. "I've made my wish, Winter. Will you do me the honor and spend your life with me, ma chérie?"

I sit on his bended knee, hug him, and tuck my face into the crook of his neck. Staring down at the stunning ring—classic with a diamond befitting a giant's wife—I reply, "You had me at Tiffany's."

Under a chuckle, he says, "So that's a yes?"

"I don't need the Empire State Building on Valentine's to know that you're the only man I want to spend the rest of my life with. So that's most definitely a yes. Yes. Yes." Dragging my hand down my throat, I teasingly moan, "Oh, God. Yes."

Popping to his feet, I'm also set down on mine. He readjusts his pants. "On that note, I'm ready to head back to the room. Did you pack the French maid's uniform?" He's so fun to tease.

"No. How do you feel about spies?"

As we walk to the door to leave, he asks, "Good spies or bad?"

"Always good."

"Do you think you can handle great?"

Stopping me, he pulls to him. "I can handle anything thrown our way."

I wrap my arms around him, and say, "Good because this is just our beginning."

EPILOGUE

Bennett

"How do you feel?"

"Like a million bucks," she replies.

"How about four?"

My joke makes her laugh—the best sound in the world. She really did get the last laugh. After Ethan bought Nobleman Inc. from her, she walked away with a cool four million, which she negotiated for shares in Everest Enterprises. With the last three deals I've sold, those shares are already worth more. Under the buyout, all Nobleman employees were absorbed into ours and given raises since they were underpaid. Everyone came out a winner.

Except for her father and brother.

Winter fulfilled her goal. She wore her mother's broach or the locket every day of their trials. Fifteen years for attempted murder, ten years for kidnapping, another five for blackmail, and fifteen for money laundering. Who knows if they'll live or die behind bars. It doesn't matter because good always prevails in the end.

One week after the sentencing and in a private ceremony with our closest friends and family, we exchanged our vows at the library.

Even though my net worth is over seven hundred million these days . . . I mean *our* net worth; we skipped a prenup. I mean, the woman is worth millions, so I totally scored. I give her a wink.

Just a few hours later, Winter rolls to her side, and asks, "Is this real life?"

"It's our life." I take her hand and kiss it.

"I love our life."

"Me too. I have to admit I was surprised by your choice of honeymoon locations, but I'm really digging it."

"I thought you might." Getting up, she straddles my waist and wiggles. When she bends down to kiss me, she says, "There's no place like home. Are you tired?"

"I'll never tire of you."

"You know . . ." She reaches over and hits a button to make the blinds close followed by the curtains. "It's only noon, but I'm always up for another round. How about you?"

"Best honeymoon ever."

"Your only honeymoon ever is more like it."

Flipping her over, I settle between her legs, definitely ready for more. "Have I told you how much I love you?"

"All the time," she replies with a soft giggle. "But tell me again."

I kiss her chest. "I thought I had everything and then you came along and turned my gray days blue." I continue to recite the vows I wrote for her while kissing between her breasts. "I promise to give you all my truths and nothing less than my best."

Kissing her stomach, I say, "To spoon you at night and feed you all the carbs you desire."

She sits up and pinches my ass. "And cheese," I add, chuckling.

"You are so ridiculous, Ben."

"Fine, I'll get back to the real vows now." When she falls back, I go lower and drag my tongue around her belly button. "I promise to love you. God, how I love you. To cherish you. To treasure you always." Goose bumps cover her skin, and I palm her breasts until I reach her sweetest spot. She sucks in a breath. "In sickness, health, and even under gunfire, I vow to not just stand by your side, but shield you with my life."

Her fingers slip into my hair, and she tugs, her signal that she wants more. I flatten my tongue and slip a finger inside her, causing her back to arch and sending that sweet moan to my ears. It's like a lightning rod to my dick, hardening even more than it already was. I can't help but start to rush the words we once exchanged. "To love you morning, noon, and night. I, Bennett, give you my heart for eternity."

I need her—to lose my mind inside her.

With deep tongue kisses, I'm able to elicit the start of her orgasm. Coaxing it, I hold her still and focus on the delicious torture between her soft lips.

"Oh God, Bennett." Her legs tense, squeezing my head between them. She tugs my hair. I push deep, so deep, I can taste the blue skies of her heaven inside. Her body gives me everything, and when her mouth falls open from the ecstasy, I move back up and kiss her again. She says, "I take you. All of you and give you all of me in return." As I sink into her, her body embraces my erection and holds me tight.

When her breathing catches up with her, we start making love as she recites her promises. "I didn't know I needed a movie star until you walked into my life. I'd lost hope until you slowly and purposely restored it."

Kisses are scattered over her neck and mine. "I promise to

always stand by your side as your best friend, lover, your wife, and your forever. I give you my heart for eternity." I lick and then suck the soft spots where she loves me. She deviates from her script. "Thank you for walking me to the corner of that street. If you hadn't shown up when you did . . . " Cupping my face, she says, "You're six foot three of solid gold insides, Bennett Everest."

"Built to love you, and love you I do. With all of me."

"I love you. Every last inch of you." She kisses me, and I start moving again. Gentle soon turns erratic as I start to lose the rhythm to chase the finale. "Fuck," I groan, just out of reach of the utopia I seek.

Slowing, I drag my hands over her shoulders and down to her wrists, then move her arms above her head. I start off slow again, wanting her to feel every part of me loving her. Her legs wrap around me as I thrust harder, her moans encouraging me to go faster.

My elbows rest on either side of my beauty. Her hair tangles around her head. With every thrust, my name comes off her tongue like a sweet melody. Too soon . . . too soon, I'm lost in the depth of her starlit abyss.

I push.

I push.

"I do."

"I do."

I push . . . until . . . I find the relief, feeding my needs. My breath escapes, and I drop my head next to hers. When my body calms, and my mind eases, I turn and kiss her cheek. She whispers, "You are everything to me."

I lean back and look into her eyes while her hand still caresses my cheek. "You are everything to me. The sun, moon, and stars. My Winter's night. You've taught me what love is."

"And that is?" she asks softly.

"Love is seeing someone and realizing they're your soul mate. We weren't just two people attracted to each other. We were two souls drawn together."

Winter kisses the tops of my cheeks and then my forehead. "Love is marrying the man of your dreams and not wanting to be anywhere else but in his arms and our own bed."

Pushing to the side of her, I bring her back to my chest and spoon her how she loves to be held while whispering in her ear, "Love is Winter Renee Everest."

An alarm goes off. *Worst timing ever.* Angling back to look at me, she says, "What's the alarm for?"

"Brownies are ready." I hate leaving this bed, but for what I have planned, it'll be worth the trip.

She laughs when I grumble as I sit up and then lies with her arms spread wide. "You wore me out."

"You have time to recover. I'll get the whipped cream."

When I click on the TV, an old black and white movie plays. She fluffs the pillows under her head, and says, "This is my favorite movie."

"*Casablanca*?" I still love learning everything about this amazing woman.

Her nails trail lightly down my arm. "Of all the bistros in Paris, you walked into mine."

"And I'd do it again." Taking her hand, I kiss each finger. "I'll always be there when you need me."

"Because you're the hero of my very own fairy tale."

"And you're the queen of mine." I steal a kiss from her lips before hopping out of bed. I detour to the bathroom to clean up before I rush to get the brownies out of the oven.

This goes to show that I have absolutely no game when it comes to sex with my wife. She makes me come too fast every fucking time. I grab the homemade cream I whipped up earlier and then check my emails while the brownies cool on the stovetop.

The third email gets my attention. Kurt is being extradited to the States. No more Brie and champagne for that motherfucker. He's about to have a rude fucking awakening. They are going to love him in prison.

He should also be thankful for those bars that protect him because if he ever walks free . . . I'll be waiting for him.

I close my computer and turn on some music, forgetting that fucker while thanking the stars for the life I have the pleasure of living with my wife. "Just Breathe" plays through the speakers, and I think about the journey Winter and I have taken to get where we are now. It's something I think about a lot.

The locket sits on the counter next to where we stripped off our clothes earlier. Knowing her mother watched over her and provided for her is helping to heal her loss after a life of feeling abandoned. This necklace has given her great comfort over the years.

It still infuriates me to think about how her own father and brother treated her. She's the flower that grew from the rubble. The rainbow that broke through the storm. *She's extraordinary.*

Needless to say, I've lost no sleep over hearing the news of Braden having a run-in the first week of prison. I didn't bother to ask what was meant by "run-in" because I'm okay with any version of it. *The bastard.*

Her father certainly hasn't been receiving any preferential treatment that we feared either. Men in prison don't take kindly to hurting children. He never got to correct them on her age. That he tried to kill his daughter was enough to have him convicted by the prisoner's jury. Karma's a bitch and has doled out her punishment.

Winter calls me her destiny and her wish come true.

Despite how often I tell her the same, she insists she's the lucky one.

She just doesn't understand the depth of my feelings. This woman has become everything to me—everything good in the world, everything worth living for.

"Hey there," she says, wrapping her arms around me from behind. When I turn around, she's wearing one of my favorite concert tees—The Crow Brothers band—who also happen to be good friends. I can't wait to introduce her to them. "I got lonely in there by myself."

Bringing her against me, I say, "C'mere and let me keep you warm."

"What should we do while we wait for the brownies to cool?"

"Your wish is my command."

"Remember when we were practically strangers?"

Running my hands over her hips and under the shirt, I say, "I sure do, but I prefer wife now."

"Me too." She kisses my chin. "I was thinking I could put on a football costume I bought the other day and you could try to score a touchdown."

"I don't need to role play when it comes to you and me." Lifting her onto the island counter, I roam my hands from her shoulders and down her arms. I find the hand with her ring on it and kiss her palm. "I already scored."

She spreads her legs, welcoming me while resting her arms around my neck. "Are you always going to be this romantic?"

"Every day and every night for as long as we both shall live."

"What about any tough times ahead? I get moody sometimes. Do you think you can handle those?"

"Thorns and all, cactus flower." Waggling my hand, I add, "This ring binds us for life."

Her heels push against my ass, and I move in as close as I can. Our lips meet, and I savor every second I get doing exactly this with this stunning woman. Parting breathless, she says, "I'm shooting for eternity."

"A woman after my own heart."

"I'm not after it. Remember, I already have it. You gave me yours, and I gave you mine."

"How could I forget? Maybe you need to remind me."

She hops off the counter. "Happily. Get the brownies and meet me in bed, movie star."

"And we live happily ever after."

You met Ethan Everest and Hutton in Force of Nature, but now is the time to get to know The Everest Brothers even better and the obstacles they have to overcome in their lives.

EVEREST (Ethan's Book): This bestselling Second Chance Romantic Suspense will charm you as well as keep you on your toes as the story unfolds. Turn the page for a sneak peek into his book. Now Available

BAD REPUTATION (Hutton's Book): Being bad never felt so good. A Second Chance Royal Romance that will have you swooning over this alpha while cheering the headstrong and fierce Princess who's determined to make her mark on history. Now Available

THE RUMORS ARE TRUE

The Everest Brothers and Winter have excellent taste in books and friends. Both of these bands were mentioned in their story. Now it's time for you to meet these rock star legends.

Johnny Outlaw/Jack Dalton - Winter's Book Boyfriend, and dreamy rock star, can be found in my New York Time's Bestseller, The Resistance. Now Available

The Crow Brothers have a fantastic bestselling series that is NOW AVAILABLE in complete. Rise to fame with these charismatic and incredible rock stars that will have you swooning and falling in love. The Crow Brothers: Now Available

THANK YOU

Reviews are love and matter so much to the success of a book and author. If you love this story, please consider sharing that love with friends and family, posting on social media, and leaving a review where you purchased the book.

Thank you!

Sincerely,
   S.L.

A PERSONAL NOTE

Force of Nature would not be possible without the support of my family, friends, readers, and team. I'm truly one of the most fortunate people in the world to be surrounded by such kindness and emotional cheerleaders.

To my family - Always. Everything and Anything for you <3 I love you!

Huge thank you's to Adriana, Amy H., Andrea, Devyn, Heather, Jenny, Kristen, Lynsey, Marion, Marla, and my amazing narrators, Ava Erickson and Sebastian York.

My readers are the best. Genuinely the best. I'm so fortunate to have such support in all my endeavors. Thank you for taking another journey with me.

To Letitia, You are the Cover Queen Magic Maker. Thank you for the stunningly beautiful cover <3

ABOUT THE AUTHOR

To keep up to date with her writing and more, her website is www.slscottauthor.com to receive her newsletter with all of her publishing adventures and giveaways, sign up for her newsletter: http://bit.ly/2TheScoop

Instagram: S.L.Scott

To receive a free book now, TEXT "slscott" to 77948

For more information, please visit
www.slscottauthor.com

ALSO BY S.L. SCOTT

To keep up to date with her writing and more, her website is
www.slscottauthor.com

To receive the Scott Scoop about all of her publishing adventures,
free books, giveaways, steals and more, sign up here:
http://bit.ly/2TheScoop

Join S.L.'s Facebook group here: S.L. Scott Books

Audiobooks on Audible

~FORCE OF NATURE AUDIO - April 2019~

The Everest Brothers (Stand-Alones)

Everest - Ethan Everest

Bad Reputation - Hutton Everest

Force of Nature - Bennett Everest

The Crow Brothers (Stand-Alones)

Spark

Tulsa

Rivers

Ridge

Hard to Resist Series (Stand-Alones)

The Resistance

The Reckoning

The Redemption

ISBN: 978-1-940071-78-7

Design: RBA Designs

Photography by Rafa G. Catala

Cover Model: Chema Malavia

Editing:

Marion Archer, Making Manuscripts

Jenny Sims, Editing 4 Indies

Marla Esposito, Proofing Style

Kristen Johnson, Proofreader

Amy Halter, Proofreader

Team Readers: Lynsey Johnson and Andrea Johnston

French Phrases: Veronique Chayer

CPSIA information can be obtained
at www.ICGtesting.com
Printed in the USA
LVHW091929140319
610685LV00001B/3/P